CW00585068

THE MECHANICS' INSTIT
ISSUE 4 AUTUMN 2007

The first Mechanics' Institute in London was founded in 1823 by George Birkbeck. 'Mechanics' then meant skilled artisans, and the purpose of the Institute was to instruct them in the principles behind their craft. The Institute became Birkbeck College, part of London University, in 1920 but still maintains one foot in the academy and one in the outside world.

The Mechanics' Institute Review
Issue 4 Autumn 2007

The Mechanics' Institute Review is published by MA Creative Writing, School of English and Humanities, Birkbeck, Malet Street, Bloomsbury, London WC1E 7HX

ISBN 978-0-9547933-4-0

Project Director: Sue Tyley

Editors:
Gabriela Blandy
Jill McGivering
Jennifer Payne
Elizabeth Sarkany
James Vincent

The Editorial Team would like to thank Russell Celyn Jones, Anne-Marie Whiting and Julia Bell for making this project possible.

For further copies or information, please contact Anne-Marie Whiting, MA Creative Writing, School of English and Humanities, Birkbeck, Malet Street, Bloomsbury, London, WC1E 7HX. Tel: 020 7079 0689. Email: a.whiting@bbk.ac.uk

Website: www.bbk.ac.uk/mir

Printed and bound by Antony Rowe Ltd., Bumpers Farm, Chippenham, Wiltshire

Cover design by Emma Forsberg

Typeset by Raffaele Teo

The Mechanics' Institute Review is typeset in Garamond

Table of Contents

PREFACE

When we five writers came together to form the editorial team for the fourth issue of *The Mechanics' Institute Review*, we expected to gain knowledge and experience of publishing a literary magazine. Our expectations were met: we discovered the work required to put a book on a shop shelf – and on a website. However, we discovered something else, too, something we did not perhaps expect to learn about writing and reading. We came to appreciate how the creations that appear in our heads as writers end up as ink on pages, between covers, being read.

Now, as the magazine goes to press, we are able to reflect on our role as editors in bringing those creations – the products of quiet isolated moments – before an audience.

We defined a vision, deciding what we wanted our magazine to represent and achieve. As writers and readers who admire and value short stories, we resolved to showcase and champion that form. Equally important, we identified our intended audience. With this framework in mind, we sought out high-quality stories from the new voices on Birkbeck's Creative Writing courses. We sifted through the quantities of submissions we received, discussed their merits and limitations and our responses to them. Each of us had our doubts and convictions, but any conflicts were resolved amicably – through asking the question, 'What's best for MIR?' – and we made our final selection as a like-minded team. Then came the task of contacting those writers whose stories we had accepted and those we had not, knowing both the pleasure and disappointment we would cause.

Our selection made, we now had to bring these carefully drawn visions to a point where the reader would see them as the authors had. Our own stories were subjected to rigorous yet considerate scrutiny by our mentor, from whom we learnt how to suggest, massage, reorganize, polish and refine – how to help realize another writer's invention; how to edit. Then, in a café or seminar room, we met a living person – the author – whom, it seemed, we already slightly knew. We asked, 'Is this what you want to show?' And sometimes they replied at length and articulately, and sometimes, with a worried look, 'I just wrote it . . .' So, with both the knowing and the instinctive writer, we worked through what their stories meant. Together we tried to ensure that these meanings would be grasped by our intended readers – be they an experienced judge, or a fresh, curious mind, both, however, searching for new ideas or unfamiliar angles on life.

We returned to the team with our reworked pieces and set out the stories by student writers, some with little knowledge or experience of bringing their work to the public. Beside these we put pieces generously provided by established authors, who perhaps recall the time they too were unpublished, and now, with their works in the bookshops, are happy to sit alongside, and lend their support to, newcomers. With our reader always in mind, we juggled and shuffled, paired and split the voices, tones, tenses, themes, locations and formats, until we had constructed a whole, a book to be dipped into or read from cover to cover. And then we dispatched these pieces, of which we had been the guardians, to the next stages of the process – copy-editing, typesetting, proof-checking – and, finally, to a printer on the other side of the country, awaiting their return in eye-catching covers and smooth paper, with attractive and clear type, as our book.

While we wait, we reflect on how this process has affected us, both as readers and as writers. We all knew what it is to open a book and immerse ourselves in its world. We knew a little, through our writing workshops and varying experiences, of what it is to be a writer, to be read and discussed. But now that we have helped nurture other writers' work for publication, we know the full process our own creations must go through to be appreciated as we first hoped they would. We know that the raw material we originally produce requires attention – continuously from us and periodically from a generous collection of others – to strike that chord we want to be heard.

So we five writers can return to our quiet solitude furnished with a new appreciation of the processes that begin and end here, with this magazine. Reading a story, we might wonder where its author started, how she pursued her idea, eventually producing a piece she felt was developed enough to be exposed to someone else's comments and suggestions. We think of the work that was done, the discussions and revisions, leading to the final version. Or perhaps, as writers, we may hatch some idea of our own, scribble it down, develop, review and make decisions about it. And we know that eventually we can take this work to someone who will commit to helping us deliver it to the reader, and that that reader, sitting alone somewhere, will nod slightly and understand.

The Editorial Team

THE ENIGMATIC ART OF SELF-CRITICISM
Joyce Carol Oates

Self-criticism, like self-administered brain surgery, is perhaps not a good idea. Can the 'self' see the 'self' with any objectivity? The harsh, repentant mood of the moment may cast its doubt back upon an entire lifetime of creativity, with cruel results: the first great poet in the English language, Chaucer, not only came to doubt the worth of his extraordinary work in later life, but, overcome by Christian repugnance for what he perceived as the sin of secular creation, repudiated it utterly. So too, the Jesuit Gerard Manley Hopkins, centuries later, who came by tortuous degrees to believe that his lushly sensuous, markedly rhythmic poetry was a violation of his priestly vows. Franz Kafka's self-criticism, always severe, seems to have developed gradually into a species of self-laceration analogous to the powerful images of his work – masochistic fantasies of punishment, mutilation, and erasure. It is hardly surprising that Kafka asked his friend Max Brod to destroy all his work, including the uncompleted novels *The Trial* and *The Castle*. (Very sensibly, since he had a clearer and more generous vision of Kafka than Kafka himself did, Brod refused to do so.)

In the long history of literary effort, what eccentric self-judgements! Despite our best intentions it's problematic that, apart from immediate, practical, technical revisions, the writer's attempt to detach himself from his work, let alone his 'oeuvre', is doomed: knowing too much may be a way of knowing too little. Or, how can we expect to know more about ourselves than we know about anything else?

Consider: in the human eye no light energy can stimulate the retina at the exit of the optic tract: all human beings carry blind spots with them in their vision. Everywhere we look there are points of invisibility, it might be said; and, since they are invisible, they can't be seen even as absence. These are the legendary 'motes' in the eye of the beholder. They have their analogue in memory, as amnesiac patches drifting like clouds through our brains. It's rare that we actively and consciously 'forget'; most of the time we have simply forgotten, with no consciousness of having forgotten. In individuals, the phenomenon is called 'denial'; in entire cultures and nations, it's usually called 'history'.

'Do you know how many years I have to be read?' – so Chekhov asked his friend Ivan Bunin, at a time when no other Russian prose writer except Tolstoy was so highly praised as Chekhov. 'Seven years.' 'Why seven?' asked Bunin. 'Well, seven and a half.' Thomas Hardy, author of *Tess of the D'Urbevilles* and *Jude the Obscure*, novels of surpassing beauty and originality, spoke slightingly of novel-writing as a mere profession, a 'temporary' but economically 'compulsory' interruption of a poetic career. And what deadly combination of egotism and humility seems to have afflicted Albert Camus soon after being awarded the Nobel Prize: as if the public celebration of a career constitutes a curse, in private life. (In *The Fall*, Camus's fictitious narrator speaks of being persecuted by a 'ridiculous' apprehension: 'One cannot die without having confessed all one's own lies . . . otherwise, be there one hidden untruth in a life, death would render it definitive . . . this absolute assassination of the truth gave me vertigo . . .')

Just get the right syllable in the proper place was Jonathan Swift's admonition, the perfectionist's credo. Yet, this credo can be the writer's nightmare. The strain of trying always to write beautifully, brilliantly, with originality, with 'exultant' force can be self-damning, paralysing. There is both vanity and humility in the despair of a perfectionist like Joseph Conrad, miserable in the composition of his most ambitious novel *Nostromo*: 'I go on as one would cycle over a precipice along a 14-inch plank. If I falter I am lost.' In a paroxysm of loathing for his task, Conrad spoke of being reduced to near-imbecility; of feeling that his brain had turned to water; and of his conviction that, for him, writing was simply the 'conversion of nervous force' into words. (Does *Nostromo* suggest such writerly strain? Unfortunately yes, overall.)

The psychological phenomenon of paralysis itself, however, can be given an ingenious theoretical twist; so that, in contemplating the difficulties of writing, one is also contemplating the universal human condition: passivity, indecision, and 'impotence' then become subjects for art, as in Mallarmé, Baudelaire, T. S. Eliot, Samuel Beckett. That sense that life has played itself out, that language is inadequate to communicate the intransigent facts of the human condition. *Why go on? Yet: we go on!* Beckett made a career of dramatizing this pseudo-tragic ennui, in poetic shorthand: 'Moments for nothing, now as always, time was never and time is over, reckoning close and story ending' (*Endgame*).

For some writers, the natural doubts of the self are amplified by critics' negative assessments: if you want confirmation of your essential worthlessness, you can always find it, somewhere. John Updike has remarked that the writer comes to feel that good reviewers are being generous while the others have really found you out. Since 1965 it has remained a perennial mystery why the much-praised J. D. Salinger ceased publishing in mid career, though Salinger has not, evidently, ceased writing; yet if one considers the jeering and dismissive tone of critical response to Salinger's last-published books, the writer's dignified withdrawal into silence is understandable. (What a feeding frenzy for critics, when Salinger's work is posthumously published . . .)

Then there is the bravado of the wounded-but-defiant: 'When reviewers like something of mine, I grow suspicious' (Gore Vidal).

More commonly, writers often have a very blurred conception of how their work is perceived by others, and what their work actually *is*. Herman Melville, for instance, the author, as a young man, of the best-sellers *Typee* and *Omoo*, seemed to believe that he had written another best-seller, a bowl of 'rural milk' for the ladies, in the static, tortuous, parodistic *Pierre: or, the Ambiguities* (a novel that comes close to strangling on its own self-loathing and was to prove as dismal an economic failure as *Moby-Dick*, the novel of Melville's that preceded it). Charles Dickens seems sincerely to have considered *Great Expectations* a comedy, boasting of the opening section as 'exceedingly droll' and 'foolish' – material that strikes most readers as horrific, tragic. Scott Fitzgerald was convinced that his flawed, conventionally rendered *Tender Is the Night* was not only a great novel, but far more experimental than James Joyce's *Ulysses*. William Faulkner was convinced that his wooden, lifeless *A Fable* was superior to his brilliantly original earlier novels *The Sound and the*

Fury, As I Lay Dying, and *Absalom, Absalom!*

James Joyce believed, or wished to believe, that *Finnegans Wake*, on which he had laboured for sixteen years, was not one of the most difficult, abstruse, and demanding novels in the English language, but a 'simple' novel: 'If anyone doesn't understand a passage, all he need do is read it aloud.' (Then again, in a less inflated mood, Joyce confessed: 'Perhaps it is insanity. One will be able to judge in a century.' Joyce offered no rejoinder to his brother Stanislaus's judgement that *Finnegans Wake* is 'unspeakably wearisome . . . the witless wandering of literature before its final extinction. I would not read a paragraph of it if I did not know you.')

No one was more uncertain about her work than Virginia Woolf, perhaps because she thought about it, analysed it, so obsessively. In November 1936 when she went over the proofs of *The Years*, the novel that had given her the most difficulty of her career, she noted in her journal that she 'read to the end of the first section in despair: stony but convinced despair . . . This is happily so bad that there can be no question about it. I must carry the proofs, like a dead cat, to L., and tell him to burn them unread.' But Leonard Woolf said he liked the book; thought it in fact 'extraordinarily good'. (Leonard is lying, but no matter: Virginia can't know.) She notes in her diary that perhaps she had exaggerated its badness. Then again, a few days later, she notes that it *is* bad. 'Never write a long book again.' But a few days later: 'There is no need whatever in my opinion to be unhappy about *The Years*. It seems to me to come off at the end. Anyhow, to be a taut, real, strenuous book. I just finished it and feel a little exalted.' Later, she concedes that it might be a failure after all – but she is finished with it. The first reviews, however, are ecstatic; Woolf is declared a 'first-rate novelist' and 'great lyrical poet'. Almost universally it is said that *The Years* is a 'masterpiece'. A day or two later Virginia notes:

> How I interest myself! Quite set up and perky today with a mind brimming because I was so damnably depressed and smacked on the cheek by Edwin Muir in the *Listener* and Scott James in *Life and Letters* on Friday. They both gave me a smart snubbing: E.M. says *The Years* is dead and disappointing. So in effect did James. All the lights sank; my reed bent to the ground. Dead and disappointing –

so I'm found out and that odious rice pudding of a book is what I thought it – a dank failure. No life in it . . . Now this pain woke me at 4 A.M. and I suffered acutely . . . But [then] it lifted; there was a good review, of 4 lines, in the *Empire Review*. The best of my books: did that help? I don't think very much. But the delight . . . is quite real. One feels braced for some reason; amused; round, combative; more than by praise.

(*The Years*, all improbably, rises to the top of the best-seller list in the United States, where it remains for four months. And we consider it, today, one of Woolf's least successful experiments, curiously dull and soporific – 'no life in it' – unlike her genuine masterpieces *To the Lighthouse*, *Mrs Dalloway*, *The Waves*, through which life flows with the quicksilver subtlety of light in a Monet painting.)

Any number of distinguished writers have been drawn into the challenge of rewriting and 'improving' early work: W. H. Auden, Marianne Moore, John Crowe Ransom immediately come to mind. The energies of youth having passed, the ageing and, it sometimes seems, vindictive elder wants to set things right: prune, revise, recast, in line with the doubtful wisdom of experience. His fellow poet George Seferis particularly denounced Auden's tampering with 'September 1, 1939' (in which the famous line 'We must love one another or die' was altered to 'We must love one another and die' – or in another version omitted altogether, along with the stanza that contained it), seeing such revision as 'immoral' and 'egotistical' since the poem had long passed out of Auden's exclusive possession. W. B. Yeats's lifelong obsession with revising – the 'making', as he called it, 'of my soul' – was, by contrast, nearly always justified; as was Henry James's, and what we know of Emily Dickinson's. (Dickinson even did numerous drafts of her seemingly tossed-off little letters.) In rewriting early work for his *Collected Poems*, D. H. Lawrence considerably improved it, perhaps because the faithful poems were so bad to begin with. (However, Lawrence was a shrewd enough critic of his own work to understand that 'a young man is afraid of his demon and puts his hand over the demon's mouth sometimes and speaks for him. So I have tried to let the demon say his say, and to remove the passages where the young man intruded.'

Note to *Collected Poems*, 1928.)

Of the innocence of raw egotism there are many, one might say too many, examples: that most macho of celebrated American writers, Ernest Hemingway, boasted of having beaten Turgenev and de Maupassant in fantasized boxing/writing matches, and of having fought two draws with Stendhal – 'I think I had an edge in the last one.' John O'Hara, the contemporary of such masters of short fiction as Thomas Mann, William Faulkner, Willa Cather, Katherine Anne Porter, Eudora Welty, and Hemingway, frequently boasted that 'no one writes short stories better than I do.' Robert Frost, even as an elder, much-honoured poet, found it difficult to sit in an audience and hear another poet read work, particularly if the work was being well received, and it was wittily said (by John Cheever) that the Russian poet Yevtushenko has an ego capable of 'cracking crystal at a distance of twenty feet'. Nabokov believed himself superior to, among others, Dostoyevski, Turgenev, Mann, Henry James, and George Orwell.

In *The Wild Duck*, Ibsen speaks of the 'life-lie' – the necessary delusion that makes life possible, gives us hope. (Even if it's an unreasonable hope.) For some writers, the 'life-lie' is essential: they must believe that they contain genius, or they can't write at all. There is nothing wrong with such a conviction, except if it collides too dramatically with actual life.

To have a reliable opinion about oneself, one must know the subject, and perhaps that isn't possible. We know how we feel about ourselves, but only from hour to hour; our moods change, like the intensity of light outside our windows. But *to feel* is not *to know*; and strong *feelings* will block *knowledge*. I seem to have virtually no opinion of myself. I only publish work that I believe to be the best I can do, and beyond that I can't judge. My life, to me, is transparent as a glass of water, and of no more interest. And my writing, which is far too various for me to contemplate, is an elusive matter, that will reside in the minds (or, as Auden more forcefully says, the guts) of others, to judge.

This essay was first published in the US in *The Faith of a Writer* (Ecco, 2003)

THE COCK THIEF
Parselelo Kantai

John Naiguran woke up suddenly and blinked, adjusting to the dimness inside the bus. There were people around him, strangers, fellow travellers. And the hand on his shoulder had been shaking him for some time.

'Alfred, Alfred, *amka*. Wake up.'

It was the student – Janet? – on her way to university in Kampala, she had said. They were on the night bus from Nairobi. She had boarded the bus in Limuru, half an hour into the journey. He had told her he was Alfred, a money-changer on his way to Busia at the border.

He felt for the bag beneath the chair. It was still there, still heavy. He sank into his seat and sighed.

'Did you know you sleep with your eyes open? You were looking at me as if I stole your grade cow.'

This girl whose name eluded him. She was skinny and small and probably more than a little high on the *miraa* bulging in her cheek. She looked very different from her voice, a rough, rousing roar of four in the morning in those dark little hovels by the roadside, the ones run by fat round women called Rhoda and Francisca who serve cheap lethal brews to broken men in oversized jackets. Now she spat suddenly into a polythene bag magically extracted from somewhere in the complicated folds of her clothes. And then she was unwrapping half of a Big G, chewing it, making rude, rhythmic clicks. She seemed to appreciate the sound more than the

11

flavour. She stared at him the whole time, her large liquid eyes shining out of the *khanga* that covered her head and framed her face; the rest of it disappeared inside a fur-lined jacket, unzipped half-way down to reveal a T-shirt tucked tight into a pair of worn jeans. Limuru, he knew, got very cold. He wondered what she would do with her jacket in the heat of Kampala. But it was the boots with their steel-tipped points that convinced him this was a *malaya*, going west to seek new flesh markets. There was no money in Kenya. Everybody was leaving, and lying about it.

'And you also talk. You're a sleep-talker.'

'No, no, no.' His left arm was dead. He shook it vigorously, felt the blood returning.

She tried to read the chewing-gum wrapper in the moonlight, holding it up in her tiny hands.

'Ingredients,' she said, reading. She made it sound like a word in her mother tongue. 'Sugar, preysurfatifs, fravareng.'

'You talktalktalktalk,' she said, the effects of *miraa* tripping up her words. Then she turned to him as if she had just remembered something. 'There is an old man who is disturbing your head.'

Lights appeared in the large windscreen up front; illuminated the driver, a large battling figure hunched over the steering-wheel; whished past. They were going uphill but Naiguran couldn't be sure where they were. The driver tried to engage a low gear. The engine protested, seized up, a winded child's soundless, frantic gulps for air. The sleeping passengers seemed to rise, and for a moment were suspended above their seats, dancing shadows. He remembered once seeing a music video, Michael Jackson, where the dead were resurrected in mist and smoke. Roused from their long sleep, they now walked the earth in silent, terrifying formations. The gears crunched in and the passengers trembled like eggs in a tray. And from deep in the belly of the bus a wail, low and desolate and full of dying machinery, began to organize itself. Then the beast sprang forward and the passengers fell back. Corporal Naiguran held onto the seat in front of him and the bus settled down to a groaning, sedate pace. He used the sleeve of his dead arm to wipe the window. It was misted with sleep-breath. He wanted to open it, but feared the cold. He turned away from the girl and peered into the darkness.

There was nothing to see outside – a vast emptiness falling away as they climbed up the shoulder of the Rift Valley. But as they came to the crest of the hill, he saw the silhouette of the Mau escarpment on the horizon, like the wall of a giant stadium, the moon a solitary floodlight. He calculated that they were past Kikopey and about half an hour from Nakuru where the bus usually stopped – at the petrol station rumoured to belong to the old man – and people grabbed something to eat at the all-night restaurant.

This empty stadium. He remembered the first time he came here, with his father and their animals, when he was an uncircumcised boy, a *layioni*, dressed in nothing but a red *shuka*. He remembered the sound of cow-bells in the dust. It was during the 1979 drought and the salt and minerals in the soil more than the grass sustained the few animals that survived. His father, tall and straight and pointing with his stick at where they had come from, how in the old days their animals had filled this valley. These were good pasturelands, but Naiguran knew that these days the land was being turned into little plots of maize. There was no room any more for men like his father, roaming with their sons and their cattle. His family had never returned here, had moved up into the Mau. He was seized by the despair of lost things.

He thought about the old man. It seemed incredible to Naiguran that it was just this morning that he had driven him to the airport. He pressed his foot down on an imaginary brake as the bus lurched over a pothole, remembered the power of the long Mercedes, the deep vibration of the steering-wheel in his hands. The old man, on his way to Khartoum for the presidents' summit, never once looked up from behind the newspaper, trusted him. He had personally recruited Naiguran when he first heard his name. The Maasai, he had said, were loyal. The old man, even now when things had become difficult, was still respected as a peacemaker. Corporal Naiguran could see him in the rear-view mirror of the Mercedes, could see the top of the balding head, the grey hair at the sides, a semi-circle of matted cottonwool.

It suddenly struck Naiguran that he had become so accustomed to that image in the rear-view mirror he could not remember the exact moment when the hair began to thin out and grey. But he knew it had been some time during the '92 election campaign, when everybody feared the old man would lose. At the airport, as he got out of the car, he had spoken directly to Naiguran, his voice grating more and more these days, as if his soul was being dragged through a cement-mixer. But he was in a good mood, and had joked: 'Naiguran, *chunga nchi mpaka nirudi, eh?* Take care of the country until I return.' Naiguran had laughed and nodded. But he had looked down, could not take the intensity of the old man's gaze, those red eyes, burning, that reached to your very core.

He knew now that he would not be seeing the old man again, not after this. If he did, if he met the old man face to face again, he would probably be just about to die, badly, with his stink all around him, begging for mercy in words and ways he could not conceive. Words would be dictated to him by fear and they would be useless words, the words that accompanied you to the other side. The old man's rage would be worse than the fear itself.

'Alfie, why were you crying?' The girl wanted to talk. She was sitting very close to him, beginning to assume intimacies. He could smell her sweat, and there was something exciting about it. Her long thin braids swung free from her headscarf and brushed against his neck as she leaned into him. He was aroused and shifted in his seat, saying nothing.

'*Uko sawa?* Are you all right?' she was asking. She was not his type at all. He faced her and glanced down at her breasts, banana-shaped and rising low in her T-shirt. He realized she was not wearing a bra; her nipples stretched the thin material. She noticed him looking, and slowly zipped up her jacket, her eyes never leaving him. He looked away, angry with himself. There was still nothing to see outside. The window had clouded over again. He found himself comparing the girl – Janey? Njambi? – to Selina, her roundness, yellow face, bouncing breasts, revolving buttocks, things you could hold onto when it mattered. But as he imagined her – his thoughts a kaleidoscope of twisting, thrashing bodies, Selina's legs tight around his waist, her jerks and yelps – the image that flashed before him was of this girl, naked, her eyes widening in surprise as he pierced her, his thing a wet piston clicking in and out like her chewing gum.

His erection bulged against his trousers. It was becoming a problem. He reached for the bag. It was heavy but he put it on his lap.

'What do you have in that bag?' she asked.

He stared at her, silent, unable to hide his dislike for her.

She continued as if he had spoken. 'You kept saying: "*Jogoo! Jogoo!*" in your sleep.' Then she leaned towards him again and said, in English, 'Cock!

Cock! Do you have a cock in that bag?' She laughed, a silent, wheezy sound like a car on low battery being cranked.

'Yes,' he said. 'A very big one. It's made of gold.'

'*Naweza kuishika?* Can I touch it?' she said suggestively, and he realized she was very high.

She reached across and began to trace her hand along the bag. He grabbed her thin wrist and squeezed. She moaned theatrically, her eyes wide as if this was all a big joke. '*Hé! Ni kubwa!* It's huge!' she said.

'It belongs to the President,' he replied without smiling. She thought this was very funny.

She was still shaking with laughter as the bus slowed down, pulled over to the side of the road and stopped. The cooked smell of the tyres came through unseen cracks and openings. Smoke rose from the beast's underbelly, betraying its agony; dust particles swam in the headlights. And there were other lights doing a firefly dance in the windscreen. Naiguran peered through the interior gloom. He saw figures in luminous green waving torches – the dancing firefly lights. Behind them the yellow metal spikes and 'Stop: Accident Ahead' sign of a roadblock. The police.

The police usually waved buses on, unless there was a problem – a highway robbery or a radio alert for escaped convicts or suspected thugs. Or a man who had stolen the President's golden cock.

The door was pulled open and a policeman clambered in, talking loudly and urgently into his radio.

Since the old man was flying back from Khartoum the next morning, one of them, probably Kipkorir, the security boss, would have sent for him.

'Where is Corporal Naiguran?'

When he failed to respond to the radio call, somebody – probably Ndambuki, because everybody knew how close he and Ndambuki were – would have been sent to his room at the base. Ndambuki would have found it padlocked from the outside. And he must have stood there staring at that lock and sensing absence – the way you walk into an empty house and feel its uninhabited silences. It would have hit him then – that Naiguran had gone ahead with the plan without him. Enraged, vindictive, he would have broken the lock, marched into the one-roomed house, knocked things around. Then he would have radioed Kipkorir back that *afande*, sir, both his gun and his radio are missing, sir. Also, *afande*, sir, most of his clothes and other valuables are missing (a lie, but nobody would bother to double-check until he was broken and pulpy on the floor at Nyati House, being ordered to confess). *Afande*, it appears that Corporal Naiguran has gone Absent Without Leave.

It would not take them long to discover that the golden *Jogoo*, the presidential cock and enduring symbol of the ruling party, was missing from the old man's bedroom. It would not take them long to put two and two together, to curse – Ndambuki especially – Corporal Naiguran, the quiet one, for having had the balls to go ahead with their collective bar-room fantasy. Can you imagine how much it would fetch when you melted it down? That was Ndambuki, one night months ago in a corner of the mess, drunk and avaricious as the rest of them. In other words, when they came after him, it would be with a large degree of professional jealousy.

What Naiguran had had on his side was time. He knew how they all let things slide when the old man was away. Assuming that he, Naiguran, was on sentry duty, Ndambuki would be busy in the servants' quarters, his trousers around his ankles, amazed at how easily Selina had yielded to him after so many years trying. Horny little Mkamba rat. That Ndambuki! He would sell his mother for pussy given half a chance. *His* Selina. Naiguran tried not to think about it. Kipkorir would be drinking with his Ministry of Lands buddies God knows where, going through registers of available property in Kileleshwa and Kilimani. Occasionally either he or Ndambuki, or maybe one of the other senior officers who had not travelled in the old man's entourage, would radio the security booth to find out how things were. But it would be a formality and they would hardly bother to listen to the reply. Everybody knew that nothing happened when the old man was away.

That's what Corporal Naiguran had been counting on. That he would have enough time to get to the border, cross by *boda boda* – it cost ten shillings on those taxi-bicycles – and eventually find one of those Indian gold merchants at Jinja.

Something had gone wrong. They had discovered he was missing earlier than he had planned them to.

*

'Fellow Kenyans, do not panic!' announced the police officer, a tall burly figure. He was smooth and reassuring, had probably attended one of those community-policing courses at the training school in Kiganjo. The barrel of his G3 rifle pointed downwards.

'We are looking for wolves in sheep's clothing, people who hide among you and want to do our country harm. Help us by producing your ID cards.' He held the radio close to his ear, but Corporal Naiguran could make out bits and pieces of the conversation over the nationwide police frequency. The radio hissed and farted and went silent. Then, as the officer came down the aisle, it suddenly came back to life.

'Secure all exits . . . border points . . . Over! He is headed for Busia!'

Even the shrrr-shrrr of radio interference could not hide that shrill voice at the other end. Ndambuki.

'*Kitambulisho tafadhali.* Your ID card, please.' The police officer was now standing by their seats, shining his torch in their faces. Naiguran reached into his shirt pocket and handed his across to the officer. The officer examined it under the torch then trained the light on Naiguran's face.

'Alfred Simiyu, eh?'

'Those are my names, *afande.*' His voice was steady but dots of sweat were forming on his brow.

'Very good. And when were you born, sir?'

Naiguran smiled, expecting the question. He began to reply. Nothing came out. His throat was very dry and he suddenly could not remember what birth date they had finally settled on. Whether the one on the ID was his or Selina's. He and Selina had been standing in that cramped printing press on Accra Road, standing there and arguing over dates. She had taken him there, said not to worry, it was owned by her cousin, a former finger-printing expert with the CID. He remembered all this clearly, remembered thinking how her voice became a squeal when she was arguing, remembered shuddering at the enormity of what he was going to do – remembered everything but the date they had settled on for his new identity.

The officer was now very still and had stopped examining the ID. A small thrill coursed through Naiguran, an orgasmic squeeze. It felt like the time during his final exams in high school – maths – when he had ten minutes left and had not even started Section B, and his panic had caused him to ejaculate. His eyes were beginning to roll and everything was liquid and sinking. The deadness in his hand had returned, was spreading through his body. He felt the girl's hands on his face. They were rough and twisted, and suddenly so familiar to him, calloused village hands of hewing wood and drawing water. He was comforted by the touch, wanted to sleep against her bosom like a child. And she was saying to the officer: 'The boy is not well, *afande* . . . malaria . . .' She sounded like a very old woman. He sensed more than heard the officer moving off. He did not find it strange, as she took her hands off his face, tenderly as if he was a baby falling asleep – he did not find it strange as his head slumped forward and his eyes swam in the sweet afterglow of a fading crisis, that the last things he saw were not her boots but a pair of tiny hooves.

He was seventeen years old again, a fervent tenor in a new white shirt damp with spreading underarm sweat, one of hundreds of students in the massed-choir bussed into the city to sing for the old man at Uhuru Park. It was his first time in Nairobi. They stood in front of the dais, a thousand shining secondary-school students singing for their leader. And right there at the centre of the podium stood a golden cock, a gift from the Queen of England to commemorate the tenth anniversary of the old man's wise and majestic rule. Her Majesty had sent a special envoy with the cock and, it was rumoured, a private letter of apology for not being able to attend herself. It was, even more than the towering bronze statue of the old man in Central Park (a gift from the Koreans), his most prized possession. Naiguran never stopped looking at the old man that day as they sang, feeling how alike they were, how it was possible to rise and change. Had not the old man once herded goats in the Rift Valley? And now the world knelt at his feet, honoured him with gifts.

The cock had become even more valued over the next few years when Her Majesty's government and the donors and diplomats started insisting on 'democracy' and 'multi-parties' and 'human rights', and froze foreign aid. It had become a souvenir of a glorious age that had faded away.

Everybody had heard of the strange, hypnotic powers the cock possessed, how the old man's angriest opponents, his most idealistic and intractable critics, would receive invitations to State House and accept them only at their own ideological peril. Strong men who spoke on behalf of the people were known to have left State House speaking a strange new language.

In their post-coital tangle (usually on the creaking spring bed in her squeezed little room in the State House compound – the smell of soap and eucalyptus leaves even now still stung his nostrils), he and Selina would often discuss how hurt the old man was by his old friends' betrayal; how the lavish dinners, the bacchanalian feasts, had dried up; how empty the parking area was these days. Selina said she even missed cooking for the Europeans. The old man only liked to eat traditional foods – maize and beans, sour milk and sweet potatoes – which meant she couldn't do anything with all her Swiss gourmet training. State House was sad these days. Selina once confided to Corporal Naiguran that she had overheard the old man talking directly to the cock in the official bedroom.

Corporal Naiguran awoke to the familiar sounds of a small town at dawn. The tooting horns of *boda boda* cyclists racing each other, straining with the first of the early-morning passengers. Franco and TPOK Jazz playing *Sandoka Sandoka*. The music came from a tribe of transistor radios that echoed up and down the dusty thoroughfare. Shopkeepers flung open the wooden shutters of their kiosks. A lone cow mooed by the roadside next to a pile of rubbish. Dogs who had ventured too close to open pots yelped and whimpered, fleeing the slipper or the heel of an irritated mistress. Children were crying. He could hear their mothers' voices, low and distinct, the sounds alone painting a picture of tea brewing on stoves in smoky wooden kitchens. Outside the window the rising sun stained the grey and smoky clouds with a childish pink-orange. It would rain in the afternoon, he knew from that colour of sky, but it would be a hot morning.

The bus had stopped and the interior lights were on. Many seats were empty. He turned to the man sitting next to him.

'Where are we?' he asked.

'Busia,' said the man. 'On the Uganda side. The Kenyans have gone to immigration for passport stamping.'

His face was buried behind a newspaper so that only the white cottony periphery of his crown was visible. It was as if he was again looking at the old man in the rear-view mirror.

19

He reached for the bag beneath his feet, weighed it in his hand and felt reassured by its heaviness. And then it hit him: Busia! He stood up, exultant, scrambled past the reading man and strode to the door. He remembered something and turned back.

'By the way, there is somebody sitting there. That seat is taken. A Kenyan student, on her way to Kampala.'

The man looked at him strangely. 'My friend, I doubt that very much. There was an old woman seated here, but she said this was where she was alighting. I even helped her get off.'

Naiguran found this odd and even more odd how much he sounded like the old man. He had obviously slept for longer than he thought. But now he was in a hurry. There was no time to waste. He made effusive noises, full of yeses and OKs and I understands, and walked up the aisle to the door.

As he stepped down from the bus, bag slung over his shoulder, his eyes were already darting about in search of a *boda boda* that would transport him into Uganda – Uganda and a new life. He had made it! He stilled the hysterical excitement building within him, swallowed back the urge to let out a whoop. He felt little delicious twitches running up and down his body. At some point, when he was settled and rich, rich and anonymous, he would find out about Selina, what had happened to her. He wondered whether he would send for her, if she had survived. He would have become Mr Alfred Simiyu by then – yes, sir! – a quiet man in a sub-location of Simiyus and Alfreds, where the stubborn modesty of the hillside villages hid the net worth of generous newcomers.

He saw a long line of *boda bodas* parked in front of a row of decrepit wooden stalls. Others whizzed past him. The *boda bodas* with their multicoloured flags and horns and mudflaps with messages and warnings: *Malipo ni humu humu!* one mudflap declared ominously – your rewards are right here on earth. Men, holding up transistor radios to receptive ears, stood beside stationary bicycles, waiting for morning travellers. For a terrible moment Corporal Naiguran was reminded of the policeman in the bus, the crackling message on his radio. But, in the morning light, he wondered whether all those things had happened – even the girl seemed unreal, part of a long nightmare, bus-sickness. It was over now. He was awake, alive and they did not know where to find him, could not; he, Alfred Simiyu, a new man. He wondered whether they would torture Selina. He felt a little guilty that he had not taken her along with him. After all, she was the one who had walked into the old man's bedroom, past those guards who smiled with nobody, taken the cock and put it in the trolley with the breakfast dishes.

He caught the eye of a particularly hefty-looking *boda boda* driver and gestured to him. The man grabbed the handlebars of his bicycle and started moving towards him, expectant.

'Good morning, chief,' Naiguran greeted him. '*Habari ya asubuhi?* How much to Uganda?'

'*Shilingi hamsini kama kawaida, bwana.* Fifty shillings as usual,' replied the *boda boda* man.

'Fifty! Since when?' Corporal Naiguran was about to start haggling and then thought better of it, buttoned up his new suit and patted it down. Rich men did not quibble over little things. 'OK,' he said a little imperiously. 'Let's go, let's go.'

He clambered onto the bicycle behind the man, felt odd about having to hold another man's waist, so placed his hands on the metal rack under him.

'Let me take your luggage for you, sir,' said the *boda boda* man.

Corporal Naiguran saw no point in protesting and handed the bag over. As he did so, he felt it move. Something stirred inside the bag as if waking up.

The man smiled as he took the bag. '*Hé, hii Jogoo ni kubwa!* This cock is huge!'

This time Corporal Naiguran was going to say something. Then the bag moved again and a cock crowed on hundreds of transistor radios – the signature tune for the National Service news bulletin. As it rose in pitch, the cocks around him began to crow. They stood majestically in scratched-out yards, in the ditch by the road, in their coops in the market. Louder and louder until the radio cocks were drowned out by the living cocks. Their crowing echoed from the no-man's land where Corporal Naiguran sat on the rear of a fifty-shilling *boda boda*, swept through the market on the Kenya side and rippled into the blue hills in the distance. But the closest one of them, the nearest cock crow, came from Corporal Naiguran's bag.

SIX PITCHES
Nadia Crandall

Pitch 1

Charmian was my climbing partner for the week and I didn't like her much. We had walked in from the Falzarego Pass well before dawn to be ahead of the weather. It was almost two hours up through steep meadows, and a forest of spruce and larch, until we reached the scree. She had chattered all the way, telling us how the rope cut into her shoulder, how her new boots rubbed, and marvelling at our progress as the valley fell away behind us. And she fiddled with her hair. Climbers don't do that. They know to conserve energy.

Up here at the base of the climb, there was nothing but wind and rock with the occasional clump of purple gentian clinging to the slopes. Across the valley and hundreds of metres below, a small village was waking to the early sunlight, but this part of the mountain was still in shadow. I wandered over to where Chris stood, and in the sharp morning chill I could feel the heat and tension radiate from his body. He was watching the horizon to the east.

'Like Tremadog?' I said. That was the cliff in Snowdonia where the weather had come in too fast and we had made an emergency bivouac on the mountain, out all night in the storm. Something had started between us there. It was something very small, but I wanted it to be in Chris's thoughts the way it was in mine.

'It's a busy sky,' was all he said. That curt, monosyllabic speech of his, I liked. It was professional and efficient. Not a word wasted. One more thing we had in common. I stayed quiet, close to him, and watched a mass of ragged grey clouds sweep across the sun. At last he nodded. 'It'll do. But we'll get a move on.'

'Tog up, then,' I said.

Charmian sat on a flat rock, applying factor 60 to her face and blue lip-block to her mouth. She had pulled her blond hair back into a pony-tail, and her helmet was wedged at an angle on top of her head, with the buckle loose. Her legs were spread out on either side of her empty pack and her kit lay in a jumble all around her. She looked up and laughed.

'Sorry,' she said. 'Bit of a mess. Couldn't find my rock shoes. Minor panic, actually. Thought I'd left them back at the hostel. And then I couldn't find the chocolate. I mean, I was starving. Had to have something.' She shrugged her narrow shoulders and looked helplessly up at Chris. 'And now it won't all go back in.'

Chris squatted calmly beside her. I was surprised he chose to help. Most likely he was thinking of the weather. With a storm on the horizon, there wasn't time to sit around.

'No problem,' he said, picking up her waterproof jacket and rolling it tight. 'You did well this morning.'

Charmian had done well, I suppose. We had walked in fast, fifteen minutes quicker than the guide time. That was mostly because with her long legs and wiry body, she had pulled ahead and I refused to fall behind. She was taller than me but I had maybe fifteen extra kilos to carry. That made a difference. And I'd slept badly the night before, restless in my bed, dreaming of Tremadog.

Charmian stuffed her chocolate and raisins into the top of the pack where she could get at them easily. For such a skinny girl, she ate a lot.

'Brilliant,' she said. 'I think that's everything.'

'Poles,' said Chris. They lay on the ground behind her.

'Oops! Almost forgot.' Charmian grabbed her trekking poles and collapsed them. She tried to push them in past the chocolate and the raisins, past the rain gear, the extra fleece, the head torch, sun block, camera, climbing boots, mobile phone, lucky elephant charm, and the lunch she'd packed. It was obvious they'd never go in that way. 'Oh, God,' she said, 'it's not going to work. I'm really sorry. I'll have to take everything out and start again.'

I thought Chris would go for her. He hated this kind of incompetence. We all did. It was dangerous, and it could mess up a day's climbing for everyone. But he said nothing. Just sighed, and shook his head.

'Look,' I said, 'we have to get going. I'll take the poles. They'll fit in my pack.'

'Are you sure?' said Charmian. 'I mean, that's brilliant. Thanks, Dot. It's really sweet of you. You're such a star.'

I shrugged and looked over at Chris for some sign of approval, but he had already stepped into his harness, and was paying out rope with neat, deft movements. While Charmian prattled on, I shifted things around inside my pack until her poles found a space. It was awkward. They protruded through the flap behind me so I couldn't easily turn my head. Still, there was nothing to be done about it now.

'I know you've told me, but tell me again,' Charmian went on. 'How many pitches are we going for?' It was the third time she'd asked that morning. She wasn't paying attention. Chris pulled out the climb map and showed it to her.

'Six pitches,' he said. 'Easily within your grade. Only tricky part is the six-plus climb at the top.'

'Six plus?' Charmian laughed. 'Am I OK to do that?' She placed a small hand on his arm. 'You'll have to haul me up, you know, if I can't make it.'

Our first pitch was easy. Just a scramble up scree, really. I told Charmian not to climb directly below, but she paid no attention, as usual. When the rocks began to slide from under my feet, she had to move fast out of their path.

Pitch 2

We turned the ropes at the belay point. There was a 4-minus pitch ahead. We traversed a slab and climbed across an arête. It was pretty exposed and Charmian kept saying it was as sharp as a dragon's back, but I told her to stop talking and think about her feet. After that, we were in the sun and the mountain was easy with plenty of good holds. I let Charmian go first. That way I could retrieve the hardware that Chris had fixed, and move her on when she got stuck. We hardly needed a rope, but we roped in anyway because she was with us, and you don't take chances with a novice.

Pitch 3

And all the time, I was remembering Tremadog. That was when I first met Chris. He was our instructor then as well, only the others hadn't shown up and it was just the two of us on the mountain. Just Chris and me. It started out an easy, sunny climb like this one, and we weren't rushing. We stopped for food around four. Bread, cheese and chocolate, which we ate sitting on that ledge five hundred metres above the valley. We even took time to mess around with rescue techniques and prusiking to reach an overhang. It wasn't that easy, hauling my seventy kilos up a rope, but I did it over and over again for drill. By the end, my arms were killing me.

But from there, Chris had found broken, rusty hardware all the way up. Vandals and amateurs littering the mountain, not bothering to pull their bloody pegs. We had to go cross country, looking for new belay points, round by the north face instead of the west. And then a fog blew in so that visibility was maybe two metres. We couldn't see to climb.

'We wait,' Chris said, 'and we stay warm.'

Then the storm came. I dumped all the karabiners, all the metal hardware, thirty metres away at the far end of the ledge, in case of lightning. And somehow, with no fuss at all, Chris pulled together a bivy for us from the tarpaulin he carried, pegged to the rock above and propped up with trekking poles. The rain began to fall in fat, black drops and the wind rose, pummelling and tearing at our shelter so that I had to talk right into Chris's ear to be heard. I smelt the sweat on him, and the distant scent of soap.

When the light faded, we made a meal from what was left in our packs. And we sat, close and quiet, wrapped in a silver space blanket, eating in the roar of the wind.

I woke sometime in the night. There was silence all around us. The storm had passed, but it was bitterly cold and I was shivering. Chris knew at once and pulled me to him.

'Scared?' he murmured.

'Nope.' How could I be, nestled against his body like that? He shifted slightly. I felt the heat of him and the hardness between his legs, and I couldn't breathe right. I knew I should do something. I wanted to do something. We lay there for a time, knowing and not saying, and when at last

I turned to him, he was asleep. There was only his breath, sweet and light against my cheek.

Now when I remember Tremadog, I reach out to touch him. I can feel his flesh. And he tells me that he longs for me, and our whispers turn to cries of passion. But then I thought it was a dream, and I didn't dare to speak. When morning came, we set up abseil ropes and came down, then walked off the mountain, watching a pair of falcons circle for food. Every pebble was alive with colour, every tussock of mountain grass green and brilliant. I had never seen the world so new. And I didn't speak to him. I didn't speak.

Pitch 4

All the way up, Charmian never stopped talking. Should she try this foothold or that? Should she go for the slab or the gully? She complained that her rock shoes pinched. She shouted up to where Chris held the ropes at the belay point. And she paid no attention at all to the mountain. There was no balance, no form. There was no respect. She scrambled up on her knees and elbows.

I took my time and chose my route carefully. I wanted to climb well, so I made sure of every foothold. I wanted Chris to see what I had learned from him about balance and strategy.

Ahead of me, Charmian was squealing up a chimney.

'Oh, God!' she cried. 'I'm stuck! How do you do this stuff anyway? There's nowhere to put my feet. Can you see another way round, Dot?'

'Get on with it, Charmian,' I called. 'You've done this before. Stick your feet on the rock, and push.'

Chimneys are all about friction. She knew that. Once she remembered, she did it well, moving quickly up, and then across. I watched until she was out of sight, and then I followed her route.

It was tighter than I thought, that chimney, and awkward to climb with a backpack. The first stretch went fine, but there was a kink where I had to turn against the mountain. There, Charmian's poles snagged. They were driven into a narrow fissure above me so that I couldn't move up and, at first, I couldn't even free myself from the rock. I tried twice more, but there was no way to get through. In the end, I had to have Chris let out rope so that I could climb down and try another route. It took an extra ten or fifteen minutes, and while I struggled with Charmian's poles, a fury rose in me that I had to hold down hard and squeeze tight into my chest.

So I was well behind them. When at last I sighted the belay point, Charmian had pulled some chocolate from her pack. She turned to Chris and offered him a square. And they leaned on their ropes, away from the mountain, juggling packs and chocolate wrappers. She was chatting to him. And he was talking back. He'd never talked to me. Not like that. Not in that way. And I could see the softness in his face as he turned to Charmian, the softness and the pleasure in his eyes. I clung to the rock, my whole body rigid.

Pitch 5

Dot. That's what I felt like. A stain, a spot, a punctuation point. Small and unimportant. Now it didn't matter how I climbed. Chris wasn't watching me. He was watching Charmian.

The temperature was falling fast and there were scattered raindrops. Wet rock is always treacherous because the rubber soles of rock shoes don't grip in the same way, and fingers slip on surfaces lubricated with rainwater. My fingers slipped often, and they grew numb with cold. I began to push up any way I could, not caring. Every movement was an effort. Every kilo of extra weight I carried seemed immeasurably heavy, an intolerable burden.

At least Charmian had finally stopped talking. She must have been exhausted. Her face had hollowed around the bones so that she looked older, pale and pinched. At the belay point, she began to shiver. Perhaps it was an early sign of exposure.

Pitch 6

It was the last and hardest pitch, a 6 plus, right at the limit of Charmian's ability. This time, I went first. I had to reach far forward across a crevasse to get onto the slab, and it was slippery now with the spattering rain. Once I was there, my hands, frozen, would not grip, and I couldn't see how to bring my legs across. Below me, there was a great gap where the mountain tumbled sharply away, and above, the holds were widely spaced and not deep enough.

I wedged my right foot into a narrow crack and swung my other knee over, banging it painfully against the ledge. I crabbed across, but there was no route. On my first try, the holds disappeared completely. On my next, a piece of loose rock came away, and I swung against the mountain, clinging on with one hand and the tip of my rock shoe. At last I found a way up, but it was very slow going.

Charmian had climbed below me, ignoring instructions. If another rock came loose, she would be right in its path. She was shivering and hanging on the rope.

'Come on, Dot,' she called. 'I'm freezing. Get a move on.'

'If I bloody could,' I yelled, 'I bloody would.'

Now it was desperation and raw strength, what was left of it. A mist was rolling in, obscuring the valley below, and I wanted to be off the mountain. Not Tremadog. Not that again. Not with her.

The last stretch, I had to fist my hand inside a fissure and lean my weight against it to move up. The rock tore at my wrist and blood trickled down my arm. Then there was a toe-hold with an impossible reach. I had to jump for it. Jump, and cling on, and belly my way onto the next outcrop.

By the time I topped out, my legs were trembling from the effort, and my breath was coming in great gasps. I couldn't even tie in properly, and Chris had to sort out my ropes for me. I sat next to him on the ledge with tears in my eyes, wanting to speak and not knowing where to start.

I thought we'd have time. I thought Charmian would take ages on the pitch. It was a stretch for me and it should have been terrifying for her. But she was no more than a minute behind. She scraped her way up in nothing flat. Elbows, knees, no form. But she did it. Chris watched her admiringly.

'She's a natural,' he said.

All those hours, days, on the climbing wall, working on technique. I was easily a 6-plus climber and she did the pitch as if it was nothing. All those hours, and never anyone to turn to me with their face soft, and pleasure in their eyes.

Now Chris had pulled the map from his pack and was checking it for the walk down. There was a new kind of urgency in him because the rain was slanting in our faces and it would make getting off the mountain a slow and treacherous business. And though there were huts along the route, no one wanted to be up here all night.

It was then, when Charmian was leaning on her rope, and Chris was concentrating on the map, that I saw she was tied in wrong. The rope was starting to slide from the clip and there was nothing to hold her. I had only to look away for a moment, and she'd be gone. I wanted her gone. She took my light from me.

I could see her stumble and tilt, her hands clawing at the mountain but finding only the wind. Chris grabs for her and misses. And screaming, she plummets onto the slab, down past the crevasse, slamming from rock to rock, until she comes to a halt, lifeless, on the stony scree below. Gone. The chattiness of her, the blond slenderness of her, the lightness of her, gone. I could see it so vividly, I almost believed it was real.

Charmian glanced over at me. Her hair, darkened by the rain, poked out from her helmet and snaked across her cheek.

'Oh, God,' she said. 'That last pitch! Scared me to death. Thought I'd never make it. Lucky you were there to find a route.'

And I couldn't let her go. Of course I'd never have let her go. I grabbed her arm with one hand and her harness with the other.

'Tied in wrong,' I said. 'Look at your bloody knot, you idiot.'

BUS TICKET REVISITED
Zoë Fairbairns

One evening in 1974, I was sitting on a train on the London Underground, trying to write a short story. I don't normally write on trains, or in any public places for that matter. I'm more of a lock-all-the-doors-and-pull-up-the-drawbridge kind of writer. But this was an emergency.

The train hurtled along the dark tunnels of the Northern Line. My destination was Belsize Park, meeting place of my women's writing group. I had agreed to bring a new story along. But it had been a busy week and I hadn't written it. What would the others say if I turned up empty-handed? They would know that I wasn't serious in my commitment to the group. They would blame me for wasting their time.

The train stopped, and I glanced up at the map to see how much longer I had to finish my story. Finish it? I hadn't even started.

Tottenham Court Road. 'Once upon a time . . .'

I chewed my pen.

Goodge Street. 'It is a truth universally acknowledged . . .'

Warren Street. 'An Englishman, a Scotsman and an Irishman went into a bar . . .'

Nothing worked. Finally, in desperation, I jotted this down:

Bus Ticket

This is a very short story about being in the women's movement every day of your life.

I travel by bus a lot, so I have a season ticket. You have to sign your name on the front and delete whichever does not apply to you of 'Mr, Mrs or Miss'. None of them applies to me, so I deleted them all and put 'Ms'.

'Ms' is accepted – well, tolerated – by such prestigious and indispensable bodies as the *Guardian*, the Passport Office, the Post Office, the Co-op Bank and Hackney Public Library. I also have high hopes of the Electricity Board, particularly as I have taken to cutting 'Miss' off my meter-reading card with scissors, and it is one of those cards that you aren't supposed to mutilate as it upsets the computer. All this notwithstanding, 'Ms' was not acceptable to the conductor of the Number 14 bus that Monday. He snatched my ticket, demanded to know whether I was Miss or Mrs, and then, when I refused to answer, glanced at my ringless left hand, crossed out 'Ms' and wrote 'Miss'.

I'm not what you'd call the retiring type, and I rarely shrink from a fight when I'm sure of my own righteousness, but there is one thing I cannot cope with, and that is unprovoked aggression. I am prepared to accept that anyone who knows me may dislike me, but when someone who cannot dislike me because they don't know me, attacks me, I collapse inside, I lose eloquence, I get frightened, sometimes I cry. So I said nothing to this conductor, just wrote down his staff number.

When it was time to get off the bus, he gave me what I thought was a friendly smile and said, 'It's all right, dear, I agree with you.' I was encouraged. 'I don't know what you are,' he went on. 'I don't know if you're a boy or a girl.' He then invited my fellow passengers to speculate on the subject.

I left the bus, went to an inspector and reported the incident. He promised to look into my complaint, and ceremoniously restored my defaced season ticket with an eraser. He suggested I confirm my complaint in writing.

I spent the day between anger and guilt. So what if I report him? So he gets disciplined or yelled at or fired. He's an oppressed worker doing a horrible job. Perhaps he heard today that he's going to be evicted, his mother is sick, his kid's been thrown out of school. Hasn't he got enough to worry about without being clobbered over the head by the injured pride of a woman fortunate enough to have the time to worry about the title on her season ticket?

Wouldn't the right thing be to write to London Transport withdrawing the complaint, and send a friendly letter to the conductor himself, explaining the meaning of 'Ms' and asking his tolerance for opinions different from his own?

Such thoughts soothed me, and then the reality of what had happened would come shooting through my consciousness like a speedboat churning up a calm sea: how dare he decree that I must wear a badge indicating, for men's convenience, whether I was available or already had an owner?

How dare he speculate on the subject, and then write his conclusions on a document that I must carry around with me and display for a month?

How dare he whip up strangers to hostility just because I didn't wear clothes clearly indicating my sex? What was it to them whether I was a woman or a man?

Then I was showered with the realization that I had spent half a working day thinking these thoughts, during which time, if I had put a foot wrong, I would have immediately proved, to some people's satisfaction, the innate unsuitability of women for this type of work; and that clinched it. I wrote the letter and confirmed the complaint. Wouldn't you?

There is now a space for 'Ms' on a London Transport season ticket.

The story is true. Every word. Well, not quite every word. You see, the conductor wasn't a he but a she. Which somehow makes it different and somehow doesn't. And I still don't know if what I did was right, and I still resent every minute I spend wondering.

I would like to be able to tell you that this story – scribbled in haste and in extremis – made my fortune. It hasn't, but as befits a story that was conceived on a bus and written on a tube, it has become one of my best-travelled pieces of work. It was the first piece of my writing to be translated into a foreign language (Dutch, in 1980) and the first to be published in the USA. It has appeared in English-language teaching materials from

Scandinavia to France to Japan, and I have met total strangers in Zimbabwe, in Germany, in Australia who know and remember this story.

All of which adds up to another argument for using public transport: not only is it better for the environment, but buses and trains are packed with stories.

Here's another one:

It was a Sunday evening in the autumn of 2002. I had been working the weekend shift. I was worn out, and looking forward to being at home.

I arrived at Victoria at around 7.30, in good time for the 7.38 to the south London suburb where I live. I paused to buy a newspaper and a take-away coffee, then went to get on the train. Ahead of me was another woman – middle-aged, white, no distinguishing characteristics. Stepping into the carriage, she turned right, then seemed to change her mind, in the way you might do if you had spotted something unsavoury close to where you had been planning to sit – excessive litter, perhaps, or a pool of sick. She turned left and went to sit at the far end, as far away as possible from whatever had bothered her.

I couldn't see anything, and there were plenty of seats at the right-hand end, so I chose one and sat down. Also in the carriage were a man in workmen's overalls who looked as if he was trying to sleep, and four twenty-something women wearing Islamic-style headscarves. The women looked to be of Arabic origin, but when one of them spoke she sounded more like a native south Londoner. A very angry native south Londoner. Her words exploded out of her: 'Did you *hear* what that woman *said*?'

Through the haze of my tiredness, I thought for a moment that she meant me. But I hadn't said anything. She was talking about the woman who had got on before me and who had gone to sit at the other end of the carriage. 'She said, "I'm not sitting with a bunch of asylum seekers."'

'She said *what*?' said her friend, who also sounded British-born.

'Asylum seekers. She called us asylum seekers.'

'*Us*?' Two of them were joining in now, indignant and incredulous. The fourth looked blank, her face politely questioning, as if she had not followed what was happening. One of the others explained the situation to her in what sounded like Arabic, and she nodded uncertainly.

33

'Who said that?'

'That old bag up there.' One of the women pointed at the culprit, who was affecting an air of indifference whilst sitting at what she clearly hoped was a safe distance. 'She did. She came in here, she nearly sat down, then she saw our headscarves and said, "I'm not sitting with a bunch of asylum seekers."'

Great, I thought. So much for my hopes of a nice quiet journey home with my *Observer* and my cappuccino with chocolate sprinkles. Two minutes before departure time and here I am trapped between four angry Muslim women at one end of the carriage and a bigot at the other. I considered changing seats – better still, changing carriages – but realized that if I did, it would make me look as if I too was refusing to sit among the women with the headscarves. While I was still trying to make up my mind, the man in the workmen's overalls who had been trying to sleep, opened his eyes. 'Keep it down, girls. You're giving me a 'eadache.'

Quick as a flash, the one who had spoken first said, 'If you've got a headache, it's because you're drunk.'

As this was almost certainly true, the man cowered. The doors slid closed and the train moved off.

Now that we were on the move, I was hoping that things would quieten down, but if anything they got worse. Perhaps the sight of a twilit Pimlico slipping past the window made the women feel they had a bigger potential audience for their grievance, if only they could shout loudly enough to reach it. 'I was born in this country! I've lived here all my life and she has the cheek to call me –' The woman stopped, as if she refused to allow the phrase to soil her lips.

Another one took over. 'My little girl is six. She wears a headscarf, and do you know what she got called in her school playground? A terrorist.'

'Because she wears a headscarf?'

'Because she wears a headscarf.'

They were egging each other on. The one who did not speak English was being kept informed in brief snatches of Arabic. Her expression was politely indignant, showing solidarity with her friends but not wanting to get involved.

They were like a chorus, telling the story over and over again, reminding each other, keeping it going. No one was disputing anything they said, but none of them wanted to be the first to fall silent.

'She comes in here –'

'I was born in this country.'

'. . . headscarves . . .'

'My little girl . . .'

'. . . *asylum seekers* . . .'

'Terrorists!'

Another voice intervened, one we had not heard before, coming from the other end of the carriage. 'I didn't say that.'

It was the culprit. The alleged culprit, I suppose I should say. Necks craned to look at her. The man next to her, who seemed to have taken her under his protection, said, 'She says she didn't say what you ladies say she said. You must have misheard.'

'What did she say, then?'

The woman had no answer, and neither had her defender. Until that moment I had had an open mind on what she had or had not said, but her truculence and obvious contempt convinced me that she was indeed guilty as charged. But she had at least disowned her words, which was as near as she seemed likely to get to an apology, so perhaps the women with the headscarves could leave it at that?

'She's a fucking liar,' shrieked the one who had spoken first.

'We heard what she said,' said another. 'Let's see her come down here and say it again.'

'Yeah, leave your fancy man behind and come back here.'

By now I had made up my mind to get off at the next station. But before we could get there, the train stopped in the middle of a bridge. The brakes sighed in the way they have of letting you know that you are going to be here for some time. Far below, the river looked dark and peaceful, with lights gleaming up at us from a passing barge. I was thinking how pleasant it would be to be down there, when I heard the clunk.

It came from under my seat – the sound of a bottle falling over, a heavy bottle, one of those big beer bottles with a metal fastening. I hadn't even realized it was there, but the slight jolt as the train stopped had caused it to topple. No one else seemed aware of it, but we all know, don't we, what happens to a bottle on its side on the floor of a train, when that train starts moving? The bottle rolls about. In this carriage full of angry people, someone might spot the bottle and pick it up. Someone might find a use for it.

The train shifted. Through the soles of my feet came a warning vibration: the bottle was on the move. I could feel it tapping at the back of my heel. I wondered how long I could keep it out of sight.

Casually I rearranged my feet. As far as I could tell, no one had noticed the bottle, certainly not the women in the headscarves who were too busy shouting, 'You come down here and say that again, you racist cow! Never mind your pimp looking after you, you just come back here –'

I said quietly, 'Not everyone thinks the same, you know.'

The woman who had spoken first turned on me. 'What?' It was less a request to know what I had said, than a sneer.

'Not everyone thinks the same.' I kept my voice quiet, remembering something a social worker friend had told me once about conflict management: never try to shout an angry person down, they'll just shout more loudly. Speak quietly and they might lower their own volume. I held out my hands with the palms upwards, which is apparently recognized the world over as a gesture of conciliation. As well as whatever subliminal significance it has, it shows that you are not holding a weapon, that your fists are not clenched.

'I didn't hear what that woman said to you,' I said. 'From what you say, it was rude and ignorant, and she was rude and ignorant to say it. But that's her problem. You don't have to make it yours.'

'Or ours,' said the man in the overalls, daring to open his mouth for the first time since being accused of being drunk. 'No one up this end said anything. Why take it out on us?'

'Exactly,' said someone from the enemy end of the train. 'We just want to get home.'

'Look,' said the woman in the headscarf. 'I'm British. I'm as British as anyone here. I was born here –'

'Yes. You said.'

'So why is it that if I want to go out in a headscarf I get called names?'
'But we didn't call you anything,' I said.

'No, well, you're a decent person, you have respect for Islam, but why can't everybody? I'm a Muslim but it doesn't stop me having respect for Christianity. I don't go around calling people terrorists just because they've got' – she looked up and down the carriage for an analogy – 'crosses round their necks,' she said finally, although no one I could see had a cross round their neck. Her friends were silent, listening to our conversation. One by one they sat down, leaving the one I was talking to the only one on her feet. She sat too. The carriage relaxed a little. The train jolted forward and the bottle rolled out. I held my head rigid, forcing myself not to look at the bottle. The woman wasn't interested in the bottle; she was saying, 'I don't make my little girl wear the headscarf. She wants to wear it. Sometimes I wish she wouldn't wear it, the way she gets treated for wearing it, but she insists. She says, it shows I'm a good Muslim, doesn't it, Mum? She just wants to be a good Muslim, and then people spit on her. She has, she's been spat on, my six-year-old daughter, for wearing a headscarf.'

'That's terrible,' I said. I knew how lame it sounded, but I couldn't think of anything else to say. In the silence that followed, the bottle rolled to the end of the carriage. No one took any notice.

'Live and let live, that's my attitude,' said the drunk man in the overalls. 'I think you girls look very attractive in your headscarves, if you don't mind me saying so.'

I sipped my cappuccino.

By now we were pulling in at Battersea Park. The woman who was supposed to have made the remark slunk off the train. I wondered if she had been meaning all along to get off here, or whether she was sentencing herself to a thirty-minute wait on the dark platform.

The women in the headscarves left the train at Clapham Junction, so I never got the chance to confirm that I do indeed respect Islam, in the same way as I respect Christianity, Judaism, Buddhism and Zoroastrianism, as well as Druids, Hare Krishnas, Moonies and people who think that bloke on the TV programme is communicating with their dead relatives.

I saw one of the women again on a train the other day, minus her friends, but still wearing her headscarf. I tried to say hello to her, but she was reading the Qur'an and didn't notice me.

First published in *How Do You Pronounce Nulliparous?* by Zoë Fairbairns
Five Leaves Publications, 2004 www.fiveleaves.co.uk

DEAD WEIGHT
Elizabeth Sarkany

A **dog lay dying in the road outside my house. From the window, I saw a** small group of people gathered round, looking down at the dog, and a laundry van abandoned with the driver's door open. I took an umbrella out there and held it up to give the dog some shade. It was the hottest July on record. Ten in the morning and you could already smell the heat rising from the dustbins.

I recognized the dog. She belonged to Ernest, an elderly man who lives a few doors up from me on the other side of the street. It was just the two of them in that place. Ernest and the dog. Ernest does have family: a scruffy, taciturn son in his forties who changes the light-bulb when it goes in Ernest's porch and takes him to Sainsbury's every couple of weeks in a battered blue Skoda. And a daughter who lives in Andalucia. Ernest showed me a picture of her once, when we were waiting in the queue at the Post Office. She was standing with three very dark, unsmiling children and all of them were dressed in riding clothes. 'She doesn't get back much,' Ernest told me. 'Can't leave her husband's business.' He smiled. 'She wants me to get email,' he said.

You only had to see them together, Ernest and the dog. You could tell how much she meant to him.

Ernest had gone inside to call the vet.

'He's been very calm about this,' said Rowena, who does some of my neighbours' gardens. '*Very* understanding.' She glared at a pale man crouched down with his hand on the dog's shuddering ribcage.

'I didn't see her,' said the man.

'What happened?' I asked.

'A cat ran out in front of my van,' he said, squinting up at me as though he'd come into blinding sunlight from a darkened room. 'I was too busy avoiding it. I didn't see the dog chasing behind.'

'Ernest is a gentleman,' said Rowena. 'If this were my dog, I'd be screaming at you.' I've never been keen on Rowena, with her freckles and her vest tops and her take-me-as-I-am underarm hair.

'He'll be in shock,' said the driver.

'Anyway,' I said, 'speaking from experience, you can never really predict how you'll react in a crisis.'

'Oh, I can,' said Rowena. 'No way would I have been polite about this. I can predict that for nothing.'

'I saw the whole thing happen,' sobbed a thin young woman dressed like an extra from an *EastEnders* funeral scene, in a black tailored jacket and skirt and a wide-brimmed black straw hat. I handed her a tissue from my apron pocket and she blew her nose. 'Right in front of me,' she whimpered. 'There was nothing I could do.'

The dog was motionless now but I saw that the driver's hand, still resting on her side, was shaking.

'You poor thing,' I said to him. 'I think this is almost worst for you.'

'She's breathing,' said the driver. 'I can feel her breathing.'

A bit of dark blood oozed out of the dog's ear.

'Things happen in life,' I said. A few years earlier my husband had killed himself while I was at work, treating psychiatric patients. 'A set of circumstances combine in some awful, unique way . . .'

'I could hold the umbrella,' offered the young woman. 'It's very important for me to feel I can do something . . .'

'The umbrella's fine,' I snapped. 'The point of the umbrella is to shade the dog and that's what it's doing.'

'I had things on my mind,' said the driver. 'I wish to God I'd taken the day off work. I felt out of sorts from the start.'

'Men and their sodding cars,' muttered Rowena. 'Take it all so sodding lightly. You shouldn't be driving if you're not up to it. This could have been a child lying here like this. When you get behind the wheel you're in charge of a lethal sodding killing machine.'

'You mustn't blame yourself,' I said to the driver. 'It achieves nothing. Hindsight is a bloody wonderful thing.'

The dog lay dying and everybody had an angle.

Everything about the dog had gone slack by the time Ernest hobbled back outside, leaning heavily on his stick. Her legs, splayed out underneath her on the hot tarmac, her open jaw, her unfurled tongue. I reached down and batted a fly away from one of her eyes and she didn't even blink.

'The vet's between surgeries,' said Ernest. 'He's on his way.'

We were all behaving as though the dog was still alive.

'You mustn't blame yourself,' said Ernest to the driver. Ernest is a very well-spoken man. Even under those circumstances, his words were level and courteous. 'I shouldn't have had her off the lead,' he said.

The two of them swapped names and phone numbers, both writing carefully on blank delivery dockets from the driver's pad.

'I'll give you a call,' said the driver, folding the piece of paper and putting it in his wallet behind a photo of a startled-looking baby. 'I'd like to know how she's doing,' he said.

I caught an expression of surprise on the vet's face when he arrived. At the way we all looked at him as though there might be something he could do. The way I was shielding the dog from the sun. I could see that he knew it was too late to save the dog before he'd even crossed to where she was. When you've seen enough death it's something you recognize. He and Ernest took her off to the surgery anyway. Rowena went too so Ernest wouldn't have to come home on his own.

'This dog's a dead weight,' said the vet, staggering to his estate car with the limp dog in his arms.

'Come inside,' I said to the driver. 'Have a cup of tea.' It didn't seem right for him to get straight back behind the wheel. Anyway, I wanted to reassure him that none of it was his fault. And I thought it might be a help if he could talk about the other things going on in his life. I miss that aspect of my work. I lost my bottle after what happened to my husband and couldn't do it any more. Nevertheless, I'm still a highly trained professional.

But the driver couldn't wait to get away. I imagine he returned the van to the depot and took the rest of the day off sick.

The young woman was properly crying by then. Each time she took a breath it caught at the top like it does in a feverishly upset child.

'I wouldn't mind that cup of tea myself,' she said.

I remembered then how much I had to do. I keep a tight grip on things in the house these days. A woman's work and all that.

When Katie and Max were little, their dad and I were one of those high-flying two-career couples. I left the house at eight every morning and came back just in time to read them a bedtime story. I used to run, panting, into parents' evenings straight from work, reading psychiatric reports while I queued for the teachers. We had an Irish nanny who baked novelty cakes for birthdays and hand-sewed pumpkin costumes for Hallowe'en. I was the envy of all my friends, with their au pairs bringing strange men back from nightclubs and lying in bed all day with period pains. I couldn't be messed about like that, not with my commitments. I paid our nanny top whack, bought her a brand-new Renault Clio and even stopped going on holiday to that lovely *pensione* in Umbria because it didn't have air-conditioning and she didn't like the bugs that came in through the windows.

Things are very different now. For a start, I can't seem to do more than one thing at a time. And I don't find uncertainty exciting. I've cut uncertainty right out. In any case, those children have been through enough. I like them to come home to the smells of casseroles and home-baked cakes. I change the sheets twice a week. I do anything I can think of that makes a house a home.

'I take everything desperately to heart,' the young woman explained, sitting on the edge of the bentwood chair in my kitchen, sipping a cup of camomile tea. She told me her name was Natalie. She'd taken her hat off and her hair was dull and matted with sweat. I was struck by the sharpness of her features, now that I could see them properly. Her face was blotchy from crying. My little electric fan hummed on the table, gamely moving the stifling air from one side of itself to the other and back again. 'My therapist says I'm one of those people that doesn't have a thick enough skin,' she said.

I felt my hackles rise. I haven't got time for navel-gazing. That's another big change. I used to worship happily at the altar of psychotherapy. Once I'd specialized in psychiatry, I used to refer my patients for it all the time, so they could work things through, resolve the issues, move on. I used to shrug and smile to myself when others talked about the dangers of opening cans of worms, the advantages of just pulling yourself together. Laypeople couldn't be expected to understand these things. That's the way I saw it then. But the truth is that therapy doesn't change the facts. And therapists, in my experience, are into expressing anger in a big way. There they are, egging you on for fifty solid minutes and then you're out the door and on your own again until next Tuesday at ten o'clock. They unleash all that and then they leave you to get on with making sure there's a football kit ready for Thursday, remembering to buy some mince for a lasagne, deciding whether to cut your losses with the broken washing machine. They leave you, your head all stirred up with rage, to try and concentrate on conversations about why the food groups matter and how Katie's friend Heather pretended she was crying *happy* tears when her dad told her his girlfriend was having a baby.

I looked at my watch and bit into a chocolate muffin. Natalie couldn't eat anything her mother hadn't specially prepared.

'I have to be so careful,' she said. 'I have allergies.'

All right for Natalie, with her thin skin and her allergies and her mother there to pick up all the pieces. Easy for Natalie, inflicting her emotional responses to every random thing on anyone that happens to be nearby. Natalie only has herself to think about. Therapy was fine – 'doing the emotional work' – that was all fine, before I understood that you have to see life in terms of . . . bottom lines. That life, when it comes down to it, is really just a very tiring and long-drawn-out exercise in survival.

I looked at my watch again. Natalie made no move to go. I wished she would.

'I'll need to run down to the shops in a minute for some ingredients,' I said. 'I thought I'd make a strawberry sponge and leave it on Ernest's step for when he gets back.'

'What do you think they'll do with the dog?' whispered Natalie. She dabbed both eyes.

I willed the phone to ring, although, nowadays, it hardly ever does.

*

I saw Natalie again that evening. I went outside to water my geraniums and she was rounding the corner at the top of the street and walking down the hill towards Ernest's house. She was holding a bunch of white lilies. Her arms were bare. They looked thin enough to snap. She walked slowly and very carefully, as though she was frightened that she might fall and break something, or that a breath of wind might take her off her feet. She was concentrating so hard that she didn't notice me. I went straight back inside and quietly closed the front door. I've nothing against the girl, obviously, but we were thrown together by circumstances. A friendship's not something I want to foster. Anyway, I have my routine. I had supper to make and homework to help with. I had baths to run. I had to get on.

I sat down at the kitchen table, and started stripping the skin off some chicken breasts. I tried to think of three positive things that had happened, which is something I used to advise my patients to do every day.

Katie's nosebleed came out of her pillowcase in a boil wash, I thought.

Each piece of chicken had one of those thick white vessels at one end, tough gristly tubes that you'd know about when you were chewing.

I had a box of paracetamol in the bathroom when I needed some for my headache, I thought.

I crossed the kitchen to fetch my sharpest little knife.

I slept OK last night, pretty much all the way through, I thought, *and I don't remember my dreams.*

I was a doctor once, of course. People don't realize that psychiatrists train first in medicine. I spent a good few years palpating abdomens, inserting drip lines and assisting with hernia repairs before I decided to specialize in the human mind. There are clues that give it away even now. The way I wash my hands to the wrists under a running tap before cooking, and dry them in a direction away from the fingers. The reassuring competence with which I excise a chicken's arteries, each in its own neat triangle of bloodless flesh.

PAROXYSM
Lucy Roeber

In the waiting room of a Harley Street clinic, a woman perches on the edge of a green armchair. Her name is Eleanor and she is thirty-three years old. She wears a dress of dark-blue silk satin with cut-velvet trimming; her light-brown hair is pulled back from her pale face. Fearful that sudden movement might unravel her, she is concentrating on being perfectly still. Only her breath flutters in her whalebone corset.

Eleanor is here at her husband's insistence that medical help is needed for her behaviour since the stillbirth of their child. Last week, he told her over dessert that something had to be done about her Condition. Looking at her with concern across the table, he informed her through his greying moustache that her Disposition was becoming increasingly Hysterical. He said that he had met a Harley Street Specialist who came highly recommended and whom he judged to be a good, reliable sort. For the first time in History, Science would be able to relieve her affliction. He smiled reassuringly into his custard. Eleanor had wanted to speak, perhaps apologize, but instead she had excused herself and left the room.

She knows her husband is right and that part of her is going astray; more than he realizes. He has not witnessed the headaches that confine her to her room all day, or heard her weeping until she cannot breathe. He is at his office on Thursday afternoons so is unaware that she no longer attends the parish meetings. She cannot tell him that she has begun to question God's will.

Before Samuel arrived dead into this world, Eleanor had considered her short marriage to be successful. She was extremely proficient at running a house, gaining confidence in entertaining; her competence pleased both her and her husband. She did not mind that he was often away on matters of business, or distracted with the latest shipment of tea from Ceylon, as she had always enjoyed her own company. He called her my little bird in private.

As an associate of her father's, he had been in the margins of her life, though scarcely registered, since childhood. Her only clear memories of him were of the red silk scarf he always wore and his particularly accomplished piano playing one Christmas Eve. So when, six years previously, he arrived at the family's town house in Hampstead asking if Eleanor were at home, no one could have predicted that he was going to propose marriage. He was unanimously agreed to be a good match: an older man, of respectable standing and irreproachable conduct. And she liked the way he spoke softly to her, and had been both flattered and impressed by his uninterest in the charms of her prettier, younger sisters.

'If you would like to come through, Mrs Bruton.' A young nurse, severely dressed in a well-starched uniform, waits in the doorway. Her dark, curious eyes look at Eleanor for longer than feels comfortable. She stands up self-consciously, her skirts brushing the parquet floor.

The Specialist rises from behind a large rosewood desk to one side of the window; the deep-red bristles on his chin are lit up by the early autumn sunlight. Eleanor takes in a picture of Queen Victoria from her Golden Jubilee four years before, pale and toad-like, on the mantelpiece; a silver ashtray in the shape of an Oriental slipper on the desk; and a series of botanical etchings and framed medical certificates lining the panelled walls. As the Specialist introduces himself by commenting on the pleasant lunch he enjoyed with her husband at their club, she notes that he is younger than she expected. She presumed he would be creaking with experience and gravitas. Instead, he has a ruddy face, piercing blue eyes and sports a well-cut navy suit with a heavy gold watch-chain tucked into a pocket. Eleanor imagines his wife as a warm, fecund woman, able to fill their leafy suburban house with child after child.

Eleanor knows she has failed as a woman. She did not conceive for five years after her wedding night and then the baby died in her womb. He arrived before term with his bloody head wrapped in tiny, paper arms, as though shielding himself from the light. The midwife was about to twist him up in a sheet and take him away. But Eleanor insisted on holding him to her breast. She could have cradled him in one hand. She called him by his name, Samuel, over and over again, and pressed his tiny nose, like an unopened daisy, against her cheek.

Eleanor sits very still opposite the Specialist. It does not matter that she is silent, as she is not asked very much. She has already been diagnosed and this consultation is a mere formality. She doesn't listen to the Specialist's monologue on Medical Science and Progress. But she notices that when he eventually mentions her treatment, a rash blossoms red under his white collar. He tells Eleanor that he has purchased only recently the electromechanical machine with which he will shortly treat her, and has been impressed by the results. He apprises her that Dr Joseph Mortimer Granville first developed the device in London in 1883 and that over the last eight years the patent has been copied in the best European and New World spas. He strongly believes it to be the long-awaited cure for the condition that debilitates many of the weaker sex: Hysteria. He informs her that he is in the middle of writing an article to that effect for *The Lancet*. Finally, he wants to reassure her that, although her affliction is also known as Womb Disease, it has nothing to do with her stillbirth. Rather, it is linked to her temperament.

'Do you have any questions, Mrs Bruton, before the nurse takes you through to the surgery?' The Specialist looks at the mahogany clock on his desk.

Eleanor wants to ask about her temperament but she cannot find the words in time.

The dark-eyed young woman is standing at the door. Eleanor follows her into the surgery. It is immaculate, and smells overpoweringly of polish and disinfectant. The wooden floor gleams; a green screen is folded neatly to the side; labelled jars and bandages are carefully stacked in a glass-fronted cabinet. The examination bed is crisp with clean linen.

The nurse unfolds the screen to create a changing area. As instructed, Eleanor starts the arduous procedure of removing her clothing. Fumblingly, she undoes the many tiny buttons that run down the front of her dress and along the forearms. The nurse tries to help, roughly unpicking her corset from behind, and Eleanor wishes she would leave her to struggle alone. Her clothes pile higher on the chair, a mountain of Victorian decency. With each layer shed, Eleanor breathes more deeply.

The new electric light above her head buzzes and casts a glossy sheen over the smooth undulations of her small breasts and narrow hips. She quickly conceals herself in the floor-length surgical gown handed her by the nurse from a chest beneath the blinded window. The nurse motions her to the examination bed. As she lies waiting for the Specialist, Eleanor wonders if the treatment will really help.

When the doctor enters, he walks straight to the far corner and starts to pull what Eleanor had taken to be a sideboard across the room towards her. The machine. It is bulky and improbable, encased in a free-standing rectangular box made of a dark, varnished wood. It is on castors for easy manoeuvre. A cable snakes behind. On the top of the machine, there is a complex arrangement of dials, knobs and switches. Beside them, what looks like a black rubber egg rests on a metal tray, along with a row of precisely aligned implements that glint in the artificial light. On one side of the box is a dull green panel.

The Specialist puts on a white coat and starts another monologue, addressing himself to the black oval which he picks up and examines with pink fingertips. He explains that she has disturbances in the womb, caused by excess liquid that needs to be drained. He tells her that she has all the classic symptoms of Pelvic Hyperaemia: melancholy, lassitude, inappropriate behaviour and weepiness. They will have a preliminary session today and, if he thinks it successful, they will continue with the full cycle of treatments. He recommends once a week for four months.

The Specialist presses down a switch and the contraption leaps into life. The wooden box hums and clanks loudly. It starts to shake on its four wheels as if preparing for a race. The green panel glows, weakly at first, then steadily brighter. The rubber egg in the doctor's hand vibrates and he adjusts a dial with a frown of expert concentration. After the initial shock, Eleanor relaxes slightly, almost smiles. There is something absurd about the doctor's quaking box. She wonders what her husband can have been thinking.

The nurse appears at the doctor's side and casually opens the lower half of Eleanor's gown, exposing her naked belly and legs and private parts to the harsh electric light. Eleanor's blush prickles from her face down her chest and arms. Even her husband has never looked at her like this. She turns her face to the wall and shuts her eyes. She tries to lose herself in the rattling hum.

The Specialist presses the vibrating oval between her legs, amid her dark pubic hair, between her lips.

Eleanor breathes in sharply, her eyes open spontaneously and her head twists towards the Specialist. He has the same look of expert concentration, his brow furrowed and his jaw set. Her body has stiffened, each muscle reacting against this affront to her privacy. Her toes and fingers have curled into tight balls; her face burns. Had her husband not been adamant that this man could help her, she might have struggled to her feet and run out of the room. But she knows she will have to endure this humiliation once. She tries to resign herself to it. To unclench her body. She closes her eyes again and attempts to slow down her ragged breathing.

Slowly. Slowly, she is aware that her tense muscles are beginning to relax. She finds herself tilting her pelvis towards the source of the vibration. A deliciously intimate sensation spreads through her body. A sensation half known, half new. She feels hot and damp between her legs, and involuntarily opens them wider. She squeezes her eyes tighter against the confusion of feelings and the heat radiating from her in waves, and tries not to move. But then the electric light, the nurse's inquisitiveness, the doctor monitoring the dials, the noise of the contraption, the sterile surgery – all recede unexpectedly. She is conscious only of her private parts becoming ripe and swollen and full.

Eleanor is unaware of the sound that comes out of her mouth as her body climaxes.

As her senses gather together, Eleanor notices that her breathing is rapid and the room is silent. She is paralysed by the abandon of her experience. She wants to ask if such loss of restraint is normal. Tentatively opening her eyes, at first she cannot see through the brightness. She feels someone closing the gown over her nakedness. Eventually she makes out the doctor, his face forcing a rigid smile in her direction. He loosens his collar with his finger, as though it were the height of summer, and clears his throat.

'Mrs Bruton, you have experienced a Hysterical Paroxysm. Your first treatment has been successful. I will see you next week.'

He leaves the room quickly. She has said nothing. Every propriety has been upheld.

Without turning her head, Eleanor watches the nurse slowly wheel the contraption back to its place, and vigorously wipe it with disinfectant.

She lies still and heavy, flooded. She is amazed and horrified by the reaction the machine has produced. That such a treatment could be sanctioned by her husband, let alone the medical profession – that she should have such an experience somewhere so impersonal, and amongst strangers, is bewildering.

Eleanor politely refuses the nurse's offer to help her get dressed, not yet able to meet her eye. There is something in the young woman's demeanour that she finds disrespectful, almost insolent. She struggles back into the layers of clothes and decency and duty, lacing her corset as best she can. With long, well-tended fingers she fastens each tiny button of her dress and smoothes her hair back into its tight bun. She collects her missing hairpins from the examination table in the palm of her hand. Looking at the wrinkled linen, she trusts that all traces of her presence will be erased by the time the next patient arrives.

She hopes that her husband will not ask her about the treatment. And at the same time, she hopes he will question her intensely. Coax it out of her. Reassure her that her response was expected, even necessary for her cure. Then, with a little relief, she remembers that her husband's cousin and his wife, from Harrogate, are coming for supper, so they won't have any time alone that evening. They will be eating stewed venison.

On the Friday following her fifth appointment with the Specialist, Eleanor retires early. She is sailing in the half moment before sleep when she hears the gentle tap on her bedroom door. Her heart thuds against her ribcage as if she has heard a ghost. It is many months since her husband came to her room.

'You may enter.' The voice sounds stronger than her own.

That morning, Eleanor had felt her husband watching her closely over their cups of tea. The newspaper lay folded and untouched by his right arm. Neither of them had spoken of her Thursday-morning visits to the Harley Street clinic but as he cleared his throat she found herself studying the violets bordering the bone-china saucer. He told her how pleased he was to see that his little bird had more colour in her cheeks. He paused. He said he was enormously relieved to learn from the Specialist that she was responding particularly well to the treatment. He smiled tightly. Eleanor knew that he found talking about it even more difficult than she did.

'It does seem to be helping,' she answered, encouraged. She looked up into his face, her nostrils flared. She considered how to phrase the many things that had been clamouring inside her. But before she could speak there was a smart knock on the dining-room door and, as was her habit, the housekeeper entered without waiting for an answer. She asked if the master would like his usual smoked kippers with porridge, whether the mistress would like a baked egg with toast and honey today. She told them that there was a hard November frost on the ground.

By the time the housekeeper left, Eleanor's husband had picked up the newspaper and was reading it intently. She decided that she could not disturb him with feelings she could scarcely explain.

She spent the rest of the day, as often of late, drifting from room to room in the quiet, spacious house. Whenever she sat still by the fire, with a book or some embroidery, she began to feel her skin tingle and was compelled to move on to another activity. She wanted to keep shifting her body until she ached. This feeling of restlessness was one of the things that she had not been able to put into words at breakfast. She has been increasingly aware that something inside her has cracked open, that there is a tide in her core that pulls her unexpectedly.

On the surface, everything is as it was in their household. Eleanor continues to plan the week's menus with the housekeeper on Mondays; writes letters to her uncle and to her sisters, now with husbands of their own, stationed across the Empire; buys flowers in the market on Wednesday; and still cries for the caress of Samuel's bud-like nose against her cheek. And yet. She has started to anticipate her Thursday-morning appointment with the Harley Street Specialist. And as she moves through the rooms or stands at the windows of her empty house, she remembers how her hairpins lay scattered on the examination table after her first treatment. She is conscious of the blush staining her neck. The heat trickling down to her belly. Then once the warmth has passed, she feels a hunger in the quick of her that compels her to reposition herself again.

And now her husband stands at the threshold of her bedroom. The grey-yellow light from the paraffin lamp in the hall illuminates him from behind and Eleanor sees only his long-gowned silhouette nearly filling the door. Her vision is blurred and she seeks out the familiar dots on the wallpaper; the squat presence of her deceased aunt's vanity table; the basin in the corner of the room and the three rectangles above it, etchings of Oxford bought at an art fair with her favourite sister the weekend before her marriage.

From her supine position, Eleanor watches as her husband perches on the edge of her bed, removes his slippers – green velvet, her gift to him on his last birthday – unties his dressing gown and slips it from his shoulders. He has left the door open, perhaps in his eagerness to resume his conjugal rights; she is unsure. She can hear his breath catching in his throat and thinks how it sounds like the Specialist's during a treatment. She is aware of a stirring inside her, of her chest released from its daily confines and her skin against the soft cotton of her nightdress.

As her husband leans over respectfully to pull back the eiderdown, heavy blankets and linen sheet that cover her, she can smell his lavender soap and the acrid hint of brandy. She does not turn her head away as he lifts up her nightdress, exposing her naked belly and legs and private parts to the dim light of her chilly room. She does not close her eyes as he leans on his left elbow to hitch his nightshirt up around his waist in an awkward movement. Or when he gently begins to part her legs with the care of someone handling a breakable object.

Eleanor's breath quickens as she reaches up and takes his hand, guides it between her legs, presses his fingers amid her dark pubic hair, between her lips.

Her husband snaps upright, pulling his hand back as though his fingers have been burnt. She can see the whites of his horrified eyes. And she watches as he silently rises, leaving his dressing gown and slippers discarded at the end of her bed, and dissolves into a shadow in the doorway. She holds her breath as she listens to him stride down the hall to his room, hears him pause customarily to look up at the portrait of his father in full military attire, painted shortly before he died in the Indian Mutiny of 1857, then close his door.

Eleanor instinctively pulls the covers over her nakedness. The fingers from her right hand rest between her bare legs.

I THINK IT'S FOR LINDSAY
James Vincent

Mum's got the biggest voice in the flats. Nan says you can hear her the length of the Old Kent Road when she gets going. Usually I like her voice, but coming in from school this afternoon, we hear her when we're on the stairs, and I know there's something going on.

It's Lindsay. She's in the living room looking at the big picture of herself on the wall, between the ones of me and Tracey that Mum kisses when she's polishing and says, 'My lovely girls.' Lindsay's got really big. She takes up all the space in front of the sofa and her back is rolls of fat where her T-shirt is tight. She's wearing the mask. It's too small and cuts right into her face. Tracey looks at me and I know she's scared. I bite my lip.

'Why aren't you at work?' Tracey asks Mum.

'Because Lindsay's here. Say hello, then.'

I kiss Lindsay on the bit of fat, sweaty cheek that sticks out from the side of the mask. Tracey does the same, but Lindsay just stands staring at her picture, like she used to stare in our bedroom mirror when she still lived with us.

We three shared a room then, and me and Tracey shared a bed. At night, Lindsay used to make us go under the covers while she changed into her pyjamas. She took ages, and I knew she was just making faces at herself in the mirror, but if we came out, she used to hold the covers over our heads really tight. It got hot so quick, I always panicked first, even though I'm older than Tracey. I used to scream and make the sheet wet with my open mouth, and then Tracey screamed too. Mum used to shout, 'Pack it in, you lot,' even though she knew it was Lindsay.

Last Sunday, me and Tracey were in our room and we could hear Mum chatting with Chrissy next door. She'd just come back from seeing Lindsay in the home and she sounded upset. She said, 'Chris, she's got so big. I don't know what they're feeding her. I mean, she was always big – I'm big, my mum's big. But the size of her, Chrissy, her arms like this, her legs. And her face is all bloated. And she's got that bloody mask on the whole time. They say it's fine for her to wear it and that she's making improvements and the environment suits her, and she does seem quieter. But I want her back with me, Chris. I just don't think I could cope, though, not with Dan how he is, and Mum wouldn't help with her. It was difficult enough before, but now . . .'

Now, seeing Lindsay in our living room again, with the mask on and not talking or anything, and looking much bigger and stronger, I want to ask Mum if she's come back to live with us.

Mum says, 'Come on, Tammy, Tracey, get those coats and shoes off. You look like you're not staying!' and she does a funny laugh, which isn't her normal one. 'Say hello to Dad, too.'

We kiss Dad and I take our coats and shoes and put them in the hall. Tracey stays, leaning against Dad's wheelchair, watching Lindsay, and Mum goes in the kitchen. I don't want to go back in the living room, so I stay in the hall and sort of hide myself between the coats on the rack. Lindsay's coat is here. It's the big silver parka that she always wears with the hood up and that smells of biscuits. She used to nick them out of the tin and hide them in her pockets until they went stale and soft. Sometimes she'd give me one.

When she lived with us, most days something would happen that meant Mum'd have to hold her by the arms until she calmed down. Me and Tracey would have to go down the play deck or next door to Chrissy's, or sit with Nan in the launderette downstairs. I used to think, why can't Lindsay go down and sit with Nan and we stay upstairs? But I never said anything. Nan said she couldn't cope with Lindsay because of The Autism, but I think she just didn't like her.

Now, I look at the front door and think I'd like to run down the stairs, through the courtyard, under the arch, and into the launderette, even though

I'm only in my socks. But Mum would be really angry, so I stay where I am.

Dad tried to explain to me about The Autism once, and showed me how to spell it. I didn't understand properly, but I tried. That was before the accident, when he could still walk and he could talk normally. Me and Tracey used to both sit on his lap – Tracey on one knee and me on the other. But then he said we were turning into great lumps, so we did it one at a time. If Lindsay came in and saw, though, she wanted to sit on him, too. Once she pulled Tracey off him and scratched all the skin up on Tracey's arm. Dad and I couldn't stop her, she was so strong.

Afterwards, Mum told us we were really really good good girls and she knew it wasn't easy, but it wasn't Lindsay's fault and we all had to try. I didn't cry, and I stopped Tracey crying by squeezing her hand. But I chewed the ends of my hair, which I don't do any more, and Mum pulled it out of my mouth and gave me a big kiss with the M noise that tickles and makes me laugh.

Mum sees me in the hall in the middle of the coats.

'What you doing, Tam? Playing forty-forty?'

'No, just standing here.'

She stops what she's doing like she's going to say something important.

'Come and help me with these things. Look, I've got cakes and choccie biscuits. Get some plates down and pass me that tray.' She's trying to make her voice quiet and I notice she's got some make-up on.

Tracey stands in the kitchen doorway. 'We've got cake? But it's not Friday and we haven't even had our tea yet.'

'I know, but Lindsay's here, so it's special.'

I don't want it to be special. I want Mum to take Lindsay back to the home and then go to work in the supermarket and everything to be like it is every day after school now that Lindsay doesn't live here.

Normally we have our tea later than the rest of the kids in the flats. They all eat theirs straight after school, then come down the play deck with sweets. Mum works at the big Tesco's till four thirty, so we have juice and a packet of crisps each to tide us over, and Dad has his big bottle with a straw. Me and Tracey fill it up, and we do a voice like Mum because we're looking after him. When she gets in she sorts him out, and then she can get round to tea. She calls us in from the balcony, and all the kids copy her big loud voice, but I don't care.

When Lindsay was at home she couldn't eat with us because of the noise of the knives and forks. She had hers first, then she finished Dad's after. Nowadays, most of his goes in the bin but Mum still puts it in front of him. When we're done, me or Tracey helps her with the washing up, while the other one watches the quizzes with Dad and shouts out the answers that he gives in his little croaky voice. He's good at it and we call through to the kitchen when he gets one right. Mum thinks he should go on one of those shows some day and win us a packet.

When she's got the kitchen straight and sorted Dad's bag and everything, that's when she makes us all a cup of tea and brings in biscuits, or on Fridays a bit of cake, and we watch something we all like, like detectives or murder or comedies. We could never watch telly properly when Lindsay was here, because she used to shout, 'Too loud, too loud,' until we had to turn it down so low nobody could hear it.

We don't watch the soaps because Mum says they're too depressing, and we can see Dad doesn't like them either because he closes his eyes or tries to pick up his paper or puzzle books. Nan loves all the soaps and they're always on at hers. But I don't like seeing a little bit of a story and not knowing what went on before or what'll happen after, and I know that it goes on for ever, not just over in a couple of weeks. Nan still watches though, so when we're there, we just get bored.

Sometimes we get a film and if it's long, Mum stops it in the middle while me and Tracey get ready for bed and then we watch the last part in our pyjamas and dressing gowns. Sometimes Tracey falls asleep and misses the end, but she says to Mum that she didn't. Then when we are in bed she gets me to whisper what happened. If the end wasn't how I wanted, I change it, and she doesn't notice.

So today we've got cake and it's not a Friday, and we haven't had our tea, and Dad can't watch his quizzes and there won't be any film, and that big fat horrible cow is in the living room in that stupid bloody mask, and I smash a plate dropping it on the floor, and I'm not sure I didn't do it on purpose. Tracey makes a noise like it hit her and Mum looks like she might get angry.

'Watch what you're doing, Tammy. Be more careful.'

We hear Dad's wheezy voice from the living room.

Mum shouts, 'It's all right, Dan, just a plate.'

*

The day the accident happened, we could hear Mum and Lindsay in our flat when we were coming through the courtyard with Chrissy. Mum was shouting, 'All right, all right, just calm down.'

Our door was open, but Chrissy knocked anyway and called through, 'It's only me, Jean. Shall I send Tammy and Tracey down to your mum? I'd take them in with me, only we've got the dentist in half an hour.'

Mum put her head out of the living room. Her hair was all coming out of her pony-tail.

'Thanks, Chrissy. Here, Tammy, there's a packet of crisps each on the kitchen side. Run through and get them and go down to Nan. Tell her Lindsay's bad.'

I ran into the kitchen and got the crisps. On the way back I looked in the living room. Dad and Lindsay were wrestling and Lindsay kind of roared and bit Dad's hand.

'Go on, Tammy,' Mum shouted. 'I'll come and get you when she's calmed down.'

We were ages in the launderette. I was thirsty after the crisps, but there was only water from the sink and Nan said she didn't have the money for drinks. We were bored. We'd played buses on the plastic orange chairs and lifted our feet up when Nan mopped the floor. Then we'd looked at each other through the glass doors on the driers until Nan told us to stop or we'd break them. So we went and stood by the front window, and watched the traffic in the Old Kent Road and picked at the backwards letters that said 'Service' from the outside. We got told off for that, too. Nan said, 'Come and help me put this lot on to dry if you want something to do.' Tracey went, but I stayed looking out, being angry with Lindsay. I knew she wasn't well, but it wasn't like flu, when you stay at home and watch telly until you're better. She was getting worse. And she was getting bigger. I had a bruise on my leg.

I saw her come running through the arch from our courtyard and out into the road. A car swerved to miss her, and then she was by the railings in the middle. She was climbing over, and I saw she had bare feet and her T-shirt was ripped. She had a bra on. I thought, I didn't know she wore a bra. Then Dad came running out after her, and I heard Mum shouting. The van came fast down off the flyover. It hit him and he went really high – not like jumping, but like someone threw a doll. He hit the railings, and landed in the road. Mum was shouting, 'Dan, Lindsay!' and all the traffic stopped and she ran over to him. I looked for Lindsay. Some bloke had hold of her on the other side, and I'm not sure now, but I think she saw me. I thought she looked like Mum a lot then. Nan pulled me away from the window, and took me down the back. The machines were whooshing with water and the driers were humming, but you could still hear Mum's voice really loud, shouting, 'Dan, Dan!'

For a while after the accident, Lindsay stopped making trouble, and hardly spoke at all, which was good because Mum was always at the hospital and Nan couldn't have coped. Then Lindsay got the mask. We don't know where she found it. I saw her one day standing in front of the mirror with it on, making noises. It's a witch mask, made of plastic that's sort of see-through, so when the person wearing it speaks or moves their face, you can still see them. I wasn't doing anything, just looking at her looking at herself. But she turned her head a bit, to find out what she looked like from the side, I suppose, and she saw me. I ran to Mum, and Lindsay came after me. When Mum saw her in the mask she swore really badly and shouted for Chrissy without even going to the door.

Mum carries the tea, and Tracey and me carry the cakes and biscuits. Lindsay turns around when she sees them and takes loads but Mum doesn't say anything. Dad manages a chocolate finger and me and Tracey have one, too. I didn't think I wanted to eat anything, but I do. I try to remember all the times Mum's told me how good I am, so I say I'm sorry about the plate and try to smile and not make Tracey or Dad worry.

Lindsay's got so big now, there's not enough room for us all on the sofa, so Tracey sits on Dad's bed. It's in the living room because it's too difficult to wheel the chair through the doors all the time. The ambulance men say, 'Peabody weren't built for wheelchairs,' when they come to get him for his hospital appointments. I wake up at night sometimes when Mum's laughing, lifting him in, telling him sleep tight and blowing a kiss from the door like she's going away.

At the weekends or on holidays we lie on his bed during the day, watching telly. There's a plastic sheet under the normal one for accidents and it crackles when you move. Tracey always asks him if it's uncomfortable and makes a face, but he doesn't answer.

Sometimes, to make him laugh, we play trampoline on it in time to songs on the telly, holding each other's hands and our hair whipping about, up and down. He can turn his head enough to watch us and he does that shaking that's him laughing. Mum always shouts at us to stop it or we'll break the bed, and tells him not to encourage us, but it isn't the angry shout, so we know we can do it some more.

Tracey does a bit of a bounce now with her bum, looking at Lindsay, and I know it's because Lindsay doesn't seem to have noticed the bed. Mum says, 'Stop that, Tracey,' but not nastily, and then she asks us what we've done at school. I'm thinking it's nice really, because we never get to see Mum at this time in the afternoon.

She looks happy, with make-up on and her hair done nice, like when she goes out for a drink with Chrissy, and Nan babysits. They usually go downstairs to The World Turned Upside Down because it's close. They both get drunk, and I wake up when they are down in the courtyard singing. Sometimes they go on the swings or the see-saw on the play deck. Chrissy fell off once and hurt herself, so Mum brought her in and put Dettol on her, but they were both laughing all the time. Nan tells them to keep their voices down, but that just makes them more silly, and I laugh too in the dark. When Nan's gone, Mum checks on Dad, and then I know she'll come in to see us. She tries to kiss us but misses, and she smells of perfume and cigarettes and beer. I don't mind. After that I generally go back to sleep, but last Saturday I heard her in her bedroom, and I could tell she was crying.

Mum cuts the cake and tells us, 'Lindsay's been in a play at her school, haven't you, Linds? Tammy was in a play, too. Show Lindsay the programme, Tammy.'

The programme is on the shelf above the telly so I have to lean over Lindsay to get it and I brush against her leg. She hates being touched sometimes, and she jerks her big leg and makes me slop my tea on her. It's only a splash, but she does a massive scream and jumps up, knocking my arm, and half the mug goes down her front. The tea's not even hot any more, so she's just wet, that's all. It isn't like when she threw the kettle at me.

It was the only time I got into a proper temper with her. Mum had gone to see the doctor about Dad so Nan came up for an hour. Nan wasn't happy because since Lindsay'd got the mask, she was worse than ever. Me and Tracey were sent down the play deck because Nan said she couldn't have us under her feet, too.

I was on a swing, and Dean from school, when I wouldn't get off for him, said we were the Addams family. Tracey was in the playhouse and didn't hear, but I made her come back upstairs with me.

I didn't tell Nan, I just said we got bored, but I could feel myself really angry inside. Then, when I was getting me and Tracey juice, Lindsay came in the kitchen and snatched the bottle off me. I grabbed it back and hit her in the face with it. I never ever hit her. The bottle was plastic and so was the mask, so it bounced off. With Tracey it would've been a game, but Lindsay picked up the kettle and threw it at me. Nan had just made tea and hot water went on my arm and some went on Lindsay's leg. It seemed like a really long time that me and Lindsay stood staring at each other and a really long time before I felt my arm hurting and then Nan and Tracey were in the kitchen. Nan hit Lindsay hard and tried to pull the mask off and it was like they were fighting. My arm was hurting more and more, and it was Tracey that made me put it under the cold tap because Mum had made her do that when she touched the iron once.

I was kept in hospital for a night and the next morning they took me down to sit beside Dad's bed. He was awake by then, but couldn't talk. It was nice sitting with him and the nurses smiling and acting like everything was normal. I had bandages and creams on my arm for weeks.

When I got home, Lindsay was gone, with most of her clothes and the suitcase we took when we stayed down the caravan. Mum told me the Social found a place to look after her – to help us out while Dad was so ill. But that night in bed, Tracey told me that the social worker had been in our flat for ages. Tracey was in the bedroom, but she could hear Mum crying and saying, 'I can't, I can't let her go.' The social worker told her she had to for safety, and that it was better for Mum to say yes, because otherwise she'd have to come back with more people and take Lindsay anyway. Mum said, 'So I've got no choice, then,' and the social worker kept saying sorry, but it was for all our safeties.

Mum dabs Lindsay all over with kitchen towel and says, 'You silly girls, you'll be the death of me, you lot.' I know it wasn't me really, but I say, 'Sorry,

Lindsay, I didn't mean to spill tea on you.' I can see her eyes through the holes in the mask, and they look like Mum's. Lindsay's looking at me a lot today, and I think that inside she has got loads and loads of words to say, even if it's not sorry, or I want to stay at home with you, or anything like that. It might be swearing or shouting, or telling us what the home is like and the other kids. But she can't say any of it, she just wobbles where Mum's rubbing her front hard.

When we've finished our tea and cake and all the biscuits are gone, Tracey asks to go down the play deck. I don't want to, and go and lay on my bed instead – on my back, crossways, with my head hanging off the edge. I do this sometimes when I want to chew my hair, because it hangs down onto the floor and won't stay in my mouth.

Looking upside down at the other bed, I think of Lindsay on it, and how she'd fall off onto the ceiling. I can hear Mum chatting to Dad and Lindsay while she's washing the cups, and after a while I feel that I'm crying, even though I didn't think I was going to. The tears make puddles under – or over – my eyebrows, then run down my forehead into my hair. I don't make any noise or sniff like you do when you cry normally. I think about why I'm crying, like when you see someone you don't know crying in the street. It's not for me, or for Mum, or even for Dad. I think it's for Lindsay.

I'm starting to feel a bit sick and dizzy, and I'm going to move, but then I hear Mum asking where I am. The door opens and I see her shoes.

'Look at you, you funny girl, all the wrong way round. What are you like that for?' Her voice is big and gentle. She kneels on the floor and looks down at me. Looking up into her face, I think of that picture of a man with a bald head and a beard and he's happy or sad, depending which way you hold it.

'Come on, you, let's get you up.' She puts her hands under me and tries to stand, but my legs twist and she falls a bit onto the bed, which makes us both giggle.

'Look at us in a big tangle,' she laughs.

I roll the right way round and we cuddle up.

'Lindsay's not coming back to live with us yet, love, just for visits,' she whispers. 'They say she's doing really well, you know. Calming down a lot, doing things. And she says she likes it.'

'Does she?' I'm surprised. Lindsay never says things like that.

'Yeah. She talks normally sometimes, Tams, you just have to know how to speak to her. Anyway, we know she's safe, and we're all OK, aren't we?'

'Yeah.'

'Do you want me to tell you that she's coming next time?'

'Yeah, please. I'll be better then.'

She wipes my eyes with a tissue and we sit quietly for a while.

'Tell you what, do you want to come in the cab with me and Linds? You can see where she's staying.'

I don't really want to, but I nod yes.

Mum phones the cab and we go downstairs and wait outside the launderette, but Nan doesn't come out and say hello. The pub sign squeaks where it's swinging in the wind. The picture is of a fish pulling a man out of the water with a rod. Nan says it's clever, that, but I don't like it. They change it sometimes, and I like to try and think of different things they could have. But not today.

When the cab comes we get in quick because there's no stopping on this bit of the road. I'm squashed in the back between Mum and Lindsay, even though there's no one in the front seat, and I feel really small between them. I'm pressed up against Lindsay's leg, but she doesn't complain this time, and I hope she'll be OK until we get to the home.

It's warm in the car, and Mum's voice is all buzzy when she's chatting to the driver. Then, when she's leaning forward, showing him where to turn, I feel something sticky in my hand. I go to pull it away, but then I realize – Lindsay's given me a chocolate finger. I keep it hidden in my palm, all melting, and look at Lindsay to give her a smile. She's turned away, though, staring out of her window. It's getting darker outside, and every now and then I see her reflection in the glass. So I smile anyway, just in case.

LOOK OUT

NEARLY BIT THE HEAD OFF A WAITRESS THIS AFTERNOON. DON'T KNOW WHAT CAME OVER ME. NEVER BADGER THE HELP, I ALWAYS SAY.

I GUESS I WAS STILL ANGRY ABOUT THE OTHER NIGHT WHEN I CAME HOME TO FIND MY PLACE BROKEN INTO. GOD, I WAS PISSED.

I WASN'T SO PISSED BECAUSE THEY TOOK MY JUNKY OLD TV OR THE CUP OF QUARTERS I USED FOR LAUNDRY. JUST HAVING SOME STRANGE FUCK IN MY HOME IS REASON ENOUGH IF YOU ASK ME.

2.

GOTTA ADMIT, THIS NEVER HAPPENED TO ME BEFORE. NOT EVEN WHEN I WAS LIVING ON THE WORST STREET IN HOPPERS.

IT'S IRONIC, THOUGH. JUST HOURS BEFORE IT HAPPENED, I WAS DAYDREAMING ABOUT THE OLD HOOD. ABOUT MY BUMMIN' SLUMMIN' TEENAGE YEARS.

EVEN MORE IRONIC, I WAS SPECIFICALLY THINKING ABOUT THE DAYS I TOOK UP THE DELICATE ART OF BREAKING AND ENTERING.

IT WAS A SUMMER WHEN MY REGULAR PARTNERS WERE AWAY ON VACATION OR SOMETHING SO I STARTED HANGING WITH THE OLDER GUYS LIKE 'LITOS AND BIG EDDIE.

WE WOULD ROAM THE STREETS REALLY LATE AT NIGHT AND PICK A DARK HOUSE AND LOOK FOR A QUIET WAY IN.

SINCE I WAS THE YOUNGEST OF THE SAUS I STOOD LOOKOUT WHILE THEY WENT TO WORK.

THEY NEVER CAME OUT WITH MUCH. IT WAS THE ACT ALONE THAT EXCITED ME.

FOR EXAMPLE, ONE NIGHT WHEN NOBODY WAS AROUND I VENTURED OUT AND DECIDED TO TACKLE A HOUSE BY MYSELF. I WASN'T LOOKING FOR LOOT, JUST SOMETHING TO KILL THE FUCKING BOREDOM.

SIR JOKER

APING MY COMPAS I GOT THE WINDOW OPEN IN LESS THAN A MINUTE.

I WALKED AROUND THE DARK HOUSE LIKE I WAS STROLLING THROUGH A GARDEN, OBSERVING THE MARIGOLDS, ETC...

I MADE MY WAY INTO THE MASTER BEDROOM WHERE A LADY SLEPT. I REMEMBER IT SMELLED LIKE HAIR PRODUCTS.

I WAS CHECKING OUT THE STUFF ON HER BUREAU WHEN SHE WOKE UP AND LET OUT A SCREAM TO WAKE THE DEAD AND THEN SOME.

COMPAS - COMPANIONS

4.

First published in *Penny Century* No. 2 (March 1998)

HAPPINESS
Michelle Singh

The saddest part of all came after she'd had the baby and they'd taken the obligatory homecoming photographs. The police tell me that it happened yesterday morning after his parents had said goodbye, driving away before the January snow grew too heavy. Fliss angered Christian when she asked him to put his meat pie and chips in the oven himself. I can imagine how her voice had sounded; her deliberate, tired whine. She had been in hospital for two days, in labour for fourteen hours. When she was readmitted she told the doctor that I was as good as her next of kin, that I should be called.

Uninvited, sitting in the fuchsia-painted front room of my spanking-new flat, the police say this is what Christian told them yesterday: he twisted Fliss's neck to one side and heard a crack like a knee-joint straightened underwater. Her back was against the shoddy, half-wallpapered hallway in their bungalow. Jack was straitjacketed in his high-chair, watching *Teletubbies*. Their baby girl was asleep in her Moses basket. Blubbing in custody, Christian had made an excuse, said he'd been so hungry and suddenly angry. He couldn't control himself. Fliss fell limply to the floor. He thought he had killed her. He lay down on the cheap carpet next to her, breathing his chemical cheese-and-onion breath into her face.

Of course the police don't tell me this, about his breath. I imagine it, that maybe he had bits of corned-beef sandwich from the day before stuck to his front teeth. He was never one to brush. And as the police talk on, I can almost see Fliss, her dark eyes wide open and, scared, her newly painted lips trembling, trying to speak. They say she could not move. I've paralysed the mother of my baby, he thought. That was one of the lines he gave them.

'Fuck it,' he said out loud. He was wearing his steel-capped work boots. He remembered days earlier he had trodden in dog shit in Chiswick. Inside, I suppose he was probably thinking something like: Let's end this once and for all. He methodically took aim.

But it seems that he is a bona fide coward, a custardy yellow-belly. He makes a habit of leaving his jobs unfinished, so it seems.

'Adele, he turned himself in,' the policewoman says to me. Her male colleague is taciturn, his eyes focussing on the spider plant on my windowsill, a gift from my parents. 'He made the call, got on the nines.' I am silent, my mouth a line. I am forced to listen to the policewoman talk clinically about Christian, how he has told them he is under pressure at work, that he can't cope, says his mind gets too full like he's going mad.

'He lays fucking carpets in west London,' I say in the end, voice low. He gets paid cash in hand and he claims dole too, I feel like telling them. But I don't.

The policewoman tells me that Fliss is on a pleasant ward, backing onto the hospital gardens. More peaceful than the maternity ward, she jokes.

'Felicity says she's not in contact with Maria any more.' The policeman doesn't even look at my face as he says this.

'Her name's Marie,' I say curtly. 'Yes, they fell out, but she's Fliss's mum. She would want to know what has happened.'

He stares at me now, and breathes out before speaking again, like he's exhausted with me.

'Felicity wants to see you. Will you visit her today?'

I nod.

'I'm so fed up with her,' I accidentally tell them, pulling things into my handbag, things I think she'll want like lipstick and chewing gum. The police look puzzled, probably thinking that these aren't the usual words from the best friend.

I can go with them in their car, they say.

'No, I'll drive.' And I take a handful of change for the parking meter. But then I remember these urban myths: a woman missed her mother's last breath because she couldn't find a space in the hospital car park. A man who left his car in neutral to walk the few steps inside to his dying wife had his wheels clamped for parking over the wrong chevrons. I relent, and get into the police car, with the stench of air freshener emanating from a damp, yellow, tree-shaped piece of card.

I wonder if Fliss has changed since I last saw her in August. She was four months pregnant then. I was thinking about what the new baby's name was a few days ago, on her due date. Fliss had said if the baby was a girl she'd be Adele after me. If it was a boy she'd name him Henry. Feeling sick now, I suppose Jack and the baby are with Christian's parents, Irene and Geoff. Irene's fat and Geoff has cheeks the colour of russet apples. He looks like a Scottie dog, smokes like a trooper, loves local football. She talks of her sore bunions, pruning back her roses, how clever Jack is. They are on a tenpin-bowling team called The Corvettes. How did they give birth to such a fuck?

'No, we haven't spoken for weeks and weeks.' I answer more questions on the way to the hospital. The police car has good brakes, I realize at the traffic lights that turn red abruptly from amber. I close my eyes against the sun, beating off the thawing roads. It snowed again in the night.

And why haven't I spoken to Felicity in so long?

'We had an argument.'

Fliss had offended every fibre in my body. She made me feel physically ill.

We drive past our old junior school, where Fliss and I first crossed paths sixteen years ago. I remember that when we first made friends, we always had to play at Fliss's house after school because she was too scared of my father to be at mine. I look at the playground, see girls red-kneed from the cold, playing hopscotch in their maroon V-neck jumpers, and heat washes over me, prickling my skin with pain. Christian nearly snuffed her out this time. I hate him so much. I want to wipe him out. The familiar thought comes into my mind: hire some contract killers; slip some cyanide into his Stella.

The police ask me about the children. When we were fifteen, I tell them, Fliss had a baby girl, Eva. Marie, in her loveliness, didn't have a clue what on earth Fliss got up to once she left the front door, and discovered too late for an abortion. We were at school. She'd been having sex with three different boyfriends who were, glamorously, in the sixth form. They thought Fliss looked like Debbie Harry in the halcyon Blondie days.

She had Eva adopted a month after the birth. She just decided. Fliss wanted to get on with things and do her GCSEs with no distractions, or so Marie explained it to me one evening after school. I'd been invited over for bangers and mash, hoping that Eva would be awake so I could play with her. Time for Fliss to enjoy being young, Marie had said. Before Eva left, Fliss's social worker told her she could send just one thing with her, for Eva to have for ever. Fliss decided against Eva's favourite pink teddy, saying it smelled of her. She wanted to keep it. Instead she gave Eva her old white leather prayer book. We were all given prayer books in a special assembly when we left primary school. Fliss didn't believe in God. I thought at the time that it was a strange gift.

Every year Fliss has to send a photograph of herself to her daughter with a note about how she is doing. Social services pass it on, even hassled Fliss when she was late sending her Christmas card because she was sitting her A-level mocks. Eva's adoptive parents in Scotland renamed her Lucille, after a long-dead grandmother in their family. Fliss had disapproved. Even though she rarely mentions Eva, Fliss has said in the past that she suspects her notes and snaps aren't even passed on any more. I don't tell the police that for fear of criticizing social workers in front of them, as if they are united serving the public good.

My mouth is dry. God, I want some water. Why didn't I bring a drink?

Wondering if I am telling them too much, whether the policeman wants me to be quiet while he drives, I admit that Fliss was adopted too. Do they want to know this? The policewoman makes encouraging noises. When Fliss was five, just after Marie's husband had died, Marie rescued her from a children's home where she'd been abandoned by her father, the one man Fliss's friends never really heard about. Fliss used to eat her own hair, chew it like liquorice. Marie would tell us proudly when we were older how well her beautiful Fliss had done, how she was light-years from that thin, bruised child who gnawed her way through her woollen sleeves. How much weight she'd put on when once you could count her ribs; she'd looked like a human xylophone. Her name used to be Felicity Boggins. What a horrible name!

Fliss hated it. When she was adopted, she took Marie's surname. She called Marie 'Mum' right away, always tasting the word like a strange sweet in her mouth, rolling it around, blurting it out all the time. My mum this, my mum that. Mum, Mum, Mum. Marie always said she'd wanted a daughter. She and her own mother had been more like sisters, or best friends, sharing secrets and clothes. Marie had lost the two of them in the same year, first her mother, then her husband.

Fliss and I used to share showers together on summer camp as teenagers because we hated the other girls; that's how much shame we had of nakedness in front of one another. Although I don't tell the police this, fearing they'll think I have a lesbian crush on Fliss, and that's why we've fallen out, because I can't bear her having sex with a man. I even let her shave her armpits with my razor once, because hers was blunt. I lent her my bar of macaroon-scented soap to froth before she shaved, a fortune it cost me, and I was surprised how little I cared about her stubble remnants turning the surface to splinters. On a Saturday night after our final A-level exam we had so much to talk about while we got ready to go out, she made me put the toilet seat down and sit on it and talk to her as she had her bath. She had lots of brown freckles on her back, and deep-red stretch marks twisting across her tummy, puckered with scars. I washed her sleek hair for her, with my expensive shampoo that I never let anyone else use. I let her share everything that was mine. I didn't complain when she drank from my can of lemonade that time she had a cold sore or when I wondered if she was stealing from my purse.

Fliss had to give up university in her final year when she was fat with Jack. She was reading to be an occupational therapist. She'd bought an extortionately expensive skeleton for her course. A real human skeleton! She ghoulishly refused to sell it, Christ knows why. She called him, originally, Bones. Bones now gathers dust in Marie's glory-hole garage, freaks her out every time she goes in for her secateurs.

'Did you go to the same university?' the policewoman asks, turning to face me. Her mascara has run slightly, I notice.

'No,' I say. 'I went away. Fliss went to university in town.' My face burns for my friend who couldn't afford to stop living with Marie even while she was a student. She was too proud to let her mum help finance her degree, said she'd done enough for her already. She thought it was great when she moved into Christian's bungalow once she was pregnant with Jack. I didn't want any of that, at least not that way. I don't want to have babies with a monster.

Jack, on that first day I met him when I lied to the nurses and said I was family, was light like air and his skin so pale you saw his blue veins veiled by jaundice. He was pure goodness pulsing through. After Eva, he was the promised land. As if on fast-forward I saw his first word, first steps, first Nobel Prize. He was so dainty, as if made of china. I was scared that he would break. Fliss, acting like a marionette with Irene and Geoff when they visited the ward, faking it and pretending she didn't know what breast pads were. What a liar. Eva and Jack were even born in the same week six years apart, little ghost ships passing in the night. Fliss shook her head wordlessly at me from her hot hospital bed as I almost said it, undid her life, popped her balloon. So that's the real reason you can't shift that first-baby weight! Funny that.

'Thanks a bunch,' I'd snapped when we were alone. 'You could have told me that Christian's parents don't know about Eva! So you mean their son hasn't even had the decency to tell them the truth?'

'Me and Christian think they don't need to know,' Fliss had replied. 'Let them think Jack's my first, like he's Christian's first.' She stopped for a bit, pulled a piece of dry flaked skin from her lower lip. 'Actually, it was Christian's idea. And don't say Eva. Her name's Lucille.'

We're at another set of traffic lights.

Why was I the last one to give up on Fliss? The policewoman wants to know what makes me different.

'I suppose I have a long fuse,' I say, shrugging. And I did feel sorry for her. I used to stick up for Fliss a lot to our other friends, before they grew weary and uninterested. She doesn't work. She has a baby. She has no time. Her boyfriend works long hours; she has to see him too. Even though he works so much, he never has any money to treat her. I remember the Christmas after Jack was born, Fliss really wanted a plum-coloured satin jacket. She'd hinted like mad to Christian, tried it on every time they went shopping. Christian had saved up all his dole money to buy Jack an enormous toy fire engine. He spent Christmas Day rolling it back and forth across the carpet, making Jack chase it, clapping and cheering every time. He'd even shelled out on hiring a Father Christmas suit, just to surprise Jack in the morning. I saw the photographs; I thought he looked grotesque. He bought Fliss some counterfeit perfume that made her skin blister. She pretended she liked it, even to me. I bought her the satin jacket myself, in the January sales.

'Fliss 'n' Chris,' she used to parrot, inanely. To try and endear Christian to us, Fliss used to fabricate about him. How he really liked her friends, how he'd love her to go out with us, have us over, go round our houses, if only they weren't so busy with the kids. What a vicious bastard, booting her, seven months gone, with a paranoia unfounded, thinking she was eyeing up some random man in the supermarket aisle. What a coward, pretending he slept through her desperate string of 3 a.m. phone calls to be picked up on a rare night out with the girls. What an animal, to barely acknowledge Marie, to never make eye contact, to smack Fliss with snide backhanders and blame doorhandles.

He's a timesheet cheater, a mummy's boy, a piece of shit. He does not deserve Fliss, Jack, his newborn. He's a monster, a buffoon, a cad with two brain cells. He's thick and lazy and rude and anal. He's tight-fisted, a selfish gambler, a thief and out-and-out liar, a spineless, gutless shit-for-brains wimp, a man bereft of vocabulary, a fraudster, charlatan, thug, hooligan, dunce, moron, waster. He's a fucking robot devoid of all sense, emotion or warmth. He's pig-like, a wanker, a bully, an ape, a dangerous thick-shit with an attitude problem. A dick. A skinhead menace. A mute, an ass, a clown, a jerk-off, a complete fucking waste of space, a bankrupt dole cheat, a benefit fraudster, a man who you curse to hell for making your friend pregnant.

And she was so beautiful, like a sultry goddess rising from the sea. He's sucked out her rosiness and left her drained and crusty and shell-like. He nicked her, and hid her soul somewhere. I have nightmares that we are kids again and that he appears and slits her throat like Bluebeard. I've heard him laugh, along to his Jim Davidson DVD. Like a machine-gun, the cartoon laugh of Chief Wigan on *The Simpsons*.

I tell the police about the time he wanted to watch a World Cup match, not even England's, wearing his mock shirt with two lions. He couldn't be bothered, at the last minute, to drive her to hospital to have her abnormal smear test repeated.

They want to know how Fliss met Christian. I don't know; bad luck, fate, chance. He was her regular customer, the elusive older man with no kids, no divorce, no hang-ups about Eva. He met Fliss when she worked the late-night tills at the petrol station, her part-time job to pay for her course books. Christian romanced Fliss over the dry-roasted peanuts and gold-and-white packs of Marlboros. She was pregnant within a few weeks, thought he was brilliant. He bought her an engagement ring. It looked like paste, as if it came out of a cheap, nasty Christmas cracker.

'Isn't he gorgeous?' she'd kept marvelling. I thought he looked like a Womble. She moved into his bungalow. He called it *his* bungalow, but Irene and Geoff paid the rent. She started talking about him, boringly, obsessively, trying to make me pity him just because his last girlfriend used to beat him up and cheat on him, made him rely on anti-depressants, gulping them like Rainbow Drops. Fliss had told me that the last girlfriend's final stand involved hurling a still-hot iron at his head. She'd relished flinging his golf clubs out of the window, pouring paint stripper on his car, splashing white spirit at his eyeballs. None of this made me pity him. Christian was a pincher and a shover, always insanely believing Fliss was staring at other men. I soon saw his thumbprints all over her, saw half a palmprint beneath the slap of fake tan.

The policewoman turns to look at me, gives me a small pink smile.

'We're nearly at St John's. You don't want Fliss seeing you crying. She's been doing enough of that already. Be brave for her. Is there anyone we can call for you?'

'What do you mean?' I think of my parents, who live miles away now.

'Anyone at home? Your husband? Your partner?'

'No, no way.' I give a short laugh. I want to thank her for kicking me when I'm down but she seems too nice to insult. 'No, thank you.'

On our way into her ward, they tell me to be prepared. Walking down the blinding strip-lit corridors I feel like I am walking to the electric chair.

'Felicity may look a bit different,' the policewoman warns me, gently holding my elbow.

And there she is. I see her face, the top half like an aubergine, nose blown up like a turnip.

'You stupid bitch,' I want to tell her. Her eyelids sealed shut as if on a rag doll's stitched face. 'You brought this all on yourself, you silly, silly girl.' I hold her hand. It feels like a hot, hairy, puffed red balloon.

'It's the drugs,' a nurse tells me. 'They make her swell up. She'll wake up in a bit.'

Oh, God. Then what will I say to her? Long time no see?

'I'll ring Marie in a bit,' I tell the police, wanting them to go.

'Why did Marie stop talking to Felicity?' The policeman has a notebook out now. They haven't been taking notes so far. How can I tell them this? Something in my face makes them relent. They'll catch up with me, maybe tomorrow. They walk away quickly, shoes squeaking on the floor, probably glad to escape.

That August day Fliss lost her final ally in me, the last time we spoke, I'd visited Marie alone at her home for lunch, to try and facilitate some peace between the two of them. Fliss and Marie had stopped speaking in June, over Fliss's latest black eye.

'How can I forgive Fliss for not stopping him, especially now she's pregnant?' Marie had quavered, dunking her dessert Garibaldi. Her voice changed, straining suddenly. 'And then little Eva, poor little Eva. She's only eight years old. What about Eva?' Marie abruptly put down her tea, her biscuit, and pressed her hands against her eyes.

And me, fearfully: 'What about Eva?'

Nothing. Dread crept up my spine like an anaesthetic. I could see every detail in Marie's cuckoo clock, hear the seconds crashing past in the stillness. I will remember everything about that moment for ever. The colour of Marie's loose, too-stretched curl at the back of her neck, her sky-blue jumper, how the sun shone through her net curtains picking out golden shafts of billions of specks of dust in the air.

'What about Eva?' I sounded strange, my voice too blaring, jumping ahead and imagining terrible, terrible things.

Marie told me, her voice strangled, that it happened six weeks ago. As she tells me, I can see it all like a horror film playing in my mind.

Christian is cooking tea. He almost never makes tea for Fliss. All he can cook is pasta, with processed cheese and value ham in strips. He acts like a hero, cooking for her when she is tired. She's watching telly, the sound turned up high, sat with Jack slumbering next to her, his little hands stretched out on her tummy. Someone rings the doorbell. Fliss asks Christian to get it. He turns his gluey pasta down on the hob, answers the door. A ramrod-backed woman is standing there, in a cream-coloured mackintosh.

'Is Felicity Marston there?'

Christian frowns, has to think. He wonders if this woman is Fliss's midwife.

She's in her forties, carries a brown patent briefcase. She looks sleek and professional. Fliss, sleuth-like, is peeking at them from the lounge door. Fliss feels the freeze of wind around her ankles.

'Why do you want her?'

'Perhaps you could give her my card? I'm here on behalf of my clients.'

Fliss is hooked now, and pads out to see, wearing her purple Mister Men slippers and her favourite raspberry-velour stay-at-home tracksuit.

'I'm Felicity,' she says cautiously, feeling that this woman looks nice with her straightened hair and expensive coat. The woman offers her hand. But Fliss, so skilled now at concealing, doesn't want to shake it in case the woman sees the purple finger marks on Fliss's forearm.

She is a private investigator visiting on behalf of Eva's adoptive parents. She's sorry to say that Eva has leukaemia and needs a bone-marrow transplant. Please can Fliss donate a sample of her bone marrow, to see if she is a match? Fliss nods her head mechanically and numbly, says yes a thousand times. And does Fliss know who Eva's father is? Can we ask him? Fliss can't ask him, and won't elaborate, because he's Matthew Picket, Lance Ramsey or Jordan Princely, and God knows where they are now.

'It's a simple enough procedure.' The woman talks at Fliss. 'They take it from your hip bone. You stay in hospital for a bit. You will take a few weeks to recover. But it's a small price to pay.'

'Why didn't Fliss tell me this?' I'd questioned Marie, shrilly. 'Was this before she was pregnant?'

'Just before she found out.'

'So she didn't have the bone-marrow operation?'

It seems not.

I wonder what was going through Fliss's head? I know what was in mine. I felt sick. Lovely little Eva. The person who made Fliss monosyllabic for a year by her absence. I remembered the delicious smell of her baby head, her surprisingly vice-like grip on my little finger. I'd always dreamt of her being thriving and young, beautiful and hearty. Not wasting away and dying.

In the end, the investigator was forced to look up Marie by ringing all of the Marstons in the telephone directory. She begged for Marie's help, explained it all. Marie had to put the phone down to vomit up her breakfast once she had heard. The morning after the visit, Christian had telephoned the private investigator.

'Fliss has changed her mind,' he'd grunted. 'Please don't contact us again.' But why, the investigator had asked. Because their happiness was all that mattered now, and Eva wasn't their problem. She asked to speak to Fliss. Christian hung up and left the telephone off the hook.

Marie told me, sobs escaping with crumbs of biscuit clumped on her lips, that if Fliss could treat her daughter like this, then Fliss was dead to her, and had for ever been a stranger to her. And stupidly, all I could think about was that they didn't stop talking to each other over a black eye after all.

After I kissed Marie goodbye I drove to Fliss's home, where she was putting up the cheap wooden shelves she'd been nagging Christian to put up for months.

'See, I can use a drill.' She was proud, answering the door revving the tool like a toy. 'God, I haven't seen you for ages, sweetheart. Are they working you too hard again? You look knackered.'

'You shouldn't be doing this kind of work, your bloody fiancé should.'

'He's at work. He's working a double shift.'

'Oh, really. That's great stuff.' My sarcasm nettled her.

'Who's rattled your cage? I was going to tell you about this gorgeous bloke who came round and offered to clean my windows for half the price. Thought I'd ask him if he was willing to take my mate out on a date instead.' She dimpled like a coquette.

'Why didn't you tell me that Eva needs a bone-marrow transplant?'

Fliss froze, her face locking down and eyes deadening.

'Talk to me!' I was screaming.

'Adele, don't shout at me, OK?'

'Why shouldn't I?'

'Because you don't know what you're talking about. A woman came over, talking to me about my old family, asking about my dad and stuff and . . . I don't know – I didn't know who she was! Am I supposed to give her what she wants?'

'What, bone marrow? Yes!'

'She wanted everything from us, all sorts of details. I didn't know if she was real or a fake.'

'I don't suppose private dicks carry about ID!'

'What if she was sent by my dad?'

I caught my breath, millions of possibilities flooding in.

'Ha, you see now?' She was almost spitting. 'He always said to me that I could never hide from him. I have to be careful – I have Jack now. I'm his mum. Anyway, you don't know the half of it. She never rang back. She said she would. She probably just wanted to find out where I'm living. You watch now, my dad'll write to me and ask for some money. Probably heard how well Christian's doing. He earned eighteen hundred quid in two months!'

'Wow! Do you really think news of his carpet-laying prowess has reached wherever the hell you came from?'

'Adele, she never called me back,' Fliss said quietly. 'She never phoned.'

'Because Christian phoned her and told her to fuck off!'

'How do you know that?' Her skin was pale. She looked anaemic.

'Marie told me!'

Fliss's expression buckled again. Then she steeled herself, her voice welling with venom. 'Well, she shouldn't get involved! She hates Christian. She'll tell so many lies just to get you to hate him too. Christian never rang her.'

'He rang that woman.'

'He never. You're wrong. He would've told me. He doesn't lie.'

'Oh fucking Jesus Christ, Fliss! Ask him!'

'I can't ask him that!'

'He fucking did it!' I was feeling deranged. 'Fliss, come on!'

'Come on what?' Jack began to wail hungrily in the next room. 'Leave it out, Adele. I've got high blood pressure as it is.'

'Don't blackmail me!'

I followed her like a stalker, into Jack's nursery, where she scooped him from his cot, and back into the front room where she cradled him, and rocked him in her lap, wiping his snot away with her finger and thumb.

'Fliss –'

'Adele, listen, listen, listen.' She was soothing me like I was her child too. She looked me straight in the eyes and spoke slowly but kindly, as if to an imbecile. 'I don't know this woman. She said she would call me. She didn't. The end. Do you believe me?'

No, I didn't believe her. And that was that.

When Fliss's eyes flutter open, she sees me there. Her lips dip down like a clown's. Her eyes are leaking, tears mingled with pus.

'I want to tell you,' she says. It's like someone's stealing her air while she speaks.

'What do you want to tell me, honey?' The words fight through my raw throat.

'We named the baby Bella.'

'Not Adele?' I joke, inappropriately.

She even tries a smile. 'No, not Adele.' A bit of a silence, then: 'That's not what I wanted to tell you.' We wait a bit longer. I listen to her haphazard breathing, watch her plum-coloured skin in sad amazement.

'Christian checks my mobile, you know,' she says, and pauses for half a minute, struggling to speak rather than cry.

I let some more hate sweep over me.

'That's not the best,' I say, not wanting to upset her more.

'He found Francesca's mobile number on my outgoing-calls list yesterday after we brought Bella home.'

'Who is Francesca?'

'That detective woman, remember? She came round just before I found out I was pregnant again.'

'And why did you ring her?'

She breathes. 'Think about it, Adele.'

I can't. It hurts me too much to think about it. My tears are molten, burning my eyes.

'He said he was scared they'd want to use Jack.'

I say nothing. If she makes any more excuses for him I will scream, kick her myself.

'It's because he loves Jack so much.'

He doesn't kick Jack in his face, I want to say to my purple-masked friend. Yet.

Did you know? I want to ask her. Did you know Christian lied to Francesca, fobbed off a life?

'Anyway, Adele,' she says now, voice crazily out of control, growing louder, 'I was a tiny bit too late. Just a teensy bit.'

She presses her lips together, trembling, and dry, dark sobs heave at her chest. I stare at my hands and bitten fingernails and remember the shape of Eva's head. I remember her red baby hands with their faint rash, and the small white leather prayer book Fliss sent with her when she left, cocooned in the white chenille shawl Fliss knitted in home economics. Perhaps it was buried with her?

THE RED SHOES
T. Rawson

In a cupboard, in a house, a pair of discarded shoes rest ashamed in the top right-hand corner underneath a paper bag filled with sanitary towels. Their shame is not because they are old or worn or the wrong colour or because they are too expensive or too cheap; it is because they are too small.

A child of nine thinks of the week before when the shoes were bought for her. She remembers the shop assistant's hair full of harsh waves and the bright red lipstick that silted up the tiny gullies around her mouth. 'How do they feel, love?' she asked her. The child hadn't answered. Instead she had looked down in wonder at the red shoes with the biscuit soles and the flowers cut through the leather. Then her mother had said, 'Do they fit?' and she nodded enthusiastically; a smile slowly filled her face.

The child's mother stands at the sink washing runner beans, looking out at the back garden. She wears a dress of colourful printed fabric, made on a very old black sewing machine that is covered in belligerent bursts of gold lettering. It's operated by a wheel on its side and when the mother turns it her body rocks backwards and forwards in a strange violent dance. The mother stops washing the runner beans and concentrates on humming to the radio. Buddy Holly is singing and she likes Buddy Holly because he looks like a Canadian soldier she met once at a dance during the war before she was married. When she sees the child's father come out of the shed into the garden she turns down the radio but still moves gently from side to side as she remembers the song in her head.

The garden is where the runner beans have been grown along with radishes, onions and cabbages. It has been a hot day and although it is cooler now, the child's father takes off his shirt. Holding up his trousers is a thick black leather belt that is very similar to the type that his father used to beat him and his brothers. A tattoo on his forearm, which says 'Mother' and won't fade, flinches with movement as he digs over the soil. He slows each movement and when he does, his body rises to muscle and then falls away again. The garden is useful for other things, not just growing vegetables, and when the child's brother (who is two years older) has to be punished, he is made to weed the garden and then dig it over. He stands in an old pair of trousers, which his mother has repaired for him, beneath the sun or rain. Sometimes he works in the garden for a few hours or a day. Once he was there for a whole week.

'Are you there?' shouts the neighbour next door. Between the houses is a brick wall, and because the neighbour is short and because the wall is tall, she has to stand on her tiptoes to speak to the mother. The child listens with disinterest until she hears the words 'new shoes', and then with enormous courage she goes into the kitchen and stands at the table.

'Do you like them?' The neighbour shows off her new shoes. They are white with a small heel and the toes are pert and at each side of them there is a rose made of fabric. 'I got them for the dance on Saturday.'

The dance is to be held for the workers of the car factory where the neighbour's husband works. Sometimes the neighbour asks the child's parents to go as well, but they can't this year. Last year the mother wore a black Lurex dress. Her body, as plump as a pillow, with wide, bouncy breasts, inflated the dress and her pale blotchy skin showed itself proudly at the low neckline. On her wrists and neck she streaked her skin with scent the colour of pink milkshake that smelt of nice medicine. She is bought a bottle every Christmas by her husband. He hands it to the younger child and says, 'Give this to your mother,' and the child takes it and the mother opens the unwrapped box and takes out the scent and places it on the table and lowers her eyes in thanks.

The child decides to leave the kitchen, but as she does she accidentally knocks the table and her mother turns round, looks at her, and then looks away.

'Do you know anyone that wants a pair of shoes? They're brand new. She said they fitted.' She pauses. 'I'd want something for them.'

The shoes are made of red leather, a quietened red; one enriched if polish was iced over them thickly and left overnight and then shined in the morning. They are the type of shoes that look good on the first day back to school when the summer sun has layered the legs with a gorgeous grubbiness, and the red shoes glisten like jewels against white ankle socks. When a tin of black or brown polish is nearly empty and the remnants are difficult to scoop out, it is gently warmed on the stove and the polish melts on the floor of the tin and becomes covered in a thin, blind, perfectly round, lake. This will never happen to the tin of red polish that has been bought specially and sits beside them.

The child walks back into the living room and starts to play with her two teddy bears, which are sitting on the settee. In a vertical line from their chins to their stomachs there is an untidy stretch of stitching made while playing hospitals with her brother. 'This teddy will die if we don't operate,' her brother says to her with his laughing eyes, and with stolen scissors their stomachs are cut open and their stuffing taken out, so they can be filled up again using old nylons that are ribbed with wear. When the child plays this game on her own the teddy bears lie on beds of folded tea towels and their heads and paws are gently bandaged, and the bears are served water in tiny cups from her tea set.

The mother finishes her conversation at the back door and opens the cupboard and takes out the new shoes, and places them on the dining-room table even though it has been laid for dinner. Then she rushes back into the kitchen because she has heard a saucepan lid fall on the floor and thinks the beans are over-boiling. The child sits and looks at the shoes, and then she looks away. When she looks back again the shoes are still there.

The father's silence comes in from the garden and sits at the table. Then the brother batters into the room, but caught in the draft of stillness, he rounds his shoulders and sits down. The father ignores the shoes even though they nearly cover his fork. The child's mother brings the father's dinner and goes back into the kitchen for the others without realizing the shoes are still on the table. Everyone begins to eat except the father. The mother looks to see what the problem is and then, alarmed, puts the shoes in the sideboard.

'Next door's wanted me, and then the runner beans boiled over,' she says hurriedly, her words clattering onto the lino. Slowly, and with great deliberation, the father picks up his knife and fork.

Everyone eats in silence. Then a shout, a loud shout, is forced through an open window and pauses at the dinner table before dissipating. The children look at each other. Joan Sullivan, an older girl of thirteen whose mother has just died and who lives opposite, is playing rounders outside with other children from the street and she wants to know if the child and her brother will join in. The child likes Joan even though she won't play hospitals with her.

'Ask to leave the table,' their mother says to them. So they do, and go outside.

Joan Sullivan whacks the ball into the privet hedge of Mrs Flynn's, who has eight children, and the scurry to retrieve the ball from her hedge makes the house restless and it expels three Flynn children who run onto the green to join in. Eventually the night crowds in and the children can't see the ball any more and have to go home.

As the child and her brother go into their house the next-door neighbour opens her door and shouts, 'Tell your mum my sister's girl will have those shoes and ask her what she wants for them.' But neither the little girl nor her brother remembers to tell their mother. Later, after the father has left for the nightshift and the mother is baking for the next day, the child says to her mother, 'Why does Linda Flynn have newspaper in her shoes?'

The mother carefully spoons out the last of the cake mix and feeds it to her daughter.

'Because they aren't the right size for her,' she replies.

'Can I see if my new shoes are the right size?'

The mother turns on the tap to wash up, and then notices a remnant of cake mix still left and scoops it up by sliding her finger around the mixing bowl, and allows the child to lick it off.

'All right, then,' she says.

The child suddenly remembers what the neighbour said and realizes this has to be done immediately.

'Can I go now?'

The child walks to the house. As soon as the front door is opened the smell, like a barrel of mouldy apples, challenges her. Linda is the same age as her but much prettier, and the fringe on her black, blunt hair is too long and gets caught up in her eyelashes. The hem on her skirt trails down and dark stains decorate the front of her blouse.

'They are too small for me,' she says.

Linda Flynn takes off her shoes to show filthy feet and shattered toenails and tries on the new shoes excitedly, then she laughs with thanks and walks up and down, gathering the hem of her dress so as to give herself wings.

When the child returns home the house smells of baking, and there is a plate of fairy cakes on the table. She picks one up and eats it, and then she goes to the cupboard and looks inside. She turns to smile at her mother who smiles back and then the child takes another cake and sits on the settee in between her mother and brother.

A NEW GRAVESTONE
FOR AN OLD GRAVE
David Bezmozgis

Shortly before Victor Shulman was to leave on his vacation his father called him at the office to say that Sander Rabinsky had died. From the tone of his father's voice, and from the simple fact that his father had felt compelled to call him at work, Victor understood he was expected to recognize the name Sander Rabinsky and also to grasp the significance of the man's passing. Not wanting to disappoint his father he held the phone and said nothing. In recent years many of his father's friends had started to take ill and die. For the most part, these were friends from his father's youth, men whom Victor could not remember, having not seen them in the twenty-five years since the Shulmans left Riga and settled in Los Angeles. For Victor they existed, if at all, in the forty-year-old photos in which they, along with his own father, appeared bare-chested and vigorous on the Baltic shore. Simka, Yashka, Vadik, Salik: athletes, womanizers, and Jewish professionals, now interred in cemeteries in Calgary, New Jersey, and Ramat Gan. Victor assumed that Sander Rabinsky was of the same company, although that didn't quite explain why his death merited a special phone call.

Sander Rabinsky was dead, which was of course sad, Leon Shulman explained, but there was more to it. Sander had been Leon's last remaining connection in Riga and the one Leon had entrusted with overseeing the erection of a new monument to his own father, Wolf Shulman. Of late, Leon and Sander had been in constant contact. Sander had been acting on Leon's behalf with the stonecutter and functioning as liaison with the Jewish cemetery. Leon had already wired one thousand dollars to Sander's bank and Sander had assured him that a new stone would be installed in a matter of weeks. But now, with Sander's death, Leon was at a loss. With nobody there to supervise the job he had no way of ensuring that it would be properly done.

'Believe me, I know how these things work. If nobody is standing over them, those thieves will just take the money and do nothing.'

'The cemetery guy and the stonecutter?'

'There are no bigger thieves.'

Little more than a year before, Leon Shulman had been forced to retire from the pharmaceutical company where he had worked for twenty-three years. The diabetes that had precipitated his own father's death had progressed to the point where it rendered Leon Shulman clinically blind. Leon was a very competent chemist, enjoyed his job, and was well liked by his co-workers, but he could hardly argue when his supervisor took him aside and began enumerating the dangers posed by a blind man in a laboratory. Since then, as his vision continued to deteriorate, Leon imposed a strict regimen upon himself. His friends were dying and he was blind: another man might have surrendered to depression, but Leon informed anyone willing to listen that he had no intention of going down that road. It wasn't that he had any illusions about mortality; he was a sick man, but sick wasn't dead. So he woke each morning at a specific hour, performed a routine of calisthenics recalled from his days in the Russian army, dressed himself, made his own breakfast, listened to the news, and then immersed himself in unfinished business. At the top of the list of unfinished business was a new gravestone for his father's grave.

On occasion, particularly when the Shulmans observed the anniversary of their arrival in Los Angeles, Leon Shulman would recount the story of his father's death. Certainly Wolf Shulman had been ill. He'd been ill for years. But the week the Shulmans were scheduled to depart he had been no worse than he'd been in five years. Just that morning Leon had seen him and the old man had made oatmeal. So there was no way Leon could have anticipated what happened. But still, the thought that he was in a black marketeer's kitchen haggling over the price of a Kiev camera – albeit a very expensive model, with excellent optics, based on the Hasselblad – while his father was dying was something for which Leon could not forgive himself. And then the frantic preparations for the funeral, and the fact that Leon had already spent all of their money on things like the camera so that they'd have something to sell in the bazaars of Vienna and Rome, made the whole cursed experience that much more unbearable. Lacking time and money, Leon grieved that he had abandoned his father, a man whom he had loved and respected, in a grave marked by a stone the size of a shoebox.

This, Victor understood, was the reason for the phone call to the office. And later that evening, after submitting himself to the indignities of rush hour on the 405 and the 101, Victor sat in the kitchen of his parents' Encino condominium and listened as his father explained how easy it would be for him to adjust his travel plans to include an extended weekend in Riga. Leon had already called a travel agent, a friend, who could – even on such short notice – arrange for a ticket from London to Riga. It was, after all, a direct flight. A matter of only a few hours. The same travel agent had also taken the liberty – just in case – of reserving a room for Victor at a very nice hotel in Jurmala, two minutes from the beach, near bars, restaurants, and the Dzintari station, where he could find a local train that would get him into Riga in a half hour.

'Ask your mother, Jurmala in July, the beach, if the weather is good, nothing is better.'

'Pa, we live in Los Angeles, if I go it won't be because of the beach.'

'I didn't say because of the beach. Of course it's not because of the beach. But you'll see. The sand is like flour. The water is calm. Before you were one year old I took you into that water. And anyway, you shouldn't worry. I'll pay for everything.'

'That's right, that's my biggest worry.'

When Victor was a sophomore in college he realized that he would need to make money. This was the same year he spent a semester abroad at Oxford – though living for three months among fledgling aristocrats had nothing to do with his decision. For Victor, having grown up in Los Angeles, the lives and privileges of rich people – English or otherwise – were no great revelation. What led to his decision were the first irrefutable signs of his father's declining health. Victor began driving his father to the offices of world-class specialists, experts in the pancreas, not one of whom had been able to arrest – never mind reverse – the advancement of Leon's blindness. It was then that Victor started the calculations that ultimately led him to law school and a position as a litigation associate at a Century City law firm. At nineteen, Victor recognized – not unlike an expectant father – the loom of impending responsibilities. He was the only son of ageing parents with a predisposition to chronic illness. His father's mother had died of a stroke before her sixtieth birthday. His mother's sister had suffered with rheumatoid arthritis before experiencing the 'women's troubles' that eventually led to her death. And diabetes stretched so far back in his lineage that his ancestors were dying of the disease long before they had a name for it. More than once Victor had joked to friends that, when confronted with forms inquiring after family medical history, he simply checked the first four boxes without looking. Still, the only reason Victor felt he could permit himself that joke was that he was thirty years old, earned one hundred and seventy thousand dollars a year, and knew that although he could not spare his parents the misery of illness he could at least spare them the misery of illness compounded by the insult of poverty.

After dinner, Victor's mother, instead of saying goodbye at the doors of the elevator, insisted on walking him down to his car. Victor had not committed to going to Riga and she wanted him to understand – if he did not already – the effect his refusal would have on his father. Both Victor and his mother knew that Leon could be obsessive about the smallest things, and considering his condition, this was in some ways a blessing. Sitting at home alone, his obsessions kept his mind occupied. He could fashion his plans and make his phone calls. At the university library where Victor's mother worked, her co-workers all recognized Leon's voice; he no longer needed to ask for her by name.

'Of course you don't know this, but he calls me five or six times a day. Over the last month all the time to consult about the preparations for the gravestone. You know how he is, he says he wants my advice. Should he send Sander all the money at once or half and half? Do I think he should make up a contract for Sander to sign or would Sander be offended? And then when they started talking about what kind of stone, what shape, what size. Finally, when it came time to compose an epitaph, he says to me: "You studied literature." There, at least, I think he actually listened to what I said.'

Standing in the street beside his car, Victor explained again why the trip would be much more complicated than his father imagined. He had only two weeks for vacation. And it wasn't the kind of vacation where he would be in one place all the time. He would be visiting the only close friend he had retained from his time at Oxford. The previous year this friend had gotten married and Victor had been unable to attend the wedding. His friend wanted Victor to meet his wife and spend some time with them. They had been planning this trip for months. Not only had his friend co-ordinated his vacation to coincide with Victor's but so had his new wife. They were to travel through Scotland, Ireland, and Wales. All the reservations had been made. So, it wasn't that Victor didn't want to help put his father's mind at ease, but that there were other people involved and he could not change his plans without inconveniencing them.

'If you tell them why, they'll understand. People have emergencies.'

'I know people have emergencies. But the grave has been there for twenty-five years. All of a sudden it's an emergency?'

'For your father it's an emergency.'

'If he waits six months, I promise I'll book a ticket and go.'

In his mother's deliberate pause, Victor heard what neither of them dared speak out loud. Leon was careful about his diet, monitored his blood sugar, and took his insulin injections. There was nothing to say that he could not continue this way for twenty years. Nevertheless, Victor felt that it was irresponsible, even ominous, to project into the future – if only six months – and presume that his father would still be there.

Meeting his mother's eyes, Victor knew that the decision had been made. And when his mother spoke it was no longer to convince him but rather to assure him that he was doing the right thing.

'I understand it will be unpleasant to disappoint your friends. But it's only three days. And, after all, this is your grandfather's and not some stranger's grave.'

Late on a Saturday night, Victor's flight made its approach to the Riga airport. On the descent Victor looked out his window at the flat, green Latvian landscape. His neighbour for the three-hour trip from Heathrow was a garrulous, ruddy-faced Latvian in his seventies – a San Diego resident since 1947. Following the collapse of Communism, the man had returned to Latvia every summer for the fishing. When Victor informed him that he was undertaking his first trip to Latvia since his family's emigration in 1978, the man invited him to his cabin. Though the man was sincere and friendly, Victor couldn't help but suspect that he was an unregenerate Nazi. To hear his parents tell it, innocent Latvians hadn't retreated with the Germans. Whether this were true or not, Victor was not exactly proud of the ease with which his mind slipped into clannish paranoia. But, to maintain the necessary objectivity wasn't easy, particularly when buckled into an airplane full of blond heads.

In fact, after Los Angeles, and even London, Latvia struck him as remarkable in its blondness. At the customs desk, a pretty blond agent checked his passport. Tall blond baggage handlers handled the baggage. And it was a blond policewoman in a knee-length grey skirt who directed Victor up to the second floor where he could find a taxi. He had returned to the city of his birth, but no place had ever seemed less familiar. He marvelled even at the sky. His flight had landed after ten and he had spent close to an hour in the terminal, but when he stepped outside he emerged into daylight. The pavement, highway, and outlying buildings were illuminated by some bright, sunless source.

At the kerb, a thin Russian hopped off the fender of a Volkswagen and reached for Victor's suitcase. He wore a New York Yankees T-shirt and Fila track pants and had the distinction of being not-blond. Identifying Victor immediately as a foreigner, he asked, 'American?' Victor responded in Russian, speaking in a terser, gruffer register than he normally used – a register he hoped would disguise the extent of his foreignness, make him appear less dupable, less likely to be quoted an exorbitant fare. And so when the cab driver said, 'Fifteen lats' – equivalent to twenty-plus American dollars – a price Victor still suspected was inflated, he growled his disapproval and, to his satisfaction, succeeded in having the fare reduced by one lat.

On the road to Jurmala, Victor sat in silence. He focussed on the passing scenery. At that hour, nearly midnight, there were few other cars on the four-lane highway. The view was unspectacular. He registered certain banal observations. The road was smooth and clean. The passing cars were German, Swedish, Japanese – and clean. The few gas stations they passed appeared to be newly constructed. Victor kept expecting to feel something, be somehow inspired. He thought: I was born here, and I'm evaluating the infrastructure.

The cab driver spoke over his shoulder and asked which hotel and Victor pronounced the name without turning his head.

'Villa Majori? Not bad. You know who owns it?'

'No.'

'The former mayor of Jurmala.' Victor gathered that the driver expected him to be impressed. 'He was mayor for six months. Now he has a hotel. The property alone is worth 250,000 lats.'

'So he's a crook.'

'Of course he's a crook.'

'Did you vote for him?'

'Did I vote for him? What difference does that make? Certain people decided he would be mayor, then later they decided he would no longer be mayor. It's not like that in America?'

'In America he'd have two hotels.'

The driver laughed, inspiring in Victor a self-congratulatory and yet fraternal feeling.

'The mayor: a crook and a bastard, but I hear the hotel is good and that the girls he hires are very attractive.'

Minutes later, Victor discovered that the hotel was indeed modern, tidy, and staffed – even at that late hour – by a pretty clerk. The hotel consisted of three floors, giving the impression that, before being converted to suit the needs of the former mayor, it had been someone's home. Victor found his room on the second floor and stood looking out the window at the flux of people on Jomas Street. The street was closed to all but pedestrian traffic and was flanked on either side by bars, restaurants, and hotels. Through his closed window he could hear the undifferentiated din of voices and music from rival bars. Had he wanted to sleep, the noise would have been infuriating, but though he'd hardly slept in two days, he felt exceedingly, even pathologically, alert. So, as he watched the sky darken literally before his eyes – a change as fluid as time-lapse photography of dusk – Victor decided to call home.

As it was Saturday afternoon in Los Angeles, his mother picked up the phone. When she realized it was Victor, she deliberately kept her voice neutral so as not to attract Leon's attention.

'You're there?'

'I'm there.'

'In the hotel?'

'In the hotel.'

'On Jomas?'

'I can see it from my window.'

'How does it look?'

'How did it look before?'

'People were strolling all day. Everyone dressed up. All year long girls thought only about getting a new dress for the summer.'

Victor heard Leon's voice, rising above his mother's, and the inevitable squabbling over possession of the phone.

'You see, if I tell him who it is he won't let me talk.'

'What do you need to talk about? You can talk when he gets home. Has he spoken to Sander's son?'

Sander Rabinsky had a son in Riga whom Victor was supposed to have contacted upon his arrival. Sander's son was named Ilya and happened, as Leon enthusiastically pointed out, also to be a lawyer. It had been Ilya who had informed Leon of Sander's death. After not hearing from Sander for several days Leon had called repeatedly, left messages, and kept calling until finally Ilya had answered the phone.

'Did you call him?'

'It's midnight.'

'Call him first thing.'

'I will.'

'Good. So how is it over there?'

'Exactly like Los Angeles. Maybe better. The women are beautiful and there are no fat people.'

'Latvians: they look good in uniforms and are wonderful at taking orders. God punished them with the Russians. The devil take them both. Don't forget to call Sander's son.'

Victor slept only a few hours and awoke at first light. He lingered in bed, trying to will himself back to sleep, but after an hour of this futility he rose, showered, dressed, and ventured outside. He found Jomas Street deserted but for a handful of elderly city workers armed with straw brooms, engaged in the removal of evidence of the previous night's revelry. It was five o'clock and Victor walked the length of the street, past the shuttered bars, small grocery stores, and souvenir shops. The only place not closed at that hour was an Internet café attended by a teenager slumped behind the counter. Victor wrote a too-lengthy email to his friend in England. He had little new to say, having parted from him and his wife less than a day before, but to kill time he reassured them that they should begin their trip without him and that he would join them as soon as he resolved the business with his grandfather's gravestone. At the very least, Victor joked, he would connect with them by the time they reached Dublin, where his friend's wife had promised to set him up with a former room-mate. Victor knew little about the girl other than her name, Nathalie, and that in a picture from his friend's wedding she appeared as a slender, attractive, dark-haired girl in a bridesmaid's dress.

By eight o'clock Victor had eaten his complimentary breakfast in the hotel's dining room and decided, even though it was still possibly too early, to call Sander's son. He dialled from his room and a woman answered. Leon had told him that Ilya was married with a young son of his own. Speaking to the woman, Victor tried to explain who he was. He mentioned Sander's name, the gravestone, and his father's name. Victor sensed a hint of displeasure in the way the woman replied, 'Yes, I know who you are,' but tried to dismiss it as cultural – Russians not generally inclined to American-grade enthusiasm – and he was relieved when he heard no trace of the same tone in Ilya's voice.

Ilya said, 'I spoke with your father. He said you would be coming.'

Victor offered his condolences over Sander's death and then accepted Ilya's invitation to stop at his apartment before proceeding to the cemetery.

As the travel agent had indicated, Victor found Dzintari station a few minutes walk from his hotel. This route – Dzintari-Riga – was identical to the route he would have taken twenty-five years earlier in the summers when his parents rented a small cottage by the seashore. Somewhere, not far from his hotel, the cottage probably still existed, although Victor didn't expect that he could find it.

For the trip, Victor assumed a window seat and watched as the train sped past the grassy banks of a river and then the russet stands of skinny pines.

Since it was a Sunday morning, and as he was heading away from the beach and toward the city, there were few other people in his car. At the far end two young men with closely cropped hair shared a quart of malt liquor, and several benches across from Victor a grandmother was holding the hand of a serious little boy dressed in shorts, red socks, and brown leather sandals no self-respecting American child would have consented to wear. Now and again, Victor caught the boy's eyes as they examined him. The boy's interest appeared to be drawn particularly by the plastic bag Victor held in his lap: a large Robinsons-May bag in which he carried a bottle of tequila for Ilya and a small rubber LA Lakers basketball for Ilya's son.

From the train station Victor followed Ilya's directions and walked through the centre of the city. Ilya lived on Bruninieku Street, formerly called Red Army Street, in the apartment Sander had occupied for over fifty years. It was there, on Red Army Street, that Sander and Leon had become acquainted. They had been classmates in the Number 22 Middle School. Leon had lived around the corner and spent many afternoons playing soccer in the very courtyard where Victor now found himself. The courtyard and the building were older than the fifty years, closer to eighty or ninety, and the dim stairwell leading to the second floor suggested the handiwork of some pre-World War II electrician. Victor climbed stone steps, sooty and tread-worn to concavity, and squinted to read graffiti of indeterminate provenance. Some was in Latvian and seemed nationalistic in nature, some was in Russian, and if he read carefully, he could make out what it meant: 'Igor was here'; 'Nadja likes cock'; 'Pushkin, Mayakovsky, Visotsky'.

Victor found the number of Ilya's apartment stencilled above the peep-hole and rang the buzzer. Through the door he heard a child's high and excited cry of 'Papa', and then Ilya opened the door. He was slightly shorter than Victor but was of the same type – a type which in America could pass for Italian or Greek but which in Latvia wasn't likely to pass for anything other than itself. Ilya wore a pair of house slippers, track pants, and a short-sleeved collared shirt. Standing at Ilya's side was a little blond girl, no older than five. The little girl seemed excited to see Victor.

'Papa, look, the man is here.'

Ilya gently put a hand on her shoulder and edged her out of the doorway. 'All right, Brigusha, let the man inside.'

Victor followed Ilya into the living room, where Ilya's wife was arranging cups, wafers, and a small teapot on the coffee table. The mystery of genes and chromosomes accounted for the nearly identical resemblance between mother and daughter and, but for a fullness at the mouth, the complete absence of the father in the little girl's face.

As Victor, Ilya, and the little girl entered the room Ilya's wife straightened up, looked at Victor, and appeared no happier at seeing him than she'd been at hearing his voice over the telephone. Ilya motioned for Victor to sit on the sofa and then performed the introductions.

'This is my wife, Salma, and Brigitta, our little girl.'

Victor smiled awkwardly. He felt that he had made the mistake of taking his seat too soon. The upholstery claimed him in a way that made it difficult for him to lean forward or to rise. Undertaking the introductions while seated seemed wrong to the point of rudeness. As it was, he already felt less than welcome. He wanted to be on his feet, not only to shake hands, but also to offer the gifts – though the prospect of rising immediately after sitting down and then that of presenting the inappropriate basketball to Ilya's daughter momentarily paralysed him. He was tempted to explain the misunderstanding about the basketball, but knew that to do so would be a betrayal of his father, portraying him as confused and inattentive, self-involved, possibly senile.

Doing his best to mask the exertion, Victor rose from the sofa and offered his hand to Salma and then, playfully, to the little girl. Because he knew that Salma didn't like him, Victor watched her face for some sign of détente but, as Brigitta's small hand gripped the tips of his fingers, Salma's smile merely devolved from token to weary. Her expression made Victor feel like a fraud even though, apart from trying to be social, he was quite sure he hadn't done anything fraudulent. Under different circumstances, Victor consoled himself, he wouldn't tolerate such a woman.

Turning his attention from her, Victor reached into his bag and retrieved first the bottle of tequila and then the ball. To his relief, the little girl took the ball with genuine pleasure and bounced it on the stone floor with both hands. Ilya, inspecting the bottle, looked up and watched as Brigitta chased the ball into the kitchen.

'Before she punctured it, she had a beach ball like that. She could bounce the thing all day. Brigusha, say thank you.'

Victor, uncertain if he'd been commended or not, said that he hoped the gift was all right.

'You couldn't get her anything better. Right, Salma?'

Salma, for the first time, looked – though not quite happy – at least somewhat less austere.

'It's very nice. Thank you.'

She then picked up the empty Robinsons-May bag that Victor had left on the floor.

'Do you need the bag back?'

'No.'

'It's a good bag.'

She called after her daughter. 'Brigusha, come here. Look at what a nice big bag the man left for you.'

Carrying the ball, Brigitta returned to admire the bag.

'See what a big, fancy bag. You could keep all your toys in here. Come show the man how you can say thank you.'

Brigitta looked up at Victor, down at her feet, and then pressed her face into Salma's hip. Ilya said, 'Now you're shy? Maybe later you can show the man how you say thank you. She can say it in four languages. Russian, Latvian, German, and English.'

Placing the tequila on the table, Ilya asked his wife to bring glasses.

'Come, we'll sit. I should have put a bottle down to begin with. What kind of alcohol is this?'

Victor resumed his place on the sofa.

'Mexican. They make it from a plant that grows in the desert. It's very popular in America.'

Salma returned with two glasses and Ilya poured. He proclaimed: 'To new friendship.'

After Salma made the tea and distributed the wafers she took Brigitta into a bedroom. From what Victor could see, that bedroom, plus another, along with the kitchen, a bathroom, and the living room, constituted the apartment. The ceilings were high, maybe twelve feet, and the floors and walls were in good repair. Also, the furniture, polished and solid, seemed to be many decades old and might have, for all Victor knew, qualified as antique.

Ilya said, 'You like the apartment?'

'It would be hard to find one as good in Los Angeles.'

'This apartment is the only home I've ever had. Now it's my inheritance. After the war my grandparents returned from the evacuation and moved here. My father grew up here, married here, and when I was born this is where he brought me from the hospital. As a boy I slept on this sofa, my parents in the smaller room, my grandparents in the larger. When my grandparents died my parents took their room and I was given the smaller one. Now it's my turn to take the big bedroom and move Brigitta into the little one. You could say I've been waiting my entire life to move into the big room. Though, if you follow the pattern, you can see where I go from there.'

'So don't move into the big room. Then maybe you'll live for ever.'

'Well, we haven't moved yet. Brigitta still calls it "Grandfather's room". She likes to go and see his white coat hanging on the hook.'

'She's a good girl.'

'Do you have children?'

'No.'

'Married?'

'No.'

'It's a different life in America.'

'Probably not that different. At my age most Americans have children. Some are even married.'

The mood had become a little too confessional for Victor's liking and he took it as a good sign when Ilya grinned.

'One day I'd like to visit America. Salma's English is very good. Until recently she even worked for an American software company. Owned by Russians from San Francisco, Jews, who left here, like you, in the 1970s. They returned to take advantage of the smart programmers and the cheap labour. But the company went bankrupt after the problems with the American stock market.'

'Unfortunately, it's a familiar story.'

'"Capitalism", as my father would have said. Though he wasn't much of a communist. But when everyone was leaving he wasn't interested. He liked it here. He was a doctor; he wanted to remain a doctor. He had no regrets. Not long ago, after your father contacted him he said to me: "You see. What if I'd left? I'd be collecting welfare in Brooklyn and who would help blind Leon Shulman with his father's gravestone?" He had a real sense of humour.'

Wolf Shulman was buried in the 'new' Jewish cemetery on Shmerle Street. An older cemetery, from before the war, could be found in the Moskovsky district, a traditionally poor, working-class neighbourhood behind the train station. Before the Nazi occupation the neighbourhood had been predominantly Jewish, and during the Nazi occupation it had served as the ghetto. Ilya said there wasn't much to see there but, if Victor liked, Ilya would show him around. The municipal courthouse, where Ilya worked as a prosecutor, was only a few minutes away by foot.

From Ilya's apartment Victor caught a bus that let out at the base of Shmerle Street – a winding tributary off the main road – which rose to the cemetery and beyond. A concrete wall painted a pale orange encircled the cemetery. Victor followed the wall to the gates, where three old Russian women minded a wooden flower stall. Business appeared less than brisk, but as Victor neared the entrance, he saw a young couple select a bouquet of yellow carnations and so he did the same. He then passed through the gates and located the small stone building that served as the cemetery manager's office. Inside, the office was one single room, with dusty casement windows, a desk for the cemetery manager, and a lectern upon which rested a thick, leather-bound book. Upon entering, Victor found a short, heavy-set man wearing faded jeans, a pink sweater, and a black yarmulke, examining a slip of paper which had been handed to him by the young couple with the yellow carnations.

Victor heard the man ask, 'Berkovitz or Perkovitz?' and the young woman reply, 'Berkovitz. Shura Efimovna Berkovitz.'

'Berkovitz, Berkovitz,' the man repeated, shuffled to the lectern, and opened the large book. 'Year of death?' he enquired and, given the year, flipped pages and ran his finger down a column of handwritten names.

Once he found the name, the manager wrote down the section and row and pointed the young couple in the appropriate direction. For his service, and for the upkeep of the cemetery, he drew their attention to a container for donations. In a practised appeal that included Victor, the man said: 'We have more dead than living. And the dead don't donate.'

When the young couple left to seek Shura Berkovitz's grave Victor introduced himself to the manager. For the second time that day he was surprised to be so effortlessly recognized. Using the same words Salma had used earlier that morning, though without the rancour, the manager said: 'Yes, I know who you are.' Flipping more pages in the book, he looked for Wolf Shulman.

'Remind me, what year did he die?'

'1978.'

'There. Shulman, Wolf Lazarovich,' the manager said, and copied the information.

'And is everything ready for the new gravestone?'

'The grave is there. It's always ready. When the stonecutter brings the new stone, he'll also remove the old one. Very easy. Tik-tak.'

'Is he here today?'

Ilya had told Victor that sometimes, particularly on Sundays, the stonecutter could be found at the cemetery. He added that Victor would be well advised to speak to him as soon as possible because the stonecutter could be a difficult man to track down. Sander had expended no small amount of energy dealing with him.

The cemetery manager said, 'I'll call him at his shop,' and dialled the number. Within seconds he was speaking to the stonecutter. He spoke partly in Yiddish and partly in Russian. After a very brief exchange, he hung up. Victor, trying to suppress his irritation, explained that he had wished to speak to the stonecutter himself.

'He said he can see you tomorrow morning. He's very busy right now, but he'll be able to speak to you then. He keeps an office at the Jewish Community Centre. He'll be waiting for you at ten thirty.'

'I understand. But, you see, I'm only here for a short time and I want to be sure there are no miscommunications.'

'You shouldn't worry. I know of the matter. He knows of the matter. There will be no miscommunications. You'll see him tomorrow and everything will be just as you wish.'

Victor paused, assumed an expression he often employed with obdurate lawyers and clients, an expression intended to imply sincere deliberation, and then said, 'Nevertheless.'

The cemetery manager raised his palms in a sign of surrender. He scribbled a number on a piece of paper.

'Here is the number. Please. I wouldn't want you to think I am interfering. I was only trying to help you. The stonecutter is one of those men who, when he is busy, doesn't like to be disturbed.'

Victor took the number and dialled. After a short while he heard a man's terse 'hello'. Before Victor could finish introducing himself the man barked, 'Tomorrow; ten thirty,' and hung up. Victor replaced the phone and turned reluctantly to face the cemetery manager's obsequious grin.

The cemetery at Shmerle had been hewn from a forest, but enough trees were spared so as to retain a sense of the arboreal. Different types of trees – birch, elm, maple, ash – provided texture and shade and resembled in their randomness the different species of gravestones – marble, granite, limestone – which sprouted from the ground as naturally as the trees. Though arranged in sections and rows, the gravestones did not follow any other order, and so large dwarfed small, traditional opposed modern, and dark contrasted light. The only commonality among them was that each stone featured a photograph of the deceased and that in each photograph the deceased possessed the same grudging expression. Soldiers, grandmothers, engineers, mathematicians: all stared into eternity with a face that declared not *I was alive*, but rather *This was my life*. After walking some distance, Victor found his grandmother and grandfather wearing this same face.

Until he saw his grandmother's grave, Victor had at some level forgotten about it. That he carried only one bouquet reminded him of the extent to which he had forgotten. His grandmother had died when he was still an infant and so he had no memory of her at all. Somewhere there was a picture of the two of them together: a baby in the arms of a stout, prematurely old woman. Her gravestone confirmed what little he knew of her: Etel Solomonovna Shulman, beloved wife, mother, and grandmother. Died before her sixtieth birthday. This information, beneath her photo, was etched into a thick, rectangular slab of black granite. And this slab, almost a metre high, towered over its partner, a limestone monument one third the size, already weather-worn and tilting slightly backward. Seeing the two gravestones side by side, Victor could understand his father's anguish. What was left for Wolf Shulman seemed a slight against a man whose solemn face

– due to the backward tilting of the stone – appealed vaguely heavenward with an expression that could also be interpreted as: *Is this all I deserve?*

After taking some pains to divide his bouquet into two equal halves, Victor paused and contemplated his grandparents' graves. They evoked in him a peculiar timbre of grief – grief not over what he had lost but over what he had never had. A baser, more selfish form of grief. The kind that permitted him only to mumble a self-conscious 'goodbye' before turning back up the path. He then retraced his steps through the cemetery, stopping at times to appraise certain gravestones, look at pictures, and read names and dates. There were other members of his family buried here, and he discovered the grave of a great-uncle as well as some other graves with the last name Shulman – although he couldn't be sure if they were definitively his relations. The only other name he recognized appeared in a section occupied by more recent graves. On a reddish marble stone he read the name RABINSKY and saw a picture of a woman who must have been Ilya's mother. The picture, like all such pictures, was not of the best quality, but Victor could discern enough to draw the obvious conclusion. And beside this grave was another, still lacking a stone; but pressed into the soft earth was a small plastic sign on which was stencilled the name S. RABINSKY.

It was only noon when Victor left the cemetery, and though he felt the sluggishness of two days without sleep he decided to take a tour of the city. He caught a bus back into the vicinity of Ilya's apartment and then walked to the heart of medieval Riga. The city had been established in the twelfth century and had, throughout its history, been the subject of every Baltic power. Germanic Knights, Poles, and Swedes had tramped through its cobblestone streets. In the twentieth century alone – but for a brief spell of interwar independence – it had belonged to the Tsar, the Kaiser, Stalin, Hitler, and then Stalin once more. The heart of Old Riga had been destroyed by the Germans in the first days of World War II, rebuilt unfaithfully by the Soviets, but corrected to some extent by the new Latvian government. And so Victor was able to observe the storeyed Blackheads House, pass through winding alleyways, and visit the Domsky Cathedral, home to a world-famous organ.

Later, by leaving the old city, he found many examples of art nouveau buildings, with their elaborate stucco figures and faces. However, not particularly interested in architecture, Victor saw just enough to get a sense of the place. And after he'd acquired this sense, he took a seat at an outdoor café and ate his lunch in view of pedestrians, vendors, drunks, policemen, and bus drivers. In its constituent parts, the city displayed itself, and seemed, with its imported cars and Western fashions, none the worse for fifty years of Soviet rule.

On the ride back to Jurmala, Victor allowed himself to drift off. It was the deepest sleep he had experienced since leaving Los Angeles, and when his cab reached the hotel, a tremendous effort was required to rouse himself. He wanted nothing other than to sleep until morning, but at the front desk there were messages waiting for him from his father and from Ilya. So, tired as he was, Victor began by calling Ilya and recounting the episode at the cemetery manager's office. The incident, according to Ilya, was consistent with the man's character.

'But you have to consider how many others are practising his trade. The man has no competition and so, unfortunately, he's become arrogant.'

Ilya wished Victor luck and then invited him to come to the courthouse after his meeting with the stonecutter. He framed the invitation in collegial terms. Ilya imagined that, as a fellow jurist, Victor possessed some professional curiosity. 'This way,' Ilya said, 'you will be able to see the fabulous workings of the Latvian legal system.'

Victor then placed his call home. This time Leon answered, after hardly a single ring, as though he had been sitting, primed, by the telephone. Whatever reservations Victor harboured about the cemetery manager and stonecutter, he knew better than to reveal them to his father. To Leon's detailed questions, he responded honestly but without elaboration. Yes, he had seen Sander's son. Yes, he had been received cordially. Yes, he had given the child the present and the child had been pleased. Yes, he had been to the cemetery, seen his grandparents' graves, and left flowers. And yes, he had also spoken with the cemetery manager and with the stonecutter – the latter of whom he had not seen personally but would the very next morning.

After the conversations with his father and with Ilya, Victor discovered – to his frustration – that he had lost his overwhelming need for sleep. The prospect of another sleepless night was unbearable and so Victor drew the blinds, climbed into bed, and resolved to nurture even the slightest vestige of fatigue. But once again his body refused to co-operate. He slept only fitfully, waking up disoriented, sometimes because of voices in the street, other times because of some malformed thought. At one point he found himself bolt upright, unsure whether or not he had indeed requested a wake-up call. He then spent what felt like an eternity, torn over whether or not to call the front desk and confirm yes or no. Later, he lost the better part of an hour recreating the scene at the cemetery manager's office and formulating alternative scenarios in which he didn't come off looking like an idiot. Eventually, in despair, he turned on the television and watched an American action movie, dubbed in Latvian with Russian subtitles.

At five in the morning, Victor was back among the sweepers on Jomas Street. The sky was cloudless and approaching full daylight. Victor made a circuit of Jomas, covering its entire length, and then turned north and walked the few blocks to the beach, which, like the streets, was largely deserted. Narrow and white, it stretched from east to west, seemingly to infinity. The tide was still high and sandpipers skittered neurotically at the fringes of the waves. A short distance away, balancing against one another and advancing gingerly out into the Baltic, were two middle-aged women in bathing suits. They had already progressed about fifty yards but the water was not yet to their waists. The sight triggered Victor's first memory of his Soviet childhood: stepping out into a dark-blue sea, conscious of danger, but feeling as though he could go a great distance before he had anything to fear.

To find the Jewish Community Centre, Victor crossed a large municipal park and looked for the spire of a Russian Orthodox church. As he was extremely early, he trolled past the community centre, made sure he was in the right place, and then sat and waited in the park until he thought it was reasonable to go and look for the stonecutter.

The community centre, contrary to Victor's expectations, was a substantial building – four storeys tall and designed in the art nouveau style. From a fairly dark and dreary-looking lobby a broad stone stairway led to the upper floors, all of which benefited from an abundance of natural light. Not knowing whom to ask or where to look, Victor climbed the staircase and roamed the hallways hoping to stumble upon something that would announce itself as the stonecutter's office. He wandered for what seemed like a long time, finding an adult choir practising Hebrew songs in a rehearsal room; a grand theatre, with crumbling plaster and a seating capacity of hundreds; the locked doors of the Latvian Jewish Museum; and a tribute dedicated to a handful of Latvians who had protected Jews during the war.

He found these things but no explicit sign of the stonecutter, and little in the way of assistance until a young Latvian woman emerged from an office and cheerily informed Victor that the stonecutter did indeed use a room in the building, but he kept no regular hours and she hadn't seen him that morning. However, keen to help, she led Victor down one floor and pointed out the stonecutter's door. She even knocked, waited, and then apologized profusely, as if she were personally responsible for the stonecutter's absence. There was a phone in her office, she said, if Victor wanted to call the stonecutter, and also magazines, if he wished to occupy himself while waiting.

Seeing no other recourse, Victor followed the woman to her office and made the pointless phone call. The stonecutter was admittedly only fifteen minutes late, and the fact that he did not pick up the phone could actually be construed as a good sign – the man was on his way – so there was, in essence, no logical reason for despair. And yet, each unanswered ring reinforced Victor's suspicion that the stonecutter would not show up.

Victor put down the phone. Beside him, the woman looked on with a doleful expression, and he dreaded that, at any moment, she would repeat her offer of the telephone and the magazines. He couldn't recall if he'd seen a pay phone down in the lobby but he was quite sure that he had seen one in the park. Calling from the park would require that he go somewhere and make change and then walk the two blocks between the community centre and the park every time he wanted to make a phone call – thereby introducing a risk of missing the stonecutter should the man make a brief appearance at his office – but all this still seemed preferable to remaining, for even one second longer, the object of this woman's sympathy. Once again, Victor walked up and down the staircase. He listened to the choir and then descended to the lobby, where he found a handful of elderly Jews convened at a table, speaking Yiddish, chewing sandwiches, and playing cards. Victor stood for a few moments, debating whether or not to go outside, until a man brushed past him, hunched, bent under the weight of some psychological burden. He wore an ancient raincoat, a beaten fedora, and carried a briefcase. The man made his way for the doors of the public toilet and Victor heard him muttering to himself: 'If only to go and shit like a human being.' Victor decided to go outside.

Sitting in the park – having run the same coin through a pay phone yet once more – Victor thought it funny that there had been a time when the purpose of his vacation had absolutely nothing to do with Latvia. That at some point he had conceived of a relaxing trip with friends, touring the UK. And when the excursion to Riga had been introduced (or, rather, imposed), he had treated it as only a minor deviation. A filial duty quickly and easily dispatched. But now, amid his exhaustion and anxiety, it seemed inconceivable that he would ever reunite with his friends and see Ireland, Scotland, and Wales. His fate was to be perpetually trapped in Latvia, pursuing a stonecutter, thinking obsessively about gravestones. Victor laughed out loud. It was possible that people at neighbouring benches turned and stared. He didn't bother to check one way or the other. He had made his phone calls, he had knocked on the stonecutter's door, he had sat and waited. It was now time to walk to the courthouse and continue the farce.

Unlike most of the buildings Victor had seen in Riga, the courthouse was new and therefore outfitted with most of the contemporary trappings. The courtroom doors locked automatically when a session was in progress, the faint whir of air-conditioning was omnipresent, and the furniture – though constructed from Latvian pine – had a vague Ikea-like quality. At the very back of the courtroom, to the right of the door, the accused sat on a bench inside a little gated prisoner's dock. Along the wall, just ahead of him, two policemen in green uniforms sat on their benches. They were both young men, barely in their twenties, but already possessing the dull, indolent posture common to all court officers. Victor had his place across the aisle from the policemen. Behind him were a young woman and a teenage boy and ahead was an old woman, presumably the defendant's family. When Victor entered the courtroom, there was no sight of the bailiff, judge, or – more to the point – Ilya. Only the defense attorney, a tall, thin woman with tired, hound-like features, was present. Ilya did not appear until the bailiff emerged from the back door and called the session to order. All were made to rise while the judge mounted his podium. He was dressed in a burgundy robe and wore a chain of ornamental, golden medallions – evidently some folkloric symbol of Latvian authority. After the judge assumed his position, there followed the routine sequence of statements and exchanges – all of them in Latvian.

Victor understood hardly anything that happened over the next hour. He had no idea what the man had done to warrant his confinement, and he couldn't determine the purpose of the proceedings. He assumed they were preliminary, since, at one point, the defendant made a plea of not guilty. However, beyond that, the sense of things was impenetrable. And so Victor paid attention only long enough to register that Ilya, in his suit and tie, seemed to be a good lawyer. He was organized, spoke succinctly, and carried himself with an aloofness that bordered on menace. All of which probably didn't bode well for the man in handcuffs who sat in the prisoner's dock, looking not so much like a criminal but rather like a weary commuter waiting for the train. Victor assumed the same attitude of forbearance from the woman and the teenage boy as he heard not a sound behind him. The only person showing any sign of distress was the old woman in the front row. She had been in tears from the outset of the proceedings, and as time wore on, her breathing became shallower and more laboured. Despite the air-conditioning, perspiration gathered in the folds of her neck. She drank water from a plastic, bear-shaped bottle – a kind manufactured to contain honey – and alternately wiped her eyes with a handkerchief and attempted to cool herself with a paper fan. But it was all to little effect as, ultimately, her breathing seized up and Victor was convinced that she was on the verge of a heart attack. It was only at this point that the judge turned his attention to her and considered a pause in the proceedings, but when she managed to collect herself things resumed as before.

The hearing was the last of the day for Ilya, and so, at its conclusion, he suggested they have lunch. They stopped at a small cafeteria where Victor bought half a dozen meat and cabbage buns and two bottles of Latvian beer. They then walked back toward the municipal park where Victor had spent much of his morning. On the way, Ilya explained what had transpired in the courtroom.

It was, as Victor had surmised, an arraignment. The man had already spent six months in custody waiting for the date. He would probably wait another several months before his next appearance. His crime was serious, though not uncommon. He was charged with attempting to murder his boss. The man was a mechanic and had worked in an auto shop. He had been on the job for three months – the standard probationary period during which a new employee is paid poorly, if at all. After three months, the boss is legally bound to either keep him on full time or let him go. Generally, to avoid the higher taxes associated with a full-time employee, a boss will let the person go and find another – there being no shortage of desperate people. In this case, the man claimed that his boss had promised to keep him. But when he came to work after his probationary period he found someone else at his post. His boss told him to go to hell, and so the man stabbed him in the neck with a screwdriver.

The boss probably had it coming, but Ilya had no choice but to prosecute. If he didn't, then every boss would be walking around with a screwdriver in his neck.

'So what will he get for stabbing his boss in the neck?'

'Hard to say. Ten years? Or nothing. He'll say it was self-defense. The boss attacked him. He supports a wife, a younger brother. Nobody really wants to put him in jail. But who knows? Maybe things will turn out badly and he'll be put away for a long time.'

'Which will probably be the end of the old woman.'

Ilya considered this and then confessed that he had his doubts about the old woman. It struck him as peculiar that while the rest of the family sat in the back, she had taken her place in the front. Obviously, the old woman was supposed to be the defendant's mother, but this wasn't something anyone had bothered to verify. So she could just as well have been any old woman off the street. Which meant that there was nothing to say that the family hadn't scraped three lats together and paid her to come to the courthouse and act hysterically. Such things were not without precedent. Though, for an arraignment, Ilya believed it a waste of money. But one couldn't blame the old woman. She probably received sixty lats a month pension. Equivalent to one hundred dollars. And, Ilya said, he didn't need to describe to Victor what it was like to live on one hundred dollars a month.

They entered the park and Ilya sought out a vacant bench in the shade. It was now early afternoon and much quieter than when Victor had been there in the morning. There were a few young mothers with children and strollers. Now and again, a businessman strode past speaking into a cell phone. A few tourists stopped to buy ice cream and study their maps. Victor sipped his beer and wondered if he should admit to Ilya that he had absolutely no idea what it meant to live on one hundred dollars a month in Riga. Judging from Ilya's tone, he gathered that one hundred dollars a month was a pathetic sum. It certainly didn't sound like a lot of money, but then again, Latvia wasn't Los Angeles and, had Ilya phrased things differently, Victor could just as easily have been convinced that, in Latvian terms, one hundred dollars was a fortune. And though Victor subscribed to a sober view of the world and of the forces that ruled it – forces for whom the financial welfare of old ladies was generally not a top priority – he was in a strange country and therefore prone to a higher level of credulity; liable, practically, to believe the opposite of everything he believed.

Ilya said, 'Do you want to know how much money I make?' and then answered his own question before Victor had a chance to object. 'Two hundred lats a month. This is considered a good salary. Just enough so that I will think twice before taking a bribe. My father made the same as a dermatologist with forty years' experience. Salma, when she worked for the Americans, made two hundred and fifty. For a time, with three salaries, a total of six hundred and fifty lats a month, we were relatively well off.'

Ilya then proceeded to quote a litany of expenses, most of which, he said, were common to everyone in the city. Rent, food, transportation, miscellaneous items for children and the elderly. The figure he quoted for rent alone exhausted the total of the old woman's pension. There was, Ilya said, really no such thing as disposable income. This was why, to cite an extreme example, most of Riga's prostitutes had abandoned the city for points west. And as for the young mothers in the park, the businessmen, the pretty girls in summer dresses – in short, the reason Victor saw no squalor – well, it was Europe, after all. Not Africa. One good suit, one designer blouse – though second-hand from Germany – represented the difference between self-respect and despondency.

Ilya recited all of this information with detachment, as though he were addressing something merely statistical, academic, impersonal. His voice contained no resentment, which was why, when he asked Victor how much money he made, Victor felt less than his normal reticence to respond.

However, he chopped fifty thousand off the number, which, given the context, still sounded obscenely excessive.

'But,' Victor qualified, 'I work for a large firm. We do most of our business with corporations. Someone doing your job would make less. And then you still have to adjust for the higher cost of living . . .'

He realized that his was not a very persuasive argument. It was, even in terms of Los Angeles, not a very persuasive argument. He made a lot of money. Probably more than he deserved. But then again, he knew of others who earned even more and deserved even less.

Ilya leaned back on the bench and regarded, as though with intense botanical interest, the leaves and branches of the shade tree.

'I have some money saved up. Enough to send Salma and Brigitta to America. As I say, Salma is an accomplished programmer and her English is very good. And Brigitta is young and will easily learn the language. I am the only impediment. But I have my job here and am prepared to wait until they are ready for me.'

Ilya then turned his attention from the tree and focussed on Victor. As Ilya prepared to speak, Victor noted an inchoate defensiveness in the set of his features, as though Ilya, like a teenage suitor, was poised for imminent rejection; prepared, at any moment, to dismiss the proposition with 'never mind'. Which was precisely what he said, but not before he said: 'I'm not asking for money.' And not before Victor replied: 'I do not practise that kind of law.'

'But perhaps someone in your firm?'

'We deal only with corporations. Trade issues. Never individual immigration cases.'

Which – other than the exceptions made for the sons and mistresses of wealthy clients – was the truth. Immigration cases were frustrating and time consuming, entailing a morass of paperwork and almost always ending in recriminations. Given the choice, he would have preferred it if Ilya actually had asked for money.

'And what about other means?'

'What other means?'

'Marriage.'

'But you are already married.'

'We could divorce. Temporarily, of course. I have heard it done.'

'And then what?'

'Salma could marry an American.'

'Just like that?'

'How else?'

'And where would she find this American?'

Which, Victor immediately understood, was a stupid question.

'Never mind,' Ilya said. 'I see that it is asking too much.'

Victor considered explaining, so far as he knew, the problems inherent in this option, to try to exonerate himself, to impress upon Ilya the impracticality; beyond that, he considered lying, consenting to fill out forms, marry the man's wife, adopt his daughter, doing whatever, since it was pitifully clear that between him and the stonecutter remained – even if only tenuously – Ilya. But he couldn't quite bring himself to do that. Instead, he sat beside Ilya and resigned himself to a punitive silence.

After some time, as if having reached a conclusion, Ilya repeated, 'Never mind,' and ended the silence. 'I realize that this isn't why you came here,' he said, with each word distancing himself from the man who had, only moments before, offered Victor his wife and child. 'Fortunately, your problem is easier to solve. I will call the stonecutter for you.'

Ilya rose and went to the phone booth, though Victor was sure that he hadn't said anything to him about his most recent frustrations. And when Victor approached the phone booth Ilya was already dialling a number. Then he was speaking in Latvian, exhibiting the same bloodless composure he had evinced in the courtroom. The conversation did not last very long and Ilya did most of the talking. Once again, as at the cemetery manager's office, Victor felt himself excluded from considerations related to his own life. His input wasn't requested except to establish the departure time of his flight the next day.

When the conversation was over, Ilya exited the phone booth and announced: 'If you like, he can see us now.'

'That was the stonecutter?'

'Yes.'

'Is he at the community centre?'

'No.'

'So, where is he?'

'At his shop. In the Moskovsky district. It's possible to walk, although I would recommend a cab. A cab would get us there in ten minutes. We can get one easily on Brivibas Street.'

Ilya half turned in the direction of the street, ready to hail the cab, as if Victor's consent were foregone and incidental. Angered by Ilya's presumptuousness, and momentarily unsure of what he wanted, Victor said: 'What if I don't want to go?'

'You don't want to go?'

'I don't understand the rush.'

'I thought you left tomorrow.'

'In the afternoon. I could see him in the morning.'

'But he can see you now.'

'I waited for him for two hours today. Where was he then?'

Ilya regarded Victor as one might a child or a dog, as some thing ruled by impulse and deficient in reason.

'I couldn't say. Though I imagine if we went you could ask him yourself.'

The flatness of Ilya's tone discouraged Victor from asking anything further. Which was fine, since Victor no longer had anything to ask. He now recognized that he was in a situation that provided for only a binary choice. He could go with Ilya and see things through to their conclusion – whatever that might be – or he could refuse and claim the transitory pleasure of refusal. Those were his choices. There was nothing else. Calling the stonecutter and repeating his mistake at the cemetery was out of the question. And though he had misgivings about the likelihood of things turning out right, he had also an almost inexorable curiosity to finally meet the man. It seemed ridiculous – and likely a symptom of his delirium – but he had begun to doubt the very fact of the stonecutter's existence. And he entertained the thought, in some sub-rational recess, that meeting the stonecutter might be like meeting God or the president or the Wizard of Oz: equal parts disappointment and reward, but at least the truth would be revealed.

Victor followed Ilya out to Brivibas Street, where, as predicted, they had no trouble finding a cab. Ilya rode up front and directed the driver while Victor sat in the back seat. The driver navigated along streets now familiar to Victor. They passed through the medieval city, looped behind the central markets and the train station, and followed a route that brought them to the courthouse and the limit of Victor's knowledge. They then continued south, into what could have been generically described as the 'bad part of town'. The change was abrupt, as though the result of a civic consensus: No tourists expected beyond this point. The streets were grey and dingy. Old buildings deteriorated unchecked. Not infrequently, Victor saw listing, wooden hovels – seemingly anomalous in an urban setting – beside concrete apartment houses. People moved about the streets, tending to their everyday affairs, but there were also shadowy figures loitering in the doorways. In America, the place would have qualified as a slum, depressing and interesting only in a sordid way. But Nazis had commanded here and perpetrated horrific crimes, the knowledge of which invested the place with a sense of historical gravity; the slum felt like more than just a slum. And, assuming he didn't get mugged or clubbed to death, Victor thought it fitting that he should come here to get to the bottom of things.

After travelling for several more minutes, Ilya pointed to a dark green cottage and instructed the driver to stop. Victor then paid the driver and joined Ilya at the cottage's entrance. They stood there for a short while, but Ilya offered nothing in the way of explanation, not even a word to assure Victor that the dilapidated structure – bearing nothing to identify it as the stonecutter's shop or as a place of business of any kind – was where they needed to be. Victor had expected to find heavy machinery and stacked rock, but there were only a peeling façade, drawn curtains, uncut grass, and a dirt path that turned ninety degrees at the front steps and wound around the side of the house. Taking this path, Ilya led Victor the length of the house and into a yard dominated by a Mitsubishi pickup truck with a sunken rear suspension. The truck had been backed into the yard so that its tailgate was only a few feet from the doors of a garage and from a large manual winch. The winch looked ancient, a relic from previous centuries, but Victor could see that it was still very much in use. By its heavy rope, it suspended a rough marble obelisk three feet in the air. The obelisk spun lazily, as though it had only recently been disturbed.

Ilya placed a hand on the obelisk, indicated the garage, and said: 'Well, here you have him.'

Victor stepped past a door and looked into the garage. Looking back at him was a man in his sixties. He wore scuffed work pants, a sleeveless undershirt, and he had the hands and arms befitting a man who spent his days working with stone. He sat on a low stool with his legs splayed out before him. In one hand he held an abrasive cloth, which he had been using to polish a granite tombstone propped against a nearby wall. He blinked sullenly and looked very much like someone who hadn't been happy to see anyone in years.

'Shimon,' Ilya said, 'I brought you your client.'

Shimon blinked again and showed no indication that he heard what Ilya had said.

Ilya gave the obelisk a firm shove, putting the weight in motion, and eliciting squeals of protest from the winch.

'Aren't you even going to say thank you, you old goat?'

'Go to the devil,' Shimon said, 'and take him with you.'

'You shouldn't talk like that. He came all the way from America just to see you.'

'All the worse for him.'

Shimon glared from Victor to Ilya as though trying to determine which of them he despised more. For a moment, Victor wondered if maybe the old man had him confused with someone else. He'd not yet said one word to the stonecutter – barely looked at him, done nothing more than show up – and yet the man seemed to loathe him in a personal way. Victor found it unsettling, like the opprobrium of a cripple or a religious person. However, it didn't appear to bother Ilya, who responded to the stonecutter's hatred with a patrician smugness.

'Listen, if you don't want the business we'll leave.'

Shimon shrugged, hatred undiminished, but evidently not prepared to lose the business. Though, what business, Victor could not quite figure out. The money had been sent months ago and the work reportedly done.

Shimon lifted his face to Victor and said: 'Well, did you come from America to stand here like a mute? What is it you want from me?'

It could only be, Victor thought, that the man had confused him with someone else. Either that or he suffered from a mental illness.

'I spoke to you yesterday. We had an appointment for this morning. I waited for you for hours. We were supposed to discuss the gravestone for my grandfather's grave. Work that I was told you had finished. Work for which you have already been paid. So, how exactly do you mean what do I want?'

'Who told you it was finished?'

'His father promised my father it would be finished. Money was wired. Are you saying it's not finished?'

'Ask your friend the parasite if it's finished.'

Shimon jerked his head toward Ilya, the parasite, who had allowed a shadow to fall over his smugness.

'You see how he talks. You see what it's like to deal with him. My father literally spent weeks trying to have a reasonable conversation with him. And though I saw the trouble he was having, my father refused to let me intervene. Now, you've seen the Latvian legal system. You have seen where I work. It's nothing to be proud of. But, for what it's worth, it gives me access to certain people. And, if absolutely necessary, I can complicate someone's life.'

Ilya frowned in the stonecutter's direction.

'Not that it's something I enjoy. What's to enjoy? Old men like him pass through the court every day. You'd have to be a sick person to enjoy making someone's miserable life even more miserable. Right?'

Ilya smiled philosophically at Victor, his eyes seeking confirmation, as though the question had not been rhetorical. Just to be clear, he repeated it.

'Right?'

'Right.'

'But what choice do I have with someone like him?'

From the roof of his skull, Victor felt the spreading of a vaporous warmth. It filled him, like helium but not exactly, making him very light and very heavy all at once. It took him a second to identify this sensation as a powerful swell of fatigue. His legs were like pillars, rooted into the ground, and yet he believed he might tip over. Out of the corner of his eye, he thought he saw a lumbering, retarded man. The man was Shimon's son. He helped his father load and unload the heavy rocks. Victor turned to get a better look, but when he did he saw only Shimon sitting by himself in the garage.

Victor turned back to Ilya and said, 'What does any of this have to do with my grandfather's gravestone?'

Ilya wavered before him, for a second blurry and then immaculately sharp.

'Let me explain it to you,' Ilya said. 'Three weeks ago my father got on a bus to go and see this man. This man who could not be relied upon to keep an appointment or return a phone call. On a hot day, after working for eight hours, at five o'clock, when the buses are full, my father had to ride across town. Before he got here he had a heart attack. They had to stop the bus. We only received a phone call when he was already in the hospital. I, my daughter, my wife, none of us even had a chance to say goodbye. This is what it has to do with your grandfather's gravestone. My father, who from the goodness of his heart agreed to help. My father, whom your father only pestered. Calling all the time. And then wanting to negotiate payment in instalments. As if my father was a thief. And later sent him a *contract* . . .'

Ilya spat out 'contract', as if a more offensive word did not exist in the Russian language.

'This is what it has to do with anything. That my father killed himself over this gravestone. This gravestone that nobody would ever even visit. And what did my father get in return? Never a thank you. Only a hundred lats for his trouble. A hundred lats that won't even buy a stone a fifth as big for his memory. Now you tell me if that's fair.'

Through the murk of fatigue, Victor heard the things Ilya said, but his brain processed only the rudiments: my father, your father, my father, your father. If there were an argument here, Victor didn't see how anyone could hope to win it. There was nothing to win. There was Sander, an old man suffering a heart attack on a cramped city bus: Ilya's father, but an abstraction to Victor. And there was Leon, an abstraction to Ilya, but as real to Victor as if he were standing before him. There he was, stumbling around the apartment, feeling the walls. There he was, every morning, in his tracksuit, doing deep knee bends and other ludicrous Soviet calisthenics. There he was, injecting himself with insulin and fretting about one thing or another at the kitchen table. His father.

'I thought I would give you a chance. If you would help,' Ilya said. 'And even now, I give you a chance. You can buy yourself another gravestone. God knows you have the money. Give this old bastard the business he doesn't deserve. And I'll send you a photo to prove it gets done.'

In a daze, Victor didn't quite remember refusing the arrangement. Because he was already picturing his cab ride and the blur of pine trees on the way to Jurmala. And he was already in his hotel room, lying in bed, asleep and having a dream in which Nathalie, the Irish bridesmaid, appeared to him either on the beach in Jurmala or on the beach in Los Angeles – maybe both – and in which she professed her undying love, had sex with him, became his wife, and then – with the confounding logic of dreams – transformed into Salma, who, stranger still, did nothing to undermine the benign quality of the dream but rather, in some illicit way, only enhanced the sense of pleasure. And then he awoke and dialled and had a conversation with his father. A conversation in which his father asked him how everything went. If he met the stonecutter. If he saw the gravestone. If everything looked as it should. And Victor answered his father, saying yes about the stonecutter, yes about the gravestone. Yes about everything. He answered him and said that everything was perfect, just the way he imagined it.

This story originally appeared in the US in *Zoetrope All-Story*
Summer 2005 Vol. 9, No. 2

ON THURSDAYS WE GO TO THE ALLOTMENT
Hilary Wilce

On Thursdays we go to the allotment. You may think this sounds easy, but you have no idea.

We order the minibus for ten o'clock, which gives us an hour for all the to-ings and fro-ings, the explanations and reassurances, the excitement and tantrums, the yelling and hollering and head-swinging and hand-flapping that go with anything – anything at all – that happens outside the daily routine.

'I sometimes wonder why we bother,' I grumbled to Chris once. And he said, quite sharply for him, 'How would you like to just come here every day and never go anywhere else?'

But I do, I thought, and turned my head away.

Today, though, when I go in, there is only Lennie sitting forlornly on a chair in his tails. He flaps an awkward hand around the classroom.

'All the others. They've gone . . .' He frowns. The thought gets away from him. He puts up his arms instead. 'Dance, Pat, dance.'

Lennie's favourite TV programme is *Celebrity Come Dancing*. He watches it in a trance, his mouth hanging open even wider than usual, dribble running down. All round his lips are permanent sores from the slobber. I put aloe vera on them during the day at school, even though legally, Chris says, it probably counts as a medicine and I'm not supposed to. His mother found him this morning suit in Oxfam, so he could look like the programme, and now he wears it all the time.

What he wants me to do is to put the music on and waltz him round the room, and I would if I had time. I love Lennie. He has a nature as open and sweet as the morning sky. Give him a task and he'll do it until you tell him to stop. He always wants to do the right thing, even though he never has a clue what it could possibly be.

But there's something else, too. Lennie was the first one that I learned to care for, and that felt like no small miracle. I only came here because I had to find a job that would let me pick Alice up from school in the afternoons. What I really wanted was to train in a florist's. I had no idea what I was letting myself in for. I had never imagined that there could be children who spent their days strapped by their foreheads into wheelchairs, or who could only grunt like animals, or who might have half a dozen fits before break time, if it was that sort of a morning. The first day I was here, I felt as if I'd fallen right through the skin of the known world.

At the end of it I went to the office and said that there was no way I could stay, but somehow Janine, the head's secretary, persuaded me to try it for a week. 'We really need people like you here,' she said. What I now know she was saying was: we really need anyone we can get.

At the end of that week I went back to her. It was the smell that was getting to me by then, sweaty and ripe. It came, I knew, from all the incontinence and the dribble, the shut-up classrooms and the whiff of school cooking that hung around in the corridors, but it seemed to get into your nose and stay there, even when you drove away at the end of the afternoon; even when you stood for half an hour in the shower trying to sluice it all off you. 'This isn't for me,' I said.

'It isn't for anyone,' said Janine. 'Not at first. Give it a month, Pat, please. At least you're with Chris. He's the best.'

I couldn't understand this thing they all seemed to have about Chris. He was the tutor of the Leavers' Group – a fancy name for the handful of misshapen teenagers at the top of the school – a small, energetic man, always dressed in tracksuit and trainers, with his hair sticking out around his head as if in distress at all the things it had to see.

I didn't notice him much at first, or rather I noticed him and then dismissed him. In the world view I held back then, men were people who wore good suits and drove BMWs and always had their eye on the main chance.

What Chris had his eye on was whoever was trying to leave the room.

'Where are you off to, Ali?'

'Toilet.'

'Well, wait a moment and Pat'll go with you.'

I was his classroom assistant. I did toilet runs, and set up the video, and sat in the circle and clapped along when it was music time. And slowly, too, I did other things, like learning to know when Ali was so distressed she was likely to start dashing her nails at her face, and knowing how, then, to take her by the hand and lead her outside and walk her round and round the scruffy little sensory garden, breaking off sprigs of rosemary for her to sniff at, until she was calm again.

'You're good, Pat,' said Chris, one afternoon. 'You're really good with them. Do you know that?'

I think it was probably the best thing that anyone has ever said to me. I've never thought I could be good at anything, and especially not lately. That day I drove away with such a feeling inside me, it would be hard to explain to anyone how it felt. But whatever it was, it seemed to be contagious, because Alice giggled and laughed in the car all the way home, and there hasn't been a lot of that in the one year and ten months since Steven has been gone. In fact there's been hardly any of it at all.

But, the allotment.

I crouch down in front of Lennie and take his hands.

'The place where we go and grow all those nice vegetables, Lennie, don't you remember? For Mrs Allen, in the kitchen? We take them to her and she cooks them and you have them for your lunch?'

Blank stare.

'Carrots and onions and beans?'

Lennie's eyes cross in concentration. 'Baked beans?'

'No, not baked beans. Green beans. Long, green beans. Like, about this long. And thin and green. Don't you remember? Last week you got lots of water for them. You took the watering can and you filled it up and you gave them water.'

Slowly his face starts to focus.

'Green beans!'

'That's right. Green beans.'

He grins so much his face could split in two, right across the sore places. 'I know, Pat!' He wrenches his hands free and claps them wildly. 'Green beans! Roast dinner!'

Chris comes in, looking distracted. His tracksuit bottoms don't match his tracksuit top and it really annoys me. He's so busy looking after the kids that he never bothers to look after himself. I long to take him into town and get him a good haircut. Janine says he had a partner once, but she went off with one of his friends and he was devastated and now he only lives for his work, and I think it must be true because I know that, one Saturday, when I decided to come in with Alice and my gardening tools, to have a go at the sensory garden, he was working away in the hall getting ready for the Monday-morning assembly. We smiled and waved, but we didn't talk, although I couldn't help but be aware of him there, just a hundred metres away, all the time I was kneeling by the beds with my secateurs and trowel.

'Where is everyone?' I ask him.

'Gone to look round the day centre, poor sods.'

Chris hates the fact that, when the kids leave his care, they drop off the end of the system, and the only future for them is the day centre. Which, he says, is no future at all. He cares for them so much, it's amazing to see, although it's all done so quietly and naturally you have to pay close attention to catch it. But when you're locked in together all day, like we are, that's the kind of thing you start to notice – the million and one little things that keep the wheels spinning, even if most of the wheels are so bent out of shape it's a miracle they can turn at all. When something good happens, like maybe he makes a joke and it almost looks like some of them get it, his whole face lights up. He's Welsh – his name's Chris Jones – and although he always looks so harassed, he has these dark eyes and white teeth and such a smile it seems to warm the whole room. Once or twice lately, when he's been smiling or laughing, I've found myself staring at him, but then when he's caught me looking he's seemed so angry and irritated I've had to look sharply away.

'I don't think Chris likes me much,' I said to Janine, one day. 'I think I annoy him.' But she hooted so loudly I felt embarrassed for her and looked around the office to see if anyone was watching.

'Like? I should think he's scared stiff of you! I mean, look at you.

Compared to the rest of us. He'll never have had anything like it in his classroom before.'

In a way, I know what she was saying. Even after all Steven did to me, or maybe because of it, I always do my hair and my nails, I'm not overweight, and I still wear the cashmere sweaters left over from back then. The kids love to pat and stroke them. Most people who work here are the size of houses and slop around in old T-shirts and leggings. But I don't think she was right about the rest of it. I mean, who could be scared of me?

Now I say to Chris, 'So it's just Lennie today?'

'No. Ricky's here, too. But something's happened at home. He's in a terrible temper. I've just spent half an hour trying to calm him down. Look.' He pushes up his sleeve to show me violent red marks, but what I mainly see is the tanned skin of his forearm, scattered with dark hairs. 'He's sitting with Janine now. I've been phoning Mum to see what's up. She's in a bad way, too. Dad's gone, apparently. Said he's had enough, and thrown in the towel. I don't think Ricky's that close to him, but he's upset because his mother's upset, and he doesn't like to see it.'

'That happens,' I say, thinking of Alice, and he looks up at the tone in my voice, but then he looks away again.

We never talk about personal things, Chris and me. But suddenly I plough on, all in a rush, 'In fact, Alice didn't really settle down again at all until I did. And that wasn't until I came here. It's funny that, isn't it, considering how much I hated it at first.'

He turns round then, and looks at me, really looks, and as he does so it feels as if the air of the fusty classroom shifts, and I almost think he might say something back to me, something that isn't just about the kids for once. But at that moment the shadows on the wall flicker and his gaze shifts outside and he says with something that sounds horribly like relief, 'Oh, look, here's the bus. We'd better get going. Remember, we need to watch Ricky like a hawk this morning. Don't let him out of your sight.'

So that's how we go to the allotment, me sitting next to Lennie, and Chris sitting across the aisle from me with Ricky, and things between the two of us more awkward and unsettled than they've ever felt before.

And I find I'm feeling so restless because of it, or maybe it's just that Ricky's agitation is getting to me – I've noticed that it often happens in our little group, emotions spreading like a virus from one to another. Ricky is a gigantic, bear-like creature with alarming black hair growing down over a sullen brow. He is unresponsive at the best of times, probably my least favourite in the whole group, and today he looks thunderous. Size-wise he could eat Chris for breakfast, although he never would, unless things went wildly awry, because Chris has this deep, natural authority that somehow makes him, to all of us, as tall and immovable as a mountain.

'Lotment,' says Lennie happily, putting his head on my shoulder and dribbling onto my hand. 'Going 'lotment. Aren't we, Pat?'

'Yes, Lennie. We'll go and pick some more beans.'

He grins some more. 'Baked beans!'

I can feel Ricky simmering away, and Chris sitting forward in his seat looking every bit as unrelaxed as I am, but there's nothing I can do about any of it, so I sit back and, like Lennie, watch the houses go past.

On this route we drive right by my front door. I used to live out by the golf course, but four months ago I sold up and now Alice and I live in a terraced house, much further in. When I was Mrs Steven Oldenfield, I never even noticed these houses existed, even though I drove past them practically every day to get to the shops. Now I'm just Pat, though, and they suit me fine.

'Look,' I imagine saying, casually, to Chris. 'That's my house. You must come over and have supper one night.' But to do that I'd have to believe that it might be an invitation someone would be glad to be offered, and Steven stripped me of that just as effectively as he stripped out our bank accounts and stripped away the happiness from all the memories we'd once shared.

I look across to Chris. It feels oddly quiet and intimate with only the two boys to look after and none of the usual hubbub from the back, so maybe this is the one day I could. But I don't dare take such a risk. I can't find the words. All the time we were married, every single day of it, Steven was with someone else. He told me so when he left. He showed me his diaries, with all the dates and the details set down as a record. He held them high up under my nose and flicked over the pages so I had to look. He seemed to want to push me so far down into everything he'd done that I'd never come up out of it again. And I suppose, in a way, that's what he did. Because for nearly a year after he went I hardly set foot out of the house at all, except to take and pick up Alice, and it was only when the money ran out that I had to come out and find myself a job and ended up here and my life began to take on some sort of shape again. So I smile rather awkwardly in Chris's direction, and say nothing, and look back out of the window.

Lennie, too, is having trouble with words. His mouth works and works. Finally he gets it out.

'Porches!' he explodes, pointing to the houses. 'Look, Pat! On the houses!' His mouth works again. '*Porches!*'

These days I get most of my pleasure from theirs. I look at the porches and see that they are, indeed, fine and wonderful things to have on the front of any house.

'That's right, Lennie. Aren't they nice?'

I'm nice, too, now, so much nicer than I was back in the days of the golf course. I know that. My heart has grown bigger. I first felt it last summer, at sports day, when the sun shone and all the parents turned out and, even though the races and so on were a complete fiasco, what with the crutches and wheelchairs and not everyone grasping which direction they were supposed to run in, it still felt so good to be part of helping to make it all happen. I walked around, and smelled the crushed grass and the hamburgers on the barbecue, and people called me Pat, and I chatted with the mums and helped the kids get ready, and I suddenly knew that, even despite all the terrible things Steven had said to me, even despite the terrible things that he'd done, my life still amounted to something. The feeling I had was, I think, that although I'd been pushed out of the human race quite some time before, and been out there on my own in some dark, lonely exile, it had now opened up and allowed me back into it again. And that this new part of it that I had been allowed back into was a much, much better place than any place I had ever been in before.

Chris is looking across at me when I come back to myself.

'What?' I ask, frightened my mouth might have been hanging open as wide as Lennie's.

'Nothing,' he says quickly, and places a hand on Ricky's arm. 'All right, Ricky? Good boy. Nearly there now.'

We drive on. Lennie searches for more porches. Chris clears his throat once or twice. Then, as we turn into the lane that leads to the allotments, he suddenly says, 'Oh, I forgot – I ought to have told you – I think there's some kids here this morning doing some weeding. Young offenders or something. Community service. I think that's what Janine said.'

We both glance instinctively at Ricky, then at each other, thinking the same thing. Ricky is not in a good mood, and he doesn't like strangers.

'I'm not sure this is a good idea,' I say.

'It'll be fine,' says Chris, but I can see he isn't certain.

'We don't have to carry on. We can always stop and turn back.'

But then, as I hear them, my words suddenly seem to mean something other than what I've said, and, like a teenager, I feel a violent blush sweep into my cheeks, and I look at him in alarm, and he quickly moves his eyes to Lennie, who is bouncing with excitement now we're nearly there, and says, 'It's not always so easy, once you've set off.' And then to my astonishment he, too, as he looks back to me, seems to start colouring up and we're left staring at each other in mortification for a moment, helpless and hopeless as our charges, before we both look quickly away.

I look down to the floor, and then out of the window. And then, as the bus swings round to park next to our little plot, I jump up ready to burst out of the door at the first possible moment. I suddenly feel desperate for fresh air.

But Lennie beats me to it. He pushes past me and stumbles down the steps just as soon as the bus has stopped, his coat-tails flying. I hurry after while, behind us, Ricky barges into Chris, catching him off guard, so that Chris pitches forward down the steps straight into me, and has to grab out to steady the two of us, and suddenly we're standing so close together, clutching at each other, that I can feel him, his vibration, all over my body – my poor, lonely body, that hasn't been loved in so long it can't even remember – and such longing and neediness surge out of me that I make a weird kind of choking noise and wrench myself free, just as two girls rise from where they have been sitting, smoking, on the raised wooden edge of our potato beds.

I see their white faces turn to take in Lennie, in his tails, and Ricky with his ape-man brow, and Chris's ill-matched tracksuit, and me gasping and jittering like a teenager. I see their mascara-ed eyes blink and their lipsticked mouths work and their cigarette smoke rise in two tiny columns as they fold their arms to stare, then I see them look at each other and snigger, and I hear one of them say, loud as anything, 'Watch out! Here come the spazzos!'

And then – to be honest, I don't know what happens then. All I can say is that somehow I'm grabbing the girl at the point where her neck meets her shoulders, digging my nails in and shaking her like I, shamefully, sometimes used to shake Alice when everything in the house was so bad that I couldn't help but lose my temper with someone; I'm shaking her until her ugly earrings knock together and her tongue-piercing clashes against her teeth; as if she is Steven, in all his wickedness, or Ricky, with his Neanderthal temper, or whatever cruel God it is that has made poor Lennie the shape he is, or Chris, in his self-containment that feels to me, in my raw, sore state like just another rejection.

'How dare you!' I scream. 'How *dare* you! You little piece of useless nothing! Don't you ever use that word again, do you hear? They are people. *People!* Just like you and me! *Better* than you and me! If I ever hear you use that word again, if I *ever* do, I promise you I will not be responsible for what I –'

'Pat!' Chris is pulling me away. 'For God's sake!'

'Did you *hear* what she said!'

'Let it go!'

'But she said –'

'It doesn't *matter*!'

But now Ricky is roaring forward, and thumping and crashing his hands down on Chris's back as Chris pulls at me, and Lennie, terrified, is whimpering like a beaten dog and scuffling backwards.

'I mean it, Pat!' says Chris, his voice raised, bringing all his authority and experience to bear on me, just as he does on the kids when they lose it like this. 'Let it go!'

And he grips my arm and holds me away from the girl with one hand, while he grapples to keep Ricky back with the other.

My heart is beating like it would burst out through my coat and jumper. I struggle and glare but he meets my eyes with his own eyes blazing. No looking away now. And I feel the great strength of him against me, some through his hand, but most through his eyes, and although I still glare back at him, I know, almost immediately, that I am beaten, and start to feel the rage shrinking back from the edges of me, until he feels it too, and he knows he can safely let go. Immediately, then, he spins around and takes Ricky with both hands, holding his arms and walking him backwards, talking to him quietly as he does so, to soothe him and calm him.

'Fucking maniac!' yells the girl. 'I could report you!'

And she jumps forward and stabs her cigarette towards my eye, almost right into it, at which Ricky, seeing what she is doing, bellows and breaks free again and lumbers at the girl on his great, splayed, sneakered feet, with his arms out like a gorilla. And the girl's look changes, as she sees him, into one of pure panic, and with good reason. Ricky could splinter her jaw with a single thump of his great fists. He could knock her sideways across the allotment so her head crashes down into the cucumber frames, or twist her arm up behind her until it pops and tears right out of its socket. And what's more, he not only could, but he would, and all this goes through my mind in a single flash, while the sun catches a corner of one of the girl's giant doorknocker earrings and her friend jabbers with fear in the background. And I'm the only one between her and him, and I've caused all this, and it's up to me, now, because if I can't do something about this, who knows what will happen . . .

'Ricky!' I roar, from somewhere deep within my chest. God knows where. 'No!'

I pull myself up, and fix him with my eyes, and put both my hands up towards him as if I'm certain he'll stop before he runs onto them, and, amazingly, after a terrifying second or so, he does exactly that. He looks astonished.

'Go!' I hiss at the girl, over my shoulder. 'Quickly. Just get away from here. The both of you. Go!'

And amazingly she, too, does what I tell her, and in a flash the two of them are fleeing out past the minibus, cigarette packets clutched in their hands and their earrings flying.

But my eyes stay on Ricky. Still standing tall, I talk to him, as Chris has shown me how to, until I feel him settle enough for me to dare to snatch a glance around for Lennie, who hates violence, and seems to have vanished altogether.

And then – oh, thank God, because I have no idea what to do next and I don't know how long I can hold him there – I hear Chris say, 'It's OK, Pat. I've got him now.'

So I put my hands down and walk shakily away towards the bus, but my legs will hardly carry me, and when I get there all I can do is to collapse on the bottom step and push my eyes down onto my knees and shudder and shake until the shock of it starts to pass. All I can think while I sit there is: suppose he hadn't stopped? And I can see my wrists snapping like matchwood and the girl being tossed like a doll away across the potato patch. But I know you can't think that like. You can't. You have to put things behind you. So eventually, just as soon as I am able, I wipe my wet face and climb up into the bus.

Lennie is on his own in there, crouched on the floor at the back, while the driver is off on the far side of the parking area, having a smoke. So there is just the two of us, and one thing I do now know is how important it is, after anything like this has happened, to look as if you are calm and in control, no matter how churned up you feel inside. So I smile at him as cheerfully as I can manage and help him up and say, 'Come on, Lennie. It's all over now. Let's go and water those beans.'

Very slowly, I coax him back towards the allotment. But it is painful progress, what with his distress and my legs, so by the time we get there Chris is sitting peacefully with Ricky on the edge of the potato bed, his arm around Ricky's broad shoulders.

'Pat the Warrier,' he says. I can't read his tone.

'Pat hit her!' blurts out Lennie.

I look at the floor.

'She did,' says Chris.

'She grabbed her!'

'That's right. She did. Never a great idea to do that to anyone, Lennie. However much they annoy you.'

At that my eyes snap up. 'You don't have to preach at me through Lennie, you know! You can just come out and say it!'

Chris looks as if he could grin.

'I'm not preaching. I'm just saying. You did, after all, assault the poor girl. Are you going to apologize?'

'What? To her?'

'Who else?'

I consider. I realize I can still feel the feeling of that great roar that I found in my chest. I can still see the moment Ricky stopped dead in his tracks. The moment that I, Pat, made him. I lift my head higher.

'No. I don't. I don't think that I am.'

His grin is definitely there now.

'I will to you, though,' I say. 'I know I shouldn't have caused all that trouble.'

'No. Well. But we got through it. And I somehow doubt that she'll sue.'

'I hope not.'

'And you were terrific with Ricky.'

'I had to be, didn't I?'

'You certainly did.'

'I was an idiot to have caused it all.'

'You certainly were.'

I look away across the potatoes. His words make me feel so stupid and small. Lennie looks at me.

'But we're all idiots sometime,' I hear Chris say. 'Let's face it. Every last one of us.'

I look back.

'What? Even you?'

'Oh, yes.' He pauses. 'Especially me.' Then, as I watch, I see him drive himself forward. 'You know that. Better than most.'

My heart gives a little lurch.

'I do?'

'Better than anyone, really.'

'Really?'

I see him swallow.

'You know that you do.'

And then he carries on looking at me, just looking, until my stomach is turning over and over, and we're staring at each other like the boneheads we've just agreed that we are, and it is as if everything since we arrived here this morning has never really happened, or maybe more as if it has, but that it, and all the other things that have happened in my life up to now, have only ever been steps on the path towards this one moment here, staring at Chris, in his mis-matched tracksuit, on the edge of the potato beds, at the allotment.

However, Lennie is tugging at my hand and pulling at me to come, so I tear my eyes from him and walk away and bend down to help Lennie fill up the watering-can.

'But anyone can learn!' Chris calls out after me, from where he is still sitting, still with his arm around Ricky.

And I begin to smile as I straighten up and help Lennie carry the can over to the beans, and Lennie smiles, too, as he tilts his head and stares at the tall green plants with astonishment and admiration.

'Baked beans,' he says, happily beginning to water his shoes. 'Aren't they, Pat? Baked beans. That's what we're growing. Baked beans.'

WHITE NOISE
Rohan Kar

What would you say to a person who asks you to scatter their ashes on the Tomb of the Christ when they die? 'You're mad,' you would say? If a Catholic, 'You're blasphemous, raving.' But Ma had asked me to do this very thing. I'd missed her death, and was left with remorse – a second, lingering death. The only things I have of her are a small silver vial of her ashes and her pocketbook copy of Frost, which I take with me everywhere.

Yesterday, in the massing crowd of the Old City, my wallet was lifted. The back of my jeans sliced clean with a blade; where there had once been a pocket there is now only a seam with loose dangling thread. Without a shekel, I feel vulnerable. My other pocket, thank God, still contains the book.

It's getting dark. Amidst reports of muggings by Palestinian child gangs and an old, black Ethiopian porter's lament about a breakdown of ordinary life, I leave the King David YMCA with a single purpose, as if pushed by an invisible hand. There is a gilded mirror in the YMCA foyer, but I can't stand to look at myself any more. My beard and hair have grown. I must look feral.

This morning a Palestinian burned the Israeli flag in a mosque. The resulting curfew means the Old City can now only be accessed in the afternoon, the first free slot in three days.

It is difficult to know what is true. Before coming to Jerusalem, I had Ma's idealized sense of this place as an old time machine: traders in ancient suks selling relics to pilgrims; a labyrinth of conflicting faiths; Christian bells; the wail of the muezzin; stones from a jumble of ages – Roman, Byzantine, Turk. Now, the Old City is full of soldiers. The acrid smell of teargas is in the air. In some areas, its vaporous fingers reach deep into the lungs making you retch.

I stand on the stone wall running along the city perimeter near the Jaffa Gate, one of eight gates into the Old City. Israeli soldiers, their heads shorn, gather below me, moving shiny steel-capped batons from hand to hand, looking edgy. Both Arabs and Jews pass by them: the Jews in Hasidic black tunics, bespectacled, dishevelled, carrying books and shopping; the Arabs in baggy pants, some wearing dark leather slippers, some barefoot even in the winter cold. The older Arabs look nervous, but the younger ones seem defiant in the face of the soldiers' suspicious gaze. Three of the squaddies are adolescents with bad skin and pouting mouths. Experience produces silence, but these Israeli soldiers are noisy, garrulous, babies. In the settlements they have had to turn on their own people. Images now come to me of children; empty homes, scattered toys.

We moved home often when I was a kid, which left me with a sense of displacement. But each time we moved and I moaned, Ma would point her long skinny pianist's forefinger at a book of verse by Frost: 'Home is the place where . . .' and then – a single parent, her feline eyebrows arched – she'd look at me, expecting me to fill in the blanks with a higher wisdom I'd yet to understand. The memory of this makes me smile. I should have told her I loved her – for saying this, for giving me the book.

To my left, the modern city: rolling hills dotted with cypress and pine trees. To the right, the Old City: staggered rooftops laden with crosses, turrets, and mosques. Dominating the skyline is the Dome of the Rock, the mosque with its roof like a giant golden light bulb. To approach the Tomb of the Christ, I will have to go back down into this labyrinth, despite my fear.

My ankles are weak, causing them to bend inwards in the winter cold. I move awkwardly, slowly towards the spiral descent to the Jaffa Gate. The vial in my pocket is heavy and clumsy, but I am so filled with her it makes me shine, like the Dome, brightly inside.

At the crematorium, I had pulled the white cloth over her shrunken face and closed the casket. I promised her then I would scatter her ashes at the

Holy Sepulchre. Sacrilegious? Yes, but when the thick metal oven door slammed shut and the sudden roar of the burners reverberated through my bones I felt her absence like the sky over the earth.

When she died I was not there. I had no chance to say goodbye. She would have liked the view up here on this wall, in her favourite season.

She'd had a window of opportunity. Six months and I could have brought her here; her cancer *healed*.

'Please take me there, Mikey,' she'd said in that persuasive, almost childlike voice I'd come to love as she got older. If I'd had the sense I would've stayed quiet, but I didn't.

It had started with her fall on the stairs. In my mind she wanted a cure only for her hip.

'Where, Ma?'

'The Holy Fire.'

'*Jerusalem?*'

She nodded, smiling like a little girl.

'Ma, stop chasing after miracles. You can't travel.'

'I'm not.' The smile gone, she crossed her arms. 'Even invalids can travel by plane, you know,' she said, trying to sit up defiantly in her wheelchair. The wrinkled white skin of the backs of her hands was peppered with moles.

I looked at her, wishing I were not alone, that I had a father and she a husband. How did she think she would manage with her chair in the Old City – or was she expecting me to carry her up all those cobbled streets on my back? Her frame seemed tiny inside her green cardigan, emaciated apart from her stomach, which stuck out as if a small football had been shoved up her top. Once, I found tablets hidden under her pillow. The white label with black print suggested a repeat prescription, but I couldn't be sure. I never found them again. But I found other things: a small blue trunk in the attic.

I refused to budge. 'You shouldn't have come down those stairs in your old slippers,' I said. The fall on the stairs had taken away the use of her legs. 'I told you to throw them away, you stubborn old fool.'

I regretted this as soon as it was out. Her eyes looked sad, a dark gaze. 'Don't talk like that, Mikey.' She turned her head away. 'Can't you hear them? Can't you hear what they're saying?'

'Hear what?'

'You'll scatter them. You promise me?' Then she looked at me as old people do. Her legs started shaking. 'I don't know what's happening to me.' She was about to say something else, but suddenly stopped.

I kept silent and just stared at her, at her skeletal form in the wheelchair. There was so much about her that remained unsaid, as if saying it would frighten me. She must have known for a long time then about the demon growing inside her.

I wanted to comfort her, but couldn't. It was only a few months ago, but I was much younger then, too focussed on myself. How many times do we make mistakes? Sometimes they fall into the white noise of life and disappear; often they don't.

Slowly, I make my way down steep stone steps so worn they dip in the middle. It is cold, the biting crisp cold she liked when younger, especially when she took me out sledging on a nearby farmer's field. I hate the cold, probably a result of my father's blood – just about the only thing I know of him. Every morning, she'd walk along that muddy track beside the raggedy cornfield to get away from the matchbox-shaped houses on the estate we were living in then. She loved the open spaces, tracing the memory of her ancestors' land. She had the hard graft of those Inverness men built into her bones, but in fact was more like a kid getting her wellies caked in mud: always curious, always welcoming.

The Tower of David rises up in front of me like a giant stone finger. It seems complex, disjointed. Nauseous, I continue on weak legs across the opening of the Jaffa Gate and towards the interior. Armed soldiers in thick fatigues stand guard by the gate's base. I keep my head down. I can't help the way I walk. It's bound to attract attention. If they body-search me and find the vial, I will have a hard time explaining I'm not the first martyr to pack a chemical weapon. They are sure to take her from me, look inside.

As I pass the gate, I hear raised voices. A tanned, blond Israeli soldier is shouting at a young Arab man. Gesticulating arms, pointing fingers; the soldier is stony faced. In one corner, just behind them, a man frying falafels on an open stand watches the scene unfold. The air fills with the sweet scent of cooked *ceci*.

And then the soldier looks at me. Fear grips my stomach. I have done nothing wrong and yet I feel the vial in my pocket radiating knowledge of the sin to come. For an instant our eyes lock and in his blue gaze I see a question arise. But distracted by the young Arab, who starts to walk away, he turns and begins shouting after him.

I tell myself I am doing this for her. I have to press on. Through the gate, steady streams of people pass in both directions. I seize my chance and scurry across the square.

An alley to my left; dark stone walls and intricate iron grilles. The wall feels icy against my back; my breath is unsteady, gasping like a fish out on sand, reminding me of my madness in agreeing to this. I'm shivering from fear. People pass the alley, but I am in the shadows away from the nervous shifting gazes and questioning looks. A small miracle to escape – or is it? I hear her now: 'Mikey, a young man who suffers with your legs must think of himself as a secretly chosen being.' No. Not me. A miracle would be an irony, as life has always carried too much reality. Belief in a God, yes, but no miracles. Faith has its limits.

Sinking to the freezing Jerusalem stone, everything coming at once, I wish she was here now, and wonder if she is, a miraculous white ghost sitting beside me, seeing and knowing my pain.

We take our health for granted. Her vulnerability when it came, sudden and harsh, made me desperate for the goodwill and duty of strangers: young doctors, nurses who had no knowledge of her as a human being – of her kindness, the support she gave to those close to her. Like most people who don't believe in miracles, I was ready to receive one. Six months after the fall, just when her hip had healed and the doctor whispered of finally discarding the wheelchair, I came home from work and found her in bed lying rigid, her mouth locked in a grotesque angle, a mocking toothy grin. She was paralysed from the neck down. But even the stroke wasn't the worst of it – in fact it concealed the real evil from me: her ovaries were the size of balloons.

But hadn't her tummy always been big? Just a year ago, I'd playfully approached her like Basil Brush, shouting 'Boom boom,' and touched it gently with my head; a ticking bomb, and for how many years? For how many years had I been blind? I told myself we had too much trouble, sometimes moving two or three times a year: a landlord kicking us out for the piano noise; shit through the letterbox; the local skinheads throwing stones at our windows or bullying me for my rolled-in ankles and funny walk. Once a gang of six skins followed us as we walked home through our estate in Hackney. One of them came up behind me and mimicked my walk, exaggerating it like a drunken penguin. And then he switched, following her, puffing his cheeks like a gecko and making like he had a huge belly. I looked across at Ma, terrified, gripping her hand, but she just looked straight ahead, completely confident, smiling and reciting in her chirpy sing-song way: 'Home is the place where, when you have to go there, They have to take you in.'

The line is now in my head and The Death of the Hired Man in my pocket next to my leg, the last thing she gave me at the hospice before she died.

The attention of a group of dark-skinned youths dressed in torn clothes and ill-fitting shoes makes me uncomfortable. Young people here scare me. They are used to more violence than I've seen in a lifetime; Arab and Jew, spilling each other's blood and yet having to share not only their holiest shrines but the folklore that goes with them. I know little of their troubles. I am here by accident. Or is it fate?

Once, I read that the stone on which God called upon Abraham to sacrifice his son Isaac is the very stone on which the Dome now stands; the same stone Muslims believe carries the imprint of Mohammed's foot as he ascended to heaven. I have often wished for a father to tell me these tales, to hear his voice teach me the truth. Arab, Jew, both of semen and ovum; it doesn't make sense. Nothing does.

The youths watch me with amusement or maybe curiosity because of my ankles. It is easy to imagine small curved Moorish knives hidden in their clothes. The hungry black gaze of one of the older boys, a tall gangly lad with arms too long for his coat, fixes upon me like an animal. I bury my hands in my pockets, fingering the pages of Frost for comfort, hurrying on to get out of sight. I turn a corner, straight into a group of five Israeli soldiers.

The soldiers approach me. They wear gas masks. I can only just see the eyes of the man in front through his Perspex visor. Silhouettes of nearby buildings reflect in shiny tinted plastic. Two old men seated on mats in a corner further along the street look vaguely at us, then quickly look away, chattering on in a harsh form of Arabic.

The soldier points his baton at my stomach, prods me. I wonder whether to gently remove it, but my legs begin to buckle, so I step aside.

Time passes slowly. The soldier's breathing sounds alien through his mask and his black gaze flashes from my jacket to my trousers, which bulge with the vial. I feel myself pray, her ashes on the Tomb now an impossible dream.

And then, just as quickly, they are gone, trotting off in their khakis, fat shaven heads with black straps bobbing up and down. My body goes numb.

I continue slowly towards the two old men, the strength returning to my legs.

'Hello, hello.' Someone shouts from behind.

Turning, I see the dark youth from earlier. He approaches with a confident swagger that makes me watchful, uncertain.

'Where you go?' the youth says, rolling his Rs with a deep Arabic sound I've come to recognize. The boy's tone is even, enquiring. I stay silent. It is just one thing after another here; a place of madness, without end.

'Where you from?' the boy persists, his intense black eyes unwavering. 'You *dark* like me.'

I stare at him. And for a moment, I want to open my mouth and howl, scream, laugh, anything to relieve the pressure within. I should have expected this, but don't know how to respond. Perhaps the boy is just as confused. Yes, I'm dark like a Palestinian, but not one; this is surely the reason why the soldiers stopped me.

What can I say to this boy about something I've never discussed, not even with Ma? There comes a time when what we call 'events' simply vanish from our memory. I don't hate my father, but I have many questions for him.

'Where you go?' the youth repeats.

I am unsure about mentioning a Christian church, given the boy looks like an Arab, possibly a Palestinian Arab. If he only knew of the sin I would soon commit.

'The Holy Sepulchre.'

'The church? Come, I take you. You go wrong way. You go this way,' he says striding off. But I remain where I stand. He stops and looks back.

'Come, I take you,' this time his inflexion suggesting a command, as if it is an insult not to follow.

I look at him, trying to measure his sincerity. I don't have any money to give this boy.

'Come, English, we go this way. Come, I take you. Do not worry, this place is my *home*, I know it.' He is confident, engaging even. He comes up to me and takes hold of my arm, pulling me in the opposite direction to the way I've been going.

There are many shadows in the light. I can smell spices, fried oil, the *narghiles* of the Arabs sitting around smoking and playing what looks like backgammon. Thick, red meat cuts hang from iron hooks.

Now would be the time to say I have no shekels, but I don't want to be abandoned with no idea how to get back. I don't know how long we will be in this quarter, a few minutes, perhaps ten or fifteen. My steps quicken.

We pass through a narrow archway into another alley. It looks safer here. Small children work as tailors, pumping on old Singer sewing machines, skilled with their hands and bare feet; tourist trinkets – shiny bead necklaces, clay lamps, belts and brassware – dangle from string in doorways. And then in the midst of all this cheap trade, I hear the sound of a piano.

It's strange to hear *this* music now, as if it is a sign. I take comfort from it. A child sitting on a small wooden stool is weaving a basket. Ma kept her favourite music in a wooden stool. To her, music was like a dream, different to waking hours. She was a reluctant performer, but I'd often make her get out Beethoven: the *Moonlight Sonata*, its sombre melody a long poem creating a sense that somehow, something is about to change.

The youth is still in front of me. His shoulders begin to slouch as if he feels more comfortable here, away from the soldiers. We are coming to the end of a long alley and I can see it will soon open onto a wider square. The sonata has faded. My fingers are still moving to its memory. She made me play classical and later I became a teacher like her. I stumble, almost falling into the boy. Stupid! With my clumsy gait, I have to keep my eyes on my feet on these uneven cobblestones. The youth has started to sing, something low and quiet in Arabic, but in tune; he has a good voice.

There is something about this voice, its loneliness or timbre that reminds me of her. She would sing to herself like this, often to clear her head. She heard voices. *His* absence did that. She got worse as she got older. She would complain that the neighbours had cameras and were watching her and that they could see into her head. Maybe she sensed what I'd done.

I found the small blue trunk hidden in the attic, covered with dust. It was one of those old-fashioned ones with brass levers and a small Champion padlock, which was easy to pick with a pair of cosmetic scissors. Inside, the musty smell of old paper, yellowing copies of *The Lady* that he must have given her, a few simple letters in faded blue ink and broken English telling her when to meet, where, how excited and happy he was to be with her. His handwriting had the sharp angles and loops of Arabic, except in Roman lettering. There was also a black-and-white photograph, partly torn, but you could still make out the face of a pretty young white girl, timid in a puffed chiffon blouse and a hat, and a man with long brown artistic hands, dressed in a pinstriped suit. His head was torn away. And then there was a crumpled letter from a GP: short, handwritten, difficult to read, telling her that she was to be admitted to a home to have a little 'rest'. It was dated the year of my birth. Her madness. And now, there but for the grace of God go I.

I look up from my feet.

The youth has disappeared. *Where?* I look crazily around the small square like a man who's lost his child. There are some trading stalls to one side. A group of children as young as three or four approach me, hovering around my legs. One of them touches the pocket with the vial. I push him away, harder than I intend. He falls back onto the ground, bumping his head on the stone. He's going to cry. I freeze.

I don't want to look up: the traders will beat me here and now. But the kid just pulls a monkey grin, revealing small, sharp black-stained teeth. He bounces up like a jumping bean, now pulling at my other trouser leg. He has a large muddy-coloured birthmark across one side of his face. I look around for the youth, but can only see Arab traders staring back.

'English, why you walk that way?'

I spin around. 'Where did you go?'

'You find church for miracle?'

'What?'

He points at my legs. I follow his gaze down to my feet, not knowing what to say. 'Transitional', the midwives said, but this boy wouldn't understand. The source of weak muscle tone that has plagued me from birth, the reason she wanted me close, a force I'd always resisted – 'Mikey, you might look poor and weak, but because of this your inner world will be richer and stronger than most.' He stares at my legs as if they are a pair of circus stilts.

'Why you go to church?' he repeats calmly.

The kids gather around him. They are now all staring at my legs. The youth has one or two of his front teeth missing and the question whistles through his remaining bad ones. Being tall and gangly there is unpredictability in his movement. Now I'm closer I can see his face has more maturity than I first thought. There are little scars around his mouth and crow's-feet around the eyes. I don't want to get too familiar with him and so pretend not to hear, but he looks at me with such a penetrating black gaze that there's little point.

'I'm going to the Sepulchre.' I imagine myself already there, fumbling with the vial and Ma's ashes. The idea makes my mouth dry. What will happen if they catch me? The Muslims cut off hands for theft. What will the priests do for blaspheming the Tomb of the Christ – of God? And yet to me, it is not an act of blasphemy, but of love.

'You are Christian?'

'Yes,' I say quietly.

The youth falls silent. I watch him very carefully, wondering whether to tell him that I too have a father who is Muslim and whom I've never seen. Suddenly, the youth waves the others away, winking at the younger child with the birthmark, who appears to be holding something. The child nods and vanishes up one of the alleyways like a genie.

We continue to walk. I keep nervously glancing at the youth's back and around at the alleyways. I look at my watch. We have to hurry if we are going to make the church in time. The sun has gone down. The evening curfew is set to start in one hour.

We pass through many streets and I settle into a routine of lifting my feet to avoid uneven stones, steep steps or small piles of rotting fruit. We've been walking for some time and my ankles hurt. I sense we are nearing the Sepulchre.

In her last months, I hired a private ambulance to take Ma to a Christian healer. It was expensive, but I was desperate. I'd gone to the hospice nearly every day, stealing time from work just to be with her, helping to turn her body and clean her mouth with pineapple juice and a tiny pink sponge on the end of a white tube, like a lollipop. With it sticking out of her mouth she looked like a child. She would stare out of the window, blinking at the grey, wintry sky and the skeletons of nude, swaying trees, their arms reaching in every direction, and I would wonder what was in her mind. Sometimes, I would clean her quickly and leave with a sense of shame, as if deserting her.

She lost the power of speech. Gradually her skin became sallow and hung from her body like folds of old paper. She ate less and less, and eventually refused even fluids. The morphine couldn't dull the pain. In solitude, with no family, I saw it all – a unique feature of hell to see down to the last detail.

I became paranoid, constantly switching between wonderment at the hospice staff for their daily compassion and suspicion they were injecting her quietly in the night, killing to free the bed. My solitude grew, becoming fat like a pig. You think I was mad? But then one day when I found her left in her own excrement, I reached the end.

The paramedic helped me wheel her out to the ambulance. It took three hours to get her to the healer. I listened to Ma groan, strapped to a stretcher. She could never stand me being distant and I wanted to touch her, comfort her, but couldn't. I sat listening to her breathe, the rain pat-patting on the roof, when suddenly both back doors flew open and the healer stood before us, like Jesus in white.

We enter the Christian Quarter, which is very different to its Muslim counterpart. I feel the anticipation in my body rise as I look upon more familiar sights: short thoroughfares decked out with neat arches and plasters, built, paradoxically, by the Ottomans.

We pass through a small archway leading to a large cobbled forecourt.

'Wait,' I say, stopping by the archway. The youth comes up to me and stands very close, almost unaware of my own space. I smell his fuggy odour: fried oil and musk. The Christ was once here: the Via Dolorosa, the route marked out by the fourteen Stations of the Cross – his last walk. I look past the boy to what seems to be a church, but cannot be sure.

'Her spirit has already left her body,' the healer told me. 'You must let her go.'

I feel the broken skin on my lower lip. In the failing light, it has begun to get very cold.

'Leave us,' I said. I couldn't let go, there was too much unresolved, too many kinks. Back at the hospice, I tried but was unable to hold her; her body was almost bone. In frustration I stepped out of the room, just for a few minutes.

'Is this . . . the Sepulchre?' I stammer, barely able to contain the tension.

Even now, I cannot understand why I left her there alone. In the time I was out, barely ten minutes, she died. In that bare, green room, as I stood staring at her just an hour after death, her face carried a gentle dignity, still holding a sense of the spirit once within her, her hands clasping a small Gideon bible. I couldn't believe the energy that gave her eyes life – their soulfulness – and her skin its luminescence could vanish without residue after only sixty-three years. I wondered then where her spirit had gone.

A wave of emotion lifts me in an endless shifting sea with no sight of solid land. I look up at the ancient stones that make up the walls of the church, a giant mosaic, an anchor. Finally, I can place Ma's ashes on the Christ's Tomb, with the miracle of the Holy Fire, a blue indefinable light, burning from the stone on which the body of Jesus is said to have been laid. She never got to touch the light, never had a chance to be healed.

I wipe my eyes so quickly the boy doesn't see.

'This is Anne's church,' the youth says flatly, spitting.

'*What?*' I shout at him. 'But I want the Sepulchre. You promised me the Sepulchre.'

The youth laughs.

'Sepulchre?' he says, his tone mocking, indicating he's known all along. He rubs the thick glob of mucus into the cobbles with his heel, reminding me I am a stranger in his land. 'That is too *far*. Look at time,' he continues, gesturing at my watch. 'You think the Israelis will let you pass *now*?' He spits again. 'Believe me, English, *Inshallah*, if God wishes, they are all the same. What does it matter what church, English?' he says, pointing at the wooden doors.

I stare at him for a long time, enough to see him look away. I crouch down. Stupid fucking boy. Fucking Arab. But then, he doesn't understand; how can the fool understand? I feel tired enough to lie down on the cobblestones and fall asleep.

'I am going into this church,' I say weakly. 'Thank you, but I'm going.'

I take the vial out of my pocket and clutch it.

The youth steps forward, blocking my way.

'I help you, English,' he says menacingly, glancing at the vial. He holds out a dirt-smeared hand. 'You give me five shekels for showing.' His gaze fixes on the silver tube now luminescent in the light.

A group of Armenian nuns pass, dressed from head to toe in black. We watch them in their silence. The boy's head turns as he watches them disappear through the archway, the tendons of his neck taut. It suddenly occurs to me whilst looking upon the dark profile of this Palestinian – just a boy like countless others from this land, which may be that of my father – that in some strange way perhaps he is right. I reach into my pocket for the book, but it has gone.

Confused, I search frantically through all my other pockets. My mind works quickly and then I realize. I look past the boy's head to the church, its stone walls dark.

My gaze flickers to the vial in my hands. For the first time since coming to this city of ghosts I feel a sort of peace. No matter what happens now, here with this boy, I know she will understand.

Home is the place where, when you have to go there, They have to take you in.

We are home.

BROACHING THE SUBJECT
David John Soulsby

I steal. But it's not like it's a major problem or anything. It's not a lifestyle choice and nothing that anyone should be worried about. Just a little bit of theft. Anyway, as my therapist encourages me to say, 'I used to steal'. Start using the past tense as soon as possible. A minor hiccup, that's all. Soon be all right again. Absolutely nothing to worry about. And I offered to pay for the goods the last time it happened, and the shop were ever so kind. Really kind, though not at first, but that's understandable. I mean, they're not supposed to be kind for that sort of thing. The manager said that the police had been called as it was company policy. There was nothing he could do about it, but it would all be sorted out. Then he offered to get me a cup of tea while I was waiting and I said a cream tea from the refurbished café would be lovely. He brought back a tea bag in a plastic cup and told me to be careful I didn't burn my mouth.

When the police did arrive, it was just my luck that one of them knew me from before. There had been a similar misunderstanding two weeks previously. He remembered me, and told me that I was being arrested for theft.

Well, of course, at that point I hit the roof. Didn't he know what type of person I was and where I lived and that I could buy the entire shop if I wanted to? And why would I be stealing?

And he said, 'That's what we hope to find out, madam.'

I said I'd sue for wrongful arrest, but he smiled and ordered what he called a 'taxi' on his radio. I said this would cause a lot of extra paperwork and waste so much time. He told me not to worry about the time; it was his to waste and he was happy to 'waste' it on me. He said that in a really pleasant way and for a moment he looked deep into my eyes. I bit my tongue, swallowed hard and then I noticed that one of the metal numbers on his left lapel was starting to come away. I told him that he would need to get that fixed.

Of course, it wasn't a taxi, it was a police van. A Ford Transit. And I was placed in the back, my head pushed down getting in so I didn't bang it. All I could think of was the song, *If My Friends Could See Me Now*. Except, if pressed, I'd have to admit that I don't have many friends.

At first I kept my head down as there were other passengers in the van. I thought that was the best way to get through the whole ghastly mistake and come out the other end, but then a woman began screaming, forcing attention in her direction. She was in her thirties, badly made up, awful clothes and cheap turquoise plastic shoes that didn't match anything else she was wearing. She was shouting what I can only describe as filth, as to how it was all a fix up and that they had got the wrong person. Apart from her appalling language, I was in complete agreement with her and began wondering if wrongful arrest was commonplace. But then she caught my eye and asked me what a posh bitch was doing locked up. She then said that I must have done something really bad and that I was probably going to go straight to Holloway where I'd end up being – and I'll use her words – 'sexed by the lesbos twenty-four seven'.

At that point a large-built black woman wearing a gorgeous blue Chanel suit with matching bag and pearl drop earrings told Plastic Shoes to shut it unless she wanted a slapping. Plastic Shoes said she wasn't taking orders from no marmalade gollywog. Chanel Suit began to get up out of her seat and I realized her hands were cuffed behind her back. She was stopped from moving any further by a truncheon pushed into her chest.

'I think everyone needs to calm down. Don't you?' said the woman PC. 'Silence, from now on.'

Plastic Shoes started to speak, but the WPC slammed the truncheon into the seat next to her. Plastic Shoes jumped and then glared at me as though it was all my fault. I looked at the floor.

At the police station I had to remove all my jewellery and hand over my phone, bag and also my belt. There was fingerprinting, a DNA swab and then photographs. Now photographs I know something about, as in the seventies my father was a photographer and my mother was a model. I used to go with her to photo-shoots when I was a child. I could hear her in my head saying, 'It's all in the lighting, darling, it's all in the lighting. You've got to watch them. Half of them have no idea what they're doing,' and then laughing while holding a champagne glass in one hand and applying heavy sky-blue eye-shadow with the other.

So I knew immediately that I was badly lit and said as much. I also adjusted my pose but was told they only wanted one head on and the other a right profile. I asked if I might be able to re-apply my make-up and whether I would get picture approval. The photographer said he would take an extra picture and give it to me if I shut up. I nodded and didn't utter another word.

After that it was a short chat with the duty officer. I was going to have to be interviewed but that wouldn't be for a couple of hours and in the meantime I was going to be put in a cell. And that was when I lost it. Completely lost it. I demanded to see my solicitor, I demanded that the whole thing be sorted out as quickly as possible and I stated clearly that I would be complaining to anyone and everyone I could think of. I also demanded pen and paper so that I could start writing down names and listing in full the degree of incompetence experienced.

'Have you finished?' said the duty officer.

'I haven't even started.'

'Well, make sure you get my name right. Meanwhile, let's find you a cell. You'll have to share. Very little room at the inn.'

He looked up at a board with names and cell numbers written on it. Plastic Shoes was shouting from inside one of the cells.

'It's cow shit. I'm not eating this.'

This was closely followed by what sounded like a tray being thrown against a wall.

The duty officer looked over at her cell, looked at me and then looked back at the board.

My cellmate was the blue-Chanel-suited woman from the van and her name was Helen. At first I sat on the bed that was built into the wall. She did as well. And there was an awkward silence. Long, drawn out. She broke this by admiring my nails and I told her where I had them done. She said she'd been there a few times and that she preferred the new branch, and that in her job broken nails were one of the hazards. I asked her what her job was and she said that she was a wrestler and dominatrix. She played up her Brazilian background and marketed herself as Amazonian. She then stood up and removed her jacket and blouse to show me her muscles, which there were quite a lot of.

Her clients were men who liked to be pinned down.

'I can barely meet the demand, darling. Definitely time to charge more ker-ching, ker-ching; for my special friends, Chanel, Dior, Yves.'

She knew she was niche and so could charge what she wanted. She'd been arrested for GBH. Broken the leg of one of her customers. Having been pinned down, Ben-Ben – real name Bernard – had made the signal to be released. Once let go, he had grabbed her again. She instinctively pushed him off and he flew across the room, fracturing his leg.

Helen phoned for an ambulance straightaway. The trouble was that her neighbours, on hearing the noise, had also called the police. There had been other complaints in the past. A history. So this time she was arrested.

'It won't stick,' she said. 'They might get me on some peace-breach thing. Darling Ben-Ben does not want to press charges, but the neighbours are, ummm . . . how do you say in English?'

'Another matter?'

'No, the neighbours are . . .'

'A different kettle of fish?'

'No, no, no, the neighbours are . . . wankers.'

Helen had already called her solicitor, also one of her clients, and he was on his way.

'So what are you in for?'

'A misunderstanding,' I said and then went through the whole story.

'You'll soon be out.'

'My husband won't be very happy.'

'He should be worried about what you're going through.'

And I talked a bit about Lazarus. How nice and kind he was when we first met and how loving. But when I began to talk about what he was like now, the words stopped and I fell silent. Helen held me and said, 'Bit of a shit, is he?'

And I lay there, encased in muscle, feeling safe.

About half an hour later the cell door opened and I was told that my solicitor had arrived.

It wasn't exactly my solicitor. It was someone appointed by Lazarus's firm. I asked where Lazarus was. Apparently he had been pulled into chairing a meeting as one of the senior managers had broken his leg. I smiled ever so slightly.

'Is something funny?' said the solicitor.

'You wouldn't understand,' I replied.

'Shall we get on?'

I nodded.

I protested my innocence strongly at first and then the solicitor said that I might want to look at some CCTV footage before I went any further. There I was, caught on the security cameras, putting the item into my bag, and then there was another clip of me leaving the store and being stopped by the security guards.

I thought about arguing that it wasn't me. That it was someone else. Someone with features similar to mine who by sheer coincidence was wearing the same outfit. As though reading my mind the solicitor said, 'It's you.'

I buried my head in my hands and let out a long sigh.

The solicitor was all business and quickly ran through my options. A caution seemed the best thing, with the promise that I would seek counselling. Over my dead body, I said, at which point the solicitor advised that if I didn't accept these terms, it would go to a magistrate's court, be in the papers and I would probably end up with a criminal record. The biggest concern was the press. 'City wife takes five-finger discount' was not the kind of publicity that the company needed, not with Lazarus at the helm, planning some big take-over in the next couple of months; this was something everyone wanted to go away.

So that was how I went from one cell to another. Once a week to a Harley Street address. Very discreet, as though nipping in for a minor cosmetic-surgery consultation. Small efficient waiting room. Soft lighting to keep everyone placid, including the therapists.

I don't quite know what to make of her. She's short, in her fifties, greying hair with a rotation of cashmere twinsets in pastels. And then there is the token piece of silver jewellery: a brooch on the left of the cardigan, so far either a cat or an owl. It's been the cat twice now, with the owl making a guest appearance for the third session.

Tissues on the table, of course. Crying out to be used; a promise of uncomfortable emotions to come. And she keeps wanting me to talk about my feelings. Every question in her soft Scottish accent seems to be, 'And how do you feel about that?'

'How I feel about that is that I wish you'd stop asking me how I felt about everything.'

'And what makes you say that?'

I told her in the second session that I called her the witch and thought that this was all a waste of time. 'What makes you say that?' she replied, smiling, and then in ten minutes she was going back over the shoplifting, subtly hammering home the fact that I was the one with the problem.

Right now she is asking me more about my marriage to Lazarus and what that is like and then onto my parents and my childhood and then back to Lazarus again. And I'm answering and answering and then she asks for more information about the stealing.

'We've touched on it before, but I want you to go into more detail.'

I am about to tell her but then clam up. She senses she is onto something and pushes a bit harder. Like I said, she's a witch.

'Tell me what you were feeling when you stole.'

I just sit there. Digging my hands down into the leather. Wanting to sink into the seat and be as small and insignificant as possible. Moving my wedding ring round on my finger and hoping that she will move on. Move onto something else, anything else. But she sits, silently. Waiting for me to fill the gap. Well, I can play that game as well. I can be silent. If it is to be a battle of wills then so be it. I play them with Lazarus all the time.

Still she sits there, looking at me with patience and all the kindness of the world in her eyes. And I look at my watch, look at her, look at her brooch, and then look at my watch again.

Then much to my embarrassment I start crying. And as the tears pour down my cheeks she leans over, reaches for the box of tissues and gently presses several into my hand.

'TIL THE MAN COMES AROUND
Nik Korpon

A hot dry wind blows dust, dirt and sun-yellowed Marlboro boxes down Lawton Street in Ningunita, Texas; past the carcass of Pete's Gas Pit and the unused pumps that look like rusted tombstones, abandoned ten years ago when Pete and his old lady Mary moved to an old folks home in Florida; past Sharp Shooters gun range and what's left of the full-body targets that wear ten-gallon wren nests on their heads; past Betty and her Lone Star Diner and its cracked-vinyl booths that don't have but four rears in them a week; past Charlie Miller standing on the wood deck of Miller's General Store.

What the hell happened to this town, he says to himself. Pretty far to the west he can see the tiny bumps of what used to be the FunLand rollercoaster, looking like a tiny rattlesnake sunning itself. Patty used to take her and Charlie's three kids there when they were still little, while Charlie was busy with the store. But that was almost twenty-five years ago, and there's not much here any more, just some ramshackle shops and miles of parched sand and patches of rock, far as his old eyes can see.

A man with a navy-blue long-sleeved shirt walks down Lawton Street shoving his hands in the big grey bag slung over his shoulder and rummaging around. Tiny tornadoes of dust swirl around in front of his boots as he walks up the step to the store.

'Heya, Charlie,' he calls out.

'Well howdy, Sam. How's life for ya these days?' Charlie answers back.

'Not too bad, buddy. Not too bad. Got some mail for you. Don't think that winning lotto ticket came yet,' Sam chuckles, handing some mail to Charlie.

'Maybe they just got the wrong address, that's all,' he says, smiling.

'Maybe, buddy. Maybe,' Sam says, pushing his sleeve across his wet forehead. 'Mind if I come in and get a soda from you and your lady?'

'Not at all, Sam. C'mon in.'

The bottom of the screen door flaps lightly in the breeze as they walk into the store. Patty's father had trusted them with the store back when Ningunita was a real town, a year after Charlie got back from Korea and a year before the oil drillers stopped drilling outside El Paso and dropped the place into the first of its two bad spells. Sam gives a short wave to the carved-rosewood cigar-store Indian standing next to the door: 'Howdy, Chief.' Charlie straightens one of the dream-catchers suction-cupped to the front window, breathes on the glass and wipes off a spot with his maple-coloured long-sleeve, then walks stiffly across the store. He looks through the mail in his cracked hands: bill, bill, junk mail, 'Have you seen me?', more junk mail, and a periwinkle-blue envelope, sent from Washington, DC. 'A card from James,' he mutters, looking at the date on his watch. 'Damn, is it our anniversary already? I'll wait to open it with Mother.' He drops the mail on a faded and torn map taped to the wood counter; about an inch from El Paso is a tiny red circle around Ningunita. The empty stapler lying open on its side catches his eye, and he starts looking around for the staples before he forgets again.

Sam goes over to the cooler pushed in the corner with a longhorn skull on top of it and pulls out a nice cool Coke. He unscrews the top and takes a long slug from the bottle, licks his lips with a satisfied 'ahh' and walks to the counter, closing the cooler door with the heel of his boot when he turns. His soles leave a trail of marks in the dust across the dirty blond wood floor.

'I'm not disturbing you or nothin', am I?' Sam says. He sets his soda on the counter next to a snow globe that has 'Washington, DC' across the bottom, then shakes the globe around, watching the plastic snow fall all around the Washington Monument.

'No sir, just tryin' to find some more staples. Where did I put those damn things?' He rubs the side of his face, weathered as an old boot that's seen its fair share of hot days and hard work, and tries to remember.

'Sure would be nice to see some snow like that,' Sam says.

'Don't wager your house on it. Hell froze over twice and we didn't even get any rain,' Charlie says. 'Maybe next time.'

Underneath the snow globe there's a yellowed newspaper article taped to the counter. 'FunLand Grand Opening' it reads, in big block letters over a faded colour picture of a smiling man in a white seersucker suit with blue pinstripes, whose comb-over is bigger than the scissors he's cutting the ribbon with. The fan behind the counter makes the torn parts of the article two-step in the hot breeze. Sam moves his head side to side. 'Damn shame what happened to those poor people,' he says.

Charlie moves the pile of mail and finds the box he's looking for. 'Here we are.' He stands tall like Chief and tilts his head back just a little to see through his bent gold-rim glasses. 'Your boy still doin' good?' he says, fooling around and trying to get the staples inside the stapler. 'These damn things. Can't make it easy for an old man now, can they?'

Sam puts his hand out to take the stapler from Charlie. 'Here, Charlie, lemme give you a hand there.'

Charlie turns his shoulder around to get in the way of Sam's hand, still messing with the stapler. 'I'll get it, don't you worry. I'm not dead yet. There we go,' as he clacks the stapler together and puts it back in its place on the counter.

Sam smiles and shows the maroon half moons under his armpits as he brings the bottle up to his mouth and takes another slug of Coke.

'How're the kids doin'? Haven't seen them for a while,' Sam asks.

'Yeah, I guess it has been a while. They're doin' just fine, though. They've all got their jobs and their families and things all over to keep them busy. And it's hard for Mother and I to visit, on account of the store and all. Just got a card from one of them today, actually.'

'That's great, Charlie. Say, I saw your screen door looks busted up. You want me to come back and tack it together for you? Only take a minute.'

'Dammit, I done told you, Sam. I'm seventy-one years old but I ain't dead yet. I can take care of things. Keep all your tools for once I die. Mother'll need someone then and you can help her 'til you're blue in the face. Lord knows she'll need someone to do all them things for her,' Charlie says sternly.

'Aw now, Charlie, she's a good woman. I think she can take care of herself quite nice.' Patty comes up behind Charlie, a woman looking about the same age as him, with a blue apron and white permed hair, and a frying pan in her hand. 'Matter of fact, I think it's her that keeps *you* movin',' he says with a great big smile.

'Hell, that woman would have me sleep for her if she could. I give it to her though, she can cook a mean BLT.'

'And I was goin' to use this fryin' pan to make you one, but I can give you a lump on the head instead.' Charlie pretends like he's surprised as Patty pipes up behind him.

'Oh, hello there, Mother. Sam and I were just talking about that Old Woman Carter down the way. You wouldn't want to wallop me now, would you?' Charlie says with a grin bigger than the bumper of his Cadillac.

'Of course not, Father.' She gives him a kiss on the cheek. 'I wouldn't want to dent my best fryin' pan now, would I? Hello, Sam. You hungry? Would you like a BLT? I was *about* to make one.' She uses special emphasis on the 'about' and turns to Charlie, who's looking sheepish.

'Well, thanks very much, Patty, but I'm headed back out to the job,' Sam says. 'I just stopped to drop off the mail and grab a soda. Damn, Charlie, I almost forgot to pay you.' He digs his hand in his jean pocket and jingles around a bunch of change, then pulls out a few silver and copper coins and drops them on the counter. 'I'll see y'all later.'

'All right, Sam,' Charlie calls out while he counts the change Sam left. 'That damn boy,' he curses, tossing the change into the register that sticks like always. 'Always leaves too much.'

'Aw, Father, leave him be. He's a good man. He wants to help when he can. Not like much of this town can do much any more nowadays.'

'This used to be a General Store,' he grumbles. 'Not a bottle of soda store.'

'You want white or wheat bread?'

'Wheat, thank you. Gotta keep this ticker healthy,' he says, banging his chest with a liver-spotted fist.

'Gently, Father, you'll bruise,' Patty says as she plants another peck on his cheek and shuffles back to the kitchen.

Charlie picks a broom up out of a leather Indian quiver with prairie scenes burned into the sides, and turquoise and silver beads and feathers all around the rim. He pauses for a minute with his face in front of the fan, then sweeps some of the dust and dirt and extra staples from behind the counter and out onto the main floor. He makes a pile or two in the middle of the room and leans the broom up against the screen door. Chief is gettin' some dust on him, Charlie notices as he pulls out a red handkerchief and flops it lightly all over the wooden Indian statue, which holds a display box with bags of Combos in its outstretched arms. After he dusts Chief, he straightens up some of the other snacks and Texan knick-knacks, then wipes off the dried rattlesnakes.

He sweeps up the rest of the floor and pulls two horseshoes in front of the screen door, then sweeps all the dust and dirt onto the porch and down the step onto the dry road that lies in front of their store. Nothing's moving outside on the street as Charlie looks up and down it again, then wipes his shiny brow with his handkerchief, putting a big grey smear of Chief's dust across his forehead. He hears Patty shout from the back and walks inside, kicking the horseshoes away with his brown work boot and letting the busted door slam shut.

'What'd you say, Mother?' he calls down the hallway to the kitchen. She nudges the red curtain that looks like a potato sack cut in half to the side with her elbow and shuffles up with a BLT on a plate in each hand.

'I said, can you bring up the tea, please?' She puts the plates down on the counter and tears off two paper towels from the roll underneath. Charlie walks into the back to fetch the tea for them.

When he comes back, Patty's picking something up from the floor and the card's open on the counter. He puts their two glasses of cold sweet tea down and picks up the card.

'Congratulations?' he says, confused that it's not a Happy Anniversary card. Maybe he got his days mixed up again. 'What the hell did we do for congratulations?'

'Oh my word,' Patty gasps from the floor. 'Oh, Father, look here!' She shoves a picture right in front of his face.

'Well I'll be,' Charlie chuckles, shaking his head and smiling. A fat little baby with dimples just like his daddy and grandaddy beams real big at Charlie. His cheeks are redder than Charlie's handkerchief and his hair is the same tobacco brown that his gram's used to be forty years ago.

'Congratulations, Mother. We're grandparents again.'

'Look at James's boy,' she says while she's reading the card.

Charlie stares at the picture, trying to pick out whose parts the baby has. His eyes have got to be from his mother. James don't have eyes like that, he thinks.

'I'll be damned,' he says, shaking his head again. 'Our first grandson, Mother. It's about time,' laughing a throaty laugh that sounds like he got half a cup of sand in his glass of sweet tea.

Patty slaps her fingers, all spread out, across her chest. 'Oh, Father,' she exhales. 'Father, James and Samantha want us to move into their house in Washington. We could help them rear the baby!'

Charlie pauses for a second then nods a few times. 'That's a real fine offer, but we're quite all right here, Mother. Tell them thanks anyway.' He sets down the picture, picks up his sandwich and takes a good bite out of the corner. He wipes the corner of his mouth with the paper towel then takes another bite. The rest of the mail sits next to his plate. He throws away the junk mail and piles the bills to the side. Sure is one hell of a cute kid, he thinks as he looks at the picture again. He sets his sandwich down and wipes off his forehead with his sleeve.

Patty stands there silent as a cactus for a minute. 'Father, you mean to tell me you're not even gonna give it one thought? Aren't you even gonna ask what I think about the whole thing?'

Charlie takes a sip of tea, gearing up for the talk again. 'I'm sorry, Mother, but we got our life here. We've got our house and our store and it's been mighty fine for the last fifty-two years, so I don't see no point in turnin' everything upside over just for this baby. We just can't do it.' He takes another sip of tea and moves the pile of bills to the other side of his plate, then turns on the little radio under the counter. He nods his head a tiny bit as Robert Johnson crackles quietly.

'Father, we don't see but ten people in here all week, and most of those are Sam dropping off our mail. And this is the first time we've seen him in two days! It's not like this store does like it used to. Hell, it's not like this whole damn town does like it used to.' Her hands curl into fists, and she jabs them into her hips, crinkling the card from James. Charlie leans back a little and adjusts his glasses on his nose. He stops nodding his head.

'Mother, everything will be OK. We've already talked about this. This place has gone to hell before and came back, right?'

'Look at it now, Charles! You gotta have customers to make money. They gotta have the money to give you and they gotta have a job to get the money! This goddamn town don't got any of it any more! How many times are we gonna —'

'I said it will be OK, Mother,' he says in a voice more worn out than the soles of his boots. 'I'll be damned if I'm gonna have your father roll over in his grave on account of us moving out to that city with all those politicians and all them crazies. Things were bad before, then they built the ride park and it got better, didn't it? It'll get better again. It always does, just like I've always told you.'

'Yeah, it got better. You're right. Everything was just fine. Ab-so-lute-ly perfect,' she says. 'Everything was fine 'til that rollercoaster went off the tracks and now nobody comes near this damn place! There's no reason to pass through here if there's nothing to pass through here to! Why can't you seem to remember that?'

Charlie bites his sandwich and chews it slowly. She stands angry for a minute, tapping her foot. She takes a couple deep breaths, then puts the card down gently and comes next to him.

'Father,' she says more softly and puts her old wrinkled hand on his. 'Charlie. Please. We've missed out on our other grandkids growin' up. And the only times they ever come out here you scare them half to death with those rattlesnakes. Elaine's already got three kids, and Daniel obviously ain't gonna have one with that man he's with. James and Samantha have been tryin' for four years to have this baby.' She squeezes his hand hard and he can feel her trying to look at him in the eyes, but he's looking through the dream-catchers at Pete's across the street. 'Please, Charlie, we can't miss this one. It's your first grandson. At least think about it. Think about all the first times we can have with him.'

Charlie sits and chews the last few bites of his sandwich. He stares out the window at the dust blowing on the street, and watches a grey bird land in a nest on one of the targets at the gun range. His fingers tap on the FunLand article, on top of the man with the scissors and the hopeful face. He looks around this store they've ran for fifty-two years, at Chief and the snakes and the knick-knacks and the longhorn skull.

'I'll think about it, Mother,' he says after a few minutes. He pats her hand a couple times before she scurries to the back. He can see her fingers rubbing the card like it was a baby's cheek.

Charlie takes a sip of sweet tea and swishes it around his mouth, pulling in his lips and swallowing, then lets out a long breath, feeling the fan blow a hot breeze on him. He rests his glasses on the register and rubs his old hands hard over his old face and stares through his fingers out onto Lawton Street looking like a ghost town, then drops them to the counter. They land next to the snow globe of Washington. He picks it up and tips it back and forth. All the plastic snow spins around the Monument like a blizzard. He watches it for a minute then smiles and tips it again, laying it down sideways on the picture, squints hard and watches his first grandson see his first blizzard for the first time.

Gardening

158

159

First published in the *Guardian* (August 2006),
then in *Three Very Small Comics* Volume 3, (Cabanon Press, 2007)

THE EXILES
Danny Birchall

'The thing I don't get about London,' said Nina, 'is the squares. London is full of beautiful little squares, all those trees and benches, but they're locked up so you can't get in. Why don't people do something about it? This is a democracy, isn't it?'

'In the end, in the little day-to-day details, the differences between a democracy and a dictatorship are not that great.' Eduardo swigged the last of his coffee and dabbed at his mouth with a paper napkin. 'Back home, we sometimes forget whether it's *el presidente* or *el general* running the country.'

'Perhaps Londoners have enough open space already,' said Cherry. 'It's a pretty green city.'

'Why don't you Londoners protest?' Nina asked.

'Personally, I don't really notice the squares,' I said.

Later, people would write books about this café, make films, pen feature articles for broadsheets; it would remain a national institution of the imagination long after wooden boards over its windows had replaced its specials board. For us, then, it was just a place with cheap tea and no music, where the voluntary rump of a subsidized course on immigration law could wedge their legs beneath an undersized table and talk.

'Are you going to finish your pie?' Cherry asked. Nina's half-eaten portion of apple pie sat in front of her, slowly absorbing brown sugar as she lit another cigarette.

'You can't have your cake and leave it,' said Ed.

'Eat it,' I said. 'You can't have your cake and *eat* it.'

'It's not cake, it's a pie,' said Cherry. 'The point is, is she going to eat it or leave it?'

'Oh, have the cake,' said Nina, pushing it towards Cherry.

Cherry made a mock-upset face and short work of the pie. A crumb stuck to her freckled cheek for a second before she brushed it off and lit her own cigarette. Six months after I quit, there were still moments when the first whiff of someone else's smoke made me almost nauseous, and edgy with fear.

Outside, as we unfurled umbrellas and shrugged into raincoats, a woman pushing an elaborate buggy stepped out into the road to avoid us. She muttered something about us being in the way.

'What was that?' asked Nina. Her translator's English was flawless, but she exaggerated her eastern-European accent for effect. The woman glanced back and scowled. 'Yeah, fuck *you*, you bitch,' barked Nina.

In the New Piccadilly, we talked about lots of things. We talked about politics – global, not local. Nina saw the fiddling fingers of the US government everywhere, and on the topic of Israel she came dangerously close to anti-Semitism. Ed found English people's ignorance of the rest of the world astounding. 'Here in London, they are surrounded by foreigners,' he said. 'People from everywhere, from Caracas to Kathmandu. And they learn nothing about them!' He banged the laminated tabletop with his broad fist, rattling forks. 'Once they hear your accent, you are wearing a sombrero in a pigeon-hole – that's it.'

Nina talked about her cat, Dosadan. She swore that he was a Former Yugoslavian too, that after she arrived in London she had had him smuggled from home to be with her, but she wouldn't tell us how she did it. 'They were extreme times, and extreme measures were called for,' was all she would say. Ed made it clear he didn't believe her. He was a disaster journalist; he wrote about NGOs, humanitarian emergencies and relief, and he knew about borders.

One day, a bored day, we talked about how we would kill ourselves. Nina said she had seen too many people die pointlessly to take her own life and this was a stupid conversation. For Cherry it was poison or pills: a slow swooning death on a bed strewn with rose petals, and a tear-stained note. I'd always fancied a tube train, fucking up everyone's journey home for the evening. Ed swore it would be a gun. He said he'd thought about it, too, and that he could get a gun in London any time, if he wanted. He knew someone in Walthamstow.

They didn't talk much about home. Each of them had reasons for being here rather than there. Nina's were obvious, Ed hinted at heroism and intrigue, and even as Cherry rolled out fond memories of mountains and hiking she hinted at romantic disappointment. We all considered ourselves to be Londoners in the truest sense of the word: we had travelcards. These were our identity papers. But when Nina wanted to know about barricaded squares, Cherry about art galleries, or Ed about etiquette in betting shops, they asked me, because I was born here. While both Nina and Cherry looked more 'English' than me (I'm what you call 'coffee-coloured', though there's a lot of milk in my latte) it was clear: I was their Londoner, and they were my foreigners.

The New Piccadilly was all of it; Tuesday mornings were our world. We made our time and our place there, the part of our lives we set aside for each other. There were only two occasions when I saw any of them anywhere other than in the New Piccadilly.

The first time, Nina arrived one wet morning with water on her face that wasn't rain. To start with, she wouldn't be drawn, ordered her coffee, and tried to talk about squares again, lighting cigarette after cigarette. Eventually, she cracked: 'Dosadan died.' He'd been acting strangely all week, she said, and she was thinking of taking him to the vet when one morning he just didn't come back in. She found him on the doorstep, a damp little rag. 'He never loved London as much as I did,' she said. 'I shouldn't have brought him here.' She asked us to help her bury him.

We met later that night, on a patch of waste ground not far off Dalston Lane. There were no fences to impede our access. It was quiet; a few kids in hoods passed by, oblivious to our presence. Cherry had brought a shovel, and her attempt to look nonchalant standing on a street corner in Hackney with a gardening implement would have been comical if anyone had been looking. Nina was the last to arrive, carrying a cardboard box in one hand and a plastic bag in the other.

She pointed to a corner overshadowed by a stunted half tree, and Cherry began to dig. Ed kept a lookout. None of us knew whether you needed permission to bury a Former Yugoslavian cat in the London Borough of Hackney, but it didn't seem to matter. Pins of rain resumed falling.

Cherry stopped digging. The hole sank about three feet into the wet clay, water already seeping in from the sides. Nina gently lowered the plastic bag into the ground and laid the cardboard box on top of it. She said something quietly to herself in her language. Ed took the shovel from Cherry and began refilling the grave.

'What was in the bag?' Cherry asked Nina.

'My video player. That cat and I used to watch a lot of films together. In truth, it belonged to him and not me. So now we are separated, he gets it. I can get a new one. It's not such a big deal.'

Ed patted the earth with the back of the shovel, then scuffed the surface with his feet. If someone was given to wonder whether people had been burying cats on this patch of mud, their eyes would not be drawn to this corner.

'There we go,' he said. 'There is some corner of a foreign field . . .'

'This is not a field,' said Nina.

She didn't invite any of us back to her flat.

The second time, I called Cherry and asked her out for a drink. She sounded surprised to hear from me when she picked up the phone, and there was something odd about the way she said yes so quickly, as if the question had been functional, another cup of tea.

We met on the South Bank, outside the National Film Theatre. She arrived dressed stunningly, in a way that I still lack the technical vocabulary to describe: belted raincoat, modest heels, a collar that was all about her face. Fashion was her thing; I often wondered why she'd ended up in London and not Paris or Milan. The only hint of disorganization was the wad of Ph.D. papers folded lengthways and crammed into her handbag.

The bar had just been refurbished, its tattered-plush familiarity replaced by reflective chrome and Scandinavian plywood chairs. We sat outside, facing each other across the fat new wooden benches in the shadow of Waterloo Bridge. Behind her, the booksellers were slowly returning two-pound crime novels and actors' biographies to their crates.

'Do you think about home?' I asked.

'Sometimes. Mostly when it's winter here and summer there I think about it.'

'Will you go back?'

'Of course. We all do, you know.'

I watched the pattern of ripples thrown up against the underside of the bridge by the setting sun. A busker with an accordion replaced a busker with a violin. Strings of bulbs swinging between lamp posts along the river's edge were beginning to warm up.

'I'd like to go there one day,' I said.

'You should,' she said. 'It's a beautiful country.'

'Perhaps I'll move there.'

'You'd get bored after six months. It's beautiful, but it's not exciting.'

'I could deal with boredom.'

'No you couldn't,' she said. 'I know you. You're a Londoner. You need stuff going on in your life all the time. You couldn't hack it.'

'You're a Londoner too, though. You've been here a year. You've got a life here.'

'That's true,' she said. 'But I've got a home as well.'

Traffic passed over the bridge above, a dull hum. Around us, people drank beer out of plastic glasses, ate sandwiches out of plastic wrappers, and chatted, babbled away. I heard someone mention Bergman. You could guarantee it here.

'And romance?' I asked, slightly later, slightly drunker. 'Ever had an Englishman?'

'Plenty,' she said. 'I never met one I could take back. They don't travel well.'

The way she looked at me I could tell that the thought of taking me home, whether to Acton or the other side of the world, had never entered her head.

Nothing lasts for ever. Not good times, not friendships, sometimes not even the countries that people are from. Cherry was the first to go, not home but to New York, a post-doctoral research post at Columbia. She promised to write postcards to us addressed to the café, even asked Lorenzo what the postcode was, but he must have misinformed her because they never arrived.

Soon after that, Nina left too. One Tuesday she was there, the next she was not. She didn't answer her phone; we didn't have her address. Three weeks in a row, Ed and I turned up and waited for her, neither of us yet ready to admit that she wasn't coming back. Perhaps she had become a Former Londoner, too.

The last time, I asked him how the journalism was going. He said so so.

'You know,' I said, 'it's confusing. When I hear about an earthquake or a hurricane, I don't know whether to feel sorry for the people it happened to, or happy for you because you've got some work.'

'It's all the same,' he said. 'What happens after a disaster goes on for a long time. You should remember to feel sorry for people six months after the earthquake. When it's snowing. That's when they really need your sympathy.'

We sat in silence for longer than was comfortable.

'Listen,' said Ed. 'The girls have gone. No girls, no point. Two guys don't meet for coffee on a Tuesday morning.'

I couldn't tell him that he was wrong, that even he would do. I just nodded. We left the New Piccadilly, and walked for a while together before he headed west towards Piccadilly Circus and I wandered towards Haymarket. I turned and saw him casually vault a crash barrier, darting between rows of oncoming traffic, towards Eros. He wasn't looking back.

A taxi honked angrily as I crossed against the lights at the bottom of Haymarket. Trafalgar Square was already full of tourists photographing each other and it struck me for the first time how like dogs the lions were, sitting in symmetrical obedience, tongues lolling, faithful. Rattling buses circumnavigated the square. I ducked behind a stalled Routemaster to get onto the Strand.

All distances to London are measured from Charing Cross. This is where London begins and ends, this is all of it. If you are looking for London, look here, and in this point on a map, this spot, this nothing, you will find it. I put my travelcard, my membership card, through the barrier and stood by the platform's edge. I thought about Eduardo's enormous hands, about apple pies, about Cherry's Ph.D. and Nina's scowl, about train tracks and spoiled journeys. Someone asked me if I was all right.

The train rolled across the river; there was no Eye then, no Millennium Bridge blinking in the distance, and as I scanned the skyline east, Gilbert Scott's power station was just another chimney, lost in the jumble of a city of bad angles and gated squares. I closed my eyes as the nearly empty carriages picked up speed past London Bridge, racing past tower blocks and over breakers' yards, and reopened them as we stopped. I leapt out and slammed the carriage door shut behind me.

On New Cross Road a man was arguing with the owner of a second-hand-furniture shop about the price of a scuffed-white melamine chest of drawers. His left hand, behind his back, clutched a brown paper bag in the shape of a can. Trapped in traffic, a skinny-faced driver let loose his speakers on *Papua New Guinea*. Outside the newsagent a small child left to wait was carefully and repeatedly kicking the metal leg of an *Evening Standard* board. These details suddenly seemed as clear to me as architecture, as if their guidebook had already been finished and annotated.

Halfway up Florence Road, I turned left down a flight of steps to a basement flat and unlocked the metal gate across the door to my own exile. Inside, the air was still thick; unwashed dishes lay in the sink; the desiccated corpse of a woodlouse lay on a table. A familiar network of cracks in the plaster connected the kitchen with the living room, the living room with the bedroom. I boiled water to make sweet tea, switched on the television and sat down.

MY SIDE OF THE RIVER
Samanthi Perera

The river is high this evening. The water touches the highest row of the metre-wide granite slabs that have held the bridge up since 1886. All but a foot or so of greenish-grey moss is submerged; it clings onto the bridge's pillars, skimming the river, yet not quite reaching the cars above. This is the only bridge in all of London that has a church at either end. A sanctuary at both sides, they say; but no one I've met here has ever found refuge within those empty walls.

The sun has bowed out from its final dance of the evening, leaving the dusky Prussian-bue sky with a single gilded streak of vibrant burnt gold that cascades downwards into an invisible pot of molten amber. A 'V' of birds glides silently overhead, across the river and over the common; they too disappear into the endless sky. Below, a rowing boat cuts through the water at an even pace; the rowers move with one smooth simultaneous action. Nothing compares with the view I have from here in the park, on my side of the river.

Across the river, two hundred metres away, 'life' is happening. The bright lights of the infamous Star & Garter pub shine piercingly onto the river, forcing an artificial daylight upon it. The river responds by reflecting the glare into the flushed, tired faces of the drinkers – the 'sociable folk'. I can just make out a few wearing their jeans – they stand out amongst the vast patches of grey and black: the city's after-work crowd enjoying the happy hour by the river. Small talk and cocktails; an affectation of candour with ice and lime. I realized a long time ago that if you're not there, over on the other side of the river, you won't be missed; and no one will care.

I once had a short-lived acquaintance with a young woman I met at the Star & Garter. A well-dressed corporate girl, tanned from her week in Bali and forward in her small talk and advances. Aided no doubt by her fifth Smirnoff and vanilla, she launched into a rant about our fellow drinkers.

'You must understand, daaarling' – her words were slurred and she swayed slightly as she spoke – 'in this tedious atmosphere, one is bound . . . one is bound to be bored tremendously . . . Tremendously! I certainly am!' Enthused by her own revelations, she slammed her glass onto the steel bar and grinned at me.

'Yes,' I agreed. 'It is quite tire –'

'It is!' she exclaimed. 'It really is! And you know . . .' She leaned in closer to me and raising her eyebrows in the manner of someone who knows all, said, 'These people, all disgracefully superficial, disgracefully. They all think they're something special. None of them are . . . All unworthy of a second glance from me!'

Thinking that perhaps amidst all the perfect sparkly diamonds I had finally uncovered a bit of irregular stone, I offered an escape. 'Well, let's get out of this wearisome hole then, shall we? A walk in the park opposite, maybe?'

She almost choked on an olive at the mere thought of damaging the heel of her newly purchased Manolo Blahnik shoes – which were, she whispered, her breath heavy with cigarette smoke and sickly sweet liquor, 'unbearably painful . . . but delightfully pretty'.

In all fairness, it may have been the alcohol that highlighted her as a caricature of the general crowd, but it was enough to ensure that our conversation was brief. I left soon afterwards with no intention of seeing her again. I was surprised, therefore, to see her stumbling alone through the park two hours later, lost both in whereabouts and balance. She did not talk much this time and again, our acquaintance was fairly brief.

Next to the pub, overlooking the pier, is the newly opened and bustling Bridge Restaurant. The exterior's sloping metal beams and tall expanses of glass are supposed to resemble a vast yacht about to be launched into the river. I hear the building has won awards from various architectural institutions. The restaurant itself isn't actually new, just the theme. Our fickle gastronomic preferences have meant that over the last three years, the cuisine has been French, Italian, Contemporary, Contemporary Italian and now, Thai. A change of décor and a promotional spin are enough to ensure that the queue of eager diners is almost as long as the building itself. Prospective patrons all longing to tell their colleagues on Monday that they sat at the hand-carved bar on the bespoke leather stools and drank the speciality drinks, whilst staring out across the full-length balcony overlooking the river in all its – pollution aside – crystal glory. There is talk of a waiting list longer than that for NHS cardiac-bypass operations, although I suspect these are rumours generated by the restaurant's own publicist.

A little further west there are dozens of rowing clubs and water-sport societies, whitewashed with royal-blue trim. All but one of the clubs are now closed for the evening. There is a lonely glow from the lower window of the small, compact white building. A dark jeep is parked outside. Two dedicated rowers in wetsuits and wellingtons haul their equipment up the rough, pebble-embedded concrete slope, a fraction of its full length due to the high tide. There is a faint scraping noise, barely audible beneath the noisy Star & Garter crowd. How solitary the rowers seem now, how lonely in comparison to the afternoon bustle of the yearly university boat race. Then, there are crowds upon crowds straining to glimpse the action on both sides of the river, even here, on this side, on my side. Here, where it is so quiet among the trees.

Glancing back at the restaurant, I can see a waitress ushering supposedly important clientele to the best seats at the front of the restaurant, at its bow, where the view is reported as being the best in 'all of south London'. I can't say I agree. Two years ago, when the restaurant was nearing the end of its French-cuisine era, I was obliged to accompany a client there for a working lunch. I had hoped the famed view would be some compensation for the ropes threaded through timber panels, the old mariners' photographs and the starched white-and-navy staff. It was not. Blocked in part by a monstrous new private residential development – twenty storeys of glass and blue lights yet again in the shape of a boat – the view was nothing remarkable. It could not even begin to compare with the view from my side of the river, from the park. The only thing remotely of interest was our waitress who, though a little too talkative and friendly for her menial position, was somewhat aesthetically pleasing. We gathered she was to finish late that evening, around eleven, and that as she was always so tired after work and did not want to walk the long way home, she often took the short cut over the bridge and through the park. My client, a husband and a father, told her to be careful as the park was a little too quiet at night. She smiled thanks as we left her a generous tip. I later learned that she did not take the tip about the park.

There is a low, distant rumble and a tiny flicker of light. The dark jeep across the river has started to move; the rowers leaving perhaps? It travels along the embankment towards the bridge. The single light in the clubhouse has been put out. I follow the vehicle as it moves slowly past the Star & Garter, then past the restaurant and onward toward the traffic lights. I wonder which way it will turn. Behind me to the left, there is a grating of metal against gravel as the resident pastor locks the church grounds for the evening. There is no rigid time for this closure and his lack of regularity means some walkers, who have left the bridge to cut through the churchyard, now have to walk by the river. It is still a short cut and indeed is a pleasant and more picturesque walk, but it is a little longer than they have anticipated and, no doubt, quieter. Consequently, there are extraordinarily few people who walk on the tow-path after dark, but I have found that there are always one or two.

The jeep has turned left and is moving along the bridge. It pulls up next to the bus stop; near one of the park's entrances. There are stone steps here that descend from the bridge to the park, some seventy metres away from me. The front passenger door opens and a woman of about my age climbs out. She is dressed sensibly for the increasingly chilly evening – a thick windbreaker and a scarf wrapped several times around her neck and she also seems to be wearing . . . mittens? Mittens seem so impractical. I press the four fingers of my right hand firmly next to each other and attempt to take my mobile phone out of the small back pocket of my jeans. Near impossible! Unworkable things, mittens.

The back door of the jeep swings open and a teenage girl climbs out. She too wears warm clothes, and again the impractical mittens. She is soon followed by another teenage girl, who is wearing a wetsuit. She must be one of the dedicated rowers. I have heard that the local private school has a fantastic rowing squad; perhaps she is one of them. The driver and the older woman are in conversation. The two girls talk briefly, hug one another and the wetsuit-clad rower climbs back into the jeep. A few more words are exchanged, a few more waves and the jeep pulls away from the kerb, back into the road. It passes out of my line of vision and I out of its.

The older woman and the teenager remain near the park entrance. More words are exchanged and after another brief embrace they part ways. The woman has descended the steps; no doubt she has seen the closed gates to the churchyard. A bus approaches the stop. The teenager turns and walks away from the entrance. I presume the woman is now walking parallel to the bridge, up towards the tow-path. I am proved correct, for the girl leans over the bridge and shouts, 'Bye, Mel! See you on Monday!' She walks towards the bus and I hear the doors open. I lean back against the tree that I have been standing next to. I hear the bus doors close; it moves away. All is quiet again.

There is a damp, musty smell of wet bark as the afternoon's shower dries into the soil. Somewhere behind me I hear a bicycle passing, its chain clanging loudly against its frame. I shall not give it much thought; it is far away so soon – already out of earshot. I move a few steps backwards off the path and rest my head against the cool trunk of a tree; I am careful not to step on the innocent bluebells at its base.

There is no moonlight this evening, no torchlight guiding romantics along the river path, as they delight both in its luminous beams and their circumstances as lovers. There is no foolish or visionary talk this night; no young intellectuals contemplating creation or its creator, whilst they imbibe their cheap wine by the river. There is only me. I do not wish for a companion with whom to contemplate, nor do I much care for the company of the moon.

I hear footsteps on the tow-path. No more than fifty feet away; a light step – perhaps a little uncertain, a little hesitant? The walker treads on a fallen briar – she gasps; she has frightened herself! I cannot help but smile. No more than twenty feet away now. I take a deep breath and exhale slowly, quietly. I wait. Mittens are really very impractical. The steps are closer now.

I wait. The steps are here. I come up behind her and place my hand over her mouth. She struggles. I wait for her to stop. Her hair smells of patchouli, richly sweet and herbaceous. There is a delicate earthiness about her that reminds me of the park. I feel alleviated. Her hands grasp at my own; the metal clasp on her watch reflects a little speck of light, a harmless firefly in the vast space and solitude of the park. I hold her close to me and wait for her to stop. It is so quiet here, on my side of the river.

HARD TO EXPLAIN FUNNY
Rosie Rogers

Mum reckons Terry Wogan's her soulmate. She wrote to him and he's reading her letter out on the radio. The volume's up so loud her words are bouncing around the kitchen. It's so loud that Max and Daisy's ears are pointing backwards like it aches their tiny skulls. They are in the hatch waiting for some Go-Cat. They don't care that Mum's letter is being read out, they just want breakfast. The letter goes like this:

Dear Terry,

I was never a great woman with the quill but I hope this letter is fit for reading on your radio show. How could you have left me here on the auld sod? And me with three hungry mouths to feed? Well, folks now tell me you've made it over there in the Land of the Oppressor – that you're nothing less than a national treasure these days. Now then, Terry, don't forget your roots and your first love. I just have one little request. Could you play our song by Foster and Allen? In memory of us. And perhaps let your mind wander back, to when, as the song goes, 'you and I were young'.

Yours truly,
Maggie (Convey)

Wogan chuckles.

'Ahhh, yes. Those misspent days of youth. This one goes out to you, Maggie.' His voice curls and lifts like he really does remember my mum. 'Back home in the old country, by way of Acton Town.' Hearing Wogan say 'Acton Town' like that makes me glad he's just a voice coming out of the radio and that he can't actually see where we live. Acton Town is where the posh houses are, near the station. We're beyond them, on the South Acton Estate. His words melt into the lyrics. 'To me you're as fair as you were, Maggie.'

Mum sings along. 'The green grove is gone from the hill.' She twirls across the parquet floor that is coming up where the washing machine flooded. 'They say we have outlived our time, Maggie.' When the song is over she pats her curls in the mirror above the sink and turns the volume down.

'Ah, thanks for that one, Woebegone. That's set me up nicely for the day, that has.' She speaks to the radio in her silly, pretend Irish accent. It's the same one she used in the letter. Underneath the accent is my real mum and I know that if she didn't put that voice on she would be dabbing away tears with one of her lacy hankies. Because what Wogan doesn't know is the song makes her think of my dad. Who really did leave her with three hungry mouths to feed.

In Mum's bedside-table drawer are the other men who could be her soulmate. There is Jeremy Irons. He sent her his picture and signed his name across it all big and like he loves himself. She's seen *The French Lieutenant's Woman* nine times. I went with her once to the cinema in Leicester Square and they let me in even though it was double-A rated. The worst bit was when Jeremy Irons and Meryl Streep were doing it. I had to shut my eyes until it was over. I wish she'd just taken me to see *Fame* like Tasha's mum did. Her mum is young and wears red suede pixie boots and helps out at school whenever she can. There is also Dave Evans in Mum's drawer. His daughter, Sophie, has been my pen-pal since last summer when me and Mum stayed with them for a week. She writes to me about her fave band, Depeche Mode, and who her latest 'bezzies' are. She's three years older than me and at big school but Sophie says that doesn't matter because I'm from London and she lives in a village in the middle of nowhere so it evens us out. She's got really neat writing and makes up her own words like 'puh-leaze' and whenever she writes 'I', she draws an eye. She lives in Norfolk, where we used to live before we ended up here. Before Dad left. Her mum and dad are still together and she lives in a big house with a never-empty fridge and Swingball in the back garden. I don't tell Sophie that her dad comes to our house sometimes when I'm at school, because her mum isn't supposed to know. Last time he was round Mum told me she hadn't been expecting him and she was in the middle of dyeing her hair with a bottle of Nice 'n Easy Auburn. She said it was embarrassing because her hair was in a plastic bag and her face wasn't on. I tried to imagine her answering the door like that, with blobs of dye coming down her neck and I was embarrassed for her too. The photograph of Dave Evans is quite nice. His hair is black and curly and he's wearing a yellow sweatshirt and smiling with the sea and some rocks behind him.

The third picture is of Morgan. I absolutely hate Morgan. In the picture, he's stood against a car, sneering at the camera in his donkey jacket. He lives on our estate in Meredith Tower. He has wispy bits of grey hair which come down to his shoulders and his nose is like Gonzo's from *The Muppets*. Me and James, who lives in Blackmore, have our own secret club and Morgan is our number-one enemy. Our mission is to get revenge on him whenever we can. Our den is in the cat park, between his block and mine. It's called the cat park because there's an old woman who feeds all the estate's cats there. Anyway, in our den, we have a warrant for Morgan's death. It's sealed with real red wax, and hidden in our special box that we hide behind the bushes, near the bins. Morgan's crimes are many, but here's a few: he says 'yurs' instead of ears, 'tuth' for tooth and 'mun' at the end of everything. That's because he's Welsh. And not nice Welsh, like Aled Jones. He's evil Welsh. Also, he coughs up big grollies and spits them out, right from the back of his throat. One time, he even flobbed a grollie at his own son, Elvis. I saw it happen. It landed bang in the middle of Elvis's forehead and slid down, onto his nose. Elvis bawled his eyes out, but Morgan just thinks things like that are funny.

'I know he's vulgar,' Mum says, 'but he's a big softie really.'

When I met the Queen, because she was opening the new Ealing Broadway Shopping Precinct, Morgan said to me, 'So, Jose, did you stick your tongue right up her arse?' He said 'right' like he really enjoyed it, rolling the r for special effect. Mum pretended to tell him off. 'Aww, Morgan. You can't say that to a kid.' But it wasn't true because I saw her thinking that he was being quite funny really. She says he fancies himself as a Communist and they don't believe in the royal family or things like manners. Morgan says that my mum is a Fascist because she reads the *Daily Mail*.

There's no picture of Dad in that drawer because he was definitely not Mum's soulmate, in the end. He's been cut out of all the photos that show him and her together. In the Jubilee biscuit tin there are lots of jagged little ovals now. Me and Dad in one picture, Mum and me in another. And sometimes just one of him on his own. In the photo of my First Holy Communion, with me in the middle, holding their hands, Mum's done an oval of him and me and another one of her, on her own. I suppose she thinks she was being fair doing that.

Mum also has her deck of tarot cards in that drawer, wrapped in a purple chiffon scarf. She does the tarot for a tenner sometimes and I sit and watch. She says I'm her little apprentice. After Dad left she was doing the tarot every day on her smoothed-out duvet. All the cards spread out in a big circle, the thirteenth one going in the middle. That's the most important one because it shows you what is going on right now and not in your past or your future. Mum always gets The Three of Swords which has three daggers piercing all the way through a glossy red heart. She says that card is heavy and nobody deserves to get it as many times as she does. She still gets The Tower a lot and she says that the two people tumbling out of the castle are like her and Dad, because they didn't build their home on sturdy foundations. It makes me think of our old house in Norfolk sinking under all that muddy seaside land. The background of The Tower is all black, with jagged lightning bolts and flames bursting out of the turret. The expression on the face of the man is open-mouthed, like he's screaming. The woman falling on the other side has an upside-down smile, which makes it look like her mouth is clamped shut. When Mum gets a Knight or an Emperor I know she's thinking he might be some new man in her life because she gets excited and says things like, 'Oh, that's a nice turn up in the seventh house.' The scariest card is Death because it's a skeleton holding up a black flag and riding a horse, but Mum says that card isn't bad at all. It just means the end of something old and the beginning of something new.

I'm eating Grape-Nuts and they are making my jaw ache. That's all we have left because it's the end of the week.

I don't get the letter. Mum was walked out on by Dad who is called Terry but is definitely not Terry Wogan. Mum says that the letter is a light-hearted joke. She says it appeals to Wogan's sense of whimsy. 'Whimsy' sounds whipped and frothy, like vanilla milkshake and not at all like how sad Mum was when Dad left.

'Anyway, why are you making out like Wogan left us?'

'It's just a joke. I'm just pretending he abandoned us for a laugh.'

'But Dad left us and Wogan doesn't even know who you are.'

'I'm merely making light of everything and anyway he likes that sort of thing.' She flicks the green J-cloth she's been wiping surfaces with at the radio. Wogan coos back to us reassuringly. I can see Tasha, Yvette and Julie threading across the path that leads from their end of the estate to school. I bet none of them had Grape-Nuts for breakfast. I bet they don't even know what Grape-Nuts are.

'Such a practical Taurean, my little girl is. Now, have a vitamin.' She pinches my cheek and rattles the Sanatogens my way. Her pinch tells me she doesn't want me to carry on about how Dad left us with Wogan listening in. It tells me she's in a jolly mood and she wants it to last.

I suck the bright orange pearl hard.

'Well, I don't get why that's funny.'

'It's hard to explain funny. You'll get it when you're older.'

I don't think I will. And I won't listen to Wogan either, with his send-you-to-sleep chat and stupid songs like *Coward of the County*.

When I get married I will have a happy marriage with lots of children. Mum said she knows this because she had my chart done when I was born and that's what it said. I don't want to have lots of children because I know what you have to do to have one. And I don't like boys much, except James, although he's been thinking about doing it way too much lately. We got his Luke Skywalker and Princess Leia to do it the other day, round at his. Then he said, 'Shall we do the same?' And I said, 'No way.'

'Not for real,' he said. 'Just pretending.'

'With you on top and me underneath?'

'Yeah,' he said. 'That's the usual way.'

'All right,' I said, 'but only for a minute.'

Then he said, 'We have to take all our clothes off.'

'No way. I don't want your thing to come out. It might go up me by accident.'

'How about just pants and knickers, then?'

'No way.'

So, in the end, we pretended to do it for way longer than a minute, with our clothes on, under his *Star Wars* duvet.

I first found out about doing it when I was in Miss Parson's class in Second Year. Peter told me and Tasha all about it. After that, Tasha went out with him for ages and then they got the lead parts in *Carousel* together. All the girls fancy Peter but I don't know why because he has a fat belly which he jiggles about, like a bowl of semolina, to show off. He said that this stuff called spunk mixes with loads of eggs in a green slime that's a bit like snot. He said you call that sex or having it off. Then he made a hole with one hand and stuck a bogey on the end of the finger of his other hand and he wiggled that finger around in the hole and said that was what sex looked like. I said it was disgusting and turned away, because seeing his bogey, which was half hard and half soft on the end of his finger, made me feel sick. Tasha didn't say anything. She just looked really into it. I said, 'How do you know?'

Peter wiped the bogey on the back of his Lord Anthony trousers and said, 'Because I saw it happen with my mum and her boyfriend.' When he said this I knew he meant the caretaker Mr Mills, who is way too old to be a boyfriend.

After that I went to the library to settle the doing-it facts. I found this book called *The Body Book* and it explained everything. I sat there on the blue carpet for a good while and got all I needed. At the back of the book there was this chapter called Reproduction. It said, 'When the man loves the woman his penis slowly stands to attention until it is very hard. This is called an erection.' It had a felt-tipish drawing of what that looked like. Then it said, 'His penis goes into the lady's vagina. This is a very special moment and it is called making love and it is very pleasurable. When the man reaches a climax lots of sperm shoot out of his penis and they swim to meet the egg inside the woman. That is how a baby is made.' I also found out that men have two holes and women have three. I thought that Peter Stanton definitely wouldn't know that.

That was ages ago but Mum must think I don't know anything about the facts of life because she thinks I'm still into Flower Fairies and My Little

Pony. I'm in Fourth Year now and next year I'll be going to secondary school. Soon I'll be a teenager and Mum says I won't want to do things with her then. She says I'll be off gallivanting with boys and too big for my Laura Ashley dresses. Anyway, if I did tell her about what Peter Stanton told me she'd be going down the school and making me feel ashamed. Like she did when we first moved here and I got picked on by Judith and her gang.

I think it's funny that she used to do it with Dad. Mum thinks Dad left because she was fat and forty. Dad's new girlfriend is a lot younger than him and she used to be a model, so it makes sense. Mum says she might change her name to Crystal when the divorce comes through because it came to her in a vision.

Mum goes to this healing centre in Northolt called Shambala. The man and woman who run it changed their names to Ra and Isis. Before that they were called Brian and Mavis. Mum says they are each other's other halves and that Ra fell in love with Isis when she was forty-six. She says, 'Isis has three children, she's been divorced, and she's *even* fatter than me. There's hope for me yet.'

Mum believes in reincarnation and that means that you don't just die but keep on coming back until you have honed the jewel of your soul. She found out that she was a Roman soldier in one of her past lives. It was at her first workshop at Shambala, and she was just sitting in the circle with all the others. Ra told them all to shut their eyes and relax. Mum says it's called meditation but it sounds to me like he might have hypnotized them. Mum swears that when she opened her eyes, she looked down and saw a big, hairy, man's arm where her own arm should have been. Then Ra took her deeper into the past life, with all the other people in the circle watching and Isis holding her hand. Then Mum said it got really far-out and it wasn't like a dream at all but just like real life. It ended when she saw that she'd killed another soldier and when she turned him over to look at his face, it was Dad.

'That's why I had to come back as his wife,' she said. 'Because I owed him, karmically.'

I'm leaving for school and the travel news has just finished. 'Bee-bee-cee Raaadio Twoooo.'

'Wogan'll be sending me a lovely signed photograph of himself, now.'

I imagine it lying on top of all the others in her bedside-table drawer.

'And don't forget to tell your teacher and all your mates that your very own mum had her letter read out on national radio this morning.'

I know that I won't be telling anyone at school but I say that I will.

I look at Mum and her face belongs to itself. She is stood in the doorway of our new maisonette in Hardy Court. I am facing her on the long balcony. On a good day, like today, you can see the Post Office Tower from up here. She's wearing her kaftan and the St Christopher that Dad bought her is sitting in the crease of her boobs. She gives me a squeeze like she always does when I go to school, a bit too hard. She watches me walk the length of the balcony and waits to return my usual wave, before I turn the corner.

A GAME OF CARDS
Rose Tremain

et me tell you the story of my friend, Anton Zwiebel.
You will soon realize that any story about Anton Zwiebel is also a story about me, Gustav Perle. In fact, I can't imagine how I could set down any account of Anton Zwiebel's life that didn't include me. I am at the heart of Anton Zwiebel's life and he is at the heart of mine.

We were both born in 1942, during the Second World War, but we were born in Switzerland, where the war didn't trespass. A little later, in 1947, when we attended kindergarten in Zorin, the village where we lived, we began learning about the war and how, beyond our country, there was this other, destroyed world, which the teachers found it difficult to talk about. We were shown pictures of ruined cities. I recall that, in one of these pictures, a white dog was sitting all alone among the rubble and the sight of this abandoned dog made me feel lonely, as though I and not the dog were the creature sitting there.

Did you know that the word 'zwiebel' means 'onion'? Herr Zwiebel translates as 'Mr Onion'. In the kindergarten days, the other kids used to laugh at Anton because he had this name, Zwiebel, but I didn't laugh; I felt sympathetic towards him. I think my mother had already taught me to show compassion towards others, because she was such a kind and understanding woman. When I first invited Anton Zwiebel home for coffee and Mutti's cinnamon cake, my mother took his hand in hers and led him out into the courtyard, where our flowering cherry tree was so weighed down with white blossom that its lower branches almost touched the stones beneath. Anton Zwiebel began stamping up and down, up and down, up and down in a little, crazy dance of wonderment. Later, after we'd had the coffee and the cinnamon cake, my mother said: 'I like this boy, Gustav. I hope he will be your friend.'

I have to move forwards now. I know this can be annoying, in stories, when you're suddenly told that twenty years have passed. You can't stop yourself from wondering what happened in all that time the author has chosen not to talk about. But let me reassure you that nothing out of the ordinary happened to Anton Zwiebel and me. We went through school. We played table tennis. We learned to skate. No tragedy came our way. I entered catering school and then acquired a job as the assistant manager of a *gasthaus* in the spa town of Matzlingen. Anton became a piano teacher at a small school, also in Matzlingen. We continued to see each other almost every day.

At the age of twenty-seven, after I'd been promoted to manager of the *gasthaus*, my modest aspirations were roughly as follows: first of all, I wanted to stay put in Switzerland, not too far from my mother's village. I had a peculiar fear of travelling outside my country, as though what I might find beyond its borders were places only partially rebuilt, where I would become lost. I enjoyed my work. The role of host, who makes everything clean and warm and convivial for those who are forced to spend their lives travelling about appealed to my conservative nature. I expected that, one day, I would own my own hotel.

As to Anton, I think I can describe with reasonable confidence what he felt when we were young men. He, too, was very fond of his country. His nature was more passionate than mine, but this intense, susceptible side of his personality found all the outlet it needed in his piano playing. He was extremely diligent about his practice and would get up every morning at six in order to play Bach for one hour. He was also working rigorously through the one hundred studies in Clementi's *Gradus ad Parnassum*, but he told me that he had no ambition to be a concert pianist. He knew he was gifted, but not exceptional. And he often joked that a concert pianist called 'Anton Onion' was an impossibility.

It was around this time, in our late twenties, that a retired English colonel, Colonel Ashley-Norton, came to stay at the *gasthaus*. He was in Matzlingen to take the spa waters and he was doing this on what he called 'the cheap', as he found that his army pension didn't go as far as he'd hoped. He spoke good German, which, he said, he had learned in the war. 'However, Herr Perle,' he said to me, 'let's not talk about the war. Do you by any chance know the English card came of gin rummy?'

It transpired that this game, which is ideal for two players, and in which scores are slowly built up and laid down on the table for all to see, was the consolation of Colonel Ashley-Norton's old age. He was addicted to it. He and his late wife used to play it for hours at a time, but now his wife was no longer there, and this was the thing about her death which caused him the greatest pain: he had lost his gin rummy partner.

Despite my managerial duties, I was able to find enough time, during the stay of Colonel Ashley-Norton, to learn this card game. After Ashley-Norton left, I taught it to Anton and we both agreed that we found it a very agreeable pastime. There is a little skill attaching to it – deciding when to hoard cards in your hand, for instance, or when to risk throwing something away in order to gain fruitful access to the discard pile at a later moment – but it's not an exacting game like bridge, where you're oppressed by the need for perpetual vigilance. It's a game which, if you are both equally good and bad at it, strengthens a friendship. And I think Anton and I knew that, in addition to table tennis and skating, we'd discovered a leisure activity which could last a lifetime.

You will be wondering by now what was happening to us in what my mother called 'the department of love'.

Although we had reached the 1960s and sometimes listened to the songs of Serge Gainsbourg, the wilder notions of that decade concerning 'free love' and 'flower power' did not seem to have quite reached Switzerland. We still behaved with a certain reserve towards girls. And I know that I speak for Anton, too, when I say that we found them confusing creatures. They seemed to be full of longing. But we felt that it was impossible to fathom what these longings were, or how they might be satisfied. The notion that we should marry two girls and then become responsible for making them happy filled us with dread. We liked to go skating with them sometimes. I certainly enjoyed watching them dancing and swooping round the Matzlingen ice rink, wearing tiny little skirts and fur hats, and afterwards drinking a glass of mulled wine with them by the rink side. Once or twice, inspired by their grace on the ice, I tried kissing one of the girls, but I have to say that this always disgusted me. Their tongues were wet, frenzied and searching. It was as though some newly hatched, blind eel had slithered its way inside my mouth. I can vividly remember lying in my bed at the *gasthaus* and thinking about the way marriage would entail repeated encounters with this newborn eel and feeling cold and sick. I anticipated, also, that any future bride of mine would pester me to rent some spacious apartment, with built-in closets to house her many skirts and embroidered blouses. And the idea that I would no longer be able to live at the *gasthaus*, in my familiar room with its Biedermeier furniture and its red-and-white check curtains was peculiarly upsetting to me. In short, I began to feel that marriage was a wretched idea.

I discussed my anxieties with Anton, during the gin rummy games. He admitted to me that he quite liked the feeling of the eel in his mouth and that he'd even gone to bed with a girl named Gisela, which he'd also enjoyed. Greatly to my relief, however, he then said: 'Marriage is probably out of the question for me, too. I need to live alone to play my music. The idea of someone listening to me while I'm practising is intolerable.'

I now have to move the story forwards again, to the time when the event of greatest significance occurred in our lives.

To most people, I've noticed, the momentous *crises* tend to happen before the age of about forty-five. And if this had been the case for us, then everything might have turned out differently. But the years of our thirties, forties and fifties went slowly by without disturbance. I was able to purchase a modest two-star hotel in Matzlingen, which I redecorated and renamed the Hotel Perle, and in which I lived very comfortably in an apartment on the top floor, with a distant view of open countryside. Anton remained in his job at the school. His name was mentioned once in our local newspaper, the *Matzlinger Zeitung*, when a former pupil of his, Mathias Zimmerli, won an international piano competition and in his speech of acceptance personally thanked 'Herr Anton Zwiebel, for being the most inspirational teacher any piano student could wish for'.

It is true that, after the 'Zimmerli incident', as I refer to it in my mind, Anton went through a period of what I would have to term wistfulness. During our games of gin rummy, for instance, I would suddenly catch him staring out of the window, instead of down at his cards. He developed the habit of sighing for no reason. He returned to the vexed question of his name, saying that it was lucky for Zimmerli he wasn't called 'Onion'. He said that the trouble with being sixty was that, now, one was able to predict how everything would end.

What neither of us anticipated was the arrival in Matzlingen of Hans Hirsch.

Hans Hirsch was the uncle of one of Anton's students and he came, in the winter of 2003, to the annual Christmas Eve concert at the school, at which performances by the pupils were traditionally followed by the playing of two or three short pieces – usually Chopin waltzes or nocturnes – by Anton himself.

You will have worked out that by 2003 Anton and I were sixty-one years old.

I can remember that it was a particularly cold and icy Christmas and I was unable to attend the concert because of problems with the central-heating boiler at the Hotel Perle. I spent the evening making sure that the emergency plumber I'd had to call out stayed until the heating system was fixed and reassuring those few residents who had booked in for Christmas that the rooms would be warm again in a few hours.

It was not until after Christmas that I learned what had happened to Anton.

He came round to my apartment with a bottle of champagne and told me that Hans Hirsch owned a small record company called CavalliSound. Hirsch had approached Anton after the concert and told him that he had never heard Chopin waltzes played 'with such sweet, underlying melancholy'. On the spot, he invited Anton to go to Zurich and record a selection of waltzes for release on the CavalliSound label.

We drank the champagne. I noted that Anton's face was flushed and that he couldn't stay still, but paced about my living room with agitated steps.

'Imagine, Gustav,' he burst out, 'imagine if, after all this time, I can have some proper recognition!'

I tried as hard as I could to feel happy for my friend. I knew that he deserved more than just being mentioned, in passing, in the *Matzlinger Zeitung*. But I now have to admit to you that what I felt about this turn of events was terror. The prospect of Anton's departure, the appalling idea that he would become famous made me feel so utterly cast down that I found it impossible to move from my armchair. In this godforsaken hour, my own life as a hotelier – from which it was far too late to escape – suddenly appeared to me as irredeemably mundane, shallow and pointless. The champagne felt bitter in my stomach. I was impatient for Anton to leave so that I could give way to my feelings in the privacy of my rooms.

Anton went away to Zurich to make his Chopin recordings in the late spring.

During his absence, my mother fell ill. I dragged myself from the hotel to the hospital and back again, sunk in a misery so deep I wished it had been I and not my beloved Mutti who was dying. It was as though the world around me, so quietly agreeable to me for so long, had turned to rubble.

I saw, too, that the Hotel Perle, where the clientele had fallen off in recent times, was in desperate need of refurbishment. The bathrooms were dingy and outmoded. Some rooms *had* no bathrooms. The dining-room carpet was stained and worn and into its walls had seeped the noxious smell of gravy. I stared at all this and knew that taking it in hand, finding the money and the will to hire builders and decorators was beyond me.

When Anton returned, full of tales about the recording studios of CavalliSound, full of hope that he might soon be invited to play recitals in Geneva or even Paris, he was disappointed by my melancholy mood and even asked me whether he'd offended me in some way.

'No. Of course you haven't, Anton,' I said, 'it's just that worry about Mutti seems to have made me wretched. Please forgive me.'

CavalliSound released Anton's recording of the Chopin waltzes in the same week in which my mother died. I tried to think only about giving Mutti a good funeral and nothing else. The dazzling recital tours which might soon take Anton away from me for ever I tried to banish from my mind.

Then, a few weeks later, I picked up the *Matzlinger Zeitung* one morning and read a headline which ran: 'Disappointment looms for Zimmerli mentor'. The article reported that national criticism of Anton Zwiebel's

Chopin recordings had been universally unfavourable. 'Across the board,' said the *Zeitung*'s arts reporter, 'music critics have attacked Zwiebel's "muddy sound" and questioned the policy of CavalliSound supremo, Hans Hirsch, of "discovering" unknowns such as local man, Zwiebel. Although, it was anticipated that recital venues would be interested in Zwiebel, once the tutor of the celebrated Mathias Zimmerli, it now looks as though this is unlikely to happen.'

I was eating my breakfast. I laid everything aside and telephoned Anton and invited him to supper. I didn't mention the article I'd just seen. I said: 'We haven't played gin rummy for a while, but we can take up where we left off. What d'you say, Anton? I'm pretty sure it was you who won the last round.'

In the years that have followed since then, we've never really talked about what happened at that time, so it's difficult for me to judge what Anton feels about it, deep down. He did say once: 'Perhaps if I'd had your name – Perle – it might have happened for me, but who knows?' But he also told me that, no matter what, he would carry on playing Bach for an hour every morning.

He's retired from the school now. And I'm contemplating selling the hotel. It's really become too much for me. When we last talked about our future, Anton and I decided that we would rather like to return to Zorin and live quietly together in the old house I've inherited from Mutti. This house remains very much as it used to be, except that the cherry tree in the stone courtyard died a long time ago.

Commissioned by BBC Radio 3 and simultaneously printed in *The Times*

THINGS YOU THINK YOU NEED
Jennifer Payne

'Will you *please* brush your teeth? Just a little? Look, watch Auntie Libby.' Libs holds the Mickey Mouse toothbrush to her mouth, bares her teeth. 'Mmm! Auntie Libby *loves* to brush her teeth!'

Brendan, astride her right knee, wrenches the toothbrush from her grip and launches it across the bathroom; Max squirms on her left thigh. 'You don't brush our teeth! Daddy does!' Libs sighs and settles back against the toilet tank. The ceramic lid rattles. She closes her eyes for a moment, then counters: 'Daddy used to. Now it's me.'

I hover in the doorway, not sure what I can say or do to help. I consider scooping the boys onto the counter, and telling them politely but firmly, 'We're doing this now. No more funny business. Open your mouths.' I don't though. Libby might think I'm undermining her, and I'm not entirely sure whether or not small children respond to polite-but-firm commands from strangers. I stand there mutely.

The boys lean together conspiratorially. I can't make sense of what Brendan is saying (it's just eighteen-month-old-baby babble to me), but his brother can, somehow, and translates for him. 'Auntie Libby.' Max tugs at her sleeve to get her full attention. 'Auntie Libby, Brendan can't remember your name.' Then Brendan turns to me, points, and loudly speaks words I do understand: 'Who's that man? I want Daddy.'

Libs turns to me. Her face has gone grey. 'Matty, will you take them, please?

Stick them in front of the TV or something. Just get them away from me.'

The next words out of my mouth confirm that I have become, since this morning, the least helpful person alive. I can't speak or act without gaffing and bringing tears to Libs' eyes. My latest faux pas is, 'But what about their teeth?'

'Fuck their teeth. Their teeth can rot for all I care. It's hardly the biggest issue, is it?'

I take the opportunity to try out my approach, even though Libby's head is bowed, her hands are clasped to her face, and I can see tears dripping, thick and fast, through her fingers. I grab Max by the wrist to prevent his escape, while man-handling Brendan onto the counter. 'Open your mouth,' I say. To my surprise, he complies immediately. The only toothbrush to hand is mine – Mickey remains abandoned in the tub – which I insert tentatively. The bristles fill the entire cavity of his mouth, and I must have pushed it to the back of his throat, because in the next moment, Brendan draws blood by crunching down on my finger. His bite is like a bear trap.

The boys seem happy to play with their trains and ignore me, so I give Libby breathing room, time to herself. I want to cook dinner, but I can't find any food here in the house, just a drawerful of take-out menus. While I debate whether she'd prefer Korean or something called Happy Veggie, I catch sight of the headline in yesterday morning's *Orange County Times*: 'Dozens Die In New Year's Eve Pile-Up'. In the accompanying photo, the fog that is being cited as the cause of the accident still lingers along the coastal highway. Hundreds of cars were involved, and police are estimating more casualties than any road-related incident in Southern California history. Vehicles and their debris cover every surface inch of the road; others dangle over the cliffs or are tilted on two wheels against the foothills. In a sidebar a man with his arm in a sling talks about how thick the fog was, like a sheet suddenly thrown against his windshield. He says that he was freaking out behind the wheel, fearing that because he couldn't see anything in front of him, he could collide with other cars or pitch into the ocean at any moment. Daniel and Rachel, Libby's brother and sister-in-law, were two of the victims who didn't walk away.

Which is why we're here. To plan a double funeral, sort out her brother's will, sell his house and I don't know what else. I tried to ask Libby during our flight down from Whistler what she plans to do about her nephews and, well, everything else – the rest of her life, our lives – but she just snapped at me. 'I can't forward plan, can I, Matty? You know that.' She then guzzled half a bottle of Pepto-Bismol (for her nausea) and an equal measure of Nyquil (for nerves) and proceeded to sleep until we hit the tarmac in Los Angeles. As we drove out of the airport parking lot and onto the freeway, she blinked in the sun and said, 'Wow, I'd really forgotten what it's like.' She hadn't set foot on Californian soil since her dad died and she moved to Canada three years ago. She'd never even met her younger nephew.

Later that night, as three thousand square feet of house sprawl around us, we all pile into the biggest set of bunk beds I've ever seen. It's like sleeping in an ark: we are paired up two by two, me and Libs with our noses practically touching the ceiling, the boys down below. With all the nightlights in the room, it's as bright as midday. I drift in and out of semi-sleep until dawn, but mostly just lie there watching the boys' reflections in the mirrored wardrobe. They kick and shift all night, whimper and sigh in their sleep. Libby, beside me, seemed comatose as soon as she lay down. She's an insomniac, normally. In the three years I've known her, seldom has she slept so peacefully without medication, or for more than two hours at a stretch.

When we first got together, we couldn't make it through a night without some parts of ourselves – fingers, ankles – entwining. We'd been dating several weeks before she told me about her dad, but she divulged her story one night, in a sudden, runny-nosed outburst, as we lay curled up together in bed. She was so overwrought that I only caught a few phrases among her rambling sentences: '. . . heart attack in front of me . . . paramedics cut his chest open . . . he was my best friend'. From that snowy November night in bed until the blooming of spring, Libby would cry herself into a few hours of fitful sleep. I would hold her, rock her, dot her neck with kisses and whisper, 'I'm here for you now. And I'll never, ever leave you.' Lately, she's been sleeping on her right side, and I spend the nights with my hand cupping the curve of her ribs and the underside of her breast. Tonight, suddenly, an army of stuffed animals has come between us. As I lie awake in the glowing room, it seems emblematic of something. Libby remains motionless, except for the shallow rise and fall of her breathing.

*

It's that time of year. Pine needles from recycled Christmas trees still litter the sidewalk. But during my first morning in California, on the 7 a.m. news, the weather reporter talks about the severe drought, which has so far lasted 177 days. The dry spell has now been coupled with other bizarre record-breaking weather phenomena – impenetrable nightly fog, and giant, violent surf. She's at the Huntington Beach Pier, and gestures at the twenty-foot waves that twist and crash behind her. I can remember the Outback winters of my childhood – a blur of disorientating, blistering sun and cracked red earth – but following a decade of the gentle rhythm of Whistler's seasons, this drought, these extremes, are something I can't make sense of.

When we left home twenty-four hours ago, the snow had been so heavy that Libby and I had been bulldozed from our ski resort to the bottom of the mountain, where a helicopter flew us to Vancover. When we arrived in California, we'd collected Max and Brendan from a babysitter a few miles inland. I'd always visualized this area of the world as teeming with wide-open spaces, fertile green hills, dense rows of palm and lemon trees. What I found, instead, as I navigated our rental car over swells and dips of foothills charred by brushfire, along an eight-lane conveyor belt of road, was that every unburned spot of hilltop had been paved over with identical stucco houses. Aside from the hazy blue of the sky, the landscape outside the windshield was a study in ash and beige.

The grass in the backyard has dehydrated into strands of hay. The boys have been rolling around out there all morning, and after refusing to join me inside or even acknowledge my presence for the first few hours of the day, while Libby remains asleep, they climb next to me on the sofa and bring me a peace offering: an orange from one of the citrus trees that line the edge of the garden, but it's as shrivelled and thin-skinned as a deflated balloon.

I follow the kids back outside, and notice the bushes and trees are pockmarked with fruit the size of marbles. I gaze over the fence towards the horizon. Even the mountains in the distance are dry, snowless peaks. My stomach starts to churn, and I wonder where Libby has put her Pepto-Bismol. Pinpricks and flashes of white light cloud my vision, and I realize I'm about to faint from the heat, or sun, or both. It's not right. Nothing about this is right. It's the third of January in the northern hemisphere, yet

I can practically feel the sun sucking the water from my body. My knees quake, and I know: I shouldn't be here. I should be giving ski lessons to a group of beginners from a school in Seattle today, not standing in an unfamiliar space, staving off the urge to be sick.

Max approaches me again, with Brendan in his shadow.

'Where's my Mommy and Daddy? Who are you?'

Libby stumbles in during the midday news, regards the latest weather update, the shots of the giant waves, with suspicion. 'What's going on? Is there a tsunami or something?'

'It's partially caused by the drought, partially by the remains of some jet stream. Some freaky El Niño thing. The news people say the waves are bigger than the pipeline in Hawaii. All these amateur surfers are going out in it, and three people have drowned already.'

'Hawaii? It's like the apocalypse.'

She has no idea.

Libby claims not to have slept at all, and demands that I go buy her half the menu at Starbucks. She's also listed gifts for Max and Brendan that she's sure will foster a speedy recovery from their parents' deaths: jump-ropes, popsicles, bubbles, costumes. In Orange County, I soon discover, you never need to leave your car. Espresso, diapers and new colouring books are all procured from drive-thru windows. I sit in the queue at Starbucks, and listen as Bing Crosby is piped in to the car. The A on the Starbucks sign has been fashioned into a Christmas tree, and my coffees are proffered in a cup-holder with cotton wool glued around the rim like snow and with a candy cane taped to the side. Even in the air-conditioned car, I'm sweating in my boardshorts, bought in haste at the airport upon arrival, and can't marry the idea of this raging heat and the holidays having just passed. Nothing natural, nothing non-commercial or non-artificial, proves this fact.

When I get back to Daniel and Rachel's house the smashed remnant of a Volkswagen van has been abandoned in the driveway. The windshield and steering wheel are gone; the front seat has been forced off its tracks and is wedged into the back panelling.

198

Libby is sitting on the playroom floor with the boys. She's still wearing the clothes she left Whistler in, and hasn't changed the boys out of their pyjamas, but she's gelled their hair into small feathery spikes. They are eating a bag of chocolate coins, and watching Marilyn Manson showcase his home on *Cribs*. Brendan glances up at me when I enter the room, his eyes as grey and dull as bullets.

'Libby, what's going on with the van? Is that your brother's?'

'Yeah. They finally removed the last of the debris from the accident site and reopened the highway today. The police called to see if I wanted to come down to the impound place to identify the van and collect Daniel's belongings, but I asked if they could bring it here instead. So they did.'

'I don't understand. Why would you want his van here?'

'I wanted to get all his stuff back. And I didn't want to have to walk around some scrapyard. That would just be . . . *grotesque*.'

I decide to look through the van myself. The side door has been crushed, and I can barely prise it open. When I do, though, I understand why Libby didn't want to give the van up so easily. It seems to have functioned as her brother's child-free haven and beachfront office. Amid the chaos, I see Daniel's surfboard, textbooks, his journal, boardshorts, flip-flops, his students' book reports. On the inside of the back panel, there is a rectangular indentation where the licence plate has been fitted. He has fashioned this into a picture frame, which contains a photo of him, Rachel, Libby and her dad in Daniel's backyard. Rachel's stomach swells underneath a maternity dress, and the orange trees are laden with fruit. Libby is turned away from the camera, on the tips of her toes, stretching to pluck an orange from a tree.

I've seen this picture once before. When Libby first moved into my chalet, she claimed one of the cupboards for herself, and insisted on keeping it locked. I spent weeks creating wild fantasies about what could be in there – cocaine, hundred-dollar bills, ass beads? One day while she was out giving a lesson, I managed to pick the lock, and fifty-odd pairs of flip-flops spilled out in an avalanche of canvas and patterned foam. Pinned to the inside of the cupboard door was the same picture Daniel had here in his van – the last one of the family together, as I would discover later. Libby caught me in the midst of shovelling her sandals back into the cupboard. I thought she would be really angry, but instead she stroked the edge of the photo and said, 'You know what? I think I'm going to go back to wearing my flip-flops. It'll make me feel like I'm at home.' It was the middle of winter, but she kept her word, and trudged practically barefoot through snowdrifts for the next four months, until one of her students, a podiatrist, told her she would eventually lose all of her toes if she kept it up. This winter, she has acquired a pair of woollen clogs which look like slippers to me, but which she insists, 'could be outdoor shoes'.

I leave everything in the van as I've found it, and join Libs and the boys in the backyard. They are sprawled head to foot on the parched grass. Max and Brendan are asleep.

'So,' I begin. I know it's only been a day since Libby got the news, but I have to ask the question. 'Have you started to think about who's going to look after the kids?'

She doesn't look up. 'Well, me. And you. Us. There's nobody else left.'

'What about Rachel? Doesn't she have any family?'

'Her great-uncle is still alive, but he's about ninety years old and like, either demented or clinically insane or something. Besides, after Dad died Daniel and I promised that we would look after each other's kids. I'm like Max and Brendan's godparent. Not literally their godparent, since they weren't christened, but you know what I mean. It's in Daniel and Rachel's will. It's the best thing for everyone.' I wonder what a social worker, any social worker, would have to say about that.

'OK, I can understand that you want to do the right thing here. But how are you actually going to raise them? Financially?'

She shrugs. 'I mean, we have this house.'

'I would assume there's a mortgage.'

'I can get a job, you know,' she tells me. 'We could both get jobs. We could work the ski season in Big Bear.' I think about the newspaper headline I saw in the recycling bin: 'White Christmas? Dream On: Ski Resorts Go Bust From Lack Of Snow'.

I only really know two things about the circumstances following Libby's dad's death, which these days she only ever obliquely refers to. First, that the sum of her and Daniel's inheritance consisted of their father's gambling debts and his fifties' bungalow in the most arid part of east San Diego County. The sale of the house more or less cancelled out his debts, but to my recollection, any remaining money had been squandered on a year's worth of Libby's college tuition. There's nothing, as far as I'm aware, to fall back on.

Second, Libby's dad died just before Max was born. The only thing she ever told me about her nephew is that from the time he was a year old, she couldn't stand the sight of him. That was the reason she'd moved away: she said Max looked so similar to her dad, it was like being in the room with a ghost.

I persist. I know I shouldn't be trying to extract information from her, poke holes in her logic, this soon, with her family not even in the ground yet, but I want to know how soon I, we, Libby and I, can get back home. 'How am I going to stay here permanently? The visa they gave me is only for ninety days.'

She refuses to look up. 'I don't know. We could go to Vegas.'

I gesture at Max and Brendan. 'They don't look like they drink or gamble.'

She doesn't laugh. 'I meant we could get married.'

'I didn't think you believe in marriage.'

'I don't. I also never believed my entire family would die before my twenty-fourth birthday.'

'Libby, look at me. I don't want to have this conversation with the back of your head.'

She rolls towards me, raises one hand to shield the sun from her eyes. I nod towards the slumbering boys. 'Libby, they haven't all died.'

'That's what I mean. That's why I think we should stay.'

'But . . .' I falter. Acid reflux kicks in again, and I have to swallow hard to keep myself from dry heaving. I'm dizzy, and don't know how to say what I need to. I lower myself to the ground, but can't regain my concentration, and the words come out wrong. 'Don't you realize that's ridiculous?'

'What's ridiculous about it? Matt, you're going to have to give a little here. You've told me a thousand times that you want us to stay together for ever, so please, help me think of a solution.'

For ever. I sigh. What can I add that won't inflame her further? I can't wait to escape this nouveau-riche, samey suburban hell? After a mere eighteen hours in their presence, I am certain I don't want to be a parent to your two demonic nephews? I feel like I'm trapped in an episode of *Desperate Housewives* and I don't like it? You're a complete fantasist? I quell these thoughts before they worm their way from between my lips. It suddenly occurs to me that maybe I'm a selfish person. Or maybe Libs is. I can't even tell any more.

'I think I'd be willing to keep them if we take them back to Whistler with us.'

'Would you now?' Mission Don't Inflame Libby has clearly failed. 'How fucking generous of you.'

'What's wrong with that? It's our home. I don't see why we should change our entire lives for children so young, when they'll never know the difference.'

'They can't move to Whistler.'

'Why not? Those Kiwis live there with their kids.'

'Those people are hippies. I'm not raising hippie children.'

I sigh. 'Well, we'll need to keep thinking of a compromise then.'

Most of the contracted North Americans leave Whistler after ski-instruction season ends, but Libby surprised me by staying on to do the summertime cash-in-hand work – dishwashing, waitressing, working a few hours at reception. For me, a career like this – something physical – felt innately destined. It was my way out of sheep farming. For Libs, with her expensive education, the fact that she remained to perform menial, thankless jobs hinted at something more complex. 'I'm not running away from anything,' she insisted one day, sensing my insecurity. 'I *want* to be here. I've met you, and I want to stay with you. This is home now.'

That night, we move into one of the guest bedrooms. Libby reaches into my boxers as soon as we lie down, licks and bites at my neck like she's starving. 'Are you sure you're ready for this?' I ask her.

'Yes,' she says, 'I need it.'

I'm on top of her, rocking back and forth as gently as I can, but Libby claws at the back of my thighs, pulls me deeper into her. She starts to melt beneath me. Her face pushes against my chest, and I can feel the heat of her tears sliding down to my stomach. I hold her closer, and realize that I'm crying, too. Salt stings my pores and my eyes hurt. We cuddle together for what seems like hours, emptying ourselves of the pain we've both been through in our lives. I try to imagine never sharing this with her again – my future without her – and I can't conjure any concrete images at all.

Libby eventually slips into sleep, but I continue to lie there, watching her in the dim light, counting the seconds until dawn. I'm cried out by this point, but my heart still beats so loudly I can hear it. My stomach swills. I close my eyes, and scenes from my childhood play out against the back of my eyelids like a home video: the sun scorching the earth; straining my back from doing farm chores too strenuous for a child – tilling the earth, carrying lambs; the heat of a leather belt slapping against my legs. I sit up in bed, and am taken back to the night Libby told me about her dad. 'So that's why you left home?' I had eventually asked. She had wiped her nose with the back of her hand. 'Yeah, it was just too painful to stay.'

I'd nodded in the dark, understanding. Now, I realize, as I sit next to her in the dark once again, with a sticky film from her tears covering my torso, she didn't reciprocate the question. In all these years, she's never asked about why I'd fled.

By our third day in California, I haven't slept in ninety-six hours, and Libby hasn't ventured further than the backyard. She's been busy phoning lawyers and crematoria, and the wrinkles that have set into her forehead tell me she needs a break. I kid-wrangle the boys into the rental car, and insist Libby join us on a trip to the beach, since I haven't actually seen the ocean during our time here, except on TV.

I drive up and down misleading lengths of cul-de-sac – I don't even know which way is west: I can find Starbucks but not the Pacific Ocean – until eventually my sighs penetrate Libby's distractedness and she directs me towards some tide pools down the coast where Max and Brendan can splash around. When we get there, we discover that the churning surf has destabilized many of the boulders that form the tide pools' perimeter. The Coast Guard has cordoned off the area with red-and-white danger flags.

Libby turns around in her seat to face the boys in the back. 'Sorry, guys, we can't visit the beach today. The waves are too high. Look.' She taps her window, pointing towards the setting sun, where despite the black flags that flutter on the lifeguard stands, a crowd of surfers is still in the water.

'Let's go see the Christmas trees!' Max suggests.

Libby agrees. 'They'll take them down soon. The kids will enjoy it.' She navigates us northwards, to a section of beach that is a bay on one side, ocean on the other, bisected by a concrete pier.

The 'Christmas trees' are simply cone-shaped buoys with strands of coloured lights. They are anchored in what I assume is normally a calm inlet, but today I watch as they bob like rollercoasters, rising and falling crazily. They seem to be functioning as lighthouses, emitting warnings.

I'm digging through my pockets for quarters for the parking meter when I hear Libby behind me.

'Matty, can you help? I think Max is stuck.' While we'd had the foresight to hire a child seat for Brendan along with the rental car, we hadn't considered Max legally requiring one, too. An infant seat was stored in the garage, and despite the warning on the bottom – MAXIMUM WEIGHT: 15 LBS! – Libby was convinced slim-hipped, gangly Max would fit fine. Now, it seems, not so: he's wedged in. Brendan has been freed from the car and is stalking a seagull that has landed beside us in the parking lot. Libby asks Max to shift his weight onto one hip so she can try to pull him upwards, but he doesn't budge. I release the fittings, and lift Max from the car, seat and all. I set him down, bent in half, long arms dangling to his toes, with the infant seat protruding like a shell on his backside. Libby holds his hands while I tug at the infant seat, and the force required to free him sends me stumbling backwards. Max looks dazed and annoyed, but Libby and I are suddenly laughing. 'You see . . .' I can barely get the words out between guffaws. 'You see *this* is why you can't become a parent,' I chastise her, but my eyes are wet with laughter. Libby kneels to Max's height, cuddles him close. 'You forgive me, don't you, pal?'

Max simply asks: 'Where's Brendan?'

I scan the parking lot – not even the seagull is still there – then the beach, which is more crowded than I had first realized. Kids are everywhere. The cove to the right of the pier, rough as it seems, is nothing compared to the tumult of the ocean on the left. I spot Brendan along the waterline, fifty metres away, toddling towards the tow of a giant wave. I'm a caribou, suddenly bounding across the sand, and manage to yank him up by the wrist just seconds before what seems like a ton of water assaults the sand.

Brendan screams, and over the thunder of the wave, I think I might hear his shoulder pop from its socket. His arm goes limp for a moment, but as I shift his bum to my hip, he makes use of it to slap me around the face. I exhale and pause in the sand, forcing my body into complete rigidity. I'm scared that if I move, I'm liable to shake the shit out of the kid.

Libby and Max are still in the parking lot. She's doubled over, one hand to her chest. 'Matt. Oh my God. He could have drowned!'

I set my mouth in a line. 'I know. What were you thinking?'

She snatches Brendan from me by his upper arms and slams him down onto the hood – too violently, we realize later, when we see the indentation that's been left – and bellows, directly into his ear, 'Don't ever run away from me again!'

Libby decides to sit in the car until she's calmed down, so I take the kids to an ice-cream shop. Brendan doesn't tantrum or cry, but he's mad. He stamps his feet and holds his breath until his cheeks are puffed out and he looks like he's just been boiled. If he internalizes anger this much at a year and a half, I can't wait to see how he copes as an adult.

Twenty minutes later Libby joins us, and we walk along the pier, each gripping one of the kids tightly by the arm. I wonder how she would have managed without me. I picture Libby doing CPR on Brendan, if not diving into a wall of water to retrieve his body. It's supposed to be low tide now, but the surf rushes across the pier, sloshing over barnacles and our bare feet. We find some crusty benches, and pull the wriggling boys into our laps as we finally relax.

'Rachel's great-uncle called earlier today. You know, the really old one?'

'The one you said has dementia? Is he coming down for the funeral?'

'No. He's pretty much an invalid. Anyway, the reason he called is that he owns a second home in Hawaii. Daniel and Rachel used to go out there every year.'

I give a half nod, not quite sure where the conversation is heading.

'Matty, he wants Max and Brendan to have it. He bought it in cash like, forty years ago, and he thinks given the circumstances it's the best for all of us to go and live there. It's just a little two-bedroom bungalow, but it's right on the beach. He says there's a nice village school they can go to, and just think: Max and Brendan can be surf babies.'

I can visualize the scene: me standing with my toes burrowed in the sand supervising the boys, a few years older than they are now, as they jump into gentle, fizzy waves and fling themselves onto their bodyboards. The surf sends them tumbling ashore on a cushion of foam, their brown bodies covered in suncream and black sand. Behind us, the teak porch on our bungalow stretches its arms out towards the Pacific. Squat trees, heavy with coconuts and pineapples, cast fat shadows across the house. Libby approaches us with a tray of cubed mahi mahi and mango. The boys abandon the ocean to slurp at the food. Their faces are sticky and glisten in the late afternoon sun. Libby wears only a bikini top and sarong, and her chestnut hair is threaded with gold-and-auburn streaks. She brushes a slice of fish against my lips, presses it onto my tongue.

'Matty.'

Her voice brings me back from my daydream. Somehow both Max and Brendan have ended up in her lap, and are snuggled against her. She kisses the top of each of their heads.

'Matty? It's perfect. How can we refuse such a wonderful offer? And I've realized, too, that although Daniel and Rachel being killed is awful and I miss them, I think it's all happened for a reason. I finally know what I've wanted since my dad died.' She grabs my hand. 'Matty, I want us to be a family.'

She's right: it is perfect. In her fantasy, in my fantasy, everything is perfect. My testicles start to ache. Waves pummel the shore.

After days of indecision, I know what I have to do.

We are in the departures lounge at the airport. The sun glares in from the five-storey-high window behind us. Libby has Max and Brendan Velcroed into the BabyProtect harnesses that she unearthed in the laundry room. They tug her in opposite directions, bucking against their restraints so hard that every few minutes she loses her footing. They jerk briefly in the same direction and actually drag Libby a few metres along the waxed floor, like huskies pulling a sled. The kids think it's a game, and Libby is either oblivious to, or is managing to ignore, their high-pitched shrieks. Everyone else is staring at them.

I touch her cheek. 'Libs, I have to get to my gate. My flight is going to leave.' She won't look at me.

'Libby, I'll see you soon. I just need to go finish out the season. The school is stuck without us, you know. They keep asking me when you'll be coming back. And I need to clean out the chalet.'

There is a pregnant pause, which I deliberately leave gestating in the silence, to allow her time to condone my decision and give me a final cuddle.

'Are those really the reasons? It's not becase I want to stay with Max and Brendan?'

'Of course not. This is just what I need to do right now. That's all.'

She picks the boys up and hefts one of them onto each hip. They yank at her hair and wipe slobber on her face. She turns toward the escalator, then calls over her shoulder as she descends, 'If those are the things you think you need, fine.'

We've left it that I'm just going back to collect our things, finish up the season; that I'll extend my American visa and we'll get married. But as my flight takes off over the Pacific, as I catch the almost imperceptible glint of a school of migrating dolphins swimming amongst the breaking points of those giant waves, I know I've lied. Ice crystals form on the window as the plane gains altitude and I settle back in my seat, waiting for the moment that I can once again feel virgin snow crumbling and swishing under my skis. I start to hum. At last my reasons for leaving become clear. I know what I think I need, what I'm dreaming of: a lifetime of white Christmases.

MUSEUM OF UNWANTABLES
Gabriela Blandy

The museum has burnt-out matches, broken flowerpots, and knives blunter than fingers. There are tubes of glue set solid, lying on desktops flecked with ink and gouged by compass points. Clothes, worn at the knees and elbows, have been nibbled to shreds by moths and mice. They dangle from rusty hangers in cupboards that won't close and barely open.

The museum also has Norman, with his scrawny arms and frizzy hair; ruddy cheeks and lop-sided dimples; his awkward scurry of a walk and hands that wriggle in his sleep as though he were working an abacus. He is sitting in the bedroom in his standard brown corduroys and striped tank-top. A leaflet rests in his lap, sweaty in one corner where he has taken it up again and again. 'Hey Ho for Hoylake's Multiplex', it reads. Norman sighs a soft lament and gazes out through the sash windows that overlook his rambling, meadow garden. Twenty-four years he has lived here. Twenty-four years! Since, at sixteen, he left the orphanage and stumbled upon this derelict manse. He remembers wandering up the long, sweeping lawn, tripping on scrambles of leaf and twig, bending down to tug at the weeds that infested the patio. Their obstinate roots had said, 'No! We're here to stay,' and he smiled and ran a hand over the cracked paving, stained with moss and years gone by.

Beyond a medley of foliage, the manse towered dark and ominous. He crept towards it with a fluttering in his stomach. The great front doors were warped with age and groaned a bleak accompaniment to Norman's staccato breaths as he opened them and stepped into the hall beyond. It was a huge space: Norman felt like a pebble rolling between the walls of a vast cavern as he entered. His shoes squelched on the sodden carpet and he looked down to see mould sprouting between the lively, paisley designs. But the rooms were empty and the house sang a whistling, creaking melody that pierced Norman's neglected soul. He danced down dim corridors, free of the nuns and sloppy suppers and, as darkness descended, claimed his first unwantable.

Crushing the bright yellow paper with its 'Hey Ho!' and cruel intention, Norman sinks back into the musty fabric of the armchair, his brow a gathering of furrows and folds. How could they level his home? What would happen to the stagnant pond at the end of his garden? The dahlias! The sinking rockery! The lavender flowing in an infinite blueness; such a cloud of heavenly scent. He clutches at the chair beneath him. What will he do with his treasures?

Norman shoves the leaflet into his pocket, stands up on two shaky legs, and makes his way downstairs. The banisters wobble and the wind hisses through the cracks in the windows. Up until now, he has felt no opposition towards him or his museum, yet it appears that the developers of Hoylake have spent the last eleven months planning a . . . an outrage! How could he not have known? There they were, tiptoeing and scheming, as he opened his doors each day and sat waiting. He picks up his coat from the back of a seatless chair and pushes open the great front doors, which moan on their hinges like cantankerous old men.

Outside, the day moves with gusto. Norman takes a series of deep breaths and checks his pockets before following the road into town. Along the way, he stops to rescue a snail that has crawled from the safety of the grassy bank onto the tarmac, all wet and inviting from rain the night before. A car drives by with a honk and Norman stumbles backwards with a thunderbolt in his chest. He stares at the grey exhaust spoiling the day as the car speeds onward, and as the engine's growl grows fainter he places the snail on a moist leaf, smoothes his clothes and continues.

When he reaches the local shop, Norman enters with a jingle and sets about grabbing a few things. He lines them up neatly on the counter and arranges the leaflet beside them.

'Did you know about this?' he asks Gladys, the ginger-haired lady who runs the store. Gladys nods and Norman thumps his hand on the counter. 'I see,' he says, and Gladys leans over and strokes his arm.

'Norman, love, I'm sorry, but things are moving on. People don't want to be reminded of imperfection nowadays. They want to enjoy themselves.' Norman closes his eyes at the warmth of her touch. 'And just think, they ought to pay a pretty penny.'

'Pay?'

'Oh, Norman,' Gladys says with a chuckle. 'You'll never change, will you?'

Norman tilts his head as he appraises her. 'Why should I want to?'

When he arrives home later that day, Norman makes himself a mug of soup, cupping his hands around its pleasant warmth and strolling through his museum: over rugs wanting tassels, clawed by cats and stained with wine; passing socks with no partners, old flat tyres and dried-up pens. Eventually, he stops in the shadowy cloakroom and from a small corner cupboard with shelves that tilt and quake he removes a pink blanket, bringing it to his face and inhaling deeply. Poor Sister Mary Clarity. How many times had he woken her in the night, the floor tiles icy beneath his feet, shivering in his pyjamas?

'Sister Mary Clarity? Are you sleeping?' he would say, watching the paleness of her lips in the darkness, their shrivelled outline; the ruins of a life without repose.

'Norman? Is that you?' Her voice was always cracked with sleep.

'There must have been something, Sister Mary Clarity,' he'd say from the doorway.

Often an owl would hoot and there'd be a flapping of wings outside the window.

'Norman, how many ways can I say it? You were in a fruit basket when we found you, wrapped only in a blanket. There was nothing else.'

'There was a sock, Sister Helen Mercy said.'

'Yes, on your head, a man's size ten. You had such wispy hair.'

Norman sighed into the shadows and outside the trees swayed in the moonlight. Sister Mary Clarity pulled herself up and lit the candle she kept for midnight moments such as these. 'A set of steps is a fine beginning,

Norman, and it was the top step, let us not forget that.'

'But Barnsley Youth Centre?'

'Indeed.'

'And it was disused even then?'

The water pipes creaked and Norman wrapped his arms around his tiny body, watching the candle's flame flicker and shimmy.

'And there really was nothing else?' he said.

'Oh, Norman, no. No things, no accessories. I've told you this. Why must you dwell?'

'But I don't dwell, that's the point. Who am I, Sister Mary Clarity? Who am I?'

She exhaled slowly and shifted on the narrow bed. 'You're Norman.'

'But Norman who?'

'There was only a first name. No things and only a first name.'

'And the blanket?'

'It was pink, Norman. Pink, pink, pink. It was pink yesterday and tomorrow it will still be pink.'

'Pink.' He echoed the word, watched it floating up into the rafters behind him, bouncing off a skylight and finally resting with a thud on one of the many bookshelves that lined the wide corridors of the orphanage.

'Why don't you go back to bed and read?' Sister Mary Clarity said. Read. It was always the same: 'Read everything and anything,' she would tell him, clapping her chapped hands together.

But how could he fill himself with the lives of others when he was stuck on himself, the fact that Norman was not Norma, and pink a perfect accessory?

Norman replaces the blanket in the cupboard and gazes down at the mishmash floor: each tile different, but united through imperfection. He smiles fondly as he traces the tip of his toe along the jagged grouting. At the orphanage, he had known boys to stake their lives on stamps and sports cards. Worthless, in Norman's opinion. What did such things mean without a wretched past? His unwantables are things of beauty; humble and gracious.

Norman brings the mug of soup to his mouth and takes a tentative slurp, the multiplex looming in his mind. He runs a twiggy finger over a broken hatstand with arms that hang downwards as if finally exhausted from a life of burdens.

Several days later, Norman takes on a solicitor: a man by the name of Anthony Mallow. A man with an enormous waist.

'We'll get you a great deal,' Anthony says, hoisting his trousers over his barrel belly and leaning on the corner of a huge mahogany desk. Norman wonders if Anthony's feet can be classed as unwantables seeing as he must have given them up years ago.

'But I don't want a deal,' Norman says, speaking a little too fast, although he'd practised his speech all the way there – the I'm Not Crazy But I Love My Rambling Manse Speech, which he forgot the moment he saw Anthony's secretary bending over to refill the photocopier: such buttocks!

She comes in just then with a tray of coffee. Norman is horrified by the heat that rushes to his cheeks, and pretends to adjust his shoelaces so that she will not see a grown man blush.

'Thanks, Hattie,' Anthony says and Norman thinks for a hideous moment that he is going to slap her behind, but he doesn't, and Norman watches as she bounces the slightest most wonderful curtsey before gliding from the room, calves and buttocks flexing in perfect synchronicity.

'Perhaps I need to come back,' Norman says, reaching for the jug of cream, which is nothing like his jugs at home: this one has a handle, and actually pours. 'I ought to come back first thing tomorrow . . . I ought to. I ought to come back.'

'Norman, Norman, Norman. Let me do my job.'

'Right. Yes. Of course,' Norman says with a sulk as buttocks and calves dangle precariously in his mind.

The negotiations continue and Norman begins to notice strange feelings, which sashay through him like dancers at a ballroom marathon who refuse to give up. He is waking in the night, calling out for a mother long gone and never known.

One morning, as he sits by the pond with a letter from Anthony in his lap, Norman feels the manse eyeing him with suspicion. There are prickles on the back of his neck, tense spasms shooting up and down his skinny arms, as his brow turns hot and then cold, hot and then cold. 'Dear Norman,' Anthony, or rather, Anthony's secretary, Hattie, has typed in a large Arial font. Despite the conservative lettering, Norman is distracted for a moment by the image of her shapely behind. But then comes the inevitable realization of his unwantability, exposing the futility of such a fantasy, and Norman's reveries pop and fizzle out.

He thinks back to those long afternoons in the orphanage, sitting in his favourite spot: a spacious window seat at the top of the main stairs. The wind was always whistling through the ill-fitting frame and from the great hall below the incessant chorus of giggles was a permanent soundtrack.

Commendable attempts at joy, Norman would think, but flawed by the very fact that such a thing cannot exist in an unwantable.

Each day he would watch another lucky child parading outside the front of the building with his new family; or a baby, oblivious in adoring arms. Couples would come while the children sat in classes drawing or making sums of bananas and apples that often caused Norman's belly to rumble. But it was always the same. No matter how well he combed his hair, no matter how smartly he tucked in his shirt and tried to hide his raggedy sleeves by folding them up to his shoulders, no matter how often he ate his greens and brushed his teeth before bed, no matter how perfectly he behaved, Norman was unable to cross that distant border. From his window seat every afternoon, he watched that painfully exclusive world, praying that one day he too would become wanted.

With a slow shake of the head, he reads on. The letter states that while Anthony is aware of Norman's standpoint, there are some offers one shouldn't refuse (the developers having doubled theirs). The letter also states that Anthony has arranged for A Specialist to come and see the museum.

A Specialist? thinks Norman. A Specialist in what?

In collections, it turns out.

Radcliff Picket is a tall, willowy man; slender enough to buckle on a gusty day. He arrives in a 1964 pale-blue Mustang and, after he climbs out of the car, gives the bonnet a little pat before heading up to the house.

Norman is pouring hot water into a cracked teapot without a lid, rubbing a hand over his stubbled cheek and wondering if he has time to shave before The Specialist arrives.

Apparently not, he thinks as he hears the tired clong of the doorbell, and leaves his steaming, lidless teapot and chugs to the front door.

They shake hands and Norman takes The Specialist's immaculate cashmere coat and lays it over a sculpture of a woman whose luscious curls are chipped and stained, and whose fingers have snapped off, leaving sad stumps. Radcliff clears his throat, bobs on the balls of his feet and commences wandering from room to room. He stops to fondle a paintbrush set rigid with acrylic, and pauses to thumb through a Sherlock Holmes novel, barking a thunderous, 'I see!' when he discovers that the final pages are missing.

Every now and then, he writes in a tiny notebook and hums to himself. Norman bends over and tries to read the exquisite script, but The Specialist starts at the shadow tumbling over him, and takes a small step to the side. Norman is left leaning like a deprived adolescent at the end of a date, who has waited with anticipation for that first kiss, only to be wrenched from his dalliance with optimism by the squeaking of the gate and the girl's footsteps on the garden path and away.

'Seven thousand,' Radcliff announces once he has walked the entire house, including Norman's en-suite bathroom, home to thirteen bars of unwanted soap salvaged from a hotel dumpster, and a neon towel rail Norman acquired at the end of a car-boot sale when a fiercely rotund lady said, 'Do you want this?' to which Norman had only one response.

'Seven thousand what?' Norman asks, straightening his arrangement of Russian dolls, which have lost all hope of coming together with their mismatched tops and bottoms.

'Seven thousand pounds to turn this collection into a collection.'

Norman scratches his tiny nose. 'If it's already a collection, why would it need investment?'

'Ah, yes, I like your logic,' The Specialist says with a light pat where the notebook rests snug in his pocket. 'Indeed, one cannot deny that this is a group of objects intended to be seen, which by its very nature makes it a collection, but there's a difference between an accumulation and an intentional gathering.'

Norman pouts. 'This is intended.'

214

'Come on, it's a heap!'

'Now steady on!' says Norman as he himself grows more tremulous.

The Specialist clears his throat and paces a small circle. 'What I am suggesting is repairs, renewal, restoration.'

Norman ponders these three Rs for a minute, aware of Radcliff's wheezy breathing next to him. 'So you think it needs some work?'

'Absolutely!' Radcliff now comes at him with the smooth, affected honesty of one on the verge of a sale. 'Just think! With themes – each room laid out to display *objets* such as household goods, books and periodicals, textiles, toys – the wistful visitor can wander through their past, even touch the products of their youth and feel, for a moment, that they are a child again.'

'So what you're suggesting is a museum of memories?'

Radcliff screws up his nose. 'We needn't be too hasty with labels here.'

'But you're making themes.'

'Yes, but I'm sticking with the sensible.'

'And I'm not?'

'Let's keep to what we know, shall we? With an affordable investment you could have a collection that is highly organized, carefully catalogued, attractively displayed and –'

'Desirable?' Norman suggests.

Radcliff beams. 'Precisely.'

That night Norman sorts through his latest box of acquisitions: a set of chipped baubles, two torn sieves, a faulty hairdryer that sucks instead of puffs, and a bent trumpet with no more toot. He tries to imagine the sort of collection that Radcliff Picket is talking about and cannot deny the eager tremblings in his chest.

Norman imagines a museum that shines and bulges with pride; a staff of attendants, neat in bottle-green blazers – perhaps berets – opening exhibits, closing exhibits; and customers, actual customers.

The following morning he calls Anthony.

'That offer from the developers,' he says. 'Does it still stand?'

There is a chuckle. 'You met Radcliff then?'

'Oh yes.'

'Pretty impressive, huh?'

'Oh yes.'

'Give me a week and I'll have all the paperwork ready.'

And that's that.

What is Norman thinking when he rests the receiver back in its cradle? He is thinking of his parents (wherever they may be) and how he might make them proud, and he is thinking of all those children at the orphanage; if they could only see him now.

Over the next few days, Radcliff visits intermittently to discuss his plans. 'There will be enough money to buy a far superior property. It's important to consider something with a conservatory where we'll be able to offer the plants some sunlight. Heavens! They may even grow a little colour.'

Norman is becoming overwhelmed. It's the right thing, he keeps telling himself, but the more he does, the more the words lose their meaning.

'What do you think?'

Norman jumps. Radcliff clutches him by the arm, an expectant expression on his face, but Norman has no idea what he has been talking about. 'Oh, yes,' he says, shuffling his feet.

'Just as I thought!' Radcliff says, clapping his hands together. 'Norman, we're going to turn your junk into a collection.'

Junk?

Norman feels his palms grow sticky and flashes appear before his eyes. He turns away and takes a deep breath. He will have to let it pass. After all, the removal men are coming in the morning to transport his collection to Radcliff's warehouse where it will undergo the three Rs.

Later, as each of the men heads to their respective cars, Radcliff to his Mustang and Norman his Reliant Robin, Norman turns to The Specialist and considers him for a moment.

'Radcliff, if I may ask, what do *you* collect?'

Radcliff cracks his knuckles and grins. 'Collectibles.' He then ducks his head, settles into his seat and revs his engine.

Collectibles!

Norman watches the Mustang driving away and seethes. Here is a man who covets the wantable, who hoards only those things designed to be hoarded. He knows *nothing* of the unwanted, the unloved, Norman and his concerns.

Radcliff is the sort of man he has spent his whole life avoiding. Norman kicks at his tyres and faces the darkening day, howling up to the clouds as they hang aloft, oblivious. He has allowed himself to be led by the enemy.

It begins to pour. Norman feels trickles down the back of his neck between his shoulders as he listens to the plunk plunk of the rain on the roof of his car.

When the removal men arrive the following morning, they find Norman sitting on the stairs, two sodden shoes next to him and a pair of damp socks draped over the banister. His greying curls are even frizzier from the rain the night before, and his eyes appear darker than their usual caramel tint.

'Morning,' says one of the men as he pushes open the door and makes out the forlorn form of Norman in the half light.

As they trundle through the dim and dusty rooms, the men glance about aghast at dented top hats, headless toys, stopped clocks, mouldy wedding cakes, used wrapping paper, expired tax discs, incorrectly assembled model airplanes, and eventually mutter a 'What a load of crap.'

As the words are released into the air, Norman sparks and fires up again. He draws away from the men and stretches his arms out wide.

'Stay back,' he says, gritting his teeth and beginning to tremble at the knees. 'Stay back, I tell you.'

The men look at each other and laugh. 'Now, sir, please,' they manage, before Norman is charging towards them and hurling himself through the air, face snarled, a high-pitched scream surging from his lips.

They move to the side, a little over a foot, and watch as Norman lands on a heap of moth-eaten rugs, a cloud of dust rising. They can make out phrases such as 'philistine mongrels', 'mannerless maniacs', 'empty-headed, worthless cretins', while Norman thrashes about as if wrestling a crocodile.

The philistines retreat to the door, each looking at the other for an indication of what to do in this astonishing situation.

'Perhaps you'd like us to come back later,' the taller of the mongrels says eventually, tapping his friend on the arm and signalling a hasty retreat.

'Call us when you're feeling better,' the smaller maniac adds.

Then there is the creak and groan of the front doors, the roar of an engine in the drive, and the cretins are gone. Norman pants and squirms for a few seconds longer and then rolls onto his back, gasping, as silent tears mooch down his face.

'I'm sorry,' he croaks. 'I'm so, so sorry.'

His unwantables lie silent in the morning sun, but he has the strangest sense that they are smiling.

Norman ventures up to the attic and settles himself in a corner. A shard of sunlight is creeping about on his thigh. The manse is silent; a world away from the noise that accompanied his favourite spot in the orphanage.

He remembers a particular afternoon; the smell of cabbage and, beyond that, garlic and onion. He'd been spying on a smart couple climbing into a fancy car with one of the babies. They sped off down the street and Norman watched them go, leaning his head back against the wall, breathing very slow, sad breaths. Sister Mary Clarity was standing at the bottom of the stairs staring up at him. She looked even worse than he felt. Every one of her features hung with the weight of her pity. He stood up and walked down the staircase.

'Oh, Norman,' Sister Mary Clarity said as he drew near. 'Perhaps next time.'

She reached out a hand to him, but he carried on past her into the great hall. Dust-ridden bookshelves towered over him, the top shelf inaccessible to even the tallest of the orphans. Norman stood staring at them for a while as boys and girls scurried past. Finally, he reached up towards a large volume, taken by the colour of its binding – deep burgundy, for valour – but then he paused and glanced behind him. Sister Mary Clarity jerked her head to the side and feigned a sudden interest in the tip of her left shoe.

Norman smiled, pulling the book from the shelf and opening it. 'The Adventures of Sir Lyle Albatross and the Dancing Plum Tree,' he read and by the time he was ensconced in his window seat he was already at the twenty-fifth page, having, little by little, walked the entire length of the orphanage, his eyes darting over words that seemed to tickle and buzz within him.

He devoured the book in what felt like a matter of moments, lost as he was in a world of knights and strange creatures. Then he chose another. And another. After that day, dreary afternoons melted away and the oblivion from which he had seemed to arrive transformed itself into an endless possibility. Norman began to entertain the idea that he was born of greatness, that his life was more than craved hugs, timed showers, a rumbling tummy and sleepless nights.

One night in autumn, Norman lay staring at the peeling walls, his bedclothes too scratchy to provide any semblance of comfort. A few of the orphans were snivelling in their beds as the wind hissed its own misery outside the windows.

'What about a story?' he said, sitting up and trying not to shiver as icy air crept about him. Blank faces took him in and there were nods and shrugs. A few of the children started whispering amongst themselves and Norman waited until everyone was quiet.

'I was born of Travelling Scientists,' he finally announced, standing on his bed, his covers pulled about him, a handkerchief around his head, as though he were a caped and crowned king. His audience marvelled. 'Travelling Scientists?' 'How voluble a title!' 'What an infinite profession!' And when he had their attention, when their eyes were round and their breathing slow, Norman continued.

'They were partners on an expedition to end suffering in the world, to discover a rare plant with healing properties we cannot imagine.'

He paused, allowing this sublime information to sink in, before going on.

'One night, in the humidity of the Ecuadorian rain forest, amid the fruitfulness of the jungle, protocol was abandoned as they merged in an accidental moment of ecstasy.' There were giggles and gasps, but Norman carried on, his story gaining momentum, his voice rising for the climax of the piece.

'For nine months my mother carried me as she worked by my father's side cataloguing flora. And then I was born, and for a blissful week the three of us slept under one tent and I fed off leaves and berries and helped them in their work. But, for the good of the trip, the service of science, mankind and their reputation, I was given up, their professional relationship resumed and countless diseases cured.'

Norman then closed his eyes, allowing himself to fall into this new world as the applause rang out around him. His life meant something. He was mighty.

As he potters in the garden the following morning, Norman feels better than he has in weeks. Finding a rusty pot of black paint, he makes his way to the sign at the front of the museum and begins to cover the gothic lettering. Later, when the paint is dry, he takes out his haphazard collection of stencils: capital Es and curly *L*s, small ᴡs and a missing f, and an ᴍ that doesn't quite go with anything. He finds a pot of white emulsion that has almost, but not quite, set dry and continues.

It is lunchtime when he finishes. As he climbs down from the ladder, which shakes and rattles with every one of his triumphant steps, Norman notices that the postman has been; a letter is sitting out in the sunshine by the mat on his porch. He picks it up and makes his way indoors.

The great hallway is bathed in light, the vast front doors open as wide as they will go. Norman rips open the envelope and pulls out the set of papers from within. They are held together with a shiny paper-clip and, on the top, a compliment slip instructs him to sign the contract and return to the offices of Anthony Mallow.

Norman spends some time studying the documents and then he finds a not-too-bent drawing-pin from the bureau beside the stairs, which sits low on the floor having lost its legs long ago, and adds the contract to his museum, pinning it on the warped noticeboard beneath a cluster of old shopping lists. He stands back and nods to himself before taking a tour of the manse. He meanders through his rooms, breathing in the fusty familiarity of every memory that is embodied here, and ends in the kitchen where he makes a sandwich from leftovers. Sitting down in the huge rocking chair that alas no longer rocks, he munches and hums to himself, a smile playing on his lips as silver particles of dust boogie back and forth around him. Afterwards, he lays the chipped plate on the floor and stares at the crumbs in his lap. These he scrapes into a neat pile and pops into his shirt pocket, tapping the area gently. An image of Radcliff Picket hovers before him, until Norman swipes him away with a flick of his mind. He cups his hands together and closes his eyes. As the sign says, he is 'thE *L*ast o thE uᴍwaᴍtab*L*Es'.

BALCONY VIEW
Laura Williams

Becky is on a balcony, five floors up in a wide block of flats. She sits on a plastic chair, her elbows leaning on the rough wooden bar that runs along the balcony's edge. Her chin rests in her hands and she gazes at the block across the courtyard. It has no balconies, just windows that Becky can barely see into. She counts them, trying to work out how many people are crammed onto this small patch of land. It is starting to get dark and a couple of lights are switched on; a few curtains have been drawn all day. The glare of televisions gives many rooms a blue glow.

Becky stops counting when she hears a faint tapping on the glass door separating the balcony from the flat. She doesn't turn around. A few moments later, the tapping starts again, louder this time. She can just about hear her name being called from inside. She turns to see Vera standing on the other side of the door, opening and closing her mouth, trying to say something, her left hand, holding a cigarette as usual, beckoning Becky inside.

'I can't hear you, Nan,' Becky mouths.

Vera shakes her head, confused, and as Becky turns away, starts to tap on the window again.

'I can't bloody hear you!' Becky shouts.

The tapping stops and Becky looks back towards the door as Vera disappears from view. Becky's limbs feel heavy, unwilling to take her inside. She's been on the balcony for hours, wishing that someone would slice the front off the block opposite so that she could see in clearly. She thinks of the people below her, eating their TV dinners; they probably wouldn't even raise their heads if someone were to jump from the building and sail past their windows.

Vera appears again, carrying a chair that she places next to the door. She hitches up her skirt and slowly lifts each of her swollen legs onto the seat. She opens the small window at the top of the door and puts her face up to it.

'What you doing out there?' she asks.

Becky shrugs and returns her gaze to the block opposite.

'I can't hear you with your back to me, can I?' persists Vera.

'I didn't say anything.'

'Do what? You're gonna have to come inside. I can't hear a bleeding word you're saying.'

Becky waits a few minutes before slowly opening the door and going inside. Vera has moved the chair back to the kitchen table and is sitting on it. A lit cigarette rests in an ashtray, creating a thin wisp of smoke which circles into the old lampshade above the table. Next to the ashtray, there are two large brandy glasses and a bottle of Teacher's whisky.

'You'll join me in a drink, won't you, love?'

Becky shakes her head and sits down in an armchair on the other side of the room, twisting her body away from Vera and towards the balcony. Vera pours herself a large measure and picks up the cigarette.

'What d'you do out there all day?'

Becky has been living in the flat for almost a month. She arrived one evening in June as a month-long heatwave broke and London's streets were washed clean with heavy drops of rain. She was exhausted; her eyes like holes in her face, her head pounding.

She hadn't slept properly for days, lying awake between Stuart's motionless body and the wall, watching the dark-orange urban sky through the window, planning her escape. On the night before she left, she did not allow herself to sleep at all, concentrating on resisting the urge to breathe to the same rhythm as Stuart's snores. She longed to be free of his bed and the sight of his open mouth, the bags already appearing beneath his eyes, the beads of sweat sitting on his upper lip and forehead.

The sky eventually turned apricot. Becky climbed over Stuart and dressed quickly, keeping a close eye on him in case he woke up and wanted an explanation for her departure. She would not have known where to start and could not be sure that the conversation wouldn't end in her pitying his fear of being left alone. But he didn't stir and Becky collected her bag and left the room.

Closing the front door quietly, she was caught in a throng of early-morning commuters dressed in suits and trainers, bounding towards the tube station. She jumped into a hot carriage as the door closed. The man next to her had sweat dripping from his chin. As the tube began to move he held up his face to welcome the slowly circulating air, thick with years of dirt, pollution and exhaled breath. Becky regretted not having had a shower before leaving. She knew that by the time she crossed London she would be conscious of her unwashed armpits and her hair that smelt of Stuart's bed.

She had intended to go to Vera's flat straightaway, on the pretence that she was just checking up on her, as her parents had asked, and then stay for a few nights to figure out her next move. Instead, she put off her journey to Battersea, spending the day in Hyde Park, lying on grass that was brown after a month with no rain.

Later in the morning, the weather broke and the sunbathers ran for shelter. Becky stayed where she was. After a while she could see no one and she felt that the park was her own. Stuart phoned her again and again but she did not answer his calls. He would not have understood pouring rain and an empty park or why she had left to stop herself burning his sofa or smashing his DVDs.

When she arrived at Waterloo station that afternoon, her eyes could focus for only enough time to read the departures board and to locate the crowd of commuters that she was to join on the platform.

In Battersea, the traffic moved slowly and loudly: cyclists, motorbikes, buses, taxis and cars, empty except for their drivers, battled to make it round the sharp bend first.

Becky crossed the road and walked towards an imposing block covered in windows open to the unpredicted downpour. She walked under the railway bridge, past a Christmas tree with branches that had turned a rusty brown in the six months it had lain there. Behind the first block, three more appeared, adorned with satellite dishes and balconies, connected by a labyrinth of brightly coloured walkways.

The streets here were almost empty, commuters from the train long dispersed under the other side of the bridge. Becky entered the second block, brushing past two teenagers sheltering from the rain in the doorway. She took a lift to the third floor, crossed a walkway that stank of decades of urine, and climbed a few flights of stairs. She turned her key in the lock.

Becky hadn't visited the flat since the funeral. She had been meaning to call in as she had promised she would, but she dreaded seeing Vera on her own. She knew now, as she opened the door, that she would not be able to pretend that she was there as the dutiful granddaughter. She walked over the hall's threadbare carpet of brown and orange swirls, running her hands along the textured wallpaper that had once been white, but was now yellow.

'Hello,' she called as she went into the living room.

Vera was asleep, her hand stretched out towards Jimmy's matching, empty, armchair. Becky remembered him sitting there, smoking, watching the snooker on television. He would miss the ashtray as he flicked the end of his cigarette, prompting Vera to vacuum around him, despite his protests about not being able to hear the commentary. 'We'd have a pile of ash to the ceiling if I didn't,' she'd say.

Not wishing to wake Vera, Becky opened the door to the balcony and went outside. It had stopped raining and people were appearing in the courtyard below. Becky watched a man as he walked past. He looked out of place in his shirt and tie, his jacket slung over his shoulder. She heard his smart city shoes against the paving slabs.

Back inside, she returned to Jimmy's armchair. The flat was as it had been for as long as she could recall: the carriage clock was still on the sideboard, the coffee table was still stained with rings from years of hot mugs. Radio 2 was still almost inaudible in the background.

Vera woke up. 'That you, Jim?'

'Nan, it's me. Becky.'

'Oh, Bec. That you? Nice of you to come and see your old nan.'

'Sorry it's been a while.'

'Has it, dear? Now you sit there. I'll put the kettle on. Make you a sandwich.'

Becky watched Vera move slowly to the kitchen. She was humming along to the radio. 'Your grandad always loved a bit of Louis Armstrong. We should have played this at his funeral. He'd have liked that.'

She came back a few minutes later with a cup of tea and a thickly sliced cheese and tomato sandwich. They sat at the table, Vera smoking, Becky eating.

'Don't eat what you don't want,' Vera said. This had been the mantra of Becky's childhood visits to Vera and Jimmy's, where she'd been allowed to gorge on the white bread and rich tea biscuits that her parents never bought.

While Becky ate, Vera talked. 'I got a postcard from your mum and dad. Spain would be too hot for me this time of year. Your grandad and I would always go a bit later. See that photo there' – Vera waved her cigarette at a photograph on the sideboard of her and Jimmy sitting on a hotel balcony, their heads thrown back, laughing – 'that was the only time he got me out on that balcony. Eighth floor we was. I thought it was bad being on the fifth. Cor, look at me. I was brown as a berry.'

That evening, Becky went to bed in the spare room. Vera tucked her in tightly under sheets and blankets, then sat on the edge of the bed and kissed her on her forehead. 'Sleep tight.'

'Thanks, Nan.'

Vera didn't get up. 'You staying a while, are you?'

Becky nodded, unable to articulate the reasons that she had been rehearsing in her head for so many weeks. Vera patted her hand and got up slowly. She switched off the light at the door. 'D'you want poached eggs in the morning?'

The poached eggs were waiting for Becky when she got up. Vera, wearing a dressing gown with stretched pockets filled with used tissues and empty cigarette packets, didn't eat.

'You can stay as long as you like. Nice for me to have someone to look after.'

'You don't have to look after me.' Becky cut into one of the eggs and the yolk spread across the plate.

'It's what I'm good at.'

Becky wiped up the yolk with a piece of toast and Vera lit a cigarette. After Becky had finished eating, Vera took her plate.

'Let me do that, Nan. You don't have to wait on me. Let me do the washing up.'

Vera waved her away. 'I'll leave it for now. Give me something to do later.'

Becky looked at Vera standing in the doorway to the kitchen but had to turn away quickly to stop herself from crying. Vera was no longer brown as a berry and no longer threw her head back in laughter. She saved the washing up as something to get her through the day.

Vera didn't get started on the dishes until late that evening. She told Becky about the latest news of her cousins, their failed relationships and ugly children. 'Of course, it runs in the blood to go after bad men.'

'What d'you mean?'

'The women in our family always go for the lousy ones.' Vera laughed.

'What about Grandad, though?'

'He was different, Jimmy. A full stop of a man. Tiny. It made him different. Not as bolshy as the others. But the rest of them weren't so lucky. Lillian's husband was a drinker. Died young, liver the size of a truck. She was heartbroken. And broke.'

'Maybe she loved him.'

'She just liked the drama.'

Becky drank her tea.

'So you not going back to him, then?' Vera asked.

Becky shook her head.

Within a few days, London's skies were bright blue again. Becky ventured out just a couple of times during her first week in the flat: to the chip shop, with its extensive menu, although everything was off except fried chicken and pukka pies.

Stuart's calls became less frequent and Becky stopped going over in her head what she would say to him if she were to answer.

The following week, she felt no need to leave the flat at all. But each morning Vera would give her five pounds. 'Get me fags and the *Mail*, Bec, love.'

Whenever she returned to the flat, Vera would be sitting in her chair at the table, smoking and doing the crossword from the previous day's paper. In the evenings, Becky spent more and more time on the balcony, getting away from the halo of smoke that followed Vera around.

Once, Becky returned to find Vera standing on tiptoes on a chair, dusting ornaments on the top shelf of a cabinet. The radio was turned up and Ella Fitzgerald's voice filled the flat.

'Is that you, Jim?' Vera called over the music.

'No. It's me, Nan.'

Vera turned to see Becky standing in the doorway, holding out the newspaper and the cigarettes. She screamed.

'Nan. Nan. It's me. Becky.'

'Help me down. Help me down.'

Becky rushed over to the cabinet and held out her arm, which Vera grabbed with both hands, placing all of her weight on it as she manoeuvred herself off the chair. They stood face to face, the light catching the thick layer of foundation on Vera's wrinkled skin. Vera's eyes were full of tears but she fought them back and went over to the sideboard, got a couple of glasses out and poured large measures of Scotch into each. She knocked one back and gave the other to Becky.

'I've lived here so long. We got this flat, me and Jimmy, when it was just the two of us again. We were so proud. I remember saving up for that settee. I know it's only a settee. I don't even sit on it much.' Vera picked up the bottle again. 'Let's have another.'

Becky emptied her glass for Vera to fill. 'Stuart never gets off his sofa.'

'It always sounded like he had his limits, that one. Even though your mum liked him.'

'I don't know what to do, Nan.'

'At least you've got me. Your old nan. Life's not so bad, you know. You wanna spread your wings a bit. I've always said that about you.'

Becky drank her second drink. It burnt the back of her throat.

The two women sit now in the living room. Vera is on her third Scotch and Becky still hasn't answered her question.

'I never wanted a balcony. Just a flat. "Let's get a balcony with a view over London," Jim said. Jim always loved a view. "Look at the view, look at the view!" he'd say. But I didn't want to look outside. I only wanted to look at him. I could have looked at him all day. In the mornings before I put on my glasses I think that I can catch a glimpse of him out there on the balcony. Looking at the bleeding view. And we ain't even high up enough for a proper one. Can't see much.' Vera lights another cigarette. 'What do you look at? All that time you spend out there. What you looking for?'

'I count the windows, sometimes.'

'Is that all?'

'And watch people.'

'You'd be better off switching on the telly.'

'Come and see for yourself.' Becky opens the door to the balcony and they hear the distant sound of cars speeding along the main road.

'I can't go out there.'

Becky goes over to Vera and offers her arm.

'Come on, Nan. You can hold on to me.'

She takes Becky's arm and, as they walk across the room, Becky notices how frail she is.

It is late evening now and most windows on the surrounding blocks are lit. The man on the adjacent balcony has his door open and they can hear canned laughter from his television. Still linking arms, Becky and Vera peer over the edge of their balcony.

'It's so high up.'

'Not high enough.'

'So how many windows are there?'

'I lost count.'

Vera laughs. They stand in silence for a while.

'Not high enough for what?'

Becky stares up at the sky, which has reached the limits of its darkness and glows with light pollution.

'For something to really look at,' she replies.

Vera squeezes Becky's arm.

'Let's count, shall we?'

GOOD PEOPLE
David Foster Wallace

They were up on a picnic table at that park by the lake, by the edge of the lake, with part of a downed tree in the shallows half hidden by the bank. Lane A. Dean, Jr., and his girlfriend, both in bluejeans and button-up shirts. They sat up on the table's top portion and had their shoes on the bench part that people sat on to picnic or fellowship together in carefree times. They'd gone to different high schools but the same junior college, where they had met in campus ministries. It was springtime, and the park's grass was very green and the air suffused with honeysuckle and lilacs both, which was almost too much. There were bees, and the angle of the sun made the water of the shallows look dark. There had been more storms that week, with some downed trees and the sound of chainsaws all up and down his parents' street. Their postures on the picnic table were both the same forward kind with their shoulders rounded and elbows on their knees. In this position the girl rocked slightly and once put her face in her hands, but she was not crying. Lane was very still and immobile and looking past the bank at the downed tree in the shallows and its ball of exposed roots going all directions and the tree's cloud of branches all half in the water. The only other individual nearby was a dozen spaced tables away, by himself, standing upright. Looking at the torn-up hole in the ground there where the tree had gone over. It was still early yet and all the shadows wheeling right and shortening. The girl wore a thin old checked cotton shirt with pearl-colored

229

snaps with the long sleeves down and always smelled very good and clean, like someone you could trust and care about even if you weren't in love. Lane Dean had liked the smell of her right away. His mother called her *down to earth* and liked her, thought she was good people, you could tell – she made this evident in little ways. The shallows lapped from different directions at the tree as if almost teething on it. Sometimes when alone and thinking or struggling to turn a matter over to Jesus Christ in prayer, he would find himself putting his fist in his palm and turning it slightly as if still playing and pounding his glove to stay sharp and alert in center. He did not do this now; it would be cruel and indecent to do this now. The older individual stood beside his picnic table – he was at it but not sitting – and looked also out of place in a suit coat or jacket and the kind of men's hat Lane's grandfather wore in photos as a young insurance man. He appeared to be looking across the lake. If he moved, Lane didn't see it. He looked more like a picture than a man. There were not any ducks in view.

One thing Lane Dean did was reassure her again that he'd go with her and be there with her. It was one of the few safe or decent things he could really say. The second time he said it again now she shook her head and laughed in an unhappy way that was more just air out her nose. Her real laugh was different. Where he'd be was the waiting room, she said. That he'd be thinking about her and feeling bad for her, she knew, but he couldn't be in there with her. This was so obviously true that he felt like a ninny that he'd kept on about it and now knew what she had thought every time he went and said it – it hadn't brought her comfort or eased the burden at all. The worse he felt, the stiller he sat. The whole thing felt balanced on a knife or wire; if he moved to put his arm up or touch her the whole thing could tip over. He hated himself for sitting so frozen. He could almost visualize himself tiptoeing past something explosive. A big stupid-looking tiptoe, like in a cartoon. The whole last black week had been this way and it was wrong. He knew it was wrong, knew something was required of him that was not this terrible frozen care and caution, but he pretended to himself he did not know what it was that was required. He pretended it had no name. He pretended that not saying aloud what he knew to be right and true was for her sake, was for the sake of her needs and feelings. He also worked dock and routing at UPS, on top of school, but had traded to get the day off after they'd decided together. Two days before, he had awakened very early and tried to pray but could not. He was freezing more and more solid, he felt like, but he had not thought of his father or the blank frozenness of his father, even in church, which had once filled him with such pity. This was the truth. Lane Dean, Jr., felt sun on one arm as he pictured in his mind an image of himself on a train, waving mechanically to something that got smaller and smaller as the train pulled away. His father and his mother's father had the same birthday, a Cancer. Sheri's hair was colored an almost corn blond, very clean, the skin through her central part pink in the sunlight. They'd sat here long enough that only their right side was shaded now. He could look at her head, but not at her. Different parts of him felt unconnected to each other. She was smarter than him and they both knew it. It wasn't just school – Lane Dean was in accounting and business and did all right; he was hanging in there. She was a year older, twenty, but it was also more – she had always seemed to Lane to be on good terms with her life in a way that age could not account for. His mother had put it that she *knew what it is she wanted*, which was nursing and not an easy program at Peoria Junior College, and plus she worked hostessing at the Embers and had bought her own car. She was serious in a way Lane liked. She had a cousin that died when she was thirteen, fourteen, that she'd loved and been close with. She only talked about it that once. He liked her smell and her downy arms and the way she exclaimed when something made her laugh. He had liked just being with her and talking to her. She was serious in her faith and values in a way that Lane had liked and now, sitting here with her on the table, found himself afraid of. This was an awful thing. He was starting to believe that he might not be serious in his faith. He might be somewhat of a hypocrite, like the Assyrians in Isaiah, which would be a far graver sin than the appointment – he had decided he believed this. He was desperate to be good people, to still be able to feel he was good. He rarely before now had thought of damnation and Hell – that part of it didn't speak to his spirit – and in worship services he more just tuned himself out and tolerated Hell when it came up, the same way you tolerate the job you've got to have to save up for what it is you want. Her tennis shoes had little things doodled on them from sitting in her class lectures. She stayed looking down like that. Little notes or reading assignments in Bic in her neat round hand on the rubber elements around the sneaker's rim. Lane A. Dean, looking now at her inclined head's side's barrettes in the shape of blue ladybugs. The appointment was for afternoon, but when the doorbell had rung so early and his mother'd called to him up the stairs, he had known, and a terrible kind of blankness had commenced falling through him.

He told her that he did not know what to do. That he knew if he was the salesman of it and forced it upon her that was awful and wrong. But he was trying to understand – they'd prayed on it and talked it through from every different angle. Lane said how sorry she knew he was, and that if he was wrong in believing they'd truly decided together when they decided to make the appointment she should please tell him, because he thought he knew how she must have felt as it got closer and closer and how she must be so scared, but that what he couldn't tell was if it was more than that. He was totally still except for moving his mouth, it felt like. She did not reply. That if they needed to pray on it more and talk it through, then he was here, he was ready, he said. The appointment could get moved back; if she just said the word they could call and push it back to take more time to be sure in the decision. It was still so early in it – they both knew that, he said. This was true, that he felt this way, and yet he also knew he was also trying to say things that would get her to open up and say enough back that he could see her and read her heart and know what to say to get her to go through with it. He knew this without admitting to himself that this was what he wanted, for it would make him a hypocrite and liar. He knew, in some locked-up little part of him, why it was that he'd gone to no one to open up and seek their life counsel, not Pastor Steve or the prayer partners at campus ministries, not his UPS friends or the spiritual counselling available through his parents' old church. But he did not know why Sheri herself had not gone to Pastor Steve – he could not read her heart. She was blank and hidden. He so fervently wished it never happened. He felt like he knew now why it was a true sin and not just a leftover rule from past society. He felt like he had been brought low by it and humbled and now did believe that the rules were there for a reason. That the rules were concerned with him personally, as an individual. He promised God he had learned his lesson. But what if that, too, was a hollow promise, from a hypocrite who repented only after, who promised submission but really only wanted a reprieve? He might not even know his own heart or be able to read and know himself. He kept thinking also of 1 Timothy and the hypocrite therein who *disputeth over words*. He felt a terrible inner resistance but could not feel what it was that it resisted. This was the truth. All the different angles and ways they had come at the decision together did not ever include it – the word – for had he once said it, avowed that he did love her, loved Sheri Fisher, then it all would have been transformed. It would not be a different stance or angle, but a difference in the very thing they were praying and deciding on together. Sometimes they had prayed together over the phone, in a kind of half code in case anybody accidentally picked up the extension. She continued to sit as if thinking, in the pose of thinking, like that one statue. They were right up next to each other on the table. He was looking over past her at the tree in the water. But he could not say he did: it was not true.

But neither did he ever open up and tell her straight out he did not love her. This might be his *lie by omission*. This might be the frozen resistance – were he to look right at her and tell her he didn't, she would keep the appointment and go. He knew this. Something in him, though, some terrible weakness or lack of values, could not tell her. It felt like a muscle he did not have. He didn't know why; he just could not do it, or even pray to do it. She believed he was good, serious in his values. Part of him seemed willing to more or less just about lie to someone with that kind of faith and trust, and what did that make him? How could such a type of individual even pray? What it really felt like was a taste of the reality of what might be meant by Hell. Lane Dean had never believed in Hell as a lake of fire or a loving God consigning folks to a burning lake of fire – he knew in his heart this was not true. What he believed in was a living God of compassion and love and the possibility of a personal relationship with Jesus Christ through whom this love was enacted in human time. But sitting here beside this girl as unknown to him now as outer space, waiting for whatever she might say to unfreeze him, now he felt like he could see the edge or outline of what a real vision of Hell might be. It was of two great and terrible armies within himself, opposed and facing each other, silent. There would be battle but no victor. Or never a battle – the armies would stay like that, motionless, looking across at each other, and seeing therein something so different and alien from themselves that they could not understand, could not hear each other's speech as even words or read anything from what their face looked like, frozen like that, opposed and uncomprehending, for all human time. Two-hearted, a hypocrite to yourself either way.

When he moved his head, a part of the lake further out flashed with sun – the water up close wasn't black now, and you could see into the shallows and see that all the water was moving but gently, this way and that – and in this same way he besought to return to himself as Sheri moved her leg and started to turn beside him. He could see the man in the suit and gray hat standing motionless now at the lake's rim, holding something under one arm and looking across at the opposite side where a row of little forms on camp chairs sat in a way that meant they had lines in the water for crappie – which mostly only your blacks from the East Side ever did – and the little white shape at the row's end a Styrofoam creel. In his moment or time at the lake now just to come, Lane Dean first felt he could take this all in whole: everything seemed distinctly lit, for the circle of the pin oak's shade had rotated off all the way, and they sat now in sun with their shadow a two-headed thing in the grass before them. He was looking or gazing again at where the downed tree's branches seemed to all bend so sharply just under the shallows' surface when he was given to know that through all this frozen silence he'd despised he had, in truth, been praying, or some little part of his heart he could not hear had, for he was answered now with a type of vision, what he would later call within his own mind a vision or *moment of grace*. He was not a hypocrite, just broken and split off like all men. Later on, he believed that what happened was he'd had a moment of almost seeing them both as Jesus saw them – as blind but groping, wanting to please God despite their inborn fallen nature. For in that same given moment he saw, quick as light, into Sheri's heart, and was made to know what would occur here as she finished turning to him and the man in the hat watched the fishing and the downed elm shed cells into the water. This down-to-earth girl that smelled good and wanted to be a nurse would take and hold one of his hands in both of hers to unfreeze him and make him look at her, and she would say that she cannot do it. That she is sorry she did not know this sooner, that she hadn't meant to lie – she agreed because she'd wanted to believe that she could, but she cannot. That she will carry this and have it; she has to. With her gaze clear and steady. That all night last night she prayed and searched inside herself and decided this is what love commands of her. That Lane should please please sweetie let her finish. That listen – this is her own decision and obliges him to nothing. That she knows he does not love her, not that way, has known it all this time, and that it's all right. That it is as it is and it's all right. She will carry this, and have it, and love it and make no claim on Lane except his good wishes and respecting what she has to do. That she releases him, all claim, and hopes he finishes up at P.J.C. and does so good in his life and has all joy and good things. Her voice will be clear and steady, and she will be lying, for Lane has been given to read her heart. To see through her. One of the opposite side's blacks raises his arm in what may be greeting, or waving off a bee. There is a mower cutting grass someplace off behind them. It will be a terrible, last-ditch gamble born out of the desperation in Sheri Fisher's soul, the knowledge that she can neither do this thing today nor carry a child alone and shame her family. Her values blocked the way either way, Lane could see, and she has no other options or choice – this lie is not a sin. Galatians 4:16, *Have I then become your enemy?* She is gambling that he is good. There on the table, neither frozen nor yet moving, Lane Dean, Jr., sees all this, and is moved with pity, and also with something more, something without any name he knows, that is given to him in the form of a question that never once in all the long week's thinking and division had even so much as occurred – why is he so sure he doesn't love her? Why is one kind of love any different? What if he has no earthly idea what love is? What would even Jesus do? For it was just now he felt her two small strong soft hands on his, to turn him. What if he was just afraid, if the truth was no more than this, and if what to pray for was not even love but simple courage, to meet both her eyes as she says it and trust his heart?

This story originally appeared in the US in *The New Yorker* (February 5, 2007)

WHEN YOUR MOTHER DIES
Paul Ryan

When your mother dies, you think it will be announced on the ten o'clock news. You expect the town where she has lived for more than forty years to miss a beat. But when she dies it is a blank Wednesday with a light, grizzly rain. Outside, bin men, commuters, school children and pensioners come and go like breaths.

When your mother dies, your father meets you at the door, thinking you already know.

'Wasn't it sudden, Sean?' he says. 'Wasn't it?' He has always been like this. Your mother said he would ambush her with news, usually bad, when she came in from shopping. She said: 'He won't even let you get your coat off before he starts giving out.'

No one knows what to do. Your sisters cry like their tears will never stop. One brother feels tears in his eyes and leaves the room. Another hunts in old albums for photos of the two of them together, which he collects in little heaps.

When she dies you gather in the room and kneel while a priest tells you what your mother was like. A sickness gnaws at the centre of your stomach.

She lies, a statue of your mother, on the pink flowered bedspread on the bed, which someone has made. One sister scolds her gently, 'Oh, Mum,' in a mouthful of tears. Another kisses her forehead and says she's cold. But you don't touch her. You are afraid of the yellowness of her skin.

236

Three days before, you sat next to her on the edge of this same bed with your arm curled round her, barely touching, a gesture she might not have allowed had she been stronger. 'I love you, Sean,' she said, the first time you remember her saying this. Then she added, in chronological order, 'And Joan and Mary and Paul and Margaret and Philip,' and fell against you in affection or fatigue.

Then she was paper, now she has turned to stone. The priest asks you all to say the rosary. You remember how they made you do this when you were children. In front of the picture of the Sacred Heart, in the tiny living room between the settee and the two armchairs, when you knew there was something good on TV. Your mother used to say, 'The family that prays together stays together,' but you can't remember the sound of her saying it.

When your mother dies, the funeral directors arrive and your father apologizes for keeping them waiting. There are four of them and the man at the front says: 'That's quite all right, sir. No problem at all,' and touches your father lightly on the forearm. The four remain in the hall, their heads bowing slightly and briefly every time one member of the family or another moves from room to room.

Outside, a car horn sounds. The hearse is blocking the road. A woman shouts: 'It ain't my fault. I've still got my bloody business to run.'

One of your uncles, Niall, goes out to talk to the men in the hall. 'She was a lovely woman. She was my sister, you know.' He has always loved to be at the centre of things. He has a word for everyone who passes in and out of your mother's room. They want to make the most of their last minutes with her, but don't know what to say or do.

Your father comes out and with an apologetic air says, 'Whenever you're ready now, thank you very much.'

Uncle Niall says, 'I'll leave you boys to it.'

When your mother dies, someone makes a show of themselves at the wake by carrying on like it was their wife who has died. There is a free bar to a limit, which quickly runs out. Cousins are caught between grief and reunion. 'These days we only meet at funerals,' one tells you. People you have seen in the street all your life and never spoken to come up, one after the other, and say, 'Sorry for your trouble,' and shake your hand. When you were a child you used to imagine what it would be like if one of your parents died. You imagined being brave.

You go back to the house with your father, the last pair to arrive. As soon as you open the door you hear voices from the living room and his face floods with anger. In his eyes there is a wild look you know too well. 'What did they want to come back here for? Did you invite them?' He marches out round the back of the house toward the garden. You know they must have heard what he was saying.

Your two aunts and uncles are on the easy chairs; your brothers and sisters have brought in kitchen chairs for themselves. Conversation stops when you walk in.

'Everything all right?' says Uncle Niall.

'Where's your father?' says his wife, Aunt Kathleen.

As she speaks, you see him appear from round the side of the house and go to the washing line. You all turn and watch him through the big, deep, bay window.

'I suppose he wants to bring them in, while there's a chance,' says Uncle John, who always gives people the benefit of the doubt.

You all watch your father move along the line of washing, which includes one of your mother's skirts.

'He was always a hard worker, your father,' says John. 'It'll help him to keep busy.'

'That's right,' says his wife, Helen.

'Even so,' says Aunt Kathleen, 'wouldn't you think today, anyway, he might be a bit more . . . natural?'

He makes an art out of unpegging the clothes. His big hands reach up and while his left rests on the line, the other releases the pressure from a peg as delicately as if he were picking strawberries. You watch him put a shirt, a pair of sheets, socks, into a basket. Gingerly, he touches the skirt and leaves it sobbing on the line.

When your mother dies, you and your brothers and sisters all go into the kitchen to boil the kettle, get out the best cups and saucers and put ham sandwiches, tomatoes and sponge cake onto plates, though it is little more than an hour since you have eaten. Through the serving hatch you hear Aunt Kathleen: 'Isn't he fierce odd?' Your father.

Your sisters hand round the sandwiches, which are accepted with reluctance: 'You're too good.' 'I couldn't eat another thing.'

You take your father out a cup of tea. The damp grass licks at the hem of his trousers. He takes the cup and asks, 'Are they still in there?' as if hours have already passed. He is facing away from the house toward the neighbour's garden.

'Is he coming in?' says Aunt Kathleen again. You make an excuse and she says, 'I don't mind but isn't it unnatural?' and laughs quickly.

'It'll be hard for him now, anyway,' says John, resting his cup and saucer awkwardly on his knee and looking out into the garden for confirmation. 'What'll he do?'

'It'll be hard on all of you,' says Aunt Kathleen.

The afternoon drags on. They ask you about jobs that you haven't had for years, a girl you used to know and whether there is any sign of children yet. There are stories about how your mother despaired of you when you were at college and arrived home with bags full of damp washing, how you would never keep your room tidy.

Aunt Kathleen says, 'You'll have to look after yourselves now,' even though half of you are already married.

You are aware, all the time, of your father outside. Not once does he even glance into the living room though he is barely a few paces from the window.

There is cake, more tea, any excuse for movement, and a fuss over the smallest thing. Everyone offers to help.

Outside a neighbour comes up and stops to talk to your father and shakes his hand.

You go out to him again, with cake.

He says: 'Are they ever going to leave us in peace? Who invited them anyway, that's what I want to know.' When you don't answer he says, 'It'll be the last time, that's for sure.'

You say nothing; you know that in this mood, there is nothing you can say. 'Well, let that be the end of it anyway,' he says.

Your uncles and aunts are first to go. They leave in a flurry, glad to be busy at last. There is a panic over coats, someone has to go to the loo at the last minute, and there is a lot of looking at watches. You all know they have plenty of time.

'Look after yourselves,' says Aunt Kathleen. She glances out into the garden.

John says: 'We'll see you again. Tell your father I'll be in to see him.'

Helen says: 'Your poor mother, she was always proud of you.'

Your Uncle Niall shakes you all by the hand in turn.

After they've gone, you open the side window onto the garden. Your sisters' husbands, who have been up the road in the pub, arrive to collect them. The sisters go out into the garden together, with their husbands trailing behind.

The eldest, his favourite, goes up to him first. 'We're going now, Dad. Take care of yourself. I'll come round next week.'

The second, who has never been so confident of his affection, says: 'I'll see you, then, Dad. The Mastersons, the Mordeys and the Reardons all said they'd be in to see you.'

'They needn't bother,' he says, and she knows she has said the wrong thing.

The youngest, the most confident and the most like him, hugs him and they leave.

Your brothers wait a while, wanting to turn on the TV but not sure if it is appropriate.

'I suppose we'd better head,' says the eldest. 'Will you be all right?' They go out into the garden to say their goodbyes, together. They stand a little distance from him and do not hug him or shake his hand.

Over the next few weeks, neighbours, your mother's friends, will come in to see your father in the afternoons. They will arrive awkwardly with offerings of cake or bread and they won't stay long. The only conversation will be your mother. They will mean to come again, but never will. Instead they will stop to speak when they see him in the street.

When your mother dies, the house empties eventually. When it is quiet again, you go up to your room. Later, your father comes inside and you hear the sound of him downstairs shuffling from room to room, checking they're gone. His footsteps end in the living room. You imagine him sitting in the armchair where he has always sat. The TV will stay turned off because he has never learned to work the remote. The plates of unfinished sandwiches and cake will still be on the table. You think of going down, but you turn the radio on in your room, quietly, under the duvet, so he won't hear.

THE SECOND CHANCE
Jill McGivering

n eleven years, this was the first time Raj had been summoned to the
Governor's office. Gupta-ji, the warder, didn't explain. He simply
marched him through the labyrinth of cell blocks, past the prison gardens
and into the hushed order of the Governor's compound.

Inside, Raj fixed his eyes on the carpet beneath his feet, a dazzling
confusion of red, white and golden swirls. A plate, discarded, lay at its edge,
littered with scraps of pakora. Vegetable pakoras, thought Raj. From the
batch he'd made fresh that morning. A good batch.

'Excellent news.' The Governor's booming voice made him tremble.
'The Gods be praised!'

Raj kept his eyes on the carpet, his head bowed respectfully. He could
hear the rustle of papers.

'Some fellow,' said the Governor, 'in Mumbai. Just convicted. Has
confessed to another murder, long ago. Yours.'

Raj heard the cardboard slap of one file falling onto another.

'So,' said the Governor. 'Over! All those hearings. Adjournments. Those
years of waiting. Long years, I know. How do you people stand it?' He
paused dramatically. 'You hear me? You're free to go.'

Raj was still dazed an hour later when Gupta-ji came to retrieve him from
the communal cell. Raj gathered together his small bundle of paintings, his

241

bedroll and his tin cup. He looked round for the last time at the pitted cement floor and out through the metal bars to the small exercise yard. It was late morning. The cells were empty, the prisoners hard at work in the laundry, kitchens and workshops. Overhead the clouds were dark with impending monsoon rain.

In the prison store, he was handed a faded cardboard box, tagged with his name and number.

'Rahul L. Raj, is it? Very fancy!' Gupta-ji hung over his shoulder, reading the label, then peering inside as Raj took off the lid. 'These aren't much use, are they? What a baby you were!'

The rags smelt dank. Raj could see they were threadbare and, Gupta-ji was right, absurdly small. He tried to remember the fifteen-year-old boy who'd worn them, picked up by police on the long hot walk home from the paddy fields. He let the box sag in his hands.

Gupta-ji was stroking his long moustache.

''Spect you could keep those for now,' he said, prodding at Raj's prison-issue clothes with his *lathi*. He nodded across at the store-wallah whose pen was poised over a yellowing ledger, neatly ruled into columns. 'Write: "Prisoner without clothing". Burn these.'

The store-wallah counted into Raj's hand five hundred rupees in torn notes, shiny with grease.

'Two of you out together,' said Gupta-ji as he locked and unlocked their way through the series of barriers before the outer wall. 'Manja as well. You know Manja?' He gave Raj a pinch as he pressed him through the small metal grille set in the final gate and added in a low voice: 'Mind him. He's trouble.'

Raj heard the grille clang shut at his back. He looked about him. The dirt road was almost deserted, just a straggle of rickshaw-wallahs dozing in the shade; a small boy, ragged, poking in the dust with a stick. Raj sank to his haunches. The air was thick with coming rain. When the clouds burst, he thought, then where would he shelter?

Manja was a thick-set man, a bully in the cells, quick tempered and vicious. Raj was afraid of him. But when he emerged a moment later through the same gate, he smiled and seized Raj's shoulder.

'*Namaste*, painting boy,' he said. 'You got rupees? *Cheliye!* Let's go!' His strong hand encircled Raj's arm and pulled him to his feet. He dragged him across the road where he kicked awake a rickshaw-wallah. 'Hey, you son of a whore! Get some work done!'

He threw back his head and laughed as the rickshaw-wallah, a thin, frightened man, scrambled to his feet. Raj found himself bundled into the back of the rickshaw. The first plump drops of rain struck his nose and cheeks.

'Painting boy,' said Manja, as the rickshaw-wallah struggled into his seat and started to pedal, 'time to make a man out of you. If that's possible!'

By the time they entered the town, the rain was falling in dirty brown sheets, beating down on the canopy stretched over their heads. The straining back of the rickshaw-wallah was sodden, a stream of water pouring down his sides. Raj shrank back against the seat. Manja had kept up a hearty monologue all the way, boasting about the beer he'd drink, the fine paan he'd chew, the fancy girls he'd lay. Raj barely listened. After the long years shut inside the prison, his senses were overwhelmed, his nerves taut. He blinked and shook his head, frightened of drowning in the torrent of sounds, smells and sights. They rose like familiar ghosts. A trotting, sniffing dog, its ears pert, tail jaunty. A chai-wallah, a scrap of a boy, dodging through the rain as drops splashed into his glasses of milky sugary tea. The modesty of a young girl, her eyes lowered, hugging the side of the road, her yellow salwar kameez clinging, wet, to her curves. Her hair, a rope of black, swung back and forth across her back.

But the changes! Raj stared. Everything looked so bright, so vivid after the dull greys of prison, even through a curtain of rain. Glossy painted signs and brash hoardings advertising items he'd never seen before. Typewriters with screens like televisions, telephones without wires, pies called pizza and fat meat sandwiches, adverts ten feet tall showing sensual young women, stylishly dressed like Westerners, in tight jeans, crisp shirts.

The rickshaw-wallah drew to a halt in a side-street, at the mouth of a gloomy alley.

'Very good choice, ji,' he said. 'Good beer here. Pukkah food. That's forty rupees, ji.'

'Forty!' Manja pulled him from his seat, slung him against the wall. Raj cringed. He heard the crack of the man's head against the crumbling brick.

'No, sir.' The man was stammering, struggling for breath. 'Nothing, sir! Please!' When Manja dropped him, he sank to his knees on the wet ground and put his palms together in a pleading *namaste*. 'Please!' he said again. Raj could see him trembling. 'I beg of you!'

Manja turned back to Raj. 'You!' he said. 'Come! We've got beer to drink.'

The alley was narrow. It stank of sewage and rotting fruit. Raj splashed through channels of water, slippery with rubbish. He longed to hide, to curl himself inside a dark dry hole and close his eyes. But where did he have to go? Already Manja was prodding him on, then grasped his wrist as he banged on a splintering door. A wizened face peered through the crack. Raj saw the dark eyes look past him to Manja and stretch in surprise.

'Manja-saab!' The voice was croaky. 'So long time! Come, come!'

Manja pushed his way inside, dragging Raj after him. 'Stupid as ever, Baba,' he said. 'Don't stand gawping. Fetch beer. Bottled beer, none of your country-made gut-rot. And good paan.'

The old man bowed, bolted the door closed and ducked to the side through a curtained doorway. They were left standing alone in a small covered courtyard. Raj let his eyes adjust to the dim light. A series of archways, roughly veiled with cloth, gave onto the cobbles. Ahead, a stone staircase led up to the open landing of a second storey. He smelt cooking rice, mingled with the rich scent of daal, underpinned by the stench of urine.

'Your home, ji?' he asked.

Manja laughed. 'Home? I wish! You never seen a place like this, have you, painting boy?' He hit him so hard on the back that Raj tottered. 'I'll gift it you,' Manja went on. 'Wash away those nancy prison boys. Come!'

He pushed aside the rag of curtain screening one of the archways. Inside, lit by a triangle of weak light, Raj saw a row of girls' faces turn towards them, thickly painted, dull and uninterested.

The beer was already befuddling him. He'd barely taken alcohol before. It tasted of the village, of his boyhood. He thought of his father, tipsy at weddings, singing raucous Hindi songs while his mother, shamed, looked on. The light at the square of window was mellow with rain and gathering dusk.

So this is what I waited for, Raj was thinking. All those years. He imagined his cell-mates, setting out their bedrolls, scratching, coughing, farting, lying side by side on the concrete floor. I should be happy, he thought. They're picturing me, here on the outside. They're longing to be me.

But instead his head was swimming, his stomach tight. He sat in silence, alone, too afraid to get up and leave this small cell-like room to which Manja had delivered him. I have nowhere to go, he thought. Not one person in this vast noisy land of India, my own homeland, who would welcome me gladly.

He could hear the rain pounding outside and, from the alley, the shouts of men brawling, the sing-song cries of hawkers as they paced to and fro, selling paan, fried snacks, toddy, chai. The loneliness of this world of outside was overwhelming. He hid his face in the spread of his hands.

'Are you ill?' Her voice was a whisper. 'You're very pale.'

He looked through the bars of his fingers. The girl in the doorway was thin and very young. Her hair, a black waterfall, fell loose over her shoulders. A gold stud shone in her nostril. Her face was rouged and powdered. Such a delicate child shouldn't be painted, thought Raj. He kept his hands to his face, peeping out shyly. She took a hesitant step towards him, stopped. Her eyes, deep brown, framed by such long eyelashes, so beautiful. He gasped. Now he daren't move his hands. He was blushing, he knew it.

'You speak Hindi or what?'

'*Haan-ji*, of course!'

'Well, stop mumbling and answer me. Are you ill?'

He smiled. So the Gods did have a plan for him! She was adorable. So determined. Such a jewel. For her, he would be a man. He let his hands fall and faced her.

'I had a sister once,' he said, 'a little like you.'

'Had, only?' She looked suspicious. 'You murdered her?'

'No, no, of course not. I murdered no one. I'm the dead one. Dead to my family, to my village. The shame, you see.' He thought of the thatched huts, sealed with patties of dung, round and soft like sweets, of his mother and father. 'But now,' he said, 'I will start a new life.' Her lovely face. It made him different, made him strong. He found himself laughing.

She stuck out her chin, defiant. She didn't seem to realize what was happening between them. 'The girls downstairs,' she said, 'they're saying you did murder someone. That's why they locked you up so long. True, isn't it?'

'They locked me up,' he said. 'That's true, little sister. But I never killed a soul.'

She looked sceptical but interested. 'What happened then?'

'I was walking home to the village, two, three hours away from that man when he was killed,' he said. 'I'd never even met him! The police-wallahs made up such nonsense! But in our country, justice and poor men don't walk the same street.'

She considered, seemed to accept what he said, nodded and came towards him. A cheap ankle bracelet tinkled as she settled herself on the floor by his feet. Her sari was stained, Raj noted, and only of man-made cloth. He would buy her such beautiful saris, the finest cotton, silk. He would –

'So now,' she said, 'how will you live?'

He looked at his fingernails. 'Don't know.'

'Can't you do something, some trade?'

'I was just a boy when they locked me up. My father is a day labourer only. I learned to cook though, in the prison kitchen. Maybe a restaurant would have me?'

'Maybe.' She loosened the pleats of her sari, giving a glimpse of petticoat. 'You can do it with me now,' she said. 'Choose what way.' She made a move towards him.

He blinked. 'What?'

She narrowed her eyes. 'Your friend's paid,' she said. 'One time only. But you can choose how.'

He shook his head. He could feel himself blushing again. As she made to pull loose her sari, he put up his hands to stop her.

'Paper,' he said. 'Fetch paper. That's how I choose.'

She was awkward at first, shuffling and fidgeting.

'Show me,' she kept saying, 'I want to see.' He could feel her suspicion. 'What're you doing? You're *pagel*, a crazy man.'

He simply smiled a little and said nothing. His pencil skimmed the paper with light, darting strokes. As they sat there together, a couple, calm settled on him like motes of dust.

'They'll call me in a minute,' she said. 'There's others due. Regulars. Won't be kept waiting.'

She shifted her weight and reached inside her *choli* to scratch one of her small breasts. He drew the lovely stretch of her throat.

'How long have you been here?' he said.

She shrugged. 'Too long.'

'How did it happen, that you came here?'

'My uncle.' She frowned. 'No good uncle. Trickster. Told my mother-ji there was good work in the city, household work. Then sold me to this place.' She turned her head to the side and spat.

He clicked his tongue. 'Can't you run away?'

'How? No rupees, no escape. And besides.' She pulled the back of her hand across her eyes. 'What use am I now? Like you say. The shame.'

He hugged his idea to himself as a secret. He would finish the drawing first. He could see sadness in her face, weighing down her features. But he drew her without that, as a beauty. He gave a final flourish and turned the paper to show her. Her eyes danced in surprise at the sight of herself.

'You could marry me,' he said. 'I too have no one.'

She didn't stir when the man below started screaming for her, his voice raucous. Raj gazed lovingly at her closed eyes, ringed with kohl, at the long lashes. He wanted to wrap his arms around her and carry her away.

'You'll see,' he whispered, 'how well I'll look after you. I promise.'

Her cheek was resting heavily against his wrist. He could feel the softness of her skin, the moist warmth of her breath between his fingers. Downstairs the shouting went on until the threats were laced with obscenities. When footsteps rang on the staircase, he woke her.

'Someone's coming,' he said, patting her shoulder. 'Look out.'

The man who burst in was broad and muscular, his hair dyed red. He was drunk. Raj could smell the toddy fumes from across the room. He was roaring abuse, making for the girl, hands clutching.

'Stupid whore! You think I'm paying you for nothing? You idle slut!'

She crouched, bending forward to protect her head with her arms. Raj was paralysed, staring. The man's hand seized a clump of her hair, jerking her backwards. Raj saw her eyes widen with fright.

'Shameless tart!'

He was ranting, barely coherent, stupid with drink. Raj got to his feet, uncertain. He was trembling. The man was bigger, stronger than him. Raj half closed his eyes and took a clumsy swing. His fist glanced off the man's chest, barely winding him. Raj blinked. A moment later, the ceiling careered over his head in a clattering rush as he was sent flying backwards into the wall. His sight shrank as one eye swelled. A trickle of blood found his tongue, viscous and cloying.

The man turned back to the girl. Raj saw him lift his hand to fumble at his *lunghi* and expose himself. That was when the girl sprang. She launched herself at him, eyes wild, mouth snarling. A tigress, thought Raj. The force of her movement caught the man by surprise and tipped him backwards. He fell like a tree. Raj saw his face blanch. Once he was down, she leapt onto him, straddling his chest and sinking her fingers in his dyed hair. She beat his skull against the stone floor, pounding it. Raj shuddered. The man's body lay, motionless, beneath her. His eyes were open but unseeing.

'Stop!' Raj heard his own voice, weak and strange. He wanted to go to her, to pin back her arms, but he was powerless to move. 'Stop that!'

She finally went limp, fell to the side and collapsed, sobbing. Raj crawled to her. He stroked her hair. She smelt of damp earth.

'Uncle,' she was sobbing. 'My own flesh.'

The spreading slick of blood around her uncle's head was already feeding a trail of ants.

The Governor was standing silhouetted against the window when Gupta-ji marched Raj in to see him. His face, when he turned, was thunderous.

'The Gods handed you a second chance,' he said. 'And you used it to take a life! You're a fool.'

Raj looked at the swirling colours of the carpet. He thought of the bullying lawyers with their endless questions, of the long dull days of waiting, handcuffed and shamed, in dank court corridors, waiting that would stretch from weeks to months to years before they even reached a verdict. Who knew how many years?

As Gupta-ji herded him back down familiar paths to the cell, Raj kept his eyes on the ground. His bedroll was a tight tube under his arm.

'You missed us then?' Gupta-ji slapped at his legs with his *lathi*. 'Must be the shortest release ever, that.'

His cell-mates looked up in dismay as Gupta-ji unlocked the gate and ushered him inside. Raj took in the concrete floor, the metal bars with their peeling paint, the pools of fresh rainwater. Sights he'd expected never to see again.

'Why'd you do it?' said Gupta-ji as he turned the key. 'An old score?'

Raj crept to the bars and pressed his face hard against them until the metal bit into his cheek. He tried to dissolve into thoughts of the long dark lashes, the soft warm skin, the sweet scent of her and, letting his head sink against the rusting iron, he closed his eyes.

NOTES ON CONTRIBUTORS

David Bezmozgis was born in Riga, Latvia in the former USSR. He holds a BA in English Literature from McGill University and an MFA in Production from the University of Southern California's School of Cinema-Television. His written work has appeared in *The New Yorker*, *Harper's*, *Zoetrope*, the *New York Times Magazine*, *The Walrus*, and other publications. *Natasha and Other Stories* (Jonathan Cape, 2004), David's first book, has been translated into more than a dozen languages.

Danny Birchall lives in London where he manages the Institute of Contemporary Arts website and writes a monthly column on online cinema for *Sight and Sound* magazine.

Gabriela Blandy has a first-class degree in History and has had fiction published in print and online journals in the US and UK. She has won the Royal Society of Literature's V. S. Pritchett Memorial Prize 2007 and twice been longlisted for the Fish Short Story Prize. She was also a winner in the Firstwriter International Short Story and Dame Lisbet Throckmorton Fiction Writing contests, and has recently completed her first novel.

Nadia Crandall holds an MA in English Literature from Oxford, an MBA from Harvard, and pursues diverse literary interests while working as a director of an investment fund. She has published articles on William Blake and contemporary illustrators, Gothic intertextuality in cyberfiction, the ideology of fairy-tale adaptations and the UK children's book business, as well as some short fiction. She is currently writing a novel.

Zoë Fairbairns' stories have been broadcast on BBC Radio 4 and have been published in *Quality Women's Fiction*, *Cosmopolitan* and anthologies including *Tales I Tell My Mother*, *By the Light of the Silvery Moon* and *Tales of Psychotherapy*. Her collection *How Do You Pronounce Nulliparous?* is published by Five Leaves. She teaches short-story writing at the City Lit in London. www.zoefairbairns.co.uk

Tom Gauld is a cartoonist and illustrator. His published books include *Guardians of the Kingdom*, *Robots, Monsters Etc.* and *Hunter & Painter*. His comic strip 'Move to the City' ran in *Time Out* 2001-2002, and his work appears each Saturday in the *Guardian*. He is noted for his work with Simone Lia, with whom he published the comics *First*, *Second* and *Both*.

Jaime Hernandez was born in California. In 1981, he and his brothers Gilbert and Mario published the first *Love & Rockets* comic, which continued for fifty issues. After solo projects, including *Whoa, Nellie!* and *Penny Century*, Jaime decided, with Gilbert, to revive *Love & Rockets*. Jaime has also worked for *The New Yorker* and the *New York Times Magazine*.

Parselelo Kantai is a Kenyan writer and investigative journalist. In 2004, he was nominated for the Caine Prize for African Writing for his debut short story 'Comrade Lemma and the Black Jerusalem Boys Band'. He has been published in the literary journal *Kwani?*. He is currently working on a novel.

Rohan Kar has had short stories published in *The New Writer* (2000) and the *Fish Anthology* (2004) and was a finalist in both the *Writers' & Artists' Yearbook* competition in 2003 and the Scottish International Open Poetry Competition in 2005. He is currently studying on Birkbeck's MA Creative Writing programme and is completing his first novel.

Nik Korpon lives in Baltimore, MD. He is currently finishing an MA in Creative Writing at Birkbeck College in London, while editing his first novel and screenplay.

Jill McGivering is a foreign correspondent with the BBC. Now based in London, she's previously served as the BBC's South Asia correspondent in Delhi, as Hong Kong correspondent and, in Washington, as State Department correspondent. She is now taking the MA in Creative Writing at Birkbeck and writing a novel set in India. 'The Second Chance' was broadcast on BBC Radio 4 earlier this year.

Joyce Carol Oates' most recent novel is *The Gravedigger's Daughter* (HarperCollins, 2007). She is a recipient of the National Book Award and the PEN/Malamud Award for Excellence in Short Fiction. She is also the recipient of the 2005 Prix Femina for *The Falls*. She is the Roger S. Berlind Distinguished Professor of the Humanities at Princeton University, and she has been a member of the American Academy of Arts and Letters since 1978.

Jennifer Payne graduated from the University of Southern California in 2002, and moved to the UK shortly afterwards. She has an MA in Gender, Culture and Politics from Birkbeck, and is currently completing the MA in Creative Writing. 'Things You Think You Need' is her first published piece.

Samanthi Perera was born and raised in London. She studied at University College London and King's College London, and now is pursuing a career in mental health. 'My Side of the River' is her first piece of published fiction.

T. Rawson has just completed the two-year Certificate in Creative Writing at Birkbeck, and is working on a novel about the social and political effects of the Industrial Revolution and how they affect one family. Her entry into this anthology is the first time she has been published. One of her ambitions is to have a radio play accepted for production.

Lucy Roeber gave up her job as assistant editor of *Prospect* magazine five years ago, moved to Paris and wrote her first novel. She's now based back in London and engaged in writing historical fiction. She is married with two children.

Rosie Rogers was born in 1973. She studied Drama at Manchester University and graduated in 1997. She teaches Drama and Film Studies in Crawley, and is currently redrafting her first novel, *In a Place Like This*. She lives in Brighton.

Paul Ryan is a first-year student on the Certificate in Creative Writing course at Birkbeck. 'When Your Mother Dies' is his first published story. He is an assistant editor on a consumer magazine and previously worked on local newspapers and as a teacher of English as a foreign language.

Elizabeth Sarkany worked as an NHS doctor between 1983 and 2002. She has had several stories published in *Quality Women's Fiction* and *Tears in the Fence* magazines, others accepted by *Parameter* and for anthologies from Earlyworks Press and Loki Books. Her story 'How Michael Stays Young' was broadcast on BBC Radio 4 in 2006.

Michelle Singh is a graduate of the University of Birmingham, where she read for a degree in English Literature. In 2000 she won the Audrey Pipe Fellowship literary award for young writers, and has had several pieces of her work published in a variety of anthologies and online. Michelle works as a media editor in the City but plans to move to the countryside this year to finish the novel she's writing.

David John Soulsby is currently in the first year of the Certificate in Creative Writing at Birbeck. He has recently been on two Arvon Foundation writing retreats and is working on the second draft of a play.

Rose Tremain is the author of nine novels and the winner of several awards, including the Dylan Thomas short story award, the *Sunday Express* Book of the Year award and the Whitbread Novel Award. She has had novels shortlisted for the Booker and Orange prizes. Her new novel, *The Road Home*, was published by Chatto & Windus in June, 2007.

James Vincent was born in south London, where he still lives. He has worked in education and financial research and currently combines freelance editing with his MA studies. He has written several short stories and is working on a novel set in Deptford featuring a seamstress who believes she is immortal.

David Foster Wallace is the author of the novels *Infinite Jest* and *The Broom of the System*, several story collections, including *Oblivion: Stories*, and books of essays – most recently, *Consider the Lobster*. He writes for *The Paris Review*, *The New Yorker* and other magazines, is the recipient of a MacArthur Fellowship and has won a number of literary prizes. He lives in California.

Hilary Wilce has won a number of awards for her short fiction, including the Mathew Prichard award, the Ian St James award and the Kent Literary Festival prize. She works as an education journalist, and has written a book for parents about schools. She is currently working on a novel.

Laura Williams is a student on the Birkbeck Certificate in Creative Writing and is currently working on her first novel about a private investigator from Tulse Hill. 'Balcony View' is her first piece of published fiction so she has yet to give up her day job as a social researcher.

Founded in 1823 and based in Bloomsbury, Birkbeck extends educational opportunities while achieving world-class research results.

Educating busy Londoners

Are you serious about creative writing and want to develop your artistic skills?

Birkbeck, University of London invites you to apply for our **MA Creative Writing** course for the 2008/09 academic year. This postgraduate degree will help you extend and experiment with your existing writing skills and develop to a professional level your own genre of fiction. The course culminates in the annual publication *The Mechanics' Institute Review*, which is widely distributed throughout the trade.

The course is taught by leading practitioners, including the novelists Russell Celyn Jones (Course Director), Julia Bell and Candida Clark. It is supported by visiting professionals (e.g. literary agents, publishers) and has master-classes by internationally regarded writers (Hari Kunzru and Maggie Gee in 2006).

With the option of studying part time over two years, or full time over one year, all classes are held in the evenings, enabling you to pursue the course without giving up daytime commitments.

Located in central London (WC1), Birkbeck is ranked as one of the leading centres of teaching and research excellence in the UK. Our tutors are not only experts in their chosen fields but they are also specialists in supporting students with work and family commitments.

Applications must be supported by a portfolio of creative writing (fiction) of approximately 5,000 words in length.

Further information and application forms are available by calling the Course Administrator on 020 7079 0689. Alternatively email: a.whiting@bbk.ac.uk or visit: www.bbk.ac.uk/eh

Visit www.bbk.ac.uk or call 0845 601 0174 to find out about the full range of part-time and full-time study opportunities at Birkbeck.

Founded in 1823 and based in Bloomsbury, Birkbeck has an excellent reputation for providing high-quality part-time courses.

Educating busy Londoners

Part-time courses in English Studies and Creative Writing

Enrol *now* to secure a place for part-time day and evening courses starting in late September at venues in and across London.

Certificate/Diploma courses

Literature
- One-year Certificate in Literature in English
- Certificate/Diploma in Literature in English

Renaissance and Victorian Studies
- Certificate/Diploma in Renaissance Studies (interdisciplinary)
- Certificate/Diploma in Victorian Studies (interdisciplinary)

Accredited short courses

Creative Writing
- Introductory courses
- Fiction
- Poetry
- Drama
- Women, Autobiography, Personal Development

English Language, Academic Writing and Study Skills
- Pre-Sessional English for Academic Purposes
- English for Academic Purposes and Academic Writing
- English for Business
- English for Social Science
- English for Legal Purposes
- Preparation for IELTS
- Advanced English Language Skills

Full details are in our Certificates, Diplomas and Short Courses Prospectus. To order your copy:

Email: info@bbk.ac.uk
Call: 0845 601 0174
Or visit: www.bbk.ac.uk/study/ce

The GIRL

ASTROF

A LOVE AND

ETS BOOK

THE COMPLETE LOVE & ROCKETS REISSUE CONTINUES...

THE GIRL FROM H.O.P.P.E.R.S.
The second volume of "Locas" stories from Love & Rockets By Jaime Hernandez

HUMAN DIASTROPHISM
The second volume of "Palomar" stories from Gilbert Hernandez

"Fantagraphics honors the groundbreaking comics of Gilbert and Jaime Hernandez with this series of reissues." — ENTERTAINMENT WEEKLY's "MUST LIST" March 2007

"Fall in Love: Fantagraphics has just released cool, convenient digest-sized volumes collecting the complete Love & Rockets by Los Bros Hernandez... These comics remain light years ahead with their exploration of gender preference and free-spirited self-exploration." — WIZARD

ALSO OUT NOW!

The all-new LOVE & ROCKETS Vol. II #20! Special double-sized anniversary issue! Featuring over 20 pages in FULL-COLOR!

FANTAGRAPHICS BOOKS

story

Visit the Short Story website for
information about forthcoming books,
competitions, events and magazines.

You can also search for published short-
story collections and read feature articles
about projects as well as news, book reviews,
opinion pieces by authors, publishers and
others involved in the world of the short story.

Plus a growing number of free stories
for you to download.

www.theshortstory.org.uk